ERIKA JOHANSEN grew up in California. She went to Swarthmore College in Pennsylvania, earned a Master of Fine Arts degree from the celebrated Iowa Writers Workshop and eventually became a lawyer, but she never stopped writing. Her acclaimed debut, *The Queen of the Tearling*, is the first book in a trilogy and became an international bestseller. The second novel, *The Invasion of the Tearling*, continues the thrilling story of Kelsea Glynn and the Tearling kingdom.

Erika lives in the San Francisco Bay Area of California.

Acclaim for Erika Johansen's *The Queen of the Tearling*

'I didn't sleep for about a week because I couldn't put the bloody thing down. It would be fair to say I became obsessed'
EMMA WATSON

'An assured and confident debut that has already been optioned for a movie to star Harry Potter's Emma Watson, featuring a strong female lead and a well-realised far-future post-apocalyptic world'
INDEPENDENT ON SUNDAY

'Did you love *The Hunger Games*? Partial to an episode of *Game of Thrones*? Then you're going to want to dive straight in to this new fantasy . . . brilliantly imagined and captivatingly written'
HEAT

'Destined to be a fantasy classic. Johansen's writing is assured, confident and thrilling. I can't wait for the next book'
AMY McCULLOCH, author of *The Oathbreaker's Shadow*

'Enjoyable, fast-paced . . . haunting, tear-jerking moments that leave you desperate to read the next instalment . . . a top summer read'
SUN

'Like *Game of Thrones* and *The Hunger Games* meets *Pulp Fiction*'
DAILY MAIL

'This book worked on me with all the subtle power of an addiction: by the time I realized I was hooked, it was far too late to stop'
LAUREN OLIVER, author of *Before I Fall*

'Erika Johansen's debut needed to cut the literary mustard. Thankfully it does'
SCIFI NOW

Also by Erika Johansen

INVASION OF THE TEARLING

THE QUEEN OF THE TEARLING

ERIKA JOHANSEN

BANTAM BOOKS

LONDON • TORONTO • SYDNEY • AUCKLAND • JOHANNESBURG

TRANSWORLD PUBLISHERS
61–63 Uxbridge Road, London W5 5SA
www.transworldbooks.co.uk

Transworld is part of the Penguin Random House group of companies
whose addresses can be found at global.penguinrandomhouse.com

First published in the United States in 2014 by Harper,
an imprint of HarperCollins

First published in Great Britain in 2014 by Bantam Press
an imprint of Transworld Publishers
Bantam edition published 2015

A CIP catalogue record for this book
is available from the British Library.

ISBN
9780857502476

Designed by Leah Carlson-Stanisic
Typeset in 10/13.5pt Ashbury by Falcon Oast Graphic Art Ltd.
Printed and bound by CPI Group (UK) Ltd, Croydon, CR0 4YY.

Penguin Random House is committed to a sustainable
future for our business, our readers and our planet. This book is made
from Forest Stewardship Council® certified paper.

13579108642

For Christian and Katie

BOOK I

——— CHAPTER 1 ———
THE TENTH HORSE

THE GLYNN QUEEN—Kelsea Raleigh Glynn, seventh Queen of the Tearling. Also known as: The Marked Queen. Fostered by Carlin and Bartholemew (Barty the Good) Glynn. Mother: Queen Elyssa Raleigh. Father: unknown. See appendix XI for speculation.

—The Early History of the Tearling,
AS TOLD BY MERWINIAN

Kelsea Glynn sat very still, watching the troop approach her homestead. The men rode as a military company, with outliers on the corners, all dressed in the grey of the Tearling royal guard. The riders' cloaks swayed as they rode, revealing their costly weapons: swords and short knives, all of them of Mortmesne steel. One man even had a mace; Kelsea could see its spiked head protruding from his saddle. The sullen way they guided their horses toward the cottage made things very clear: they didn't want to be here.

Kelsea sat, cloaked and hooded, in the fork of a tree some thirty feet from her front door. She was dressed in deep green from her hood down to her pine-colored boots. A sapphire

13

dangled from a pure silver chain around her neck. This jewel had an annoying habit of popping out of Kelsea's shirt minutes after she had tucked it in, which seemed fitting, for today the sapphire was the source of her trouble.

Nine men, ten horses.

The soldiers reached the raked patch of earth in front of the cottage and dismounted. As they threw back their hoods, Kelsea saw that they were nowhere near her own age. These men were in their thirties and forties, and they shared a hard, weathered look that bespoke the toll of combat. The soldier with the mace muttered something, and their hands went automatically to their swords.

"Best be done quickly." The speaker, a tall, lean man whose authoritative tone marked him as the leader, stepped forward and knocked three times on the front door. It opened immediately, as if Barty had been waiting there all along. Even from her vantage point, Kelsea could see that Barty's round face was lined, his eyes red and swollen. He'd sent Kelsea out into the woods that morning, unwilling to have her witness his grief. Kelsea had protested, but Barty wouldn't hear refusal and finally simply pushed her out the door, saying, "Go and say goodbye to the woods, girl. It'll likely be a long time before they'll let you wander at will again."

Kelsea had gone then, and spent the morning roaming the forest, climbing over fallen trees and stopping every now and again to listen to the stillness of the woods, that perfect silence so at odds with the abundance of life it contained. She'd even snared a rabbit, for something to do, before letting it go; Barty and Carlin had no need for meat, and she took no pleasure in killing. Watching the rabbit bound off and vanish into the woods where she had spent so much of her childhood, Kelsea tried the word again, though it felt like dust in her mouth: *Queen*. An ominous word, foretelling a grim future.

"Barty." The leader of the troop greeted him. "A long time."

Barty muttered something indistinguishable.

"We're here for the girl."

Barty nodded, put two fingers in his mouth, and whistled, high and piercing. Kelsea dropped soundlessly from the tree and walked out of the cover of the woods, her pulse thrumming. She knew how to defend herself against a single attacker with her knife; Barty had taken care of that. But she was intimidated by the heavily armed troop. She felt all of these men's eyes on her, measuring. She looked nothing like a queen and she knew it.

The leader, a hard-faced man with a scar down the edge of his chin, bowed low in front of her. "Your Highness. I'm Carroll, Captain of the late Queen's Guard."

A moment passed before the rest bowed as well. The guard with the mace bent perhaps an inch, with the slightest perceptible dip of his chin.

"We must see the marking," muttered one of the guards, his face nearly concealed behind a red beard. "And the jewel."

"You think I would swindle the kingdom, man?" Barty rasped.

"She looks nothing like her mother," the red-bearded man replied sharply.

Kelsea flushed. According to Carlin, Queen Elyssa had been a classic Tearling beauty, tall and blonde and lithe. Kelsea was tall as well, but she was dark in coloring, with a face that could charitably be described as plain. She wasn't statuesque by any stretch of the word, either; she got plenty of exercise, but she had a healthy appetite too.

"She has the Raleigh eyes," another guard remarked.

"I would prefer to see the jewel and the scar," replied the leader, and the red-haired man nodded as well.

"Show them, Kel."

Kelsea pulled the sapphire pendant from beneath her shirt and held it up to the light. The necklace had lain around her neck ever since she could remember, and right now she wanted nothing so much as to tear the thing off and give it back to them. But Barty and Carlin had already explained that they wouldn't let her do that. She was the crown princess of the Tearling, and this was her nineteenth birthday, the age of ascension for Tearling monarchs all the way back to Jonathan Tear. The Queen's Guard would cart her back to the Keep kicking and screaming, if need be, and imprison her on the throne, and there she would sit, hung with velvet and silk, until she was assassinated.

The leader nodded at the jewel, and Kelsea shook back the left sleeve of her cloak, exposing her forearm, where a distended scar in the shape of a knife blade marched from her wrist to her bicep. One or two of the men muttered at the sight of it, their hands relaxing from their weapons for the first time since they'd arrived.

"That's it, then," Carroll declared gruffly. "We go now."

"One moment." Carlin stepped into the doorway, gently nudging Barty out of the way. She did so with her wrists, not her fingers; the arthritis must be very bad today. Her appearance was impeccable as always, her white hair pinned up neatly off her neck. Kelsea was surprised to see that her eyes, too, were slightly red. Carlin wasn't one for tears; she rarely demonstrated any emotion at all.

Several of the guards straightened at the sight of Carlin. One or two even took a step back, including the man with the mace. Kelsea had always thought that Carlin looked like royalty herself, but she was surprised to see these men with all of their swords daunted by one old woman.

Thank God I'm not the only one.

"Prove yourselves!" Carlin demanded. "How do we know you come from the Keep?"

"Who else would know where to find her on this day?" Carroll asked.

"Assassins."

Several of the soldiers chuckled unkindly. But the soldier with the mace stepped forward, fumbling inside his cloak.

Carlin stared at him for a moment. "I do know you."

"I brought the Queen's instructions," he told her, producing a thick envelope, yellowed with age. "In case you didn't remember."

"I doubt many people forget you, Lazarus," Carlin replied, her voice tinged with disapproval. She unwrapped the paper quickly, though it must have played hell with her arthritis, and scanned its contents. Kelsea stared at the letter, fascinated. Her mother was long dead, and yet here was something she had written, actually touched.

Carlin seemed satisfied. She handed the piece of paper back to the guard. "Kelsea needs to gather her things."

"A few minutes only, Highness. We must go." Carroll spoke to Kelsea now, bowing again, and she saw that he'd already dismissed Carlin from the proceedings. Carlin had seen the transition as well; her face was like stone. Kelsea often wished that Carlin would get angry, instead of withdrawing into that inner, silent part of herself, so cold and remote. Carlin's silences were terrible things.

Kelsea slipped past the standing horses and into the cottage. Her clothing was packed into her saddlebags already, but she made no move to approach them, moving to stand in the doorway of Carlin's library. The walls were lined with books; Barty had constructed the shelves himself, of Tearling oak, and given them to Carlin on Kelsea's fourth Christmas. In a time of vague memory, that day was pure and bright in Kelsea's mind: she had helped Carlin shelve the books, and cried a little when Carlin wouldn't let her organize them by color. Many years had passed, but Kelsea still loved the books, loved seeing them side by side, with every single volume in its own place.

But the library had been a schoolroom as well, often an unpleasant one. Rudimentary mathematics, her Tear grammar, geography, and later the languages of surrounding countries, their odd accents first difficult and then easier, faster, until Kelsea and Carlin could switch easily from tongue to tongue, hopping from Mort to Cadarese and back again to the simpler, less dramatic language of the Tearling without missing a syllable. Most of all, history, the history of humanity stretching back before the Crossing. Carlin often said that history was everything, for it was in man's nature to make the same mistakes over and over. She would look hard at Kelsea when she said so, her white eyebrows folding down, preparing to disapprove. Carlin was fair, but she was also hard. If Kelsea completed all of her schoolwork by dinner-time, her reward was to be allowed to pick a book from the library and stay up reading until she had finished. Stories moved Kelsea most, stories of things that never were, stories that transported her beyond the changeless world of the cottage. One night she'd stayed up until dawn reading a particularly long novel, and she had been allowed to skip her chores and sleep away most of the next day. But there had also been entire months where Kelsea became tired of the constant schooling and simply shut down. And then there were no stories, no library, only housework, loneliness, and the granite disapproval of Carlin's face. Eventually, Kelsea always went back to school.

Barty shut the door and approached her, every other footstep dragging. He had been a Queen's Guard a lifetime ago, before a sword to the back of his knee had left him lame. He placed a firm hand on her shoulder. "You can't delay, Kel."

Kelsea turned and found Carlin looking away, out the window. In front of the cottage, the soldiers shifted uneasily, darting quick glances around the woods.

They're accustomed to enclosure, thought Kelsea; *open space alarms them.* The implications of this, the life it foreboded for her at the Keep, almost overwhelmed her, just when she'd thought that all of her crying was done.

"This is a dangerous time, Kelsea." Carlin spoke to the window, her voice distant. "Beware of the Regent, uncle or no; he's wanted that throne for himself since he was in the womb. But your mother's Guard are good men, and they'll surely look after you."

"They dislike me, Carlin," Kelsea blurted out. "You said it would be an honor for them to be my escort. But they don't want to be here."

Carlin and Barty exchanged a look, and Kelsea saw the ghost of many old arguments between them. Theirs was an odd marriage; Carlin was at least ten years older than Barty, nearing seventy. It took no extraordinary imagination to see that she had once been beautiful, but now her beauty had hardened into austerity. Barty was not beautiful, shorter than Carlin and decidedly rounder, but he had a good-humored face and smiling eyes beneath his grey hair. Barty didn't care for books at all, and Kelsea often wondered what he and

19

Carlin found to talk about when she wasn't in the room. Perhaps nothing; perhaps Kelsea was the common interest that kept them together. If so, what would become of them now?

Carlin finally replied, "We swore to your mother that we would not tell you of her failures, Kelsea, and we've kept our promise. But not everything at the Keep will be as you thought. Barty and I have given you good tools; that was our charge. But once you sit on the throne, you'll have to make your own hard decisions."

Barty sniffed in disapproval and limped over to pick up Kelsea's saddlebags. Carlin shot him a sharp look, which he ignored, and so she turned it on Kelsea, her eyebrows drawing together. Kelsea looked down, her stomach tightening. Once, long ago out in the forest, they had been in the middle of a lesson on the uses of red moss when Barty had blurted out, apropos of nothing: "If it was up to me, Kel, I'd break my damned vows and tell you everything you want to know."

"Why isn't it up to you?"

Barty had looked helplessly down at the moss in his hands, and after a moment Kelsea understood. Nothing in the cottage was up to Barty; Carlin was in charge. Carlin was smarter, Carlin was physically whole. Barty came second. Carlin was not cruel, but Kelsea had felt the pinch of that iron will often enough that she could understand the shape of Barty's bitterness, almost feel it as her own. But Carlin's will had ruled in this matter. There were large gaps in Kelsea's knowledge of history, and information about her mother's reign that Kelsea simply didn't have. She had been kept from the village and the answers it might have provided; hers had been a true childhood in exile. But more than once she had heard Barty and Carlin talking at night, long after they thought Kelsea was asleep, and now she understood at least part of the mystery. For years now, the Regent's guards had ranged over every part of the country, looking for a child with the necklace and the scar. Looking for Kelsea.

"I've left a gift in your saddlebags," Carlin continued, bringing her back to the present.

"What gift?"

"A gift you'll discover for yourself after you leave this place."

For a moment Kelsea felt her anger resurface; Carlin was always keeping secrets! But a moment later Kelsea was ashamed. Barty and Carlin were grieving ... not only for Kelsea, but for their home. Even now, the Regent's trackers were probably tracing the Queen's Guard across the Tearling. Barty and Carlin couldn't stay here; shortly after Kelsea's departure, they would be leaving themselves, off to Petaluma, a southern village near the Cadarese border where Barty had grown up. Barty would be lost without his forest, but there were other forests for him to learn. Carlin was making the greater sacrifice: her library. These books were her life's collection, saved and hoarded by settlors in the Crossing, preserved through centuries. She couldn't take them with her; a wagon would be too easy to track. All of these volumes, gone.

Kelsea picked up her night pack and shrugged it onto her shoulders, looking out the window to the tenth horse. "There's so much I don't know."

"You know what you need to," Barty replied. "Do you have your knife?"

"Yes."

"Keep it about you always. And be careful what you eat and where it comes from."

Kelsea put her arms around him. Despite Barty's girth, his

body was shaking with fatigue, and Kelsea realized suddenly how tired he'd become, how completely her education had taxed energy that Barty should have conserved for growing old. His thick arms tightened about her for a moment, and then he pulled away, his blue eyes fierce. "You've never killed anyone, Kel, and that's well and good, but from this day onward, you're hunted, understand? You have to behave so."

Kelsea expected Carlin to contradict Barty, Carlin who always said that force was for fools. But Carlin nodded in agreement. "I've raised you to be a thinking queen, Kelsea, and so you will be. But you've entered a time when survival must trump all else. These men will have an honest charge to see that you get back to the Keep safely. After that, Barty's lessons may help you more than mine."

She left her post by the window and placed a gentle hand on Kelsea's back, making her jump. Carlin rarely touched anyone. The most she seemed capable of was a pat on the back, and those occasions were like rain in the desert. "But don't allow reliance on weapons to impair your mind, Kelsea. Your wits have always been sound; see that you don't lose them along the way. It's easy to do so when you pick up a sword."

A mailed fist thudded against the front door.

"Your Highness?" Carroll called. "Daylight fails."

Barty and Carlin stepped back, and Barty picked up the last piece of Kelsea's baggage. They both looked terribly old. Kelsea didn't want to leave them here, these two people who'd raised her and taught her everything she knew. The irrational side of her mind briefly considered dropping her luggage and simply bolting out the back door, a bright and tempting fantasy that lasted two seconds before it faded.

"When will it be safe to send you a message?" she asked. "When can you come out of hiding?"

Barty and Carlin looked at each other, a quick glance that struck Kelsea as furtive. It was Barty who finally replied. "Not for a while, Kel. You see—"

"You will have other things to worry about," Carlin broke in sharply. "Think about your people, about fixing this kingdom. It may be a long while before you see us again."

"Carlin—"

"It's time to go."

The soldiers had remounted their horses; as Kelsea emerged from the cottage, they stared down at her, one or two of them with outright contempt. The soldier with the mace, Lazarus, wasn't looking at her at all but staring off into the distance. Kelsea began to load her baggage onto the horse, a roan mare that seemed somewhat gentler than Barty's stallion.

"I assume you can ride, Your Highness?" asked the soldier holding her reins. He made the word *highness* sound like an infection, and Kelsea snatched the reins from him. "Yes, I ride."

She switched the reins from hand to hand as she put on her green winter cloak and buttoned it closed, then mounted her horse and looked down at Barty, trying to overcome an awful premonition of finality. He was grown old before his time, but there was no reason he shouldn't live for a number of years yet. And premonitions often came to nothing. According to Barty, the Mort Queen's own seer had predicted that Kelsea wouldn't reach her nineteenth birthday, and yet here she was.

She gave Barty what she hoped was a brave smile. "I'll send for you soon."

He nodded, his own smile bright and forced. Carlin had turned so white that Kelsea thought she might faint dead away, but instead she stepped forward and reached out a hand. This gesture was so unexpected that Kelsea stared at the hand for a moment before she realized that she was supposed to take it. In all her years in the cottage, Carlin had never held her hand.

"In time, you'll see," Carlin told her, clenching her hand tightly. "You'll see why all of this was necessary. Beware the past, Kelsea. Be a steward."

Even now, Carlin wouldn't speak plainly. Kelsea had always known that she wasn't the child Carlin would have chosen to train, that she'd disappointed Carlin with her ungovernable temper, her lax commitment to the enormous responsibility lying on her shoulders. Kelsea tugged her hand away, then glanced at Barty and felt her irritation vanish. He was crying openly now, tracks of tears glinting on his face. Kelsea felt her own eyes wanting to water again, but she took the reins and turned the horse toward Carroll. "We can go now, Captain."

"At your command, Lady."

He shook the reins and started down the path. "All of you, in kite, square around the Queen," he called back over his shoulder. "We ride until sunset."

Queen. There was the word again. Kelsea tried to think of herself as a queen and simply couldn't. She set her pace to match the guards', resolutely not looking back. She turned around only once, just before they rounded the bend, and found Barty and Carlin still standing in the cottage doorway, watching her go, like an old woodsman couple in some tale long forgotten. Then the trees hid them from view.

Kelsea's mare was apparently a sturdy one, for she took the uneven terrain surefootedly. Barty's stallion had always had problems in the woods; Barty said that his horse was an aristocrat, that anything less than an open straightaway was beneath him. But even on the stallion, Kelsea had never ventured more than a few miles from the cottage. Those were Carlin's orders. Whenever Kelsea spoke longingly of the things she knew were out there in the wider world, Carlin would impress upon her the necessity of secrecy, the importance of the queenship she would inherit. Carlin had no patience with Kelsea's fear of failure. Carlin didn't want to hear about doubts. Kelsea's job was to learn, to be content without other children, other people, without the wider world.

Once, when she was thirteen, Kelsea had ridden Barty's stallion into the woods as usual and gotten lost, finding herself in unfamiliar forest. She didn't know the trees or the two streams she'd passed. She'd ended up riding in circles, and was about to give up and cry when she looked toward the horizon and saw smoke from a chimney, some hundred feet away.

Moving closer, she found a cottage, poorer than Barty's and Carlin's, made of wood instead of stone. In front of the cottage had been two little boys, a few years younger than Kelsea, playing a make-believe game of swords, and she had watched them for a very long time, sensing something she'd never considered before: an entirely different upbringing from her own. Until that moment, she had somehow thought that all children had the same life. The boys' clothes were ragged, but they both wore comfortable-looking shirts with short sleeves that ended at the bicep. Kelsea could only wear high-necked shirts with tight, long sleeves, so that no chance passersby would ever get a look at her arm or the necklace she wasn't allowed to remove. She listened to the two boys' chatter and found that they could barely speak proper Tear;

no one had sat them down every morning and drilled them on grammar. It was the middle of the afternoon, but they weren't in school.

"You's Mort, Emmett. I's Tear!" the older boy proclaimed proudly.

"I's not Mort! Mort's short!" the littler one shouted. "Mum said you supposed to make me Tear sometime!"

"Fine. You's Tear, but I's using magic!"

After watching the two boys for a while, Kelsea marked the real difference, the one that commanded her attention: these children had each other. She was only fifty yards away, but the companionship between the two boys made her feel as distant as the moon. The distance was only compounded when their mother, a round woman with none of Carlin's stately grace, came outside to gather them up for dinner.

"Ew! Martin! Come wash up!"

"No!" the little one replied. "We ain't done."

Picking up a stick from the bundle on the ground, the mother jumped into the middle of their game, battling them both while the boys giggled and shrieked. Finally, the mother pulled each child up and then held them both close to her body as they walked inside together, a continuous walking hug. The dusk was deepening, and although Kelsea knew she should try to find her way home, she couldn't tear herself away from the scene. Carlin didn't show affection, not even to Barty, and the best Kelsea could hope to earn was a smile. She was the heir to the Tear throne, yes, and Carlin had told her many times what a great and important honor that was. But on the long ride home, Kelsea couldn't shake the feeling that these two children had more than she did.

When she finally found her way home, she had missed dinner. Barty and Carlin were both worried; Barty had yelled a bit, but behind the yelling Kelsea could see relief in his face, and he'd given her a hug before sending her up to her room. Carlin had merely stared at Kelsea before informing her that her library privileges were rescinded for the week and that night Kelsea had lain in bed, frozen in the revelation that she had been utterly, monstrously cheated. Before that day, Kelsea had thought of Carlin as her foster mother, if not the real thing. But now she understood that she had no mother at all, only a cold old woman who demanded, then withheld.

Two days later Kelsea broke Carlin's boundary again, on purpose this time, intending to find the cottage in the woods again. But halfway there, she gave up and turned around. Disobedience wasn't satisfying, it was terrifying; she seemed to feel Carlin's eyes on the back of her neck. Kelsea had never broken the boundary line again, so there was no wider world. All of her experience came from the woods around the cottage, and she knew every inch of them by the time she was ten. Now, as the troop of guards moved into distant woods with Kelsea in their center, she smiled secretly and turned her attention to this country that she had never seen.

They were riding south through the deepest heart of the Reddick Forest, which covered hundreds of square miles on the northwestern part of the country. Tearling oak was every- where, some of the trees fifty or sixty feet tall, forming a canopy of green that overspread their heads. There was some low underbrush too, unfamiliar to Kelsea. The branches looked like creeproot, which had antihistamine properties and was good for making poultices. But these leaves were longer, green and curling, with a reddish tinge that warned of poison oak. Kelsea tried to avoid putting her mare through the foliage, but in some places it couldn't be helped; the

27

thicket was deepening as the land sloped downhill. They were now far from the path, but as they rode over a crackling golden carpet of discarded oak leaves, Kelsea felt as though the entire world must be able to hear their passage.

The guards ranged themselves around her in a diamond, remaining equidistant even with the changes of speed demanded by the shifting terrain. Lazarus, the guard with the mace, was somewhere behind her, out of sight. On her right was the distrustful guard with the red beard; Kelsea watched him with covert interest as they rode. Red hair was a recessive gene, and in the three centuries since the Crossing, it had bred slowly and steadily out of the population. Carlin had told Kelsea that some women, and even some men, liked to dye their hair red, since the rare commodity was always valuable. But after about an hour of sneaking looks at the guard, Kelsea became certain that she was looking at a true head of red hair. No dye was that good. The man wore a small gold crucifix that bounced and glimmered as he rode, and this too gave Kelsea pause. The crucifix was the symbol of God's Church, and Carlin had told her many times that the Church and its priests weren't to be trusted.

Behind the redhead was a blond man, so extraordinarily good-looking that Kelsea was forced to sneak several looks at him, even though he was far too old for her, well over forty. He had a face like those of the painted angels in Carlin's books of pre-Crossing art. But he also looked tired, his eyes ringed with hollows that suggested he hadn't slept in some time. Somehow, these touches of exhaustion only made him better-looking. He turned and caught her staring and Kelsea snapped her head forward, blood flaming in her cheeks.

On her left was a tall guard with dark hair and enormous

shoulders. He looked like the sort of man you would threaten someone with. Ahead of him was a much shorter man, almost slight, with light brown hair. Kelsea watched this guard closely, for he looked nearer to her age, perhaps not even thirty yet. She tried to listen for his name, but whenever the two guards spoke, it was in low tones that Kelsea was clearly not meant to hear.

Carroll, the leader, rode at the head of the diamond. All Kelsea could see of him was his grey cloak. Occasionally he would bark out an order, and the entire company would make an incremental change in direction. He rode confidently, not seeking anyone's guidance, and Kelsea trusted him to get her where she was to go. This ability to command was probably a necessary quality in a guard captain; Carroll was a man she would need if she was to survive. But how could she win the loyalty of any of these men? They probably thought her weak. Perhaps they thought all women so.

A hawk screamed somewhere above them, and Kelsea pulled her hood down over her forehead. Hawks were beautiful creatures, and good food as well, but Barty had told her that in Mortmesne, and even on the Tear border, hawks were trained as weapons of assassination. He'd mentioned it in passing, a bit of trivia, but it was something Kelsea had never forgotten.

"South, lads!" Carroll shouted, and the company angled again. The sun was sinking rapidly below the horizon, the wind icy with oncoming night. Kelsea hoped they would stop soon, but she would freeze in her saddle before she complained. Loyalty began with respect.

"No ruler has ever held power for long without the respect of the governed," Carlin had told her countless times. "Rulers who attempt to control an unwilling populace govern nothing, and often find their heads atop a pike to boot."

Barty's advice had been even more succinct: "You win your people or you lose your throne."

Good words, and Kelsea saw their wisdom even more now. But she had no idea what to do. How was she to command anyone?

I'm nineteen. I'm not supposed to be frightened anymore.

But she was.

She gripped the reins tighter, wishing she'd thought to put on her riding gloves, but she'd been too anxious to get away from that uncomfortable tableau in front of the cottage. Now the tips of her fingers were numb, her palms raw and reddened from the rough leather of the reins. She did her best to tuck the sleeves of her cloak over her knuckles and rode onward.

An hour later, Carroll called the company to a halt. They were in a small clearing, ringed with Tearling oak and a thick layer of underbrush composed of creeproot and that mysterious red-leaved plant. Kelsea wondered if any of the Guard knew what it was. Every Guard unit had at least one medic, and medics were supposed to know plants. Barty had been a medic himself, and while he wasn't supposed to be teaching Kelsea botany, she had quickly learned that almost any lesson could be sidetracked by discovery of an interesting plant.

The guards closed in around Kelsea and waited as Carroll circled back. He trotted up to her, taking in her reddened face and death grip on the reins. "We can stop for the night, if you like, Your Highness. We made good time."

With some effort, Kelsea released the reins and pushed back her hood, trying to keep her teeth from chattering. Her voice, when it came out, was hoarse and unsteady. "I trust your judgment, Captain. We'll go as far as you think necessary."

Carroll stared at her for a moment and then looked around the small clearing. "This'll do, Lady. We must rise early anyway, and we've been long on the road."

The men dismounted. Kelsea, stiff and unused to long riding, made a clumsy hop to the ground, nearly fell, then stumbled around until she regained her footing.

"Pen, the tent. Elston and Kibb, go for wood. The rest of you take care of defenses. Mhurn, go catch us something to eat. Lazarus, the Queen's horse."

"I tend my own horse, Captain."

"As you like, Lady. Lazarus will give you what you need."

The soldiers dispersed, moving off on their various errands. Kelsea bent to the ground, relishing the cracking in her spine. Her thighs ached as if they'd taken several sharp blows, but she wasn't going to do any sort of serious thigh-stretching in front of all of these men. They were old, certainly, too old for Kelsea to find them attractive. But they *were* men, and Kelsea found herself suddenly uncomfortable in front of them, in a way she had never been in front of Barty.

Leading her mare over to a tree at the far edge of the clearing, she looped the reins in a loose knot around a branch. She stroked the mare's silken neck gently, but the horse tossed her head and whinnied, unwilling to be petted, and Kelsea backed off. "Fine, girl. No doubt I'll have to earn your goodwill as well."

"Highness," a voice growled behind her.

Kelsea turned and saw Lazarus, a curry comb in hand. He wasn't as old as she'd first thought; his dark hair had just begun to recede, and he might still be on the early side of

31

forty. But his face was well lined, his expression grim. His hands were seamed with scars, but it was the mace at his belt that drew her eye: a blunt ball of iron covered with steel spikes, each sharpened to a pinpoint.

A natural killer, she thought. A mace was merely window dressing unless wielded with the ferocity to make it effective. The weapon should have chilled her, but instead she was comforted by the presence of this man who had clearly lived with violence for so much of his life. She took the comb, noting that he kept his eyes on the ground. "Thank you. I don't suppose you know the mare's name."

"You're the Queen, Lady. Her name is whatever you choose." His flat gaze met hers briefly, then slid away.

"It's not for me to give her a new name. What is she called?"

"It's for you to do anything you like."

"Her name, please." Kelsea's temper kindled. The men all thought so badly of her. Why?

"No proper name, Lady. I've always called her May."

"Thank you. A good name."

He began to walk away. Kelsea took a breath for courage and said softly, "I didn't dismiss you, Lazarus."

He turned back, expressionless. "I'm sorry. Was there something else, Lady?"

"Why did they bring me a mare, when you all ride stallions?"

"We didn't know if you'd be able to ride, Lady," he replied, and this time there was no mistaking the mockery in his voice. "We didn't know if you could control a stallion."

Kelsea narrowed her eyes. "What the hell did you think I was doing out there in the woods all these years?"

"Playing with dolls, Lady. Putting up your hair. Trying on dresses, perhaps."

"Do I *look* like a girl's girl to you, Lazarus?" Kelsea felt her voice rising. Several heads had turned toward them now. "Do I look like I spend hours in front of the mirror?"

"Not in the slightest."

Kelsea smiled, a brittle smile that cost some effort. Barty and Carlin had never had any mirrors around the cottage, and for a long time Kelsea had thought that it was to prevent her from becoming vain. But one day when she was twelve, she had caught a glimpse of her face in the clear pool behind the cottage, and then she had understood, all too well. She was as plain as the water beneath.

"Am I dismissed, Lady?"

She stared at him for a moment, considering, then replied, "It depends, Lazarus. I have a saddlebag full of dolls and dresses to play with. Do you want to do my hair?"

He stood still for a moment, his dark eyes unreadable. Then, unexpectedly, he bowed, an exaggerated gesture that was too deep to be sincere. "You can call me Mace if you like, Lady. Most do."

Then he was gone, his pale grey cloak vanishing into the dusk-shadows of the clearing. Kelsea remembered the comb in her hand and turned to take care of the mare, her mind moving like a wild thing while she worked.

Perhaps daring will win them.

You'll never win the respect of these people. You'll be lucky not to die before you reach the Keep.

Maybe. But I have to try something.

You speak as though you have options. All you can do is what they tell you.

I'm the Queen. I'm not bound by them.

So think most queens, right until the moment the axe falls.

D inner was venison, stringy and only barely edible after roasting over the fire. The deer must have been very old. Kelsea had seen only a few birds and squirrels on their ride through the Reddick, though the greenery was very lush; there could be no lack of water. Kelsea wanted to ask the men about the lack of animals, but she worried that it would be taken as a complaint about the meal. So she chewed the tough meat in silence and tried very hard not to stare at the guards around her, the weapons hanging from their belts. The men didn't talk, and Kelsea couldn't help thinking that their silence was because of her, that she was keeping them from the entertaining conversation they could otherwise be having.

After dinner, she remembered the present from Carlin. Taking one of the several lit lanterns sitting around the fire, she went to retrieve her night bag from her mare's saddle. Two guards, Lazarus and the taller, broad-shouldered man she had noticed on the ride, detached themselves from the camp-fire and followed her to the makeshift paddock, their tread nearly silent. After years of solitude, Kelsea realized, she would likely never be alone again. The idea should perhaps have been comforting, but it created a cold feeling in the pit of her stomach. She recalled a weekend when she was seven, when Barty had been preparing to travel to the village to trade meat and furs. He made this trip every three or four months, but this time Kelsea had decided that she wanted to go with him, wanted to so badly that she honestly thought she would die if she didn't go. She'd thrown a full tantrum on the library carpet, complete with tears and screaming, even kicking her feet against the floor in frustration.

Carlin had no patience with theatrics; she tried to reason with Kelsea for only a few minutes before disappearing into her library. It was Barty who'd wiped Kelsea's face and sat her on his knee until she cried herself out.

"You're valuable, Kel," he told her. "You're valuable like leather, or gold. And if anyone knew we had you here, they'd try to steal you. You wouldn't want to be stolen, would you?"

"But if nobody knows I'm here, then I'm all alone," Kelsea replied, sobbing. She had been very certain of this proposition: she was a secret, and so she was alone.

Barty had shaken his head with a smile. "It's true, Kel, nobody knows you're here. But the whole world knows who you are. Think about that for a minute. How can you be alone when the whole world is out there thinking about you every day?"

Even at seven, Kelsea had found this an extremely slippery answer for Barty. It had been enough to dry her tears and calm her anger, but many times in the subsequent weeks she had turned his statement over, seeking the flaw that she knew was there. It was only a year or so later, reading one of Carlin's books, that she found the word she'd been seeking all along: not alone, but anonymous. She had been kept anonymous all those years, and for a long time she had thought that Carlin, if not Barty, had hidden her out of cruelty. But now, with the two tall men right on her heels, she wondered if her anonymity had been a gift. If so, it was now a gift long gone.

The men would sleep around the fire, but they had put up a tent for Kelsea, some twenty feet away on the edge of the clearing. As she stepped inside and tied the flap closed, she heard the two guards stationing themselves on either side of the opening, and after that there was silence.

Dumping her pack on the floor, Kelsea dug through clothes until she found an envelope of white vellum, one of Carlin's few luxuries. Something shifted and slithered lightly inside. Kelsea sat down on the bedding and stared at the letter, willing it to be filled with answers. She had been taken from the Keep when she was barely a year old, and she had no memory of her real mother. Over the years, she'd been able to glean a few bits of hard fact about Queen Elyssa: she was beautiful, she didn't like to read, she had died when she was twenty-eight years old. Kelsea had no idea how her mother had died; that was forbidden territory. Every line of questioning Kelsea undertook about her mother ended at the same place: Carlin shaking her head and murmuring, "I promised." Whatever Carlin had promised, perhaps it ended today. Kelsea stared at the envelope for another long moment, then picked it up and broke Carlin's seal.

Out slid a blue jewel on a fine silver chain.

Kelsea picked up the chain and dangled it from her fingers, staring at it in the lamplight. It was a twin of the necklace that had been around her neck all of her life: an emerald-cut sapphire on a thin, almost dainty silver chain. The sapphire glimmered merrily in the lamplight, casting intermittent blue flickers around the inside of the tent.

Kelsea reached into the envelope again, looking for a letter. Nothing. She checked both corners. She tilted the envelope up, peering inside against the light, and saw a single word scrawled in Carlin's writing beneath the seal.

Careful.

A sudden burst of laughter from the campfire made Kelsea jump. Heart racing, she listened for any sound from the two guards just outside her tent, but heard nothing.

She took off her own necklace and held the two side by side. They were indeed identical, perfect twins right down to the minutiae of the chains. It would be all too easy to mix them up. Kelsea quickly put her own necklace back on.

She held up the new necklace again, watching the jewel swing back and forth, puzzled. Carlin had told her that each heir to the Tearling throne wore the sapphire from the day they were born. Popular legend held the jewel to be a sort of charm against death. When Kelsea was younger, she had thought more than once about trying to take the necklace off, but superstition was stronger; suppose she were struck with lightning on the spot? So she had never dared to remove it. Carlin had never mentioned a second jewel, and yet she must have had it in her possession this whole time. Secrets . . . everything about Carlin was secret. Kelsea didn't know why she had been entrusted to Carlin for fostering, or even who Carlin had been in her old life. Someone of importance, Kelsea assumed; Carlin carried herself with too much grandeur to live in a cottage. Even Barty's presence seemed to fade when Carlin entered the room.

Kelsea stared at the word inside the envelope: *Careful*. Was it another reminder to be careful in her new life? Kelsea didn't think so; she'd heard chapter and verse on that subject in the past few weeks. It seemed more likely that the new necklace was different in some way, perhaps even dangerous. But how? Kelsea's necklace certainly wasn't dangerous; Barty and Carlin would hardly have allowed her to wear it each day otherwise.

She stared at the companion jewel, but it simply dangled there smugly, dim lamplight glinting from its many facets. Feeling silly, Kelsea tucked the necklace deep into the breast pocket of her cloak. Perhaps in the daylight it would be easier to see some difference between the two. The envelope went inside the casing of the lamp, and Kelsea watched the flames devour the thick paper, her mind pulsing with low anger. Leave it to Carlin to create more questions than answers.

She stretched out, looking up at the ceiling of the tent. Despite the men outside, she felt entirely isolated. Every other night of her life, she'd known that Barty and Carlin were downstairs, still awake, Carlin with a book in her hand and Barty whittling or playing with some plant he had found, mixing it up into a useful anesthetic or antibiotic. Now Barty and Carlin were far away, already heading south.

It's only me.

Another low rumble of laughter sounded from around the campfire. Kelsea briefly debated going out there and attempting to at least speak to the guards, but she discarded the idea. They spoke of women, or battles, or perhaps old companions . . . her presence wouldn't be welcome. Besides, she was exhausted from the ride and the cold, and her thigh muscles ached horribly. She blew out the lamp and turned over on her side to wait for uneasy sleep.

The next day they rode more slowly, for the weather had turned murky. The air had lost its icy feel, but now a thin, sickly mist clung to everything, wrapping around tree trunks and moving over the ground in visible tides. The country was gradually flattening, the woods growing sparser each hour, trees giving way to thick undergrowth. More animals, most of them strange to Kelsea, began to appear: smaller squirrels and drooling, doglike creatures that would have seemed like wolves but that they were docile and fled at the sight of the troop. But they didn't see a single deer, and when the morning was well over, Kelsea identified another source of her growing uneasiness: not a single note of birdsong.

The guards seemed subdued as well. Kelsea had been awakened several times during the night by the continuous laughter from the campfire and had wondered whether they would ever shut up and go to sleep. Now all of their mirth seemed to have departed with the bright weather. As the day wore on, Kelsea noticed more and more of the guards shooting hunted glances behind them, though she could see nothing but trees.

Near midday, they stopped to water the horses at a small stream that bisected the forest. Carroll pulled out a map and huddled around it with several guards; from the snatches of conversation she overheard, Kelsea gathered that the mist was causing problems, making landmarks difficult to see.

She limped over to a large, flat rock beside the stream. Sitting down was excruciating, her hip muscles seeming to peel away from the bone when she bent her knees. With some maneuvering, she got herself sitting cross-legged, only to find that her bottom was also aching from hours on the saddle.

Elston, the hulking, broad-shouldered guard who had ridden beside Kelsea for much of the journey, followed her to the rock and stationed himself five feet away. When she looked up, he grinned unpleasantly, showing a mouthful of broken teeth. She tried to ignore him and stretched out one of her legs, reaching toward her foot. Her thigh muscles felt as though they were being shredded.

"Sore?" Elston asked her. His teeth gave him difficulty with enunciating; Kelsea had to think for a moment to figure out what he'd meant.

"Not at all."

"Hell, you can barely move." He chuckled, then added, "Lady."

Kelsea reached out and grabbed her toes. Her thigh muscles screamed, and Kelsea felt them as raw flesh, seams that opened and bled inside her body. She held her toes for perhaps five seconds and then released them. When she looked up at Elston again, she found him still smiling his jagged smile. He didn't say anything else, only stood there until it was time for them to mount up again.

They made camp near sunset. Kelsea had barely dropped to the ground when her reins were plucked from her hand; she turned and found Mace guiding the mare away. She opened her mouth to protest, but thought better of that and turned back to the rest of the Guard, who were also going about their various tasks. She noticed the youngest guard pulling the makings of her tent from his saddlebags.

"I'll do it!" she called and strode across the clearing, holding out her hand for some tool, perhaps some weapon, she didn't care which. She'd never felt more useless.

The guard handed her a flat-headed mallet and remarked, "The tent does require two people, Highness. May I help you?"

"Of course," Kelsea replied, pleased.

Given one person to hold things and one to pound them in, the tent was a simple enough business, and Kelsea talked to the guard as she moved along with the mallet. His name was Pen, and he was indeed relatively young; he appeared to be no more than thirty, and his face held none of the wrinkles or wear that seemed tunneled into the faces of the rest of the guards. He was handsome, with dark hair and an open, good-natured face. But then again, they were all handsome, her mother's guards, even those over forty, even

Elston (when his mouth was closed). Surely her mother wouldn't have chosen her guards only for their looks?

Kelsea found Pen easy to talk to. When she asked his age, he told her he'd just had his thirtieth birthday four days since.

"You're too young to have been in my mother's guard."

"That's right, Lady. I never knew your mother."

"Then why did they bring you on this errand?"

Pen shrugged and made a self-explanatory gesture toward his sword.

"How long have you been a guard?"

"Mace found me when I was fourteen years old, Lady. I've been in training ever since."

"With no ruler in residence? Have you been guarding my uncle?"

"No, Lady." A shadow of distaste crossed Pen's face, so quickly Kelsea might have imagined it. "The Regent keeps his own guard."

"I see." Kelsea finished pounding a stake into the ground, then stood up and stretched with a grimace, feeling her back pop.

"Are you adjusting to the pace, Highness? I assume you've undertaken few long journeys on horseback."

"The pace is fine. And necessary, I understand."

"True enough, Lady." Pen lowered his voice, glancing around them. "We're being tracked hard."

"How do you know?"

"The hawks." Pen pointed skyward. "They've been behind us since we left the Keep. We arrived late yesterday because we took several detours to throw off pursuit. But the hawks can't be fooled. Whoever controls them will be behind us now—"

41

Pen paused. Kelsea reached out for another stake and remarked casually, "I heard no hawks today."

"Mort hawks make no sound, Lady. They're trained for silence. But every now and again, you might see them in the sky if you're looking out for them. They're devilish quick."

"Why don't they attack?"

"Our numbers." Pen spread out the last corner of the tent so that Kelsea could stake it. "The Mort train their hawks as you would soldiers, and they won't waste themselves by attacking a superior force. They'll try to pick us off one by one if they can."

Pen paused again, and Kelsea waved the mallet at him. "You needn't worry about frightening me. I must fear death no matter which stories you choose to tell."

"Perhaps, Lady, but fear can be hobbling in its own way."

"These pursuers, do they come from my uncle?"

"Likely, Lady, but the hawks suggest that your uncle has help."

"Explain."

Pen looked over his shoulder, muttering, "It was a direct order. Should Carroll ask, I'll tell him so. Your uncle has dealt with the Red Queen for years. Some say they've made alliance in secret."

The Queen of Mortmesne. No one knew who she was, or where she came from, but she had become a powerful monarch, presiding over a long and bloody reign for well over a century now. Carlin considered Mortmesne a threat; an alliance with the neighboring kingdom could be a good thing. Before Kelsea could ask further questions, Pen had moved on. "The Mort aren't supposed to sell their weaponry to the Tear, but anyone with enough money can get hold of

Mort hawks on the black market. My guess is, we have Caden behind us."

"The assassins' guild?"

Pen snorted. "A guild. That's assigning them too much organization, Lady. But yes, they're assassins, and very competent ones. Rumor is that your uncle has offered a large reward to anyone who can track you down. The Caden live for such challenges."

"Will our numbers not stop *them*?"

"No."

Kelsea digested this information, looking around her. In the middle of the camp, three guards were hunched around the pile of gathered firewood, cursing assiduously as it refused to light. The others were dragging felled trees together to make a crude enclosure around the camp. The purpose behind all of these defenses was clear enough now, and Kelsea felt a helpless trickle of fear, mixed with guilt. Nine men, all of them now targeted along with her.

"Sir!"

Carroll came stomping out of the trees. "What is it?"

"Hawk, sir. From the northwest."

"Well-spotted, Kibb." Carroll rubbed his forehead and, after a moment's deliberation, approached the tent.

"Pen, go help them with dinner."

Pen gave Kelsea a brief, mischievous smile that seemed to convey goodwill and disappeared into the dusk.

Carroll's eyes were dark circles. "They come for us, Lady. We're being tracked."

Kelsea nodded.

"Can you fight?"

"I can defend myself against a single attacker with my knife. But I know little of swords." And, Kelsea realized suddenly, she had been trained in self-defense by Barty, whose reflexes were not those of a young man. "I'm no fighter."

Carroll tilted his head, a flash of humor in his dark eyes. "I don't know about that, Lady. I've watched you on this journey; you hide your discomfort well. But we're coming to the point" – Carroll looked around and lowered his voice, then continued – "we're coming to the point where I may need to split my men to evade pursuit. If so, my choice of bodyguard for you will depend much on your own abilities."

"Well, I'm a fast reader, and I know how to make stew."

Carroll nodded in approval. "You've a sense of humor about all this, Lady. You'll need one. You're entering a life of great danger."

"You've all placed yourselves in great danger to escort me to the Keep, yes?"

"Your mother charged us with this task, Lady," Carroll replied stiffly. "Our own honor would allow nothing less."

"You were my mother's man, were you not?"

"I was."

"Once I'm delivered to the Keep, will you be the Regent's man?"

"I haven't decided, Lady."

"Can I do anything to influence that decision?"

He looked away, clearly uncomfortable. "Lady . . ."

"Speak freely."

Carroll made a helpless gesture with his hands. "Lady, I think you're made of much stronger stuff than you appear. You strike me as one who might make a real queen one day, but you're marked for death, and so are those who follow you. I have family, Lady. Children. I wouldn't use my children as a stake in a game of cards; I can't set their lives at hazard by following you, not in the face of such odds."

Kelsea nodded, hiding her disappointment. "I understand."

Carroll seemed relieved. Perhaps he had expected her to begin blubbering. "Because of my station, I would know nothing of any specific plot against you. You may have better luck asking Lazarus, our Mace; he's always been able to discover what others can't."

"We've met."

"Be wary of God's Church. I doubt the Holy Father bears any special love for the Regent, but he must love the person who sits on the throne and holds the keys to the treasury. He'll play the odds, just as we must."

Kelsea nodded again. Carlin had said something very similar, only a few days ago.

"All of these men in my troop are good men. I stake my life on it. Your executioner, when he comes, won't be one of us."

"Thank you, Captain." Kelsea watched as the guards finally lit a fire and began to fan the small flame. "I guess it will be a hard road from now on."

"So your mother said, eighteen years ago, when she charged me to bring you back."

Kelsea blinked. "Didn't she charge you to take me away?"

"No. It was Lazarus who smuggled you out of the castle when you were a baby. He's invaluable that way."

Carroll smiled, remembering something Kelsea couldn't share. He had a nice smile, but again Kelsea noted the gauntness about his face, and wondered whether he might be ill. His gaze lingered on the sapphire, which had once again escaped from Kelsea's shirt. He abruptly turned away, leaving her with a muddle of information to sort through. She dug deep into the pocket of her cloak and felt the second jewel nestled there.

"Your Highness!" Pen called from the campfire, which was burning brightly now. "There's a small stream to the east, if you wish to clean up."

Kelsea nodded, still turning Carroll's advice over in her mind, trying to analyze it as a practical problem. She would need a bodyguard and a staff of her own. Where was she to find people loyal enough to resist the Regent's threats and bribes? Loyalty couldn't be built on nothing, and it certainly couldn't be bought, but in the meantime, she would have to eat.

She wished she had thought to ask Carroll about her mother. He had guarded Queen Elyssa for years; he must know all about her. But no, every Queen's Guard took a vow of secrecy. He wouldn't divulge anything, not even to Kelsea. She gritted her teeth. She had automatically assumed that the transition to a new life would bring an end to all secrets; after all, she would be the Queen. But these men would be no more willing than Carlin to give her the information she sought.

She had meant to try to take a bath tonight after they stopped riding; her hair was oily, and she was beginning to smell her own sweat whenever she moved. The nearby stream would serve her purpose, but the thought of bathing under the watchful eyes of Pen or Elston, or worse, Lazarus, was unthinkable. She would just have to bear the filth, and take some comfort in the fact that her guards certainly didn't smell any better. She gathered her greasy hair and fastened it into a bun, then hopped off the rock to go and find the stream.

That night the guards were boisterous around the campfire again. Kelsea lay in her tent, first trying to sleep and then fuming. It was hard enough to nod off when her brain was crammed with questions, but the constant bursts of drunken laughter made it impossible. She wrapped her cloak around her head, determined to ignore them. But when they broke into a filthy song about a woman with a rose tattoo, Kelsea finally tore the cloak off her head, put it on, and left the tent.

The guards had set up bedrolls around the fire, but none of them appeared to have seen any use yet. The air was heavy with an unpleasant, yeasty smell that Kelsea deduced must be beer, although there had never been any alcohol at the cottage. Carlin wouldn't allow it.

Only Carroll and Mace stood when she approached. They appeared to be sober, but the rest of the Guard simply regarded her unblinkingly. Elston, she saw, had fallen asleep with his head on a thick oak log.

"Did you need something, Lady?" Carroll asked.

Kelsea wanted to shriek at them, to let out two pent-up hours' worth of sleeplessness. But then she looked around at their reddened faces and thought better of it. Carlin said that it was easier to reason with a toddler than with a drunk. Besides, drunken people in books often disclosed secrets. Perhaps Kelsea could actually get them to talk to her.

She tucked her cloak beneath herself and sat down between Elston and Pen. "I want to know what happens when we reach New London."

Pen turned a bleary gaze toward her. "What happens?"

"Will my uncle try to kill me when we get to the Keep?"

They all stared at her for a moment, until Mace finally answered, "Probably."

"Your uncle couldn't kill anybody," Coryn muttered. "I'd be more worried about the Caden."

"We don't *know* they're behind us," the red-bearded man argued.

"We don't know anything," Carroll announced in a shut-up voice, and turned back to Kelsea. "Lady, wouldn't you rather simply trust us to protect you?"

"Your mother always did," added the red-bearded man.

Kelsea narrowed her eyes. "What's your name?"

"Dyer, Lady."

"Well, Dyer, you're not dealing with my mother. You're dealing with me."

Dyer blinked owlishly in the dim light. After a moment, he murmured, "I meant no offense, Lady."

She nodded and turned back to Carroll. "I was asking what happens when we get there."

"I doubt we'll actually have to fight our way into the Keep, Lady. We'll bring you in in high daylight; the city will be crowded this weekend, and the Regent isn't brave enough to kill you in front of the wide world. But they'll come for you in the Keep, without doubt."

"Who is they?"

Mace spoke up. "Your uncle isn't the only one who wants you dead, Lady. The Red Queen has everything to gain by keeping the Regent on the throne."

"Isn't the castle inside the Keep secure?"

"There's no castle. The Keep's enormous, but it's a single structure: your castle."

Kelsea blushed. "I didn't know that. No one told me much about the Keep."

"What the hell were you learning all these years?" asked Dyer.

Carroll chuckled. "You know Barty. He was a great medic,

but not much of a details man. Not unless he was talking about his precious plants."

Kelsea didn't want to hear about other people's experiences with Barty. She cut Dyer off before he could reply and asked, "What about our pursuers?"

Carroll shrugged. "Caden, probably, with a little Mort assistance. The hawks we've spotted may be merely hawks, but I think not. Your uncle isn't above taking help from the Mort."

"Of course not," slurred Elston, sitting up from his log and wiping drool from the corner of his mouth. "Surprised the Regent doesn't use his own women as shields."

"I thought the Tearling was poor," Kelsea interrupted. "What would my uncle give in return for such an alliance? Lumber?"

The guards glanced at each other, and Kelsea felt them unite against her in silence, as plainly as if they'd had a conversation.

"Lady," Carroll said apologetically, "many of us spent our lives guarding your mother. We don't cease to protect her just because she's dead."

"I was never in Queen Elyssa's Guard," Pen ventured. "Couldn't I—"

"Pen, you're a Queen's Guard."

Pen shut up.

Kelsea looked around the circle. "Do all of you know who my father is?"

They stared back at her in mute rebellion. Kelsea felt her temper begin to rise, and bit down hard on the inside of her right cheek, an old reflex. Carlin had cautioned her many times that a wild temper was something a ruler couldn't afford, so Kelsea had learned to control her temper around

Carlin, and Carlin had fallen for it. But Barty had known better. He was the one who'd suggested Kelsea bite down on something. Pain counteracted the anger, at least temporarily, sent it somewhere else. But the frustration didn't go anywhere. It was like being back in the schoolroom with Carlin. These men knew so many things, and they wouldn't tell her a single one. "Well, then, what can you tell me about the Red Queen?"

"She's a witch," the handsome blond guard announced flatly. It was the first time Kelsea had heard him speak. The fire highlighted his face, chiseled and symmetrical. His eyes were a pure, wintry blue. *Had* her mother chosen them for their looks? Kelsea shied away from the thought. She had a very specific idea of what her mother should have been like, an idea created in her earliest days and then woven, embellished, each year she remained trapped in the cottage. Her mother was a beautiful, kind woman, warm and reachable where Carlin was cold and distant. Her mother never withheld. Her mother would be coming for her someday, to take her away from the cottage and its endless routines of learning and practicing and preparation in a grand rescue. It was just taking a bit longer than expected.

When Kelsea was seven, Carlin sat her down in the library one day and told her that her mother was long dead. This put an end to the dreams of escape, but it didn't stop Kelsea from constructing new and more elaborate fantasies: Queen Elyssa had been a great queen, beloved by all of her people, a hero who made sure that the poor were fed and the sick doctored. Queen Elyssa sat on her throne and dispensed justice to those who couldn't seek justice for themselves. When she died, they carried her body in a parade through the streets of the city while the people wept and a battalion of the Tear army clashed its swords in salute. Kelsea had honed and polished this vision until she could invoke it at any moment. It dulled her own fear of being Queen, to think that when she returned to the city at nineteen to take the throne, they would give her a parade also, and Kelsea would ride to the Keep surrounded by cheers and weeping, waving benevolently the whole way.

Now, looking around at the group of men around the campfire, Kelsea felt a trickle of unease. What did she really know about her mother, the Queen? What could she really know, when Carlin had always refused to say?

"Come on, Mhurn," Dyer replied to the blond man, shaking his head. "No one ever proved that the Red Queen's actually a witch."

Mhurn glared at him. "She is a witch. Doesn't matter whether she's got the powers or not. Anyone who lived through the Mort invasion knows she's a witch."

"What about the Mort invasion?" Kelsea asked, interested. Carlin had never explained the invasion or its causes very well. Twenty years ago the Mort had entered the Tearling, carved their way through the country, and reached the very walls of the Keep. And then . . . nothing. The invasion was over. Whatever had happened, Carlin skipped right over it in each history lesson.

Mhurn ignored Carroll, who had begun to scowl at him, and continued, "Lady, I have a friend who went through the Battle of the Crithe. The Red Queen sent three legions of Mort army into the Tearling and gave them free rein en route to New London. The Crithe was wholesale slaughter. Tear villagers armed with wooden clubs fought Mort soldiers armed with iron and steel, and when the men were dead every female between five and eighty—"

"Mhurn," Carroll murmured. "Remember who you're talking to."

Elston spoke up unexpectedly. "I've been watching her all day, sir. Believe me, she's a tough little thing."

Kelsea nearly smiled, but the impulse dried up quickly as Mhurn continued, staring at the fire as though hypnotized. "My friend fled his village with his family as the Mort army approached. He tried to cross the Crithe and make for the villages in the north, but he wasn't fast enough, and unfortunately for him, he had a young and pretty wife. She died before his eyes, with the tenth Mort soldier still inside her."

"Christ, Mhurn!" Dyer got up and staggered off toward the edge of the camp.

"Where are you going?" Carroll called.

"Where do you think? I've got to take a piss."

Kelsea suspected that Mhurn had told his tale merely to shock her, and so she kept her face still. But the moment their attention was diverted from her, she swallowed hard, tasting something sour in the back of her throat. Mhurn's story was very different from reading about unrestricted warfare in a book.

Mhurn looked around the campfire, his blond head lowered aggressively. "Anyone else think this is information the new queen shouldn't have?"

"I only question your timing, you ass," Carroll replied softly. "There'll be plenty of time for your tales once she gets on the throne."

"If she gets there." Mhurn had located his mug and now he took a great gulp, swallowing convulsively. His eyes were bloodshot, and he looked so tired that Kelsea wondered if he should stop drinking, but could think of no way to suggest it. "Rape and murder went on in every village in their path,

Lady, in a straight line through the country, all the way from the Argive to the walls of New London. They even slaughtered the babies. A Mort general named Ducarte went from the Almont Plain to the walls of New London with a Tear baby's corpse strapped to his shield."

Kelsea wanted to ask what had happened at the walls of New London, for that was where Carlin's tales always stopped. But she agreed with Carroll: Mhurn needed to be reined in. Besides, she wasn't sure she could handle any more first-person history. "What's your point?"

"My point is that soldiers, most soldiers, aren't born wanting to act that way. They aren't even trained to act that way. War crimes come from one of two sources, situation or leadership. It wasn't the situation; the Mort army went through the Tearling like a knife through warm butter. It was a holiday for them. Brutality and massacre happened because that's what the Red Queen *wanted* to happen. The last census found over two million people in the Tearling, and I'm not sure they know how precarious their position is. But, Lady, I thought that *you* should know."

Kelsea swallowed, then asked, "What happened to your friend?"

"They stabbed him in the gut and left him to bleed to death when they moved on. They did a poor job, and he survived. But the Mort army took his ten-year-old daughter in their train. He never saw her alive again."

Dyer came sauntering back from the trees and plopped down on his bedroll. Kelsea stared into the fire, remembering one morning at her desk in Carlin's library. Carlin showed her an old map of the border between the Tearling and New Europe, a ragged line that ran down the eastern end of the Reddick Forest and the Almont Plain. Carlin was a great admirer of New Europe. Even in the early wake of the Crossing, when borders were barely drawn and the southern New World was a battlefield for warlords, New Europe had been a thriving representative democracy with nearly universal participation in elections. But the Red Queen had changed many things; now New Europe was Mortmesne, and democracy had vanished.

"What does the Red Queen want, then?" Kelsea had asked Carlin. She had no interest in maps and wanted to wrap up the lesson.

"What conquerors always want, Kelsea: everything, with no end in sight."

Carlin's tone had left Kelsea with a certainty: Carlin, who feared nothing, feared the Red Queen. Queen's Guards were supposed to fear nothing as well, but as Kelsea looked around now, she saw a different story in their faces. She strove for a lighter tone. "Well, then, I'd best not let the Red Queen invade again."

Dyer snorted. "Precious little you could do, Lady, if she took it into her head."

Carroll clapped his hands. "Now that we've had our bedtime story from Mhurn, it's time to sleep. And if any of you want a good-night kiss from Elston, let him know."

Elston chortled into his mug and then spread his huge arms. "Aye, for all who enjoy the tough love."

Kelsea stood up, tightening her cloak. "Won't you all be hung over in the morning?"

"Probably," muttered the dark-haired guard named Kibb.

"Is it really a good idea for so many of you to be drunk on this journey?"

Carroll snorted. "Lazarus and I are the real Guard, Lady. These other seven are window dressing."

All of them burst out laughing, and Kelsea, feeling excluded again, turned and wandered back toward her tent. None of the men followed her, and she wondered whether anyone would guard the tent tonight. But when she turned around, Mace was right behind her, his tall silhouette unmistakable even in the dark.

"How do you do that?"

He shrugged. "It's a gift."

Kelsea ducked into her tent and fastened the flap. Stretching out on her bedding, she tucked a hand beneath her cheek. She had put on a bravura front by the campfire, but now she was shivering, first in her chest and then spreading to the rest of her body. According to Carlin, Mortmesne loomed large over its neighbors. The Red Queen demanded control, and she had it. If the Regent had truly allied with her, she even had control of the Tearling.

A hacking cough came from the direction of the campfire, but this time Kelsea didn't find the noise irritating. Digging inside her cloak, she took out the second necklace and squeezed it tightly in one hand, her own sapphire in the other. Staring at the apex of the tent, she thought of women raped and babies on the points of swords, and sleep didn't come for a very long time.

CHAPTER 2
THE PURSUIT

The Tearling is not a large kingdom, but it embraces a wide variety of geography and climate. The heart of the country is flat and temperate, much of it rich farmland. In the west, the kingdom is bordered by the Tearling Gulf, and beyond that God's Ocean, which remained uncrossed until well into the Glynn Queen's reign. In the south, the country becomes dusty and dry as it reaches the borders of Cadare. On the northern border, above the Reddick Forest, foothills climb into the Fairwitch, an impassable mountain range. And in the east, of course, the Tearling runs a jagged border with Mortmesne. As years passed and the Red Reign of Mortmesne progressed, Tearling monarchs watched this eastern border with deepening unease . . . and for good reason.

—The Tearling as a Military Nation, CALLOW THE MARTYR

Early in the morning, before the sun even thought of breaking the horizon, the Queen of Mortmesne woke from a nightmare.

She lay frozen for a moment, her breath coming quickly, until she recognized the familiar scarlet of her own apartments. The walls were paneled in Tear oak, and everywhere the wood was embossed with dragons, the pattern dyed red. The Queen's bed was enormous, draped in scarlet silk, seamless and comfortable. But now the pillow beneath her head was soaked with sweat. It was the dream, the same dream that had woken her for two weeks now: the girl, the fire, the man in pale grey with the face she could never quite see, and finally the last flight to the borders of her land.

The Queen rose and moved to the bank of windows that overlooked the city. The borders of the panes were opaque with frost, but her apartments were quite warm. The glassmakers in Cadare created such a marvel of insulation that many claimed they used magic, but the Queen knew this to be false. There was no magic in the surrounding kingdoms but that which she permitted, and she had given the Cadarese no license to enchant their glass or anything else. But the insulation was an impressive achievement. Each year, Mortmesne took a significant portion of Cadare's tribute in glass.

Below the Queen lay the Crown city of Demesne, silent and mostly dark. A glance at the sky told her it was just before the fourth hour; only the bakers would be awake. The castle beneath her was dead silent, for all of them knew that the Queen never rose before the sun.

Until now.

The girl, the girl. She was the hidden child, Elyssa's child, she could be no one else. In the Queen's dreams she was sturdy and dark-haired, with a strong, determined face and her mother's green Raleigh eyes. But unlike Elyssa, she was a plain thing, and somehow that seemed the worst detail of all, the one that conveyed the most reality. The rest of the dream was a blur of pursuit, thoughts of nothing but escape while the Queen attempted to outrun the man in grey and what appeared to be a conflagration behind him. But when she woke, it was the girl's face that remained: round and unremarkable, just as her own had once been.

The Queen would have had one of her seers interpret the dream, but they were all merely frauds who enjoyed dressing in veils. Liriane had been the only one with any true gift, and now Liriane was dead. There was no need of the sight anyway. In broad stroke if not in detail, the meaning of the dream was plain enough: disaster.

A thick, guttural sound came from behind her, and the Queen whirled around. But it was only the slave in her bed. She had forgotten about him. He'd performed well, and she'd kept him for the night; a good fuck chased the dreams right away. But she loathed snoring. She watched him with narrowed eyes for a moment, waiting to see if he would do it again. But he only grunted softly and rolled over, and after a moment the Queen turned to stare out the window again, her thoughts already distant.

The girl. If not dead already, she would be soon. But it rankled, to have been unable to find the jewels all these years. Even Liriane had seen nothing of the girl's whereabouts, and Liriane had known Elyssa well, better than the Queen herself. It was maddening . . . a girl child of known age, with a singular marking on her arm? Even if the child kept the jewels hidden, it should have been an easy search. The Tearling wasn't a large kingdom.

Where did you hide her, you bitch?

Possibly outside the Tearling, but that would have shown considerable imagination for Elyssa. Besides, any hiding place outside the Tearling would have brought the child under greater dominion of Mortmesne. Elyssa had assumed until the very end that the greatest threat to her child would come from outside the Tearling, and that was another error of judgment. No, the girl was still in the Tearling somewhere; she had to be.

Another snorting rumble came from the bed.

The Queen shut her eyes and rubbed her temples. She *hated* snoring. She looked longingly at her fire, considered lighting it. The dark thing might give her answers, if she was brave enough to ask questions. But it didn't like to be summoned, except in the gravest need, and it had no use for weakness. To ask it for help would be to admit doubt of her own ability to find the child.

Not a child anymore. I must stop thinking of her that way. The girl would be nineteen now, and Elyssa hadn't been a complete fool. Wherever the girl had gone, someone had been training her to survive. To rule.

And I can't see the jewels.

Another disquieting thought. In the dreams, the girl never wore a necklace; there was no sign of either sapphire. What did that mean? Had Elyssa hidden the jewels somewhere else?

The slave was now snoring steadily, waves that began innocuously enough but built to a crescendo of sound that was probably audible in the bakeries twenty floors below. The Queen had handpicked him for his dark skin and aquiline nose, a clear sign of Mort blood. He was one of the Exiled, a descendant of Mort traitors banished to the western protectorate of Callae. Although she had sent them to Callae herself, the Queen still found the idea of the Exiled strangely exciting. But a slave who snored was no use to anyone.

On the wall beside the window were two buttons, one black and one red. The Queen considered for a moment and then pushed the black button.

Four men came through the door, nearly soundless, clad in the black of the palace guard. All of them had swords drawn. Ghislaine, her guard captain, was not among them, but of course he wouldn't be. He was too old to work nights anymore.

The Queen pointed to the bed. The guards pounced, laying hold of the snoring man, one to each limb. The slave awoke with a gasp and began to struggle. He kicked a guard with his left leg and rolled over, fighting his way toward the end of the bed.

"Majesty?" asked the ranking guard, gritting his teeth as he held on to a flailing arm.

"Take him down to the lab. Have them remove his tongue and uvula. And sever his vocal cords, just in case."

The slave screamed and struggled harder as her guard worked to pin him to the bed. One had to admire his strength; he freed his right arm and left leg before one of her guards planted an elbow in the small of his back. The slave gave a shriek of agony and ceased his struggles.

"And after surgery, Majesty?"

"Once he's healed, offer him to Lady Dumont with our compliments. If she doesn't want him, give him to Lafitte."

She turned back to the window as her guard hauled the still-screaming man from the room. Helene Dumont might well want him; being too stupid to hold up a conversation, she liked her men quiet. The shrieks became abruptly muffled as the guards closed the door, and soon they faded altogether.

The Queen tapped her fingers on the windowsill, considering. The fireplace beckoned her, almost begging her to light it, but she was certain that would be the wrong course. The situation wasn't that dire. The Regent had hired the

Caden, and despite her disdain of all things Tear, even the Queen didn't underestimate the Caden. Besides, if the girl did somehow manage to reach New London alive, Thorne's people would take care of her. One way or another, by March, the Queen would have the girl's head on her wall and both necklaces in hand, and then she would be able to sleep, dreamless. She stretched out both hands, palms up, and snapped her fingers. Far out on the western horizon, near the Tear border, lightning flickered.

She turned and went back to her bed.

The third day of the journey began well before sunrise. Kelsea rose when she heard the clink of arms in the darkness outside her tent and began to dress, determined to break down the tent herself before one of the guards tried to do it for her. She was about to light the lamp when she realized that she could already see. Everything in the tent was lit with a thin, sickly glow, and she easily spotted her shirt in the corner. But her shirt looked blue.

She looked around cautiously, seeking the source of the light. It took two complete turns before she realized that she was casting no shadow on the tent walls, that the light was coming from her. The sapphire around her neck was glowing, giving off its own light, not the cobalt glitter that it always reflected in firelight but a deep aquamarine blaze that seemed to come from within the jewel itself. She clutched the pendant in her palm and made a second discovery: the thing was giving off actual heat. It was at least twenty degrees hotter than her body temperature.

Uncovering the stone, she watched the blue light dance across the canvas interior of the tent. The sapphire had lain around her neck all of her life, and other than its annoying habit of popping free of her clothing, it had never done anything remarkable. But now it was radiant in the darkness.

Magic, Kelsea thought wonderingly, staring at the cerulean light. *Like something out of one of Carlin's books.*

Reaching down, she grabbed her cloak and dug into the pocket for the other necklace. She pulled it out eagerly, then sank back in disappointment. The companion jewel looked exactly the same, a large blue sapphire in the palm of her hand. It gave off no light.

"Galen! Help me saddle!"

The voice outside, a gruff rumble that Kelsea already recognized as Mace's, brought her back to herself. There was no time to marvel at the light; rather, she needed to conceal it. She dug in her bags for her thickest, darkest shirt, burgundy wool, put it on and tucked the necklace beneath, then pinned her hair into a tight bun and covered it with a thick knitted hat. The jewel lay like a tiny warm coal between her breasts, radiating a pleasant heat that cut into the bitter cold of early morning. Still, it wouldn't keep her warm all day; she donned an extra layer of clothing and her gloves before venturing outside.

The eastern sky showed only a thin line of cornflower against the shadow of the hills. As Kelsea approached, Galen broke from the group packing the horses and brought her several pieces of half-cooked bacon, which she wolfed hungrily. She broke her tent down alone, pleased that no one came to help. Carroll gave her a nod of greeting on his way to the small copse that held the horses, but his face was still shadowed, and he looked as though he hadn't slept at all.

Kelsea packed the tent onto Pen's horse before turning to her own saddlebags. Even May the mare seemed to have softened toward her overnight; Kelsea held out a carrot from a pile that Mace produced, and May seemed content to eat from her hand.

"Hawk, sir! Two of them on the eastern horizon!"

Kelsea scanned the lightening sky but saw nothing. The stillness was unnerving. She had grown up in a forest filled with hawks, and their high, savage cries had always chilled her blood. But this silence was worse.

Carroll had been tightening saddlebags onto his horse. Now he stopped and stared at the sky overhead, mulling something over. After a moment he called, "All of you! Over here now! Pen, finish getting that fire out!"

The men gathered around, most of them carrying supplies. Pen came last, his face smudged with ash. They began to distribute the supplies among the various saddlebags, but Carroll barked, "Leave them!"

He rubbed his bleary eyes. "We're being hunted, lads. And my heart tells me they're drawing close."

Several of the guards nodded.

"Pen, you're the smallest. Give the Queen your cloak and armor."

Pen's face tightened, but he nodded, unclasped his cloak, and began to shed his armor. Kelsea reached into her pocket and grabbed the second necklace, burying it in her fist, before drawing off her own cloak. They began to buckle Pen's armor onto her body, one piece at a time. The iron was incredibly heavy; several times Kelsea had to stifle a grunt as each new piece settled upon her frame.

"We'll split up," Carroll announced. "They won't be a large company, and we have to hope they can't track us all in force. Go in any direction you please, so long as you don't go together. We regroup on the Keep Lawn."

He turned to Pen. "Pen, you'll trade horses with the Queen

as well. If we're fortunate, they'll put all their energy into tracking the mare."

Kelsea swayed slightly as Mhurn settled a breastplate against her shoulders. It was flat, made for a man, and her breasts throbbed painfully as he began to buckle it in the back.

"Who goes with the Queen?" asked Dyer, looking as though he prayed it was anyone else.

"Lazarus does."

Kelsea looked up at Mace, who stood behind Carroll at the edge of the group. His expression was as disinterested as ever; Carroll might as well have instructed him to guard a particularly important tree. Some of Kelsea's doubt must have shown in her face, for Mace raised his eyebrows, clearly daring her to argue.

She didn't.

Carroll smiled bravely at the group of men, but his face was haunted; Kelsea felt death on him, could almost see it as a black shadow that waited over his shoulder. "This errand is our last together, but the most important. The Queen must reach the Keep, even if we fall seeing it done."

He made a sign of dismissal, and the men turned to leave. Kelsea summoned as much force as she could. "Hold!"

"Lady?" Carroll turned back, and the rest stopped on their way to their horses. Kelsea looked around at them all, their faces hard and resolved in the ashlight of morning, some of them hating her, she knew, deep down where their honor wouldn't allow them to admit it.

"I know that none of you chose this errand, but I thank you for it. I would welcome any of you in my guard, but either way, your families will be taken care of. I swear . . . for what it's worth."

She turned back to Carroll, who was watching her with an expression she couldn't read. "We can go now, Captain."

"Lady." He nodded, and the men began to mount their horses. "Lazarus, a word!"

Mace stomped up to the two of them. "You'll not take my horse, Captain."

"I wouldn't dare." A small smile creased Carroll's face. "Stay with the Queen, Lazarus, but distant enough that you'll not be tracked as a pair. I would make for the Caddell and then follow it to the city. The tide will cover your tracks."

Mace nodded, but Kelsea had an odd flash of intuition: he'd already evaluated and rejected Carroll's advice in a heartbeat, choosing his own direction instead.

"You've no time for stories, Lady, but our Lazarus is a renowned escape artist. If we're lucky, he may perform his greatest trick."

Kelsea's armory was complete. Pen shrugged his green cloak over his shoulders, where it sat tightly. "Godspeed, Lady," he murmured, then was gone.

"Captain." Kelsea thought of Carlin and Barty standing in the doorway of the cottage, their dreadful false optimism. "I'll see you shortly in front of my throne."

"No, Lady, you won't. I've seen my own death on this journey. Enough for me that you sit there." Carroll mounted his horse, his face drawn with a terrible and hopeless purpose. Mace reached up a hand, and he grasped it. "See her safe, Lazarus."

He spurred his horse into a trot and vanished into the forest.

Kelsea and Mace were left standing alone. Their horses' breath steamed the air, and Kelsea realized anew how cold it was. She picked up Pen's grey cloak, found a pocket inside the breast, and shoved the second necklace deep inside before putting the cloak on. The camp around them seemed very empty, nothing but a pile of dead leaves, the wisps of smoke from the fire, and the skeletal branches of trees above their heads.

"Where do I go?" she asked.

"Through that treebreak to your left." Mace helped her mount Pen's horse, a deep brown stallion a good hand taller than her mare. Even with Mace's help, Kelsea groaned at the effort to haul both her body and Pen's armor into the saddle. "You'll ride north for only a few hundred feet, Lady, and then circle back east until you ride due south. You won't see me, but I'll be near at hand."

Feeling the great size of the horse beneath her, Kelsea admitted, "I don't ride very well, Lazarus. And I've never really ridden fast at all."

"I've noticed, Lady. But Rake is one of our gentlest stallions. Ride him with a slack rein and he won't attempt to throw you, though you're unfamiliar to him." Mace's head whipped up sharply, his gaze fixed above Kelsea. "Go now, Lady. They're coming."

Kelsea hesitated.

"Christ!" Mace slapped the horse's rump and Rake leaped forward, the reins nearly jerked from Kelsea's hands. Behind her, she heard him call out, "Dolls and dresses, Lady! You'll need to be tougher than this!"

Then she was off into the woods.

It was a terrible ride. She took the stallion in the wide circle Mace had described, her whole body itching for the moment when she could go straight and pick up speed. When she judged the circle wide enough, she checked the moss on the rocks and began to ride south, Pen's grey cloak flying behind her. For a few minutes the armor weighed heavily, seeming to rattle her whole body each time Rake landed on his front hooves. But after a bit she found that she could no longer feel the weight of the metal at all. There was nothing but speed, a pure, clean speed that she had never achieved with Barty's aging stallion. The forest flew by her, trees sometimes far off and sometimes so close that the tips of branches whipped against her mailed body. A freezing wind screamed in her ears, and she tasted the bitterness of adrenaline in the back of her throat.

There was no sign of Mace, but she knew he was there, and his last comment recurred to her every few minutes while she rode, making her face flush with warmth even beneath the numbness imparted by the wind. She had thought that she'd been very strong and very brave during this journey; she had let herself believe that she had impressed them. Carlin had always told Kelsea that her face was an open book; what if they had all seen her pride? Would she ever be able to face them again?

Stop that nonsense right now!

Carlin's voice thundered inside her head, stronger than any humiliation, stronger than doubt. Kelsea clamped her thighs more tightly against Rake's sides and urged him to go faster, and when her cheeks threatened to turn warm again, she reached up and slapped herself across the face.

After perhaps an hour of hard riding, the woods cleared for good and Kelsea was suddenly down into pure farmland, the Almont Plain. Carefully tilled rows of green stretched out as far as she could see, and she mourned inside at the very flatness of the land, its sameness. There were a few trees, but they were only thin leafless trunks that twisted upward toward the sky, none of them sturdy enough to provide any cover. Kelsea rode on, finding lanes between the rows of crops, cutting across fields only when there was no other way through. The farming acres were dotted with low homesteads made of wood and hay-thatched roofs, most of them little more than huts. In the distance Kelsea could also see several taller, stronger wooden dwellings, probably the houses of overseers, if not nobles.

She saw many farmers; some of them straightened to get a look at her, or waved as she flew by. But most, more concerned with their crops, simply ignored her. The Tear economy ran on farming; farmers worked the fields in exchange for the right to occupy the noble's land, but the noble took all of the profits, except for taxes paid to the Crown. Kelsea could hear Carlin's voice in the library now, her tone of deep disapproval echoing against the wall of books: "Serfdom, Kelsea, that's all it is. Worse, it's serfdom condoned by the state. These people are forced to work themselves to the bone for a noble's comfortable lifestyle, and if they're lucky, they're rewarded with survival. William Tear came to the New World with a dream of pure socialism, and this is where we ended up."

Carlin had hammered this point home many times, but it was very different for Kelsea to see the system in front of her. The people working the fields looked hungry; most of them wore shapeless clothes that seemed to hang from their bones. The overseers, easily identifiable on horses high above the rows of crops, did not look hungry. They wore broad, flat hats, and each carried a thick wooden stick whose purpose was painfully clear; when Kelsea rode close to one of them, she saw that the end of his stick was stained a deep maroon.

To the east, Kelsea spotted what must be the house of a

noble: a high tower made of red brick. Real brick! Tearling brick was a notoriously poor building material compared to Mortmesne's, which was made with better mortar and commanded at least a pound per kilo. Carlin had an oven made of real bricks, built for her by Barty, and Kelsea had wondered more than once whether Barty had bought the bricks off the black market from Mortmesne. Mort craftsmen weren't supposed to sell their wares to the Tear, but Mort luxuries commanded a great price across the border, and Barty had told Kelsea that anything was available for the right price. But even if Barty wasn't above doing a bit of black market business, he and Carlin would never have been able to afford a brick house. The noble who lived there must be extraordinarily wealthy. Kelsea's gaze roved over the people who dotted the fields, their scarecrow cheeks and necks, and dim anger surfaced in her mind. She had dreaded being a queen most of her life, and she was ill equipped for the task, she knew, though Barty and Carlin had done their best. She hadn't grown up in a castle, hadn't been raised in that privileged life. The land she would rule frightened her in its vastness, but at the sight of the men and women working in the fields, something inside her seemed to turn over and breathe deeply for the first time. All of these people were her responsibility.

The sun broke the horizon on Kelsea's left. She turned to watch it rise and saw a black shape streak across the blinding sky, there and then gone without a sound.

A Mort hawk!

She dug her heels into Rake's sides and relaxed her grip on the reins as far as she dared. The stallion picked up pace, but it was futile; no manned horse could outrun a hawk in hunt. She glanced around wildly in all directions and saw nothing, not even a stand of trees to give them cover, only endless farmland and ahead, in the distance, the blue gleam of a river. She dug beneath her cloak for her knife.

"Down! Get down!" Mace shouted behind her. Kelsea ducked and heard the harsh whistle of talons hitting the air where her head had been.

"Lazarus!"

"Go, Lady!"

She crouched against Rake's neck and took all pressure off his reins. They were tearing down the length of the country now, so fast that Kelsea could no longer distinguish the farmers in the fields, only a continuous blur of brown and green. It was only a matter of time, she thought, before the horse threw her and she broke her neck. But even that idea brought its own strange freedom . . . who could have predicted she would survive this long? She found herself laughing, wild, out-of-control laughter that was instantly cut to shreds by the wind.

The hawk swooped in from her right and Kelsea ducked again, but not soon enough. Talons punctured her neck and ripped through the skin. Blood, thick and warm, oozed down to her collarbone. The hawk soared off to her left. Kelsea turned to track it and felt the gash in her neck pull wide open, sending a shot of pain all the way down her right side.

Hooves were pounding up behind her on the right, but Kelsea didn't dare turn around; the hawk was circling in front of her now, preparing to come for her eyes. It was far larger than any hawk she'd ever seen, a deep, dark black rather than the usual brown, almost akin to a vulture. Suddenly it dived for her again, talons outstretched. Kelsea ducked a third time, throwing up her arm to protect her face.

A sound of muffled impact thudded above her head.

Kelsea felt no pain, waited a moment, and then peeked above her. Nothing.

She glanced to her right, her eyes tearing with the pain of movement, and found Mace alongside her. The hawk's body dangled from the spiked head of his mace, a pulpy mass of blood, feathers, and gleaming innards. He shook the handle truculently until the bird fell off.

"Mort hawk?" she called over the wind, trying to keep her voice steady.

"For certain, Lady. They're like no other hawks in the world, black as midnight and big as dogs. God knows how she's breeding them." Mace slowed his stallion and looked Kelsea over, his gaze assessing. "You're wounded."

"Only my neck."

"The hawks are killers, but they're also scouts. A party of assassins will be behind us now. Can you still ride?"

"Yes, but the blood will leave a trail."

"About ten miles southwest is the stronghold of a noblewoman who was loyal to your mother. Can you make it that far?"

Kelsea glared at him. "What sort of weak, housebound woman do you think I am, Lazarus? I'm bleeding, that's all. And I've never had such a fine time as on this journey."

Mace's dark eyes brightened with understanding. "You're young and reckless, Lady. It's a desirable quality in a warrior, but not in a queen."

Kelsea frowned.

"Let's go, Lady. Southwest."

By now the sun had risen fully over the horizon, and Kelsea thought she could see their destination: another brick tower outlined against the blue shimmer of the river. From this distance, the tower had the dimensions of a toy, but she knew that upon approach it would rear many stories high. Kelsea wondered if the noblewoman who lived there took toll from the river; Carlin had told her that many nobles who were situated next to a river or road took the opportunity to squeeze extra money from those who passed by.

Mace's head swung back and forth, as though on a swivel, while they rode. He had tucked his mace back into his belt without even bothering to clean it, and the hawk's innards gleamed in the morning sunlight. The sight made Kelsea feel slightly sick, and she turned to study the country around her, ignoring the pain in her neck. They were undoubtedly in the center of the Almont, the great farming plains of the Tearling, with nothing but flat land in every direction. The river up ahead was either the Caddell or the Crithe, but Kelsea couldn't determine which without knowing how far west they'd ridden. Far to the southwest, she saw a smudge of brown hills and a darker stain of black against it, possibly the city of New London. But then sweat dripped into her eye, and by the time she could see again, the brown hills had vanished like a mirage and green land stretched as far as she could see. The Tearling felt enormous, much more so than it had ever looked on any of Carlin's maps.

They had covered perhaps half the distance to the tower when Mace reached out and slapped Rake's rump, hard. The stallion whinnied in protest but lengthened his stride, tearing off toward the river so suddenly that Kelsea nearly fell from her saddle. She tried to jog with the stallion's movement, but the wound in her neck seemed to tear open each time Rake's hooves hit the earth, and Kelsea fought to ignore a dizziness that rose and fell like the tide.

For a time she could hear only Mace behind her, but gradually her ears picked up the unmistakable sound of hooves, at least several sets in pursuit. They were gaining, and the river was approaching at an alarming pace. Peeking over her shoulder, Kelsea saw her worst fears confirmed: Caden, four of them, perhaps fifty yards back, their bright red cloaks flying in the wind. Hearing of the Caden in her childhood, Kelsea had asked Barty why professional assassins would wear such a bright and distinguishable color. Barty's answer was not comforting: the Caden were such confident killers that they could afford to wear bright red and come in daylight. Those cloaks sent a clear message; something inside Kelsea froze at the sight of them.

Behind her, Mace snarled a curse before shouting, "On the right!"

Looking around, Kelsea now saw a second group of men, perhaps four or five strong, cloaked in black, bearing down from the northwest, angling to intercept them before they reached the river. Even if Rake was strong enough to outrun both parties in pursuit, Kelsea would be cut off when the river forced her to turn. The river was wide, perhaps twenty yards across, and even from this distance, Kelsea could see that the deep green water flowed rapidly along, occasional spits and sprays betraying underwater rocks. It was too fast and wild to swim, and no boats were visible. Kelsea saw no option, but still her thoughts wandered back helplessly across that vast green land that stretched to all horizons, the fields covered with people. Her responsibility.

If she could gallop west along the riverbank, she thought, both packs of pursuers would be forced to follow her along the water's edge; there would be no more angles for them to cut her off. They would probably catch her anyway, but it would extend the time during which a miracle was possible. She tightened her grip and rode headlong for the river. Blood from the wound on her neck spattered across her chin and cheek with each stride.

When the water was perhaps fifty feet away, Kelsea yanked on the reins, trying to take the other riders by surprise with a right turn. But Rake misinterpreted the movement and stopped short, and Kelsea went flying, taking in a confused muddle of inverted river and sky before she landed flat on her stomach. Her wind had been knocked out so completely that she could only chuff out small puffs of air. She pushed herself up, but her legs wouldn't respond. She tried to force breath in and only managed a hitching gasp. The sound of approaching horses seemed to fill the world.

To her left, a man shouted, "The girl! The girl, damn you! Deal with the Mace later, take the girl!"

Something crashed to the ground in front of her. Kelsea looked up and saw Mace, his sword raised in one hand and his mace in the other, facing down four men in red cloaks. The Caden were all quite different in appearance, dark and light, tall and short. One even had a mustache. But each face had the same hard, blank look: disciplined ferocity. The light-skinned assassin got through Mace's guard and raked the point of a sword across his collarbone. Blood spattered across the Caden's face and sank into the scarlet of his cloak, but Mace ignored the wound, reached out with one hand, and jabbed his attacker in the throat. The man in red collapsed with a gargling, choking sound, his windpipe crushed.

Mace backed up to stand directly in front of Kelsea now, waiting, a weapon raised in each fist. Another Caden rushed him and Mace dropped to his knees, his sword slicing through the air. The Caden fell to the ground, shrieking in agony. His right leg had been severed just below the knee;

blood fountained from the stump in bursts, soaking the riverbank a deep red. After a moment, Kelsea realized that she was watching the rhythm of the man's dying pulse, his heart pumping out his lifeblood onto the sand.

Dimly, she realized that she should do something. But her legs still weren't responding, and her ribs ached horribly. The two remaining Caden came at Mace from each side, but Mace ducked them neatly and buried his mace in the side of one man's head, crushing it in a spray of blood and bone. Mace didn't recover quickly enough; the last assassin reached him and sliced him up the hip, his sword tearing cleanly through the leather band at Mace's waist. Mace dove beneath him, rolled once, and came to his feet with the grace of an animal, swinging the mace with crushing force against the assassin's spine. Kelsea heard a snap, a sound like Barty breaking a branch of greenwood, and the Caden thumped to the ground.

Behind Mace, Kelsea saw that the black-cloaked men had arrived and dropped from their horses with swords already drawn. Mace whirled and charged forward to meet them while Kelsea watched with a sense of disappointed wonder ... it seemed such a waste for him to die here. She'd never heard of anyone beating one Caden swordsman before, let alone four. She took her hand from her neck and found it slick with blood. Was it possible to bleed to death from a shallow wound? Barty had never covered death or dying.

Someone reached beneath Kelsea's arms and flipped her onto her back. Black spots danced in front of her eyes. The gash in her neck tore wider and began to pulse with warm blood. Her legs splayed out, the feeling in them reawakened to horrible life as though shards of glass were being driven into her calves. A face loomed just above hers, a face the color of pale death with fathomless black holes for eyes and a bloodstained mouth, and Kelsea screamed before she could help it, before she realized that it was only a mask.

"Sir. The Mace."

Kelsea looked up and saw a second masked man standing in front of her, though his mask was a mercifully plain black.

"Knock him out," ordered the man in the white mask. "We'll take him with us."

"Sir?"

"Look around you, How. Four Caden, all by himself! He'll be trouble, for certain, but it would be criminal to waste such a fighter. He comes with us."

Kelsea hauled herself up, though her neck shrieked in protest, and reached a sitting position in time to see Mace, bleeding from numerous wounds now, surrounded by several black-masked men. One of them darted forward, quick as a weasel, and brought his sword hilt down on the back of Mace's head.

"Don't!" Kelsea cried as Mace crumpled to the ground.

"He'll be fine, girl," said the white-masked man above her. "Get yourself together."

Kelsea dragged herself to her feet. "What do you want with me?"

"You're in no position to demand answers, girl." He held out a flask of water, but she ignored it. Black eyes gleamed behind the mask's eyeholes as he studied her, peering closely at her neck. "Nasty. How did that happen?"

"A Mort hawk," Kelsea replied grudgingly.

"God bless your uncle. His taste in allies is no better than his taste in clothing."

"Sir! More Caden! From the north!"

Kelsea turned northward. A cloud of dust was visible

across the acres of farmland, deceptively small at this distance, but Kelsea thought that the party in pursuit must be at least ten men strong, a reddish mass against the horizon.

"Any more hawks?" asked the leader.

"No. How shot one down."

"Thank Christ for that. Tie up the horses; we'll take them with us."

Kelsea turned to look at the river. It was deep and wild, the far bank covered in trees and shrubs that overhung the water for at least five hundred yards downstream. If she could swim the width of the river, she could probably manage to pull herself out.

"What a coveted prize you are," the leader remarked beside her. "You don't look like much."

Kelsea whirled toward the river. She didn't make three steps before he grabbed her elbow and threw her toward a second man, nearly the size of a bear, who caught her neatly beneath the arms.

"Don't try to run from us, girl," the leader told her, his voice cold. "We might kill you, yes, but the Caden *will* kill you, and give the Regent your head as a prize."

Kelsea weighed her options and decided she had none. Five masked men surrounded her. Mace lay on the ground twenty feet away; Kelsea could see him breathing, but his body was limp. When one of the men finished binding Mace's hands, two more picked him up and began to bundle him onto his horse. Kelsea had no sword, and didn't know how to use one anyway. She turned back to the leader and nodded her consent.

"Morgan, take her on your horse." The leader turned and mounted his own horse, raising his voice as he did so. "Quickly now! Watch for outriders!"

"Up, Lady," Morgan said, his voice surprisingly gentle in contrast to his massive frame and black mask. "Here."

Kelsea placed her foot in the makeshift stirrup of his hands and hauled herself onto his horse. Her neck was bleeding freely again; the right shoulder of her shirt was soaked, and scarlet rivulets had begun to drip down her forearm. She could smell her own blood, a coppery odor like the old pennies Barty kept in his keepsake box at home. Once a week, he would polish them meticulously and then show them to Kelsea: dull round copper coins with a stately bearded man on the face, remnants of a time long gone. It seemed strange that a good memory could be triggered by the smell of blood.

Morgan climbed up behind her; Kelsea felt the horse settle appreciably under his weight. His arms provided a sturdy frame on either side. Kelsea ripped the fabric of her sleeve until she had a patch to press against her neck. The wound definitely needed stitches, and soon, but she was determined not to leave a blood trail on the ground.

They galloped along the river's edge. Kelsea wondered where they could go, for the river certainly ran too fast and wild for the horses to swim, and there was no sign of a bridge. Glancing north, Kelsea saw that the group of red cloaks had changed direction and were now on a direct course to intercept. But the masked men around her gave no hint of where they were going, whether they had a plan of escape. The leader rode in front, and behind him another man rode Mace's stallion with Mace thrown across the saddle, his inert form bouncing with each of the horse's strides. Kelsea could see only a little blood, but his grey cloak covered the bulk of his body. All of the masked men seemed singularly focused on the road ahead; they didn't even turn to track the progress of her pursuers, nor did they look at Kelsea, and she felt another pang at her own helplessness. On her own, she would have been dead in a heartbeat.

"Now!" the leader shouted.

The earth turned beneath Morgan's horse and they galloped headlong into the river. Kelsea shut her eyes and held her breath, preparing for the icy water, but it didn't come. All around them the current roared wildly, freezing droplets scattering in the air and soaking Kelsea's pants to the knees. But when she opened her eyes, she found that they were incomprehensibly crossing the river, the horses' hooves splashing with each step, yet striking solid ground.

Impossible, she thought, her eyes wide with astonishment. But the proof was before her: they were cutting a broad diagonal across the river, each step bringing them closer to the far bank. They passed between two boulders jutting upward from the water, so close that Kelsea could see patches of deep emerald moss slicked across the surface. She thought of the glowing jewel around her neck, and almost laughed. The day had been full of wonders.

When they reached dry ground, the group of horses immediately cut into the woods. For the second time that day, Kelsea found her face whipped and snapped by trees, but she tucked her chin into her chest and made no sound.

Deep in the shade of a massive oak, the leader raised his hand and they brought their horses to a stop. Behind them, the river was barely visible through the trees. The leader brought his horse around in a circle and then sat motionless, staring back toward the far bank.

"That should puzzle them for a while," one of the men muttered.

Kelsea turned, ignoring a wave of dizziness, and peered

through the branches of the oak. She could see nothing, only the gleam of sunlight off the water. But one of the black-masked men chuckled. "They're stumped, all right. They'll be there for hours."

Now she could hear their pursuers: raised voices and an answering shout of "I don't know!"

"The lady needs stitching," Morgan announced behind Kelsea, startling her. "She's losing too much blood."

"Indeed," the leader replied, fixing Kelsea with his black eyes. She stared back, trying to ignore his mask. The face was a harlequin, but much more sinister, awful in some way that she couldn't put her finger on. It reminded her of nightmares she'd had as a child. Nevertheless, she forced herself to sit up straight and stare back at him while blood pooled in the crook of her arm. "Who are you?"

"I am the long death of the Tearling. Forgive us." He nodded, looking over her head, and before Kelsea could turn around, the world went dark.

CHAPTER 3
THE FETCH

The mark of the true hero is that the most heroic of his deeds is done in secret. We never hear of it. And yet somehow, my friends, we know.

—*Father Tyler's Collected Sermons,*
FROM THE ARVATH ARCHIVE

Wake up, girl."

Kelsea opened her eyes to a sky of such brilliant blue that she thought she must still be dreaming. But a quick glance around showed her that it was a tent. She was lying on the ground, wrapped in the skin of some animal. Not deer, which she would have recognized, but it was warm, so warm that she was reluctant to rise.

She looked up at the speaker, a man dressed entirely in dark blue. His voice was a pleasant baritone, distinctive enough that she recognized him even without his awful mask. He was clean-shaven and handsome, with sharp cheekbones and good humor in the set of his mouth. He was also considerably younger than she had guessed on the riverbank, certainly no more than twenty-five, his hair still thick and dark and his unlined face dominated by a pair of large black eyes that gave Kelsea pause; those eyes were much older than twenty-five.

"Where's your handsome face today?"

"I'm home now," he replied easily. "No point in dressing up."

Kelsea busied herself with sitting upright, though the movement brought a strong warning twinge from the right side of her neck. Exploring the area gently with her fingers, she found a stitched gash, covered with some sort of sticky poultice.

"It will heal well. I tended you myself."

"Thank you," Kelsea replied, then realized that she wasn't wearing her own clothing, but a gown of some sort of white cloth, linen perhaps. She reached up to touch her hair and found it smooth and soft; someone had given her a bath. She looked up at him, her cheeks reddening.

"Yes, me as well." His smile widened. "But you needn't worry, girl. You're far too plain for my taste."

The words hurt, and badly, but Kelsea hid the sting with only a slight tightening of her face. "Where's my cloak?"

"Over there." He flicked his thumb toward a pile of clothing in the corner. "But there's nothing in it. It would take a better man than me to resist hunting for this."

He held out one hand to display a dangling sapphire necklace. Kelsea reached up and found her own necklace still around her neck.

"They're optimistic, girl, to let you have both. Some said the King's jewel had been lost altogether."

Kelsea restrained herself from reaching for the second necklace, since he so obviously wished her to. But her eyes followed the sapphire as it swung back and forth.

"You've never worn this necklace," he remarked.

"How do you know?"

"If you had worn it, the jewel would never have allowed me to take it from you."

"What?"

He gave her an incredulous look. "Don't you know anything of these jewels?"

"I know they're mine."

"And what have you done to earn them? Born to a second-rate queen with a burn on your arm."

Second-rate. What did that mean? Kelsea filed the comment away, speaking carefully. "I would not have wished for any of this."

"Perhaps not."

Something in his tone chilled Kelsea, warned her that she was in danger here. And yet why should that be, when he had saved her life on the riverbank? She watched the jewel, blue sparkles reflecting across her skin, while she concentrated on the problem. Bargaining required something to bargain with. She needed information. "May I ask your name, sir?"

"Unimportant. You may call me the Fetch." He leaned back, awaiting her reaction.

"The name means nothing to me."

"Really?"

"I was raised in isolation, you see."

"Well, you would know my name otherwise. The Regent has a high price on my head, growing all the time."

"For what?"

"I stole his horse. Among other things."

"You're a thief?"

"The world is full of thieves. If anything, I am the father of thieves."

Kelsea smiled against her will. "Is that why you all wear masks?"

"Of course. People are envious of the gifts they don't have."

"Perhaps they just don't like criminals."

"One needn't be a criminal to get in trouble, girl. There's a handsome reward for your head as well."

"My head," Kelsea repeated faintly.

"Yes, your head. Your uncle offers twice as much if it's recognizable upon delivery. A present for the Mort bitch, no doubt; I suppose she wishes to hang it somewhere. But your uncle demands the jewels and your arm, as proof."

Carlin's words about the fates of rulers reappeared in Kelsea's mind. She tried to picture her head atop a pike and couldn't. Carlin and Barty rarely spoke about the Raleigh Regent, Kelsea's uncle, but there was no mistaking their tone. They held him in low esteem, and that low esteem had trickled down to Kelsea. The fact that her uncle wanted to kill her had never bothered her; he had never seemed important, not the way her mother was important. He was only an obstacle to be surmounted. She returned her attention to the Fetch and took a deep breath; he had drawn his knife now. It sat balanced on one knee.

"So, girl," the Fetch continued in a deceptively pleasant voice, "what to do with you?"

Kelsea's stomach tightened further, her mind racing. This man wouldn't want her to beg.

I must prove that I'm worth something. Quickly.

"If you're such a wanted man, I'll be in a position to offer you clemency."

"You will indeed, should you survive to sit on the throne for more than a few hours, and I doubt you will."

"But I may," Kelsea replied firmly. The wound on her neck gave a hard twinge, but she ignored it, recalling Carroll's words in the clearing. "I'm made of stronger stuff than I appear."

The Fetch stared at her, long and intently. He wanted something from her, Kelsea realized, though she couldn't imagine what it might be. With each passing second, she became more uncomfortable, but she couldn't look away. Finally, she blurted out the question in the back of her mind. "Why did you call my mother a second-rate queen?"

"You think she was first-rate, I suppose."

"I don't know anything about her. No one would tell me."

His eyes widened. "Impossible. Carlin Glynn is an extraordinarily capable woman. We could have picked no one better."

Kelsea's mouth dropped open. No one but her mother's guard knew where she'd been raised, or the Regent's men would have been at the door of their cottage years before. She waited for the Fetch to continue, but he said nothing. Finally she asked, "How is it that you knew where I was, but the Mort and the Caden didn't?"

He waved a dismissive hand. "The Mort are thugs, and the Caden didn't start looking for you until your uncle grew desperate enough to pay their rates, which are exorbitant. If the Caden had been looking for you from the beginning, you'd have been dead years ago. Your mother didn't hide you that well; she lacked imagination."

Kelsea managed to hold her face still, but it wasn't easy. He talked about her mother so contemptuously, but Carlin had never said anything bad about Queen Elyssa.

But she wouldn't have, would she? Kelsea's mind whispered unpleasantly. *She promised.*

"Why do you dislike my mother so much? Did she wrong you somehow?"

The Fetch tipped his head to one side, his gaze calculating. "You're very young, girl. Incredibly young to be a queen."

"Will you tell me your grievance with my mother?"

"I see no reason to."

"Fine." Kelsea crossed her arms. "Then I'll continue to think of her as first-rate."

The Fetch smiled appreciatively. "Young you may be, but you have more brains than your mother ever had on a good day."

Kelsea's wound was aching badly now. A fine mist of sweat had sprung up on her brow, and he seemed to notice it only a moment after she did herself. "Tip your head."

Kelsea did so without thinking. The Fetch reached into his clothing and pulled out a pouch, then began to apply something wet to her neck. Kelsea braced herself for the sting that didn't come. His fingers were soft on her skin. Within a few seconds, Kelsea realized that she should have been more protective of her person, and shut her eyes, resigned. A phrase from one of Carlin's books occurred to her: *any plausible scoundrel . . .* Her own foolishness made her toes clench.

The anesthetic worked quickly; within a few seconds, the pain had dulled to a low pulse. The Fetch released Kelsea's neck and pocketed the pouch. "Later, some mead should take care of the rest of the pain."

"Don't patronize me!" Kelsea snapped; she was angry at herself for finding this man attractive, and it seemed very important that he not know. "If you mean to kill me, be done with it!"

"In my own time." The Fetch's black eyes gleamed with something that Kelsea thought might be respect. "You surprise me, girl."

"Did you expect me to beg?"

"Had you done so, I would have killed you on the spot."

"Why?"

"Your mother was a beggar."

"I'm not my mother."

"Perhaps not."

"Why don't you tell me what it is you want?"

"We want you to be a queen."

Kelsea heard the implication easily. "As my mother was not?"

"Have you any idea who your father was?"

"No, and I don't care."

"I do. I've a bet with one of my men."

"A bet?"

His eyes twinkled. "Your paternity is one of the great wagering items in this kingdom. I know an old woman living in a village far to the south who backed her horse almost twenty years ago, and she's been waiting for the truth to come out ever since. The field is, shall we say, quite wide."

"How charming."

"You're royalty, girl. Nothing in your life will be personal anymore."

Kelsea pursed her lips, annoyed at the turn of the conversation. Her father, like her uncle, had never seemed particularly important. Her mother was the important one, the woman who ruled the kingdom. Whoever Kelsea's father was, he had apparently abandoned her at birth . . . but that abandonment had never hurt the way her mother's had. Kelsea remembered days spent waiting in front of the picture window in the front room of the cottage; eventually, the sun would always set, and still her mother hadn't come.

"We've waited a long time to see what you were made of, girl," the Fetch remarked. "I cajole and threaten by turns, and now I'm no further. You're not what we expected."

"Who is we?"

The Fetch gestured behind him. Kelsea realized that she could hear men's voices outside the tent, and, slightly more distant, someone chopping wood.

"What holds your group together?"

"That's a perceptive question, so of course you'll get no answer." He sprang to his feet, the movement so sudden that Kelsea flinched and drew her knees together. Had she a knife and he nothing at all, this man would still have her dead in less than a minute. He reminded her of Mace: a man of latent violence, its employment all the more deadly for the fact that he held it in such low esteem. She'd forgotten to ask about Mace, she realized, but now wasn't the time. She felt dim relief when the Fetch tucked his knife back into the band at his waist.

"Dress yourself, girl, and come outside."

When he had disappeared through the tent flap, Kelsea turned her attention to the pile of dark-hued clothing on the ground. Men's clothes, and far too big for her, but perhaps that was for the best. Kelsea didn't flatter herself that she had a shapely figure.

Who cares about your figure?

No one, she answered Carlin grumpily, pulling the

crumpled linen gown over her head. She wasn't fool enough to miss the danger here: a man who was handsome, intelligent, and more than slightly bad. Not all of Carlin's books had been nonfiction.

But I'm doing no harm, she insisted. *If I know the danger, it lessens the harm.*

Even inside her head, this statement didn't ring entirely true. The Fetch had left moments ago, but she was already anxious to follow him outside and see him again.

Don't be a fool, her mind snapped. *You're too ugly for him, he said so.*

She had finished dressing now. Combing her fingers through her hair, she stood and peered out of the tent.

They must have brought her a long way south. The country surrounding the camp was no longer forest or even farmland; they were on top of a high, flat hill covered with weedy grass parched yellow by the sun. Similar hills surrounded them on all sides, a sea of rolling yellow. The land hadn't yet begun to drop into desert, but they couldn't be far from the Cadarese border.

At first glance, Kelsea would have taken the camp for that of a circus troupe: several tents dyed gaudy shades of red, yellow, and blue, situated around a stone fire pit. Something was cooking, for smoke drifted lazily into the air and Kelsea could smell roasting meat. On the other side of the pit, a short blond man dressed in the same sort of shapeless clothing as Kelsea herself was chopping wood.

Closer to Kelsea's tent, three men were huddled together, talking in low voices. One of them was the Fetch; another, judging by his height and shoulders, could only be the enormous Morgan. He had blond hair and a round face that remained friendly as Kelsea approached. The third man was black, which gave Kelsea pause for a moment. She'd never seen a black person before, and she was fascinated by the man's skin, which gleamed in the sunlight.

None of them bowed to her, not that Kelsea had expected them to. The Fetch beckoned her, and Kelsea moved forward, taking plenty of time about it so that he knew she didn't jump to his command. As she drew nearer, he gestured to his two companions. "My associates, Morgan and Lear. They won't harm you."

"Unless you tell them to."

"Of course."

Kelsea squatted down and found the three of them gazing at her with an assessment that she could only describe as clinical. Her sense of danger doubled. But if they killed her, she reasoned, her uncle would remain on the throne. He might even become king, since he was the last of the line. It wasn't much of a bargaining chip, but it was something. According to Carlin, the Regent was not loved in the Tearling, but maybe Carlin had lied to her about that too. Kelsea looked off into the distance, trying to tamp down her frustration. Her mother, the Regent, the Red Queen . . . she needed someone to tell her the truth.

What if the truth isn't anything you want to hear?

She still wanted to know. And, she realized, someone did have answers. "Where's Lazarus?"

"Your Mace? Over there." The Fetch gestured toward a bright red tent some thirty feet away. One of his men, broad and sandy-haired, stood on guard.

"Can I see him?"

"Be my guest, girl. See if you can get him to settle down; he's been making a nuisance of himself."

Kelsea headed for the tent, a bit worried. They didn't seem to be vicious men, but they were hard, and Mace didn't strike her as a model prisoner. The man in front of the red tent stared at her, but she nodded at him and he allowed her to pass.

Mace was lying on the floor, blindfolded and bound securely to a peg in the ground. His wounds appeared to have been stitched just as skillfully as Kelsea's, but ropes were coiled around his wrists and ankles, and a secondary line had been tied up around his neck in a noose. Kelsea hissed involuntarily, and at the sound Mace turned his head. "Have you been harmed, Lady?"

"No." Mindful of the man stationed outside the tent, Kelsea seated herself cross-legged on the floor beside him and spoke in a low voice. "Only a few threats against my life."

"If they were going to kill you, you'd be dead. Your uncle has no use for you alive."

"They're not—" Kelsea lowered her voice even further, struggling to express the strange impression she'd received. "I don't think they're sent from my uncle. They want something from me, but they won't tell me what it is."

"I don't suppose you could untie me? They've found a knot I can't slip."

"I don't think further flight is the way, Lazarus. We wouldn't escape these men."

"Wouldn't you rather call me Mace?"

"Carroll didn't."

"Carroll and I, Lady, have a long history."

"I don't doubt that." Kelsea considered it, realizing that she always thought of him as Mace in her head. "Still, I prefer Lazarus. It's a name of good omen."

"As you like." Mace shifted, the ropes binding his wrists and ankles visibly expanding as he tried to stretch his muscles.

"Are you in pain?"

"Discomfort. Certainly I've been in worse places. How did we escape from the river?"

"Magic."

"What sort of—"

"Lazarus," Kelsea cut in firmly. "I need some answers."

He winced visibly, shifting against his bonds.

"I know my uncle placed a price on my head. But what has he done to the Tearling?"

"Pick something, Lady. Your uncle's probably done it."

"Explain."

"No."

"Why not?"

"I won't have this discussion with you, Lady."

"Why? Were you in my uncle's guard?"

"No."

She waited for him to elaborate, but he merely lay there. Somehow Kelsea knew that his eyes were shut tightly, even beneath the blindfold, like a man under heavy interrogation. She bit down on her cheek, hard, trying to keep a rein on her temper. "I don't understand how I'm supposed to make smart decisions without knowing everything."

"Why dwell on the past, Lady? You have the power to make your own future."

"What of my dolls and dresses?"

"I poked you with a stick to see if you'd fight back. And you did."

"What if I order you to tell me?"

"Order away, Lady, and see how far you get."

She thought for a moment, then decided not to. It was the wrong road to take with Mace; order though she might, he would be guided by his own judgment. After watching him shift restlessly in his bindings for another minute, Kelsea felt the last of her annoyance give way to pity. They'd trussed him up very hard; he barely had room to stretch.

"How's your head?"

"It's fine. Bastard hit me just hard enough, in just the right place. A good shot."

"Have they fed you?"

"Yes."

"Carroll told me that you were the one who smuggled me from the Keep when I was a baby."

"I was."

"Have you always been a Queen's Guard?"

"Since my fifteenth year."

"Have you ever regretted choosing this life?"

"Not once." Mace moved again, his legs stretching and then relaxing, and Kelsea watched, astonished, as one foot slipped free of its coil of ropes.

"How did you do that?"

"Anyone can do it, Lady, if they take the trouble to practice." He flexed his foot, working the stiffness out. "Another hour and I'll have a hand out as well."

Kelsea stared at him for a moment, then scrambled to her feet. "Do you have family, Lazarus?"

"No, Lady."

"I want you for my Captain of Guard. Think on it while you escape."

She left the tent before he could reply.

The sun was beginning to sink, leaving only a dark line of cloud topped with orange on the horizon. Looking around the camp, Kelsea found the Fetch leaning against a tree, staring at her, his gaze flat and speculative. When she met his eye, he smiled, a dark and frozen smile that made her flinch.

Not just a thief, but a murderer as well. Beneath the handsome man, Kelsea sensed another man, a terrible one, with a life as black as the water in an ice-covered lake. *A murderer many, many times.*

The idea should have brought horror. Kelsea waited for a long moment, but what came instead was an even worse realization: it didn't matter at all.

Dinner was an unexpectedly lavish affair. The meat Kelsea had smelled earlier turned out to be venison, and a much better specimen than she'd eaten several days ago. There were boiled eggs, which surprised Kelsea until she caught sight of a small chicken coop out behind her own tent. Morgan had been baking bread over the fire pit for most of the day, and it turned out perfect, crusted on the outside and soft on the inside. The sandy-haired man, Howell, poured her a cup of mead, which Kelsea had never tasted and treated with great wariness. Alcohol and governing went together badly; her books seemed to indicate that alcohol went badly with everything.

She ate little. For the first time in a very long while, she was conscious of her weight. The cottage had always been well stocked with food, and Kelsea usually had second helpings at dinner without a thought. But now she pecked at her meal, not wanting them to think she was a glutton. Not wanting *him* to think so. He sat beside her, and there might as well have been an invisible cord that tugged at her when he smiled or laughed.

The Fetch urged Kelsea to tell them of her childhood in the cottage. She couldn't imagine why he would be interested, but he pressed her, and so she told them, blushing occasionally at the intensity of their gazes. The mead must have loosened her tongue, for she suddenly had many things to say. She told them about Barty and Carlin, about the cottage, about her lessons. Every day, Barty had her in the morning until lunch, and then Carlin had her until dinnertime. Carlin taught her from books, Barty taught her outside. She told them that she knew how to skin a deer and smoke the meat to last for months, that she could snare a rabbit in a homemade cage, that she was handy with her knife but not fast enough. She told them that every night after dinner, she began a book of fiction, reading just for herself, and usually finished it before bedtime.

"A fast reader, are you?" Morgan asked.

"Very fast," Kelsea replied, blushing.

"It doesn't sound like you've had much fun."

"I don't think the point was for me to have fun." Kelsea took another sip of mead. "I'm certainly making up for it now, anyway."

"We've rarely been accused of being fun," the Fetch remarked. "You clearly have no head for alcohol."

Kelsea frowned and put her cup back down on the table. "I do like this stuff, though."

"Apparently. But slow down, or I'll have How cut you off."

Kelsea blushed again, and they all laughed.

At the urging of the others, the black man, Lear, stood up and told the tale of the White Ship, which had sunk in the

Crossing and taken most of American medical expertise with it. Lear told the tale well, much better than Carlin, who was no storyteller, and Kelsea found herself with tears in her eyes as the ship went down.

"Why did they put all of the doctors in one ship?" she asked. "Wouldn't it have made more sense for each ship to have its own doctor?"

"The equipment," Lear replied, with a slight sniff that told Kelsea he liked to tell stories, but didn't appreciate having to answer questions afterward. "Lifesaving medical equipment was the one technology that William Tear allowed them to bring on the Crossing. But it was lost all the same, along with the rest of medicine."

"Not entirely lost," Kelsea replied. "Carlin told me that there's birth control available in the Tear."

"Indigenous birth control. They had to rediscover it when they landed, mostly by trial and error with local plant life. Real science has never existed in the Tearling."

Kelsea frowned, wondering why Carlin hadn't told her that. But of course, to Carlin, birth control was just one of many figures to take into account on a population chart. The Fetch sat down beside her and she felt blood rush to her cheeks. It was a dangerous subject to think about while he was next to her in the dark.

After dinner was cleared, they pushed two tables together and taught her how to play at poker. Kelsea, who had never even seen playing cards before, took a pure pleasure in the game, the first time she'd taken real pleasure in anything since the Queen's Guard had come to Carlin's door.

The Fetch sat beside her and peered at her cards. Kelsea found herself blushing from time to time, and prayed that he wouldn't notice. He was undeniably attractive, but the real source of his charm was something very different: he obviously didn't care one whit what Kelsea thought of him. She wondered if he cared what anyone thought.

After a few hands, she seemed to be getting the hang of the game, though it was difficult to remember the many ways to get the high hand. The Fetch ceased to comment on her discard choices, which Kelsea took as a compliment. However, she continued to lose each hand and couldn't understand why. The mechanics of the game were simple enough, and most of the time prudence counseled that she fold. Each time she did so, however, the hand was usually won by a lower set of cards, and each time, the Fetch chortled into his mug.

Finally a scruffy blond man (Kelsea was fairly certain his name was Alain), while collecting the cards to shuffle and deal, caught Kelsea's eye and commented, "You have dire need of a poker face."

"Agreed, girl," said the Fetch. "Every thought you have is written plain in your eyes."

Kelsea took another gulp of mead. "Carlin says I'm an open book."

"Well, you'd better fix that, and fast. Should we decide not to kill you, you'll find yourself in a den of snakes. Honesty will serve you ill."

His casual talk of killing her made Kelsea's stomach clench, but she attempted to school her face to blankness.

"Better," the Fetch remarked.

"Why can't you make this decision about killing me and be done with it?" Kelsea asked. The mead seemed to have cleared her head even while muddling it, and she longed for a straight answer.

"We wanted to see what sort of queen you look to be."

"Why not just give me a test, then?"

"A test!" The Fetch's grin broadened, and his black eyes gleamed. "What an interesting idea."

"This is a fine game," grumbled Howell. He had a wide, painful-looking scar on his right hand that appeared to be a burn mark. Of course he wanted to get back to play; he won the most often, with the worst cards.

"We're going to play a different game now," the Fetch announced, pushing Kelsea none too gently off the bench. "It's a proper examination, girl. Get yourself over there."

"I've had too much mead to take an examination."

"Too bad."

Kelsea glared at him but moved away from the bench, noticing with slight astonishment that she was unsteady on her feet. The five men turned from the table to watch her. Alain, who had been dealing, snapped the cards in one last shuffle and then pocketed them in a movement too quick to follow.

The Fetch leaned forward and placed his hands beneath his chin, studying her closely. "What will you do should you become a queen indeed?"

"What will I do?"

"Have you any policy in mind?"

The Fetch spoke lightly, but his black eyes were grave. Beneath the question, Kelsea sensed an infinite and deadly patience, perversely coupled with a desperate need for her answer. A test indeed, and she knew instinctively that if she answered incorrectly, the conversation was done.

She opened her mouth, not knowing what she would say, and Carlin's words spilled out into the darkness, Carlin's vision, reiterated so often in the library that Kelsea now spoke the words in a litany as practiced as though she read from the Bible of God's Church. "I'll govern for the good of the governed. I'll make sure that every citizen is properly educated and doctored. I'll cease wasteful spending and ease the burden on the poor through redistribution of land and goods and taxation. I'll restore the rule of law in this kingdom and drive out the influence of Mortmesne—"

"So you do know of it!" Lear barked.

"Of Mortmesne?" She looked at him blankly. "I know that Mortmesne's hold over this kingdom grows all the time."

"What else of Mortmesne?" boomed Morgan, his huge form bearlike in the firelight.

Kelsea shrugged. "I've read of the early years of the Red Reign. And I've been told that my uncle has likely made alliance with the Red Queen."

"Anything else?"

"Not really. Some information on Mort customs."

"The Mort Treaty?"

"What's that?"

"Great God," murmured Howell.

"Even her guardians sworn to secrecy," the Fetch told the rest of them, shaking his head. "We should have known."

Kelsea thought of Carlin's face, her voice, always so laden with regret: *I promised.*

"What is the Mort Treaty?"

"You do at least know of the Mort invasion?"

"Yes," Kelsea replied eagerly, glad to finally know something. "They made it all the way to the walls of the Keep."

"And then what?"

"I don't know."

The Fetch turned away from her and stared off into the darkness. Kelsea looked up at the night sky, and she saw thousands upon thousands of stars. They were miles from everything out here, and the sky was enormous. When she looked back at the group of men, she was dizzy, and nearly stumbled before catching herself.

"No more mead for you," Howell announced, shaking his head.

"She's not drunk," Morgan disagreed. "She's lost her legs, but there's nothing wrong with her wits."

The Fetch returned to them then, with the decisive air of a man who had made a difficult decision. "Lear, tell us a story."

"What story?"

"A Brief History of the Mort Invasion, from Crossing to Disaster."

Kelsea narrowed her eyes; he was treating her like a child again. He turned to her and grinned, almost as though he'd read her thoughts.

"I've never told that as a story," Lear remarked.

"Well, make a good tale of it, if you can."

Lear cleared his throat, took a sip of mead, and locked his gaze on Kelsea. There was no charity there, none at all, and Kelsea had to fight not to look down at her feet.

"Once upon a time, there was a kingdom called the Tearling. It was founded by a man named William Tear, a utopian who dreamed of a land of plenty for all. But ironically, the Tearling was a kingdom of scarce resources, for the British and Americans had not been fortunate in their choice of landing place. The Tearling had no ores, no manufacturing. The Tear were farmers; all they had to offer was the food they grew, the meat they raised, and a limited amount of good lumber from their indigenous oaks. Life was difficult, basic necessities were hard to come by, and over the years many Tear became poor and illiterate. They had to buy everything else from the lands surrounding, and since they were stuck in a hard place, the price wasn't cheap.

"The neighboring kingdom had been luckier in the Crossing. It had everything that the Tearling lacked. It had doctors with access to centuries of European knowledge. It had masons, decent horses, and some of the technology that William Tear had forbidden. Most important of all, it had vast deposits of iron and tin in the ground, so it had not only mining but an army with superior weapons of steel edge. This kingdom was New Europe, and for a long time it was content to be rich and invulnerable, to have its citizens live and die in health and comfort."

Kelsea nodded; she knew all of this already. But Lear's voice was deep and hypnotic, and he did make it sound like a fairy tale, like something from Carlin's *Complete Brothers Grimm* back at home. Kelsea wondered if Mace could hear the tale in his tent, whether he'd worked his other hand free. Her mind felt wildly out of focus, and she shook her head to clear it as Lear continued.

"But toward the end of the second Tear century a sorceress appeared, seeking the rule of New Europe for herself. She slaughtered the democratically elected representatives, their wives, even their children in cradles. Citizens who resisted woke to find their families dead, their homes on fire. It took nearly half a century to subdue the populace, but eventually democracy gave way to dictatorship, and everyone in the surrounding kingdoms forgot that this rich land had once been New Europe; instead it became Mortmesne, the Dead Hand. And likewise, everyone forgot that this sorceress had no name. She became the Red Queen of Mortmesne, and today, one hundred and thirteen years later, she still holds her throne.

"But unlike her predecessors, the Red Queen wasn't content to control only her own kingdom; she wanted the entire New World. After consolidating her rule, she turned her attention to the Mort army, building it into a vast and powerful machine that could not be defeated. And some forty years ago, she began to move beyond her own borders. She took Cadare first, then Callae. These countries surrendered easily, and now they're subject to Mortmesne. They pay tribute, as any good colony would. They allow Mort garrisons to quarter in their homes and patrol their streets. There is no resistance."

"That's not true, though," Kelsea objected. "Mortmesne had an uprising. Carlin told me about it. The Red Queen sent all the rebels to Callae, into exile."

Lear glared at her, and the Fetch chuckled. "You can't interrupt him when he's telling a tale, girl. The Callae uprising lasted about twenty minutes; he's right to omit it."

Kelsea bit her lip, embarrassed. Lear gave her a warning glance before continuing. "But when the Red Queen had reduced these nations to colonies and finally turned her attention to the Tearling, she found trouble in the form of Queen Arla."

My grandmother, Kelsea thought. *Arla the Just.*

"Queen Arla was sickly all her life, but she had brains and courage, and she liked being the queen of a free nation. All of the landowners in the kingdom, particularly God's Church, were worried about their land, and they demanded that she reach a settlement with the Red Queen. The Tearling army was weak and poorly organized, utterly outmatched by the Mort. Nevertheless, Queen Arla refused all Mort overtures and challenged the Red Queen to take this kingdom by force. So Mortmesne invaded the eastern Tearling.

"The Tearling army fought well, perhaps better than anyone could have anticipated. But they had weapons of wood and a few black-market swords, while the Mort army was armed and armored with iron. They had steel-edged blades and steel arrowheads, and they carved their way through the Tear with little difficulty. The Mort had already taken the eastern half of the country by the time Queen Arla died of pneumonia in the winter of 284. She left two surviving children: the Crown Princess Elyssa, and her younger brother Thomas. Elyssa began to make overtures of peace to the Mort Queen almost immediately upon taking the throne. But she couldn't offer tribute, even if she'd been so inclined. There simply wasn't enough money."

"Why not lumber?" Kelsea asked. "I thought the surrounding kingdoms valued Tear oak."

Lear glared at her; she had interrupted him again. "Not enough. Mort pine is of poorer quality than Tear oak, but you can build with it if you need to. Negotiations failed, and the Mort army made straight for New London. The road to the capital was wholesale rape and slaughter, and the Mort left a trail of burned villages in their wake."

Kelsea thought of Mhurn's story, of the man who had lost his wife and child. She stared up at the night sky. Where were the rest of her guards now?

"The situation was desperate. The Mort army was about to breach the walls of the Keep when Queen Elyssa finally came to an agreement with the Red Queen. The Mort Treaty was signed only a few days later, and it's kept the peace ever since."

"And the Mort? Did they withdraw?"

"Yes. Under the terms of the treaty, they left the city several days later and withdrew across the countryside. Strictly speaking, there were no further casualties."

"Lear," the Fetch cut in. "Have some more ale."

Kelsea's insides warmed with pride. Why had Carlin never told her any of this? This was the sort of tale she'd always wanted to hear. Queen Elyssa, the hero! She imagined her mother, barricaded in the Keep with the Mort hordes just outside and her food stores dwindling, sending secret messages back and forth to Demesne. Victory snatched from the very jaws of disaster. It was like something from one of Carlin's books. And yet . . . and yet . . . as she looked around the table, she saw that none of the men were smiling.

"It's a good story," she ventured, turning to Lear. "And you told it very well. But what does it have to do with me?"

"Look at me, girl."

She turned and found the Fetch staring at her, his gaze as grim as the rest.

"Why haven't you begged for your life?"

Kelsea's brow furrowed. What on earth did he want from her? "Why would I beg?"

"It's the accepted course for captives, to offer everything in return for their lives."

He was playing with her again, Kelsea realized, and the idea set off a flare of anger deep inside her. She drew a long, shaky breath before replying, "You know, Barty told me a story once. In the early years after the Crossing, there was a Tear farmer whose son took gravely ill. This was before the British ships arrived in the Tearling, so there were no doctors at all. The son grew sicker and sicker, and the father believed that he would die. He was consumed by grief.

"But one day a tall man in a black cloak showed up. He

said he was a healer, that he could cure the son's illness, but only for a price: the father must give him one of the son's fingers to appease the man's god. The father had his doubts about the man's abilities, but he thought it a good bargain: one useless little finger for his son's life, and of course the healer would only take the finger if he succeeded. The father watched for two days as the healer worked over his son with spells and herbs, and lo and behold, the son was cured.

"The father tried to think of a way to go back on the bargain, but he couldn't, for the man in the black cloak had begun to frighten him very much. So he waited until his son was asleep, then he fetched a knife and sliced off the little finger of the boy's left hand. He wrapped the hand with cloth and staunched the bleeding. But without antibiotics, the wound soon became infected with gangrene, and the son died all the same.

"The father turned to the healer, furious, and demanded an explanation. The healer drew off his black cloak to reveal a terrible darkness, a scarecrow shape of nothing. The father cowered, covering his face, but the shape only announced, 'I am Death. I come quickly, I come slowly, but I am not cheated.'"

Lear was nodding slowly, the first smile she had ever seen flickering about his mouth.

"What's your point?" the Fetch asked.

"Everyone dies eventually. I think it's better to die clean."

He watched her a moment longer, then leaned forward and held up the second necklace so that the sapphire swung back and forth above the table, catching the firelight. The jewel seemed very large, so deep that Kelsea could look beneath its surface and see something moving, dark and far away. She reached for it, but the Fetch pulled the necklace back.

"You've passed half of the test, girl. You've said all of the right things. We're going to let you live."

The men around the table seemed to relax all at once. Alain took the cards out and began shuffling them again. Howell got up and went for more ale.

"But," the Fetch continued in a low voice, "words are the easy part."

Kelsea waited. He spoke lightly, but his eyes were grave in the firelight.

"I don't think you'll survive long enough to truly rule this kingdom. You're bright and good-hearted, perhaps even brave. But you're also young and woefully naive. The protection of the Mace may extend your life beyond its appointed time, but he can't save you. However . . ."

He took Kelsea's chin in one hand, spearing her with his black gaze. "Should you ever gain the throne in truth, I expect to see your policies implemented. They're much in need of refinement, and likely doomed to failure in execution, but they're good policies, and they show an understanding of political history that most monarchs never take the trouble to achieve. You'll rule by the principles you've outlined, and you'll attempt to cure the blight on this land, no matter what it costs you. This is *my* test, and if you fail, you will answer to me."

Kelsea raised her eyebrows, trying to hide the shiver that passed through her. "You think you could get to me once I'm in the Keep?"

"I can get to anyone in this kingdom. I am more danger-ous than the Mort, more dangerous than the Caden. I've stolen many things from the Regent, and he's been under my knife. I could've killed him many times over, but that I had to wait."

"For what?"

"For you, Tear Queen."

Then he was up and gone from the table in one fluid motion, and Kelsea was left staring after him, her face burning where his fingers had been.

CHAPTER 4
THE ROAD TO THE KEEP

O Tearling, o Tearling,
The years you have seen,
Your patience, your sorrow,
You cry for a Queen.
           —*"Lament for the Mothers,"* ANONYMOUS

Kelsea woke with an aching head and a parched mouth, but it wasn't until breakfast that she realized it was her first hangover. Despite the discomfort, she was charmed to experience something that she'd only read about in a book. An upset stomach was a small price to pay for fiction made real. The party had gone on well into the night, and she couldn't remember how much mead she had drunk. It was tasty stuff; she should avoid it in the future.

Once she was dressed, the Fetch produced a shaving mirror so that she could look at the long, ugly gash that wandered down the right side of her neck. It had been neatly sewn closed with fine black thread.

"Good stitchery," Kelsea told him. "But it will scar anyway, won't it?"

The Fetch nodded. "I'm not God, nor am I the queen's surgeon." He gave her a mocking bow. "But it won't fester, and you can tell people that you took the wound in battle."

"Battle?"

"It was a battle getting all that armor off you, and I'll tell the world so."

Kelsea smiled, put down the mirror, and turned to him. "Thank you, sir. You've given me many kindnesses, my life not the least of them. I plan to grant you clemency."

He looked at her for a moment, his eyes dancing with amusement.

"You don't want clemency."

He smiled. Kelsea marveled at the change in him; the grim man she'd seen last night seemed to have vanished with the sun. "Even if you pardoned me, Tear Queen, I'd simply throw it away by stealing something else."

"Have you never wanted another life?"

"There's no other life for me. Anyway, clemency wouldn't begin to repay your debt. I've given you a greater gift than you know."

"What gift?"

"You'll find out. In return, I expect you to keep it safe."

Kelsea turned back to the mirror. "Great God, tell me you didn't impregnate me while I slept."

The Fetch threw back his head and roared with laughter. He placed a friendly hand on Kelsea's back, making her skin prickle. "Tear Queen, you'll either be dead within a week or you'll be the most fearsome ruler this kingdom has ever known. I see no middle ground."

While she brushed her hair, Kelsea glanced at herself in the mirror. She had seen her own reflection in the pond at home, but this was very different; the mirror showed her what she really looked like. It wasn't good. She thought her eyes were very nice, almond-shaped and bright green, part of her Raleigh heritage. Carlin had told her that all of her mother's family had the same cat-green eyes. But her face was as round and ruddy as a tomato, and – there was no other word for it – plain.

The Fetch had given her some pins for her hair, beautiful amethyst pins in the shape of butterflies. Kelsea's hair needed washing again, but the pins made it serviceable. She wondered if the Fetch had stolen them right out of some noblewoman's hair. His smile deepened in the mirror, and Kelsea knew that he had read her mind. "You're a rogue," she remarked, clipping the last pin in place. "I should increase the price on your head."

"Do so. It would only augment my fame."

"What was your life before this? Despite the severity of my education, I think you have an even finer grasp of grammar and vocabulary than I do."

He replied to her in Cadarese. "Of Tear, perhaps. But you'll doubtless outshine me in Mort and Cadarese. I was late to begin learning both, and my accent is imperfect."

"Don't evade the question. I'll find out when I get to the Keep anyway."

"Then there's no reason I should waste my valuable energy telling you now." He reverted to Tear with a rueful smile. "I couldn't remember the Cadarese for energy. I'm out of practice."

Kelsea tilted her head and looked at him, questioning. "Is there nothing I can do for you or your men once I take the throne? Even a small thing?"

"Nothing comes to mind. Anyway, you have a monstrous

task before you, Lady. I wouldn't seek out any additional charge."

"Since you won't allow me to put a hold on your eventual decapitation, I suppose you *would* look foolish asking for a herd of sheep or a new crossbow."

"I'll collect on the debt someday, Tear Queen; don't doubt it. And my price will be steep."

Kelsea looked sharply at him. But his gaze was distant, outside her tent and over the trees. Toward the Keep.

All at once, she realized the great necessity of getting far away from him. He was a criminal, an outlaw, an indisputable threat to the very rule of law she hoped to establish. And yet she didn't know if she would even have the will to imprison him someday, let alone give him the death sentence he surely deserved.

Some other man must come along and take my mind from him. A more acceptable man. That's how it must work.

She set the mirror down. "Can I leave now?"

Mace (the Fetch told Kelsea) had made two more escape attempts in the night. Today, when they finally released him from his tent, he'd worked both legs free again. He was still blindfolded, but as they marched him forward, he delivered a sudden, vicious kick to Alain's legs, and Alain went down to the ground, cursing and clutching his shin. Howell and Morgan hoisted Mace into his saddle, completing the operation with only minor mishap. They left his hands tied, and the murderous expression on his face remained plain beneath the blindfold.

Kelsea bade the Fetch and his men good-bye, an awkward sort of good-bye that seemed unnecessarily grave. She was gratified when Morgan seemed reluctant to see her go; he shook her hand in a manlike fashion and gave her an extra vial of anesthetic for her neck.

"What is this stuff?" Kelsea asked him, tucking the vial into her cloak. "It works wonders for a topical."

"Opium."

Kelsea raised her eyebrows. "*Liquid* opium? Is there such a thing?"

"You've led a sheltered life, Lady."

"I thought opium was a controlled substance in the Tear."

"That's why God made the black market."

The Fetch accompanied Kelsea and Mace for the first few miles, but insisted that Mace remain bound and blindfolded until they were some distance from the camp, so Kelsea had to lead Mace's horse. Oddly enough, the Fetch had allowed them both to keep their stallions. Rake was a decent animal, but Mace's stallion was a Cadarese beauty that must be worth a fortune. Kelsea wondered at this generosity, but didn't ask.

Beneath her cloak, she wore Pen's heavy armor. She'd been reluctant to leave it behind, and the Fetch agreed that she should keep it on. With some chagrin, Kelsea realized that she would need to get herself into more rugged physical condition, as armor would likely be part of her wardrobe for some time.

The Fetch halted atop a slope and pointed down to the countryside ahead, where a thin track wound its way through the yellow hills. "That's the main road through these parts. It will eventually connect to the Mort Road, which takes you straight to New London. Whether you take the road or not is up to you, but even if you don't, you should remain within sight of it. You'll enter quagmire country late tonight, and without a sense of direction you might wander in a swamp forever."

Kelsea stared out across the land. The hills hid much of the road, but eventually the beige line reemerged in the country beyond, neatly bisecting the farming plains and marching toward another set of hills, these brown. Hundreds of buildings clustered across them, all of them over-shadowed by a gigantic grey monolith. The Keep.

"Would you take the road?" she asked the Fetch.

He considered for a moment, then replied, "I would take the road. I'm not in such great danger as you are at the moment, but still, I find that the direct way is often the right way, for reasons that can't be foreseen."

"If he would only remove this blindfold," Mace growled, "I could decide the best way and be damned to him."

"You will not, if you please," the Fetch replied, "remove the blindfold until I'm gone."

Kelsea looked at him curiously. "Is there some grievance between you two?"

The Fetch smiled, but his eyes, staring at the Keep, had hardened. "Not in the way you mean."

He turned his horse and extended a hand. It was a firm, businesslike handshake, and yet Kelsea knew that it was a moment that would be with her all her life, whether she saw him again or no.

"One more thing, Lady."

Kelsea started at the title; she was so used to him calling her "girl." The Fetch reached into his shirt and pulled out the second necklace, which Kelsea had forgotten all about. Again she felt the urgency of getting away from him, this man who made her forget everything that was ordinary and important.

"This necklace is yours; I don't claim it for myself. But I'm going to hold on to it."

"Until when?"

"Until you earn it back with your deeds."

Kelsea opened her mouth to argue, thought better, and shut it. Here was a man who did almost nothing spontaneously; everything was deliberate, so the chances of changing his mind with words were slim. Reaching up, she found that her own necklace had escaped from her shirt again, and she tucked it back in.

"Good luck, Tear Queen. I shall watch you with great interest." He gave her a smile of goodwill and rode away, his horse gaining speed as he went down the slope. Within a minute he was over the next hill and out of sight.

Kelsea stared at the path he left for a bit longer; what Mace didn't know wouldn't hurt him. But after a few minutes even the dust from the Fetch's passage had cleared, and Kelsea turned back to Mace, bringing her horse up alongside his and working quickly on the knots binding his wrists. When his hands were free, Mace tore the blindfold off his head, blinking rapidly. "Christ, that's bright."

"You showed remarkable restraint, Lazarus. With your reputation, I thought you would chew through your bonds and murder several people on the way here."

Mace said nothing, only rubbed his wrists, which still showed deep bruising from the ropes.

"You were very impressive at the river," she continued. "Where did you learn to fight like that?"

"We should be moving along."

Kelsea looked at him for a moment and then turned back toward the city. "You're pledged to see me safely to the Keep, I know. But I release you from that pledge. You've done enough."

"My vow was made to a dead woman, Lady. You can't release me from it."

"What if we ride to our death?"

"Then we'll be a fey pair indeed."

Kelsea turned her face back into the gentle sting of the wind. "Unless you have a better idea, let's take the road."

Mace looked out over the countryside for a moment, his eyes eventually returning to New London, and he nodded. "We'll take the road."

Kelsea clicked to her horse, and they set off down the hill.

After they'd ridden hard for several hours, the small path the Fetch had showed them fed into the Mort Road, a broad avenue some fifty feet wide. This road took the bulk of trading traffic between the Tearling and Mortmesne, and the dirt was so tamped down that there was barely any dust. The path was crowded, and Kelsea thought it fortunate that she was wrapped in the deep purple cloak the Fetch had given her. Mace's Guard grey was gone, replaced by a long black cloak, and if he still had his mace (she hoped he did), he'd prudently tucked it somewhere out of sight. Most of the people traveling in the direction of the Keep were also cloaked and hooded, and all seemed to want to keep their business to themselves. Kelsea kept her eyes out for figures that might be the Caden, or any trace of the grey worn by her Guard. But after a while, they saw so many people that Kelsea was unable to concentrate on any one for very long, and she thought that Mace would have a better sense of hidden danger. She trusted his eyes and concentrated on the road ahead.

The Fetch had told her that it would be an easy two days' ride to New London. Kelsea considered trying to take the journey in one jaunt, but rejected the idea by sundown. She would need to sleep, and her wound was beginning to ache. She mentioned this in a low voice to Mace, and he nodded.

"I don't really sleep, Lady. Therefore, you may."

"You have to sleep sometime."

"Not really. The world's too dangerous to fall asleep in."

"What about when you were a child?"

"I was never a child."

A man jostled against Kelsea's horse, muttering, "Sorry, sir," before moving away. The road had become densely packed. People rode or walked on all sides of Kelsea, and the stench of unwashed flesh hit her nostrils like a slap. But of course this road came from the south, where there was no water for bathing.

Ahead was a cart containing what appeared to be an entire family: parents and two small children. The children, a boy and girl no older than eight years, had gathered a pile of grasses and roots and were playing a cooking game on the floor of the cart. Kelsea watched them, fascinated. All of her imaginary games had been solitary; she had always been the hero, having to invent the cheering masses around her, and even the friends by her side. Still, the urge to see other children, to be with them, had never faded. Kelsea watched the two children so long that the mother began to look back at her with a suspicious lowering of the brows, and Kelsea whispered to Mace that they should fall back a bit.

"Why is the road so crowded?" she asked, once the wagon had passed out of sight.

"This is the only direct road to New London south of the Crithe. Many footpaths feed it."

"But this is a trading road. How does anyone get a caravan through?"

"It's not always so crowded, Lady."

They rode past sunset and well into the night, long after most other travelers had made camp. For a while, fires dotted the sides of the road, and Kelsea could hear talking and singing as they passed, but soon the fires began to go out. From time to time, Kelsea thought she heard hooves far behind them, but she could never be sure, and when she turned around there was only darkness. As they rode, she asked Mace various questions about the current state of her government. He answered each one, but Kelsea sensed that he was being very circumspect, each answer heavily edited. Still, the little information she got was grim.

Most of the Tear population was hungry. The agriculture that Kelsea had seen spread out across the Almont Plain was subsistence farming at best; all extra food went to the landowner, who then sold the produce on for profit, either in the markets of New London or, via the black market, to Mortmesne. There was little justice to be found for the poor. The judicial system had largely broken down under the weight of corruption, and most of the honest judges had been conscripted into other government jobs. Kelsea felt her own poor preparation, almost a physical weight now upon her shoulders. These were problems that needed to be fixed, and quickly, but she didn't know how to do it. Carlin had taught her so much history, but not enough politics. Kelsea had no idea how to wrangle anyone to do her will.

"You said we were fey, Lazarus. I don't know that word; what does it mean?"

"My ancestors were pre-Crossing Scottish. 'Fey' means seeing your own death and exulting in it."

"That doesn't sound like me."

"Perhaps it's only something in your eyes, Lady."

As they rounded another bend, Kelsea thought she heard hooves again. It wasn't her imagination; Mace halted his horse abruptly and twisted around to stare behind them.

"Someone's back there. Several riders."

Kelsea couldn't see anything. There was only a hint of moon in the sky, and she'd never had very good night vision; Barty could run rings around her in the dark. "How far?"

"Maybe a mile." Mace tapped his fingers on his saddle for a moment, debating. "There isn't enough foliage here to provide good cover, and it's safer for us to travel most of the night and then rest in the morning. We'll go on, but if they begin to close the distance, we'll leave the road and take our chances. Let's speed up a bit."

He started forward again, and Kelsea followed. "Couldn't we leave the road now and let them pass by?"

"Risky, Lady, if they're tracking us. But I doubt they're Caden or even Mort. I've seen no hawks, and I think our trail is cold. Your rescuer, whoever he was, did the job admirably."

Mention of the Fetch jolted Kelsea, and she realized, not without some self-satisfaction, that she hadn't thought of him in at least a few hours. Her wish for more information about him warred with the desire to keep his identity a secret for her alone, a brief battle before she crushed the second impulse, furious at herself. "He told me he was called the Fetch."

Mace chuckled. "I had my suspicions, even blindfolded."

"Is he such a great thief as he claimed?"

"Greater, Lady. Tear history boasts plenty of outlaws, but none like the Fetch. He's stolen more goods from your uncle than I've owned in my lifetime."

"He said there was a high price on his head."

"Fifty thousand pounds, at last count."

"But who is he?"

"No one knows, Lady. He first appeared some twenty years ago, mask and all."

"Twenty years?"

"Aye, Lady. Twenty years precisely. I remember it well, because he stole one of your uncle's favorite women when she went shopping in the city. Then, several months later, your mother announced her pregnancy." Mace chuckled. "Probably the worst year of your uncle's life."

Kelsea mulled this information over. The Fetch must be far older than he appeared. "Why hasn't he been caught, Lazarus? Even if he has the luck of the devil, that sort of flamboyance should have brought him down long ago."

"Well, he's a hero to the common people, Lady. Anytime someone manages to rob the Regent, or one of the nobles, the world assumes it's the Fetch. Every piece of rich man's fortune lost endears him to the poor."

"Does he distribute the money to the poor?"

"No, Lady."

Kelsea settled back into her saddle, disappointed. "Has he stolen a great amount?"

"Hundreds of thousands of pounds worth."

"Then what does he do with that money? For certain, I saw none of it in that camp. They were living in tents, and their clothing had seen better days. I'm not even sure they—"

Mace clamped a hand on her arm, silencing her mid-sentence. "You saw?"

"What?"

"You weren't blindfolded."

"I'm not such a fearsome warrior as you are."

119

"Did you see his face? The Fetch?"

"I'm not blind, Lazarus."

"You misunderstand, Lady. They didn't blindfold me for the ferocity of my reputation. The Regent can't catch the Fetch because he's never been able to procure a likeness of him, nor any of his men. The Fetch has nearly killed the Regent twice in my memory, but even he couldn't get a glimpse of the Fetch's face. No one knows what the man looks like, unless it's those who wouldn't betray him for any number of pounds."

Kelsea looked up at the stars, bright points blanketing the sky over her head. They gave her no answers. She'd been growing sleepy, swaying in her saddle, but now she found herself wide-awake again. She should create a likeness of the Fetch at the earliest opportunity, or describe him to someone who could truly draw. And yet she knew that she would do neither of these things.

"Lady?"

Kelsea took a deep breath. "*I* wouldn't betray him for any number of pounds."

"Ah, Christ." Mace halted his horse in the middle of the road and simply sat there for a moment. Kelsea could feel his disapproval; it was like being in the corner of Carlin's library, where Kelsea used to curl up and try to hunch into as small a ball as possible when she didn't know the answer. How Carlin would react to this latest development? Kelsea decided not to imagine it.

"I'm not proud of it," she muttered defensively. "But I see no gain in pretending it's not so."

"Do you know what a fetch is, Lady?

"A retrieval."

"No. A fetch is a creature of ancient myth, a harbinger of

death. The Fetch is an extraordinary thief, but many of his other deeds won't bear close scrutiny."

"I have no wish to hear about the Fetch's other deeds at this time, Lazarus." Suddenly *all* she wanted to hear about was his other deeds. "I told you only because we should have an understanding about this."

"Well," Mace replied after a moment, his voice resigned, "the man is a disruptive influence. Perhaps we shouldn't speak of him again."

"Agreed." Kelsea tugged lightly on the reins, guiding her horse forward. She cast around for some other topic besides the Fetch. "My uncle has no wife, Carlin told me. What's this about one of his women?"

With some reluctance, Mace explained that the Regent had set himself up in the manner of the Cadarese rulers, with a harem culled from young women sold to the palace by poor families. On top of the fact that her kingdom was now steeped in corruption, Kelsea had inherited a brothel into the bargain. She asked Mace to teach her some foul words such as soldiers used, but he refused, so she could find no language bad enough to vent her rage. Women bought and sold! That particular evil was supposed to have been eradicated in the Crossing.

"All of my uncle's actions as Regent reflect on my throne. It's as though I sanctioned this traffic myself."

"Perhaps not, Lady. No one really likes your uncle."

This didn't help Kelsea's anger at all. But beneath her anger, there was also a deep sense of unease. From Mace's description, this practice had been going on since before Kelsea was born. Why had her mother done nothing? She began to ask Mace, then stopped. Of course he wouldn't answer.

"I will have to get rid of the Regent," she said decisively.

"He's your uncle, Lady."

"I don't care. The minute I'm on the throne, I'll throw him out of the Keep."

"Your uncle is high in the favor of the Red Queen, Lady. If you simply kick him out of power, it could destabilize relations with Mortmesne."

"Destabilize? I thought we had a treaty."

"We do, Lady." Mace cleared his throat. "But peace with Mortmesne is always fragile. Open hostility could be disastrous."

"Why?"

"This kingdom hasn't the trained fighting men to deal with any army, let alone that of Mortmesne. And we don't have the steel."

"So we need weapons and a real army."

"No army will challenge Mortmesne, Lady. I'm not a superstitious man, but I believe the rumors about the Red Queen. I chanced to actually see her some years ago—"

"How?"

"The Regent sent a full diplomatic embassy to Demesne. I was in the guard. The Red Queen has held her kingdom for well over a century now, but I swear to you, Lady, she looked no more than your mother's age when you were born."

"And yet she's only one woman, ageless though she may be." Kelsea's voice was steady, but she was unnerved all the same. Discussions of a witch queen were a poor idea on a deserted road in the deep of night. The campfires that had dotted the sides of the road had disappeared entirely, and now it felt as though she and Mace were truly alone in the dark. A sickly-sweet stench of rot had begun to overtake the road; there must be a marsh nearby.

"Be very careful, Lady. Good as your intentions may be, the direct way isn't always best."

"And yet here we are on the road, Lazarus."

"Yes, for want of a better option."

They made camp not long before dawn, still some four or five hours' ride from the city. Mace forbade Kelsea to build a fire, and as a precaution he situated their camp behind a large blackberry thicket that blocked the view from the road. The riders behind them must have finally made camp themselves, for Kelsea heard no more hooves. She asked Mace if she could shed her armor for sleep, and he nodded.

"But you'll wear armor tomorrow, Lady, since we'll enter the city in high daylight. Armor's not much without a sword, but it's better than nothing."

"Whatever you say," Kelsea murmured, already half asleep despite the insistent throb in her neck. She must sleep. All things narrowed toward tomorrow. *Fey*, she thought. Riding toward death. She slept and dreamed of endless fields, the fields she had seen running out before her across the Almont Plain, covered with men and women, ragged scarecrow figures working the land. Beyond the fields the sun was rising, and the sky was on fire.

Kelsea moved closer to the nearest of the farm women. The woman turned and Kelsea saw that she was beautiful, with strong features and dark, tangled hair, her face surprisingly young. As Kelsea approached, the woman held out a bundle of wheat, as though for Kelsea's inspection.

"Red," the woman whispered crookedly, her eyes bright with madness. "All red."

Kelsea looked down again and saw that the woman was

holding not a sheaf of wheat but the broken, bleeding body of a small girl. The child's eyes were torn out, the sockets filled with blood. Kelsea opened her mouth to scream and Mace shook her awake.

CHAPTER 5
WIDE AS GOD'S OCEAN

Many families waited in front of the Keep that day, preparing themselves for grief. They couldn't know that they were about to become players on the stage of history, and some to hold parts greater than they could ever have imagined.

—The Early History of the Tearling,
AS TOLD BY MERWINIAN

They entered New London several hours after midday. Kelsea was groggy with the heat, the punishing weight of her armor, and lack of sleep, but as they crossed the New London Bridge, the sheer size of the city slapped her awake.

The bridge had a toll gate, two men on either side making the collection. Mace produced ten pence from his cloak and managed the admirable trick of paying the gatekeeper while keeping his face covered. Kelsea studied the bridge. It was a marvel of engineering: at least fifty yards long, carved from grey blocks of granite and supported by six enormous pillars that jutted upward from the Caddell River. The Caddell would continue around the outer edge of the city, meandering some fifty miles southwest before it descended in falls over the cliffs and emptied into the Tearling Gulf. The water beneath the bridge was a deep azure.

"Don't look too long at the water," Mace murmured, and Kelsea jerked around to face forward.

New London had originally started as a small town, built by early settlers on one of the lower foothills of the Rice Mountains. But as the town grew into a city, it had spread from hill to hill, eventually becoming the Tear capital. Now New London covered the entire stretch of foothills, its buildings and streets rolling gently up and down to accommodate the topography. The Keep rose from the center of the city, an enormous obelisk of grey stone that dwarfed the buildings surrounding. In her mind, Kelsea had always pictured the Keep as an orderly structure, but the castle ascended ziggurat fashion, without symmetry: battlements and balconies on various levels, multiple nooks and crannies capable of concealment. The Keep had been constructed during the reign of Jonathan the Good, the second king of the Tearling; no one knew the name of the architect, but he must have been a marvel.

The rest of the city was less marvelous. Most of the buildings were poorly constructed of cheap wood, and they leaned haphazardly every which way. One good fire, Kelsea thought, and half the city would burn down.

Near the Keep, perhaps a mile distant, was another tower, pure white and perhaps half as tall, topped with a golden cross. That must be the Arvath, the seat of God's Church. Close to the Keep, of course, although Mace had told her that the Regent had given in and allowed the Holy Father to build a private chapel within the Keep walls as well. Kelsea couldn't tell if the cross atop the Arvath was gilded or made of real gold, but it shone brilliantly in the sun, and Kelsea narrowed her eyes at the sight. William Tear had forbidden the practice of organized religion in his utopia; according to Carlin, he had even thrown one man right over the side of his flagship when he found out the man had been proselytizing in secret. But now Christianity had rebounded as strongly as ever. Kelsea couldn't say what her attitude toward God's Church would have been if she'd grown up in a different house, if her values had not been so shaped by Carlin's atheism. But it was too late; Kelsea's distrust of the golden cross was instinctive and visceral, even though she knew that she would have to come to some sort of compromise with what it represented. She had never been good at compromise, even during the easy conflicts that arose in the cottage.

Mace rode silently beside her, occasionally pointing for a change of direction, as the bridge ended and the crowded thoroughfare entered the city proper. They both remained heavily cloaked and hooded. Mace believed that all routes to the Keep would be guarded, and Kelsea sensed the watchfulness in him, the way he occasionally shifted his position to place himself between her and something that had put his wind up.

Kelsea couldn't detect anything out of the ordinary, but how could she know what was ordinary? The streets were lined with stalls, merchants hawking everything from simple fruits and vegetables to exotic birds. An open-air market, Kelsea realized, one that grew ever more densely packed as she and Mace attempted to maneuver their horses farther into the city. There were shops as well, each with a gaily-colored placard out front, and Kelsea saw a tailor, a baker, a healer, a hairdresser, even a haberdasher! What sort of vanity supported a milliner?

The crowd astounded her. After years with only Barty and Carlin, it was hard to accept so much humanity in one place. People were everywhere, and they came in so many varieties, tall and short, old and young, dark and fair, thin and round. Kelsea had met plenty of new people in the past few days, but she had never really considered before how many possibilities were presented by a single human face. She saw a man with a long, hooked nose, almost like the beak of a bird; a woman with long, wavy blonde hair that seemed to reflect the sun in thousands of sparkles. Everything seemed overly bright, enough to make Kelsea's eyes water. And the sounds! All around Kelsea was the roar of innumerable voices raised at once, a clamor that she had never heard before. Individual voices pressed in on her from time to time, merchants shouting their wares or acquaintances greeting each other across the confusion of the road, but their voices were nothing compared to the overall roar of the crowd. It attacked Kelsea's ears with a physical force that threatened to crush her eardrums, yet she found the chaos oddly comforting.

As they rounded one corner, a street performer caught Kelsea's eye. He placed a rose in a vase, made an identical vase appear from nowhere, then made the rose vanish and reappear instantaneously in the second vase. Kelsea slowed her horse to watch. The magician vanished the rose and both vases entirely, and then reached into his own mouth and produced a snow-white kitten. The animal was clearly alive; it squirmed in his hands while the crowd applauded. The magician then presented the kitten to a small girl in the audience, who squealed with excitement.

Kelsea smiled, charmed. Most likely he was gifted only with extraordinary dexterity, not true magic, but she could see no slip in the flawless transition of objects.

"We court danger here, Lady," murmured Mace.

"What danger?"

"Only a feeling. But my feelings on such matters are usually right."

Kelsea shook the reins and her horse began to trot forward again. "The magician, Lazarus. Mark him for me."

"Lady."

As the day drew on, Kelsea began to share Mace's anxiety. The novelty of the crowd was diminishing, and everywhere Kelsea looked, she sensed people staring at her. She felt more and more hunted, and wished simply for the journey to be over. She had no doubt Mace had chosen the best route, but still she began to long for an open, clear space where threats could arrive cleanly, an honest fight.

But she didn't know how to fight.

Although New London had the feel of a labyrinth, some neighborhoods were clearly better off than others. The higher-end areas had well-tended roads and well-dressed citizens on the streets, even a few brick buildings with glass windows. But other areas had tightly packed pinewood buildings with no windows and denizens who slouched along the walls in a creeping, furtive manner. Sometimes Kelsea and Mace were forced to ride through a cloud of stench that suggested that the houses were plumbed poorly, or not at all.

This is what it smells like in February, Kelsea thought, sickened. What must it be like in high summer?

Halfway through a particularly run-down section, Kelsea realized she was in a blue district. The street was so narrow that it was really an alley. The buildings were all made of some cheap wood that Kelsea couldn't even identify, and many buildings listed so far sideways that it seemed a miracle they were still standing. Occasionally Kelsea heard screams and the sound of things breaking as they passed. The air rang with laughter, a cold laughter that made her skin break out in gooseflesh.

Poorly dressed women appeared from the crooked doorways and leaned against walls, while Kelsea stared at them in helpless fascination from beneath the shelter of her hood. There was an indefinable air of squalor about the prostitutes, something that couldn't be pinpointed. It wasn't their clothing; certainly their dresses were neither more nor less fancy than many Kelsea had seen, and despite the considerable amount of flesh they displayed, it wasn't the cut of the garments either. It was something in the eyes, in the way the eyes seemed to eat up the faces of even the heaviest women. They looked worn, the young as well as the old. Many of them appeared to have scars. Kelsea didn't want to imagine the lives they must lead, but she couldn't help it.

I'll close this entire section down, she thought. *Close it down and give them all real employment.*

Carlin's voice spoke up in her head. *Will you regulate the length of their dresses as well? Perhaps forbid novels deemed too pornographic?*

There's a difference.

No difference. Blue laws are blue laws. If you wish to dictate private morality, march yourself over to the Arvath.

Mace directed her to the left, between two buildings, and Kelsea was relieved when they emerged onto a wide boulevard lined with neatly kept shops. The grey facade of the Keep was closer now, blotting out the surrounding mountains and most of the sky. Despite the width of the boulevard, it was so crowded that Kelsea and Mace were boxed in again, and could only muddle along at the crowd's pace. There was more sunlight here, and Kelsea felt uneasy, exposed despite her cloak and hood. No one knew what she looked like, but Mace must cut a recognizable figure anywhere. He seemed to share the feeling, for he spurred his stallion forward until he was literally nudging the crowd of riders and pedestrians out of the way. A path opened before them, with some grumbling on either side.

"Straight ahead," Mace muttered, "as quickly as we can."

Still their progress was slow. Rake, who had behaved well throughout the journey, seemed to sense Kelsea's anxiety and now began to resist her direction. Her efforts to control the horse quickly became exhausting in combination with the weight of Pen's armor. She was sweating in thick drips that trickled down her neck and back, and Mace's darting glances behind them became more frequent as they went. The crowds continued to pack them in more and more tightly as they approached the Keep.

"Can't we take another way?"

"There's no other way," Mace replied. He was controlling his horse with only one hand now; the other was on his sword. "We're out of time, Lady. Push on; not much farther now."

For the next few minutes, Kelsea struggled to stay conscious. The late-afternoon sun bore down on her dark cloak, and the close quarters created by the crowd did nothing to relieve the feeling of suffocation. Twice she swayed in her saddle, and was only restored by Mace's tight grip on her shoulder.

Finally the boulevard ended, branching off onto a wide field of grass that circled the Keep and its moat. At the sight of the Keep Lawn, Kelsea felt a moment of atavistic excitement. Here the Mort soldiers had gathered with their siege equipment, had nearly breached the walls, and then had been turned away at the last minute. The lawn sloped gently downhill toward the Keep, and almost directly below Kelsea, a wide stone bridge crossed the water, leading to the Keep Gate. Two lines of guards were stationed at even intervals along the edges of the bridge. The grey monolith of the Keep itself towered almost directly over Kelsea's head, and staring at the top made her dizzy, forced her to look away.

The Keep Lawn was covered with people, and Kelsea's first reaction was surprise: wasn't her arrival supposed to be a secret? Adults, children, even the elderly streamed like water across the grass and down toward the moat. But this wasn't at all how Kelsea had pictured this day in her daydreams. Where were the cheering masses, the flowers thrown? Some of these people were weeping, but not the happy tears that Kelsea had imagined. Like the farmers in the Almont, all of these people looked as though they could use several hundred good meals. They wore the same sort of clothing Kelsea had seen in the Almont as well: dark and shapeless wool. Deep misery was etched into each face. Kelsea felt a sudden wave of powerful anxiety. Something wasn't right.

Another scan of the lawn revealed that while many of the people on the lawn were milling around, apparently loitering, some of them had organized into long, straight lines that stretched down to the edge of the moat. When the crowd parted, Kelsea saw that there were several tables down there, tables with men standing behind them, probably officials, given the deep, identical blue of their clothing. Kelsea felt relief, tinged with slight disappointment. These people hadn't come to see her at all. They were here for something else. The lines were very long, and they weren't moving. The entire crowd appeared to be waiting.

But for what?

She turned to Mace, who was keeping a sharp eye on the lawn, one hand clenched on the hilt of his sword. "Lazarus, what are all these people doing here?"

He didn't answer, wouldn't meet her eye. A cold noose seemed to tighten around her heart. The crowd shifted again, and Kelsea spotted something new, some sort of metal contraption beside the moat. She stood up in her stirrups to get a better look and saw a series of structures: low rectangular boxes, about ten feet tall. The tops and bottoms were wood, and the sides were metal. There were nine of them in a line, stretching all the way down the lawn toward the far corner of the Keep. Kelsea squinted (her eyesight had never been very good) and saw that the walls of the boxes were actually a series of metal bars. Time suddenly slipped backward, and she saw Barty, heard his voice as clearly as if he was beside her, his fingers cleverly weaving wire through a series of holes punched in a piece of sanded wood. "Now, Kel, we make the wire tight enough that the rabbit can't get away, but not so tight that the poor little bastard suffocates before we find him. people have to trap to survive, but a good trapper makes sure the animal suffers as little as possible."

Kelsea's eyes ran over the line of metal boxes again, assessing, and she felt everything inside her go cold, all at once.

Not boxes. Cages.

She gripped Mace's arm, heedless of the wounds that she knew lay beneath his cloak. When she spoke, her voice didn't entirely sound like her own. "Lazarus. You tell me what's going on here. Now."

This time he finally met her eye, and his bleak expression was all the confirmation that Kelsea needed. "It's the shipment, Lady. Two hundred and fifty people, once a month, like clockwork."

"Shipment to where?"

"To Mortmesne."

Kelsea turned back to the lawn. Her mind seemed to have gone blank. The lines had begun moving now, slowly but surely, toward the tables down beside the moat. While Kelsea watched, one of the officials marched a woman away from the table, toward the cages. He stopped at the third cage and gestured to a man in a black uniform (the Tear army uniform, Kelsea realized faintly), who then pulled open a cleverly concealed door at the cage end. The woman marched meekly inside, and the soldier in black closed and locked the door.

"The Mort Treaty," Kelsea murmured numbly. "This is how my mother made peace."

"The Red Queen wanted tribute, Lady. The Tearling had nothing else to offer."

A sharp pain arrowed through Kelsea's chest, and she pressed a clenched fist between her breasts. Peeking beneath her shirt, she saw that her sapphire was glowing, a bright and angry blue. She gathered the jewel in a handful of the cloth and found that the thing was scalding, deep heat that burned her palm through the cloth. The sapphire continued to burn her hand, but the pain was nothing compared to the burn inside her chest, which continued, deepening with each passing second until it began to change, moving toward something different. Not pain . . . something else. She didn't question the feeling, for she seemed to be beyond any capacity for wonder now, and could only stare mutely at the scene in front of her.

More officials were escorting people toward the cages. The

134

crowd had backed up to allow them space, and Kelsea saw now that each cage had enormous wheels of wood. Tear soldiers had already begun to tether a team of mules to the cage at the far end of the Keep. Even from a distance, Kelsea could tell that the cages had seen hard use; several of the bars were visibly scarred, as if they'd been attacked.

Rescue attempts, her mind murmured. *There must have been at least a few.* She suddenly remembered standing in front of the big picture window at the cottage as a child, crying about something – a skinned knee, perhaps, or a chore she hadn't wanted to do – staring at the forest, certain that this was the day when her mother would finally come. Kelsea couldn't have been more than three or four, but she remembered her certainty very well: her mother would come, she would hold Kelsea in her arms, and she would be nothing but good.

I was a fool.

"Why these people?" she asked Mace. "How do they choose them?"

"By lottery, Lady."

"Lottery," she repeated faintly. "I see."

Family members had begun to gather around the cages now, speaking to people inside, holding hands, or merely loitering. Several of the black-clad soldiers had been stationed next to each cage, and they watched the crowd stonily, clearly anticipating the moment when a family member presented a threat. But the onlookers were passive, and to Kelsea that seemed the worst thing of all. They were beaten, her people. It was clear in the long, straight lines that stretched from the official table, the way families merely stood beside the cages, waiting for their loved ones to depart.

Kelsea's attention caught and held on the two cages

nearest the table. These cages were shorter than the others, their steel bars set more tightly in their frames. Already, each cage held several small forms. Kelsea blinked and found that her eyes had filled with tears. They coursed slowly down her face until she tasted salt.

"Even children?" she asked Mace. "Why don't the parents just flee?"

"When one of the allotted runs, his entire family is forfeit in the next lottery. Look around you, Lady. These are large families. Often they must sacrifice the welfare of one child, thinking of the other eight."

"This is my mother's system?"

"No. The architect of the lottery is down there." Mace pointed toward the officials' table. "Arlen Thorne."

"But my mother approved it?"

"She did."

"She did," Kelsea repeated faintly. The world tipped crazily in front of her and she dug her fingernails into her arm, drawing blood, until the haze disappeared. In its wake came fury, a terrible, cheated anger that threatened to overwhelm her. Elyssa the Benevolent, Elyssa the Peacemaker. Kelsea's mother, who had sold her people off wholesale.

"All's not lost, Lady," Mace said unexpectedly, putting a hand on her arm. "I swear to you, you're nothing like her."

Kelsea gritted her teeth. "You're right. I won't allow this to continue."

"Lady, the Mort Treaty is specific. There is no appeals process, no outside arbiter. If a single shipment fails to arrive in Demesne on time, the Mort Queen has the right to invade this country and wreak terror. I lived through the last Mort invasion, Lady, and I assure you, Mhurn wasn't exaggerating the carnage. Before you take action, consider the consequences."

Somewhere a woman had begun wailing, a high, eldritch shrieking that reminded Kelsea of a story Barty used to tell her as a child: the banshee, a terrible creature that summoned one to her death. The screams echoed over the crowd, and Kelsea finally pinpointed the source: a woman who was trying desperately to reach the first cage. Her husband was trying just as hard to drag her away, but he was heavyset and she was too quick for him, wriggling out of his grasp and pushing her way toward the enclosure. The husband buried a hand in her hair and simply yanked, pulling her from her feet. The woman went down to the ground in a pile, but a moment later she was up again, straining toward the cage.

The four soldiers on guard around the cage were visibly on edge; they watched the mother uneasily, not certain whether to get involved. Her voice was giving way, her shrieks fading to a bruised cawing like a crow's, and her strength also appeared to be giving out. While Kelsea watched, the husband finally won the battle and got a grip on her wool dress. He pulled her away to a safe distance from the cage, and the soldiers settled back into their formerly relaxed postures.

But the mother continued to croak brokenly, the sound audible even from Kelsea's distance. Husband and wife stood watching the cage, surrounded by several children. Kelsea's vision was blurred, and her hands were shaking on the reins. She sensed something terrible within her, not the girl hidden in the cottage: someone on fire, burning. The sapphire branded her chest. She wondered if it was possible for her own skin to break open, revealing another person entirely.

Mace touched her shoulder gently, and she spun around

to him with wild eyes. He held out his sword. "Right or wrong, Lady, I see that you mean to take action. Hold this."

Kelsea took the hilt in her hand, liking the heft of it, though the blade was too long for her build. "What about you?"

"I have many weapons, and we have friends here. The sword is for appearance only."

"What friends?"

Slowly and casually, Mace raised an open palm into the air, clenched it into a fist, and dropped his arm again. Kelsea waited a moment, half expecting the sky to break open. She sensed some shifting in the crowd around her, but nothing distinct. Mace, however, seemed satisfied, and turned back to her. Kelsea looked at him for a moment, this man who'd guarded her life for days now, and said, "You were right, Lazarus. I see my own death, and exalt in it. But before I go, I'm going to cut a wide swath here, wide as God's Ocean. If you don't want to die with me, you should leave now."

"Lady, your mother wasn't a good queen, but she wasn't evil. She was a weak queen. She would never have been able to walk straight into death. A fey streak carries enormous power, but be very certain that the havoc you wreak is for your people, not against your mother's memory. This is the difference between a queen and an angry child."

Kelsea tried to focus on his words, the way she would have considered any problem set before her, but what popped into her mind instead were illustrations from Carlin's history books. People of deep brown skin, an old and infamous brutality that had darkened an age. Carlin had dwelled long on this period in history, and Kelsea had wondered more than once why it should be relevant. Behind her closed eyes, she saw stories and illustrations: people in chains. Men caught fleeing and roasted alive. Girls raped at so young an age that their wombs never recovered. Children stolen out of their mothers' arms and sold at auction. State-sponsored slavery.

In my kingdom.

Carlin had known, but she hadn't been allowed to tell. Yet she had done her job, almost too well, for now years of extraordinary cruelty flickered through Kelsea's mind in less than a second. "I will end this."

"You're certain?" Mace asked.

"I'm certain."

"Then I vow to guard you against death."

Kelsea blinked. "You do?"

Mace nodded, resolve clear in his weathered face. "You have possibility in you, Lady. Carroll and I could both sense it. I have nothing to lose, and I would rather die attempting to eradicate a great evil, for I sense that's Your Majesty's purpose."

Majesty. The word seemed to ripple through her. "I haven't been crowned, Lazarus."

"No matter, Lady. I see the queenship in you, and I never saw it in your mother, not one day of her life."

Kelsea looked away, moved to fresh tears. She had won a guard. Only one, but he was the most important. She wiped her leaking eyes and tightened her grip on the sword. "If I shout, will they hear me?"

"Let me do the shouting, Lady, since you don't have a proper herald yet. You'll have their full attention in a moment. Keep your hand on that sword, and don't move any closer to the Keep. I see no archers, but they may be there, all the same."

Kelsea nodded firmly, though inwardly she groaned. She

was a mess. The simple, clean gown that the Fetch had given her was now streaked with mud, the hem of her pants torn. Pen's armor was twice as heavy as it had been that morning. Her long, unwashed hair fell from its pins to dangle in dark brown clumps around her face, and sweat poured down her forehead, stinging her eyes. She remembered her childhood dream of entering the city on a white pony with a crown on her head. Today she looked nothing like a queen.

The mother in front of the children's cage had begun weeping again, oblivious to the small children who looked fearfully up at her. Kelsea cursed herself. *Who cares about your hair, you fool? Look what's been done here.*

"What are those cages made of, Lazarus?"

"Mort iron."

"But the wheels and undercarriage are wood."

"Tearling oak, Lady. What are you getting at?"

Staring down at the table full of blue-clad officials in front of the Keep, Kelsea took a deep breath. This was her last moment to be anonymous. Everything was about to change. "The cages. After we empty them, we're going to set them on fire."

Javel was fighting sleep. Guarding the Keep Gate was not a challenging job. It had been at least eighteen months since anyone had tried to rush the gate, and that attempt had been halfhearted, a drunk who stumbled up at two in the morning with a grievance over his taxes. Nothing had happened, and nothing was going to happen. That was the life of a Gate Guard.

Besides being sleepy, Javel was miserable. He had never enjoyed his job, but he positively loathed it during the shipment. The crowd as a whole didn't present a security problem; they stood around like cows waiting for the slaughter. But there was always some incident at the children's cages, which were closest to the gate, and today was no exception. Javel had breathed a sigh of relief when they finally got the woman quieted down. There was always a parent like that, usually a mother, and only Keller, true dyed-in-the-wool sadist that he was, enjoyed hearing a woman scream. For the rest of the Gate Guard, the shipment was bad duty. Even if another guard was willing to trade, it took two regular shifts to balance it out.

The second problem was that the shipment brought two troops of the Tear army onto the Keep Lawn. The army thought Gate Guard was a soft option, a refuge for those who weren't skilled enough or brave enough to be soldiers. It wasn't always true; across the drawbridge, directly in front of Javel, stood Vil, who'd received two commendations from Queen Elyssa after the Mort invasion and been rewarded with command of the gate. But they weren't all Vil, and the Tear army never let them forget it. Even now, when Javel cut his eyes to the left, he could see two of the soldiers snickering, and he was certain they were laughing at him.

The worst thing about the shipment was that it reminded him of Allie. Most of the time he didn't think about Allie, and when he did start to think of her, he could find the nearest bottle of whiskey and put an end to that. But he couldn't drink on duty; even if Vil wasn't on watch, the other guards wouldn't tolerate it. There wasn't much loyalty in the Gate Guard, but there was plenty of solidarity, a solidarity based on the understanding that none of them was perfect. They all looked the other way for Ethan's incessant gambling, Marco's illiteracy, and even Keller's habit of roughing up the whores down in the Gut. But none of those problems impaired their job performance. If Javel wanted to drink, he had to wait until he was off duty.

Fortunately, the sun was beginning to set and the cages were almost full. The priest from the Arvath had risen from his place at the table, and now he stood beside the first cage, his white robes rippling in the late-afternoon wind. Javel didn't recognize this official, a great, thick fellow with jowls that hung down almost to his neck. Piety was good, so the saying went, but it was especially good with everything else. Javel loathed the sight of the priest, this man who never had to face the lottery. Perhaps he had even joined God's Church for that reason; many men did. Javel remembered the day the Regent had granted the Church exemption; there had been an outcry. The lottery was an indiscriminate predator; it took everyone it could get its hands on. It was indiscriminate, but it was fair, and God's Church only took men. Yes, there had been an outcry, but like all outcries, it soon quieted.

Javel fidgeted with his sleeves, wishing the time would pass faster. It couldn't be long now. The priest would bless the shipment, Thorne would give the signal, and then the cages would begin to roll. It was technically the Gate Guard's job to disperse the crowd, but Javel knew this routine as well: the crowd would disperse itself, following the shipment when it left the lawn. Most of the families would go at least as far as the New London Bridge, but eventually they would give up. Javel closed his eyes, feeling a sudden pain behind his ribs. When Allie's name had been pulled from the lot, they had talked about fleeing, and at some point they'd almost done it. But Javel had been young and a Gate Guard, and in the end he had convinced Allie that it was their duty to stay. Javel believed in the lottery, in loyalty to the Raleigh house, in the sacrifices that needed to be made for a larger peace. If his name had been pulled from the lot instead, he would have gone without question. Everything had seemed so clear then, and it was only when he saw Allie in the cage that his certainty crumbled. He thought longingly of the burn in his throat, the way it would hit his stomach like an anchor, setting everything in its place. Whiskey always put Allie back in the past, where she belonged.

"People of the Tearling!"

The man's voice, sonorous and powerful, rolled down the slope and across the lawn before reverberating against the walls of the Keep. The crowd hushed. Gate Guards weren't supposed to have their eyes anywhere but the bridge, but all of them, Javel included, turned to peer toward the top of the lawn.

"The Mace is back," Martin murmured.

He was right. The figure at the top of the slope was unmistakably Lazarus of the Mace: tall, broad, and terrifying. Whenever he passed by Javel on the gate, Javel did his best to be as invisible as possible. He was always afraid that those deep, calculating eyes might linger on him, and Javel didn't want to be even a speck in the smallest corner of the Mace's mind.

Beside the Mace was a smaller figure, cloaked and hooded in purple. Probably Pen Alcott. Queen's Guards were usually tall and well built, but they'd taken Alcott despite his slim build; he was reputed to be very good with a sword. But then Alcott pushed back his hood, and Javel saw that it was a woman, a plain woman with long, tangled dark hair.

"I am Lazarus of the Queen's Guard!" the Mace's voice boomed again. "Welcome Queen Kelsea of the Tearling!"

Javel's jaw dropped. He'd heard rumors that the Regent

had intensified the search in recent months, but he hadn't paid much attention. Songs about the girl's return sometimes went around, but Javel dismissed these. After all, musicians had to write about something, and the Regent's enemies liked to keep people's hopes alive. But there wasn't even any proof that the princess had ever escaped the city. Most of New London, including Javel, assumed that she was long dead.

"All of them," Martin muttered. "Look!"

Craning his neck, Javel saw that a group of grey-cloaked figures had formed a ring around the woman, and as they pushed back their own hoods, Javel recognized Galen and Dyer, then Elston and Kibb, Mhurn and Coryn. It was the remainder of the old Queen's Guard. Even Pen Alcott was there, just in front of the woman with his sword drawn, wearing a green cloak. According to rumor, the Regent had tried to kick them all out of the Keep several times by stopping their salaries or assigning them to other duties. But he never managed to get rid of them for more than a few months or so, and they always came back. Carroll and the Mace held plenty of clout with the Tear nobles, but the real problem was deeper: no one feared the Regent, at least not the way they feared the Mace.

The crowd began to murmur, a buzzing that grew louder with each passing second. Javel felt the mood shifting around him. The shipment ran like clockwork each month: the check-in, the loading, the departure, Arlen Thorne at the head of the Census table in his usual fashion as though he was the grand emperor of the New World. Even the inevitable screaming parent eventually quieted down and left the lawn, weeping, when the cages had vanished into the city. It was all part of an orchestrated piece.

But now Thorne leaned over and began speaking urgently to one of his deputies. The entire Census table was moving, like rodents who scented danger. Javel was pleased to see that the soldiers around the cages were eyeing the crowd uneasily, that most of them had their hands on their swords. The priest from the Arvath had leaned in as well, his jowls shaking with each word as he argued with Thorne. The priests of God's Church preached obedience to the Census, and in return, the Arvath received a healthy tax exemption from the Regent. The Arvath's head bursar, Cardinal Walker, did a lot of drinking down in the Gut, and he wasn't particular about who he did it with; Javel had heard several reminiscences about the Holy Father's dealings that chilled his blood.

But like most of the Holy Father's moves, this had been a shrewd one. Church doctrine did seem to make the Census run more smoothly. Javel could almost pinpoint the devout families by the resignation on their faces; long before their loved ones ever went into the cage, they had accepted it as their duty to country and God. Javel himself had attended the Church, long ago, but he had only done it to keep Allie happy, and he hadn't been back since the day she shipped. The priest's face grew more choleric the longer he argued with Thorne. Javel imagined going over and giving the fat man a good kick in the gut.

Suddenly a man's voice rose above the low hum of the crowd, pleading: "Give me back my sister, Majesty!"

Then they were all shouting at once.

"Please, Lady, pity!"

"Your Majesty can stop this!"

"Give me back my son!"

The Queen held up her hands for silence. At that moment, Javel knew for certain that she truly was the Queen, though he never knew why or how he knew. She stood up in her stirrups, not tall but imposing nonetheless, her head thrown back combatively and her hair streaming around her face. Even raised in a shout, her voice was dark and deliberate, like syrup. Or whiskey.

"I am the Queen of the Tearling! Open the cages!"

The crowd erupted in a roar that hit Javel with the impact of a physical blow. Several soldiers moved to obey, pulling keys from their belts, but Thorne barked sharply, "Hold your positions!"

Javel had always thought Arlen Thorne the scrawniest human being he'd ever seen. The man was a collection of long, sticklike limbs, and the deep navy of the Census uniform did nothing to augment his girth. Watching Thorne rise from the table was like watching a spider uncoil itself and prepare to hunt. Javel shook his head. Queen or no, the girl was never going to get those cages open. Thorne had grown up in the Gut, raised by whores and thieves, and he'd clambered his way to the top of that particular shitheap to become the most profitable slave trader in the Tear. He didn't see the world in the same way that most people did. Two years ago, a family named Morrell had tried to flee the Tearling when their daughter's name came up in the lot. Thorne had hired the Caden, who found the Morrells in a cave within a day's ride of the Cadarese border. But it was Thorne himself who tortured the child to death before her parents' eyes. Thorne made no secret of these dealings. He wanted the world to know.

Vil, braver than the rest of them, had asked Thorne what he hoped to accomplish, reporting back: "Thorne said it was an object lesson. He said you couldn't underestimate the value of a good object lesson."

The object lesson had worked; so far as Javel knew, no one had tried to smuggle out one of the allotted since. Both Morrells had gone to Mortmesne in the next shipment, and Javel remembered that departure well enough: the mother was one of the first to march into the cage, docile as a rabbit. Looking into her blank eyes, Javel had seen that she was dead already. Much later, he'd heard that she'd succumbed to pneumonia on the journey, that Thorne had left her body for the vultures on the side of the Mort Road.

"The Queen of the Tearling has been dead these many years," Thorne announced. "If you claim to be the un-crowned princess, this kingdom will require better proof than your word."

"Your name, sir!" the Queen demanded.

Thorne stood up straight and drew in a deep breath; even from twenty feet away, Javel could see his pigeon chest expand. "I'm Arlen Thorne, Overseer of the Census!"

While Thorne was speaking, the Queen had reached up behind her neck and begun fiddling there, in the way a woman did when there was something wrong with her hair. It was a gesture Allie used to make, when the day was hot or when she was exasperated about something, and it pained Javel to see it on another woman. Memory cut infinitely deeper than swords; that was God's truth. Javel closed his eyes and saw Allie for the last time, six years ago, that final glimpse of her bright blonde hair before she vanished over the Pike Hill into Mortmesne. He'd never wanted a drink so badly in his life.

The Queen held something high in the air. Javel squinted and saw a flash of blue in the last of the dying sunlight, there and then gone. But the crowd erupted again in bedlam. So many hands went into the air that the Queen was momentarily blocked from view.

"Jeremy!" called Ethan from up the bridge. "Is it the Heir's Jewel?"

Jeremy, who had better eyesight than any of them, shrugged and called back, "It's *a* blue jewel! Never seen the real one!"

Several groups of people had begun to push forward toward the cage of children. The soldiers pulled swords and turned them back easily, but the area around the cage was in a tumult now, and none of the swords returned to their scabbards. Javel grinned; it was good to see the army forced to work for once, even if the small rebellion was doomed. The troops who guarded the shipment were entitled to a bonus from the Regent. They didn't reap as much reward from the shipment as the nobles who took toll from the Mort Road, but it was a fair chunk of money, from what Javel had heard. Good money for bad work; it seemed fitting to Javel that they should meet with some difficulty along the way.

"Anyone can hang a necklace around a child's neck," Thorne replied, ignoring the crowd. "How do we know it's the true jewel?"

Javel turned back to the Queen, but before she could react, the Mace was shouting at Thorne. "I am a Queen's Guard, and my word has been bonded to this kingdom! That is the Heir's Jewel, just as I last saw it eighteen years ago!" The Mace leaned forward against his horse's neck, his voice carrying an undercurrent of ferocity that made Javel recoil. "I've bound myself to this Queen, Thorne, to guard her life! Do you question my loyalty to the Tear?"

The Queen sliced the air with her hand, and the gesture silenced the Mace immediately. The Queen leaned forward and shouted, "All of you down there! You're part of *my* government, and *my* army! You will open the cages!"

The soldiers looked blankly at each other and then turned back to Thorne, who shook his head. And then Javel saw something extraordinary: the Queen's jewel, almost invisible moments ago, now flared a bright aquamarine, so bright that Javel had to squint, even at this distance. The necklace swung, a glowing blue pendulum over the Queen's head, and she seemed to grow taller, her skin lit from within. She was no longer a round-faced girl in a worn cloak; for a moment she seemed to fill the whole world, a tall, grave woman with a crown on her head.

Javel grabbed Martin's shoulder. "Do you see that?"

"See what?"

"Nothing," Javel muttered, not wanting Martin to think him drunk. The Queen had begun speaking again, her voice angry but controlled, reason on top and fury underneath.

"I may sit on the throne for only one day, but if you don't open those cages right now, I swear before Great God that my sole act as Queen will be to watch every one of you die for treason! You will not live to see another sun set! *Will you test my word?*"

For a moment, the scene before the cages remained frozen. Javel held his breath, waiting for Thorne to do something, for an earthquake to break the Keep Lawn wide open. The sapphire above the Queen's head was now glowing so brightly that he had to raise a hand to shield his eyes. For a moment, he had the irrational feeling that the jewel was *looking* at him, that it saw everything: Allie and the bottle, the years he'd spent with the two of them tangled inside his head.

Then the soldiers began to move. Only a few at first, then

several more, and more after that. Despite Thorne, who had begun to hiss at them in a furious undertone, the two commanders took keys from their belts and began to unlock the cages.

Javel released his breath, staring at this phenomenon. He'd never seen the cages opened once they'd been locked; he supposed no one but the Mort had. He knew of several people, including himself, who had followed the shipment all the way to the Argive Pass. But few dared to cross the Mort border, and no one followed the shipment all the way to its final destination in Demesne. If the Mort army found any Tear hanging around the cages, they would kill him outright as a saboteur.

One by one, men and women began to clamber out of the cages. The crowd received them into what seemed to be an enormous embrace. An old woman ten feet from the Census table simply collapsed and began weeping on the ground.

Thorne braced both arms on the table, his voice acid. "And what of Mortmesne, then, Princess? Will you bring the Red Queen's army down on us all?"

Javel turned back to the Queen and was relieved to find that she was simply a girl again, just a teenager with an unremarkable face and disheveled hair. His vision, if that's what it had been, was gone. But her voice had not diminished; if anything, it was louder now, clear anger ringing across the Keep Lawn. "I haven't named you a foreign policy adviser, Arlen Thorne. Nor have I ridden halfway across this kingdom to engage in pointless debate with a bureaucrat on my own front lawn. I consider the good of my people first and foremost in this, as in everything."

The Mace leaned over to whisper in the Queen's ear. She nodded and pointed at Thorne. "You! Overseer! I hold you responsible to see that each child is returned to his family. Should I hear complaint of a lost child, it will rest at your feet. Do you understand me?"

"Yes, Lady," Thorne intoned colorlessly, and Javel was suddenly very glad that he couldn't see the man's face. The Queen might think she'd leashed this particular dog, but Arlen Thorne had no leash, and she'd find that out soon enough.

"Praise for the Queen!" someone cried from the far side of the cages, and the crowd roared its approval. Families were reuniting in front of the cages, people calling joyfully to each other across the expanse of the lawn. But most of all, Javel heard weeping, a sound he hated. Their loved ones were being returned; what the hell did they have to cry about?

"There will be no more shipments to Mortmesne!" the Queen shouted, and the crowd answered in another incoherent roar. Javel blinked and saw Allie's face floating just behind his closed eyes. Some days he feared he had forgotten her face; no matter how hard he tried, it wouldn't come clear in his mind. He would fixate on one feature he thought he remembered, something easy like Allie's chin, and then it would shimmer and blur like a mirage. But every so often would come a day like this, when he could recall every angle of Allie's face, the curve of her cheekbone, the determined set of her jaw, and he would realize that the forgetting had actually been a kindness. He looked up at the sky and saw, relieved, that it was purpled with dusk. The sun had disappeared behind the Keep.

"Vil!" he called across the bridge. "Aren't we off duty?"

Vil turned to him, his round face astonished. "You want to leave *now*?"

"No . . . no, I was just asking."

"Well, hold it together," Vil replied, his voice shaded with mockery. "You can drown your sorrows later."

Javel's face flamed, and he looked at the ground, clenching his hand into a fist. A hand clapped on his back; he looked up and saw Martin, his friendly face sympathetic. Javel nodded to show that he was all right, and Martin scuttled back to his position.

Two Queen's Guards, one large and one small, both cloaked in grey, were moving around the cages with a bucket. Elston and Kibb, most likely; the two of them were inseparable. Javel couldn't tell what they were doing, but it didn't really matter. Most of the cages were empty now. Thorne had instituted some sort of careful procedure at the children's cages, releasing the children one at a time and questioning parents who came forward before handing off a child. Probably a good idea; there was a loose confederacy of pimps and madams down in the Gut who catered to all tastes, and they weren't above snatching a child from time to time. Javel, who spent plenty of time in the Gut, had thought more than once about trying to find the people who did these things, trying to bring them to some sort of justice. But his resolve always weakened as night fell, and besides, that was a charge for someone else. Someone brave.

Anyone but me.

Kelsea was exhausted. She clutched the hilt of Mace's sword, trying to look regal and unconcerned, but her heart was hammering and her muscles felt drawn with fatigue. She reclasped the necklace around her throat and found that she hadn't imagined it: the sapphire was burning, as though it had been heated in a forge. For a few moments there, arguing with Arlen Thorne, she had felt as though she could reach out and break the sky in half. But now all of that power had gone, drained away, leaving her muscles slack. If they didn't get inside soon, she thought she might fall off her horse.

The sun had disappeared, and the entire lawn beneath the Keep was bathed in shadow, the temperature sinking rapidly. But they couldn't go yet; Mace had sent several guards out into the crowd on various errands, and so far none of them had come back. Kelsea was relieved to see so many of her mother's Guard alive, though she'd already done a quick count and realized, her heart sinking, that Carroll wasn't there. But several new guards had shown up as well, men who hadn't been with them on their journey. There might be as many as fifteen guards surrounding her now, but Kelsea couldn't be sure without turning around. Somehow it seemed very important not to look back.

Perhaps a third of the people who'd originally been on the lawn had drifted away, likely fearing trouble, but most stayed. Some families were still tearfully reuniting with their loved ones, but others were merely spectators now, watching Kelsea curiously. The pressure of their eyes was a monstrous weight.

They expect me to do something extraordinary, she realized. *Now, and every day for the rest of my life.*

The idea was terrifying.

She turned to Mace. "We need to get inside."

"Only a moment more, Lady."

"What are we waiting for?"

"Your Majesty's rescuer said a true thing, and one that's stayed with me. Often the direct way is the right way, for reasons that can't be foreseen."

"Meaning what?"

Mace pointed to the edge of the circle of guards, and Kelsea saw four women and several children waiting there. One of them was the woman who had been screaming down in front of the cage. A small girl, perhaps three years old, was clutched in her arms, and four other children surrounded her. Her long hair fell over her face as she bent to her daughter.

"Your attention!" Mace called.

The woman looked up, and Kelsea's breath caught. It was the madwoman from her dream, the one who had held the destroyed child in her arms. She had the same long, dark hair and pale complexion, the same high forehead. If the woman spoke, Kelsea thought she would even recognize the voice.

But I've never been able to see the future, Kelsea thought, bewildered. *Not once in my life.* As a child, she'd often wished for the sight; Carlin had told her several stories of the Red Queen's seer, a truly gifted woman who had predicted many great happenings that eventually came to pass. But Kelsea had only the present.

"The Queen requires a service corps!" Mace announced, and Kelsea jumped, refocusing her attention on the scene in front of her. "She'll require—"

"Hold." Kelsea held up her hand, seeing the sudden fear in the eyes of the women. Mace's idea was a good one, but if he mishandled that fear, all the bribes in the world would be of small use.

"I will command no one into my service," she announced firmly, attempting to look each of the four women in the eye. "However, for those who join my household, I promise that you and your loved ones will receive every protection at my disposal. Not only protection, but all that my own children will one day receive. Education, the best of food and medical care, and the ability to learn any trade they choose. I also give you my word that anyone who wishes to leave my service will be allowed to do so at any time, without delay."

She tried to think of something else to say, but she was so tired, and she'd already discovered that she loathed making speeches. A statement about loyalty seemed necessary here, but what was there to say? Surely they all knew that in service to her, they would be in a position to bring about her death, and more likely to see their own. She gave up, spread her hands wide, and announced, "Make your choice in the next minute. I can delay no longer."

The women began to deliberate. For most of them, this seemed to consist of staring helplessly at their children. Kelsea noted the lack of men and guessed that Mace had specifically chosen women without husbands. But that wasn't entirely true; her gaze went back to the madwoman from her dream, and then out into the crowd, searching for the husband. She found him standing some ten feet back, his feet spread and his muscled arms crossed.

She leaned over to Mace. "Why the dark-haired woman in blue?"

"If convinced, Lady, she'll be the most loyal servant you have."

"Who is she?"

"No idea. But I've a knack for these things, just take my word."

"She may not be entirely sane."

"Many women behave so when their young children ship. It's those who let them go without a murmur that I distrust."

"What of the husband?"

"Look closely, Lady."

Kelsea stared at the woman's husband, but saw nothing

out of the ordinary. He watched the proceedings balefully, a tall dark-haired man with an unkempt beard and broad arms that revealed him to be a laborer of some kind. His black eyes were narrowed in a pouty way that was easy to read: he didn't like to be cut out of decisions. Kelsea returned her gaze to his wife, whose eyes darted between her husband and the group of children around her. She was very thin, with arms like twigs; blackened marks on her forearm revealed where her husband had hauled her away from the cage. Then Kelsea spotted more bruises: one high up on her cheek and a large dark smudge on her collarbone when her daughter pulled at the neck of her dress.

"Christ, Lazarus, your eyes are sharp. I have a mind to take her with us either way."

"I think she'll come on her own, Lady. Watch and wait."

Pen and one of the new guards had already maneuvered themselves between the burly black-eyed man and his wife. They were very quick, very competent, and despite the danger all around her, Kelsea felt almost hopeful . . . perhaps she would survive. Then the hope collapsed, and she was merely exhausted again. She waited a few more moments before announcing, "We'll enter the Keep now. Those who wish to accompany me are welcome."

Kelsea watched the madwoman out of the corner of her eye as the company began to ride down the slope. The woman pulled her children close to her, gathering them until they surrounded her like a broad skirt. Then she nodded, murmuring some kind of encouragement, and the entire group began to move down the lawn. The husband leaped forward with an incoherent yell, but halted at the point of Pen's sword. Kelsea jerked her horse to a stop.

"Keep riding, Lady. They'll control him."

"Can I take children from their father, Lazarus?"

"You can do whatever you like, Lady. You're the Queen."

"What will we do with all these children?"

"Children are good, Lady. They make women predictable. Now keep your head down."

Kelsea turned to face the Keep. Although she found it difficult to let her guards handle everything behind her – she heard raised voices arguing and the muted sounds of a scuffle – she knew that Mace was right: interference would show a lack of faith in her Guard. She rode on, keeping her gaze resolutely forward, even when a woman's voice rose in a shriek.

As they approached the cages, Kelsea saw that a crowd fanned in an outer ring beyond her guards. The people had pressed so close that some of them were lined up against the horses' flanks. All of them seemed to be speaking to her, but she could understand none of their words.

"Archers!" Mace barked. "Eyes on the battlements!"

Two of her guard produced bows and nocked arrows. One of them was very young and fair; Kelsea thought he might be even younger than she. His face was white with anxiety, his jaw clenched in concentration as he stared up at the Keep. Kelsea wanted to say something reassuring, but then Mace repeated, "On the battlements, dammit!" and she clamped her mouth shut.

When they drew level with the cages, Mace grabbed hold of Rake's bridle and brought the horse to a sudden stop. He signaled to Kibb, who presented a flaming torch. Mace offered it to Kelsea. "The first page in your history, Lady. Make it good."

She hesitated, then took the torch and rode toward the nearest cage. The crowd and her guards shifted like a single great organism to allow her access. Mace had sent Elston and Kibb ahead to the cages with a bucket of oil; hopefully they'd done it properly, or she was about to look extremely stupid. She took a good grip on the torch, but before she could throw it, her eye happened on one of the two cages built for children. The fire inside her chest reignited, spreading heat across her skin.

Everything I've done so far can be undone. But if I do this, there's no going back. If the shipment did not come, the Red Queen would invade. Kelsea thought of Mhurn, her handsome blond guard, of his tale about the last Mort invasion. Thousands had suffered and died. But here in front of her was a cage built especially for the young, the helpless, built to carry them hundreds of miles from home so that they could be worked, raped, starved. Kelsea closed her eyes and saw her mother, the woman she had pictured throughout her childhood, the white queen on the horse. But the vision had already darkened. The people who cheered the Queen were scarecrows, gaunt with long starvation. The wreath of flowers on her head had withered. Her horse's mouth was rotting away with disease. And the woman herself ... a crawling, servile thing, her skin white as a corpse and yet bathed in shadow. A collaborator. Kelsea blinked the image away, but it had already propelled her onward to the next step. Barty's story of Death recurred in her head; it had never really left her since that night beside the campfire. Barty was right; it was better to die clean. She reared back and flung the torch at the children's cage.

The movement pulled the wound in her neck wide open, but she stifled a cry as the crowd roared and the under-carriage ignited. Kelsea had never seen fire so hungry; flames spread over the floor of the cage and then began, improbably, to climb the iron bars. A burst of heat blew across the lawn, scattering the few people who had ventured too close to the cage. It was like being in front of a lit oven.

The crowd surged toward the fire, shrieking curses. Even the children were screaming, infected with their parents' hysteria, their eyes lit red. Watching the flames, Kelsea felt the wild thing inside her chest fold its wings and disappear, and was both relieved and disappointed. The sensation had been like having a stranger inside, a stranger who somehow knew everything about her.

"Cae!" Mace called over his shoulder.

"Sir?"

"Make sure the rest burn."

At Mace's signal, they rode on, leaving the cages behind. When they reached the drawbridge, the stink of the moat hit Kelsea's nostrils: a rank smell, like rotting vegetables. The water was a deep, dark green, and a layer of nearly opaque slime had gelled on the surface. The fetid smell grew stronger the farther they progressed across the bridge.

"Is the water not drained?"

"No questions now, Lady, forgive me." Mace's eyes were darting everywhere, over the Keep's surface and into the darkness ahead, across the moat to the far side, lingering on the guards who lined either side of the bridge. These guards made no move to stop the procession, and several of them even bowed as Kelsea went by. But when the crowd tried to follow her into the Keep, the men grudgingly moved into action, blocking off the bridge and herding people back to the far bank.

Ahead, the Keep Gate was a dark hole with vague flickers of torchlight inside. Kelsea shut her eyes and opened them again, an action that seemed to take all of her strength. Her uncle was waiting inside, but she didn't know how she could stand in front of him now. Her bloodline, once a secret source of pride, now seemed little more than a cesspool. Her uncle was filth, and her mother... it was like sliding down the face of a precipice from which all handholds had vanished.

"I can't face my uncle tonight, Lazarus. I'm too tired. Can we delay?"

"If Her Majesty will only be quiet."

Kelsea laughed, surprising herself, as they passed through the grim archway of the Keep Gate.

Two hundred feet away, the Fetch watched the girl and her entourage cross the bridge, a small smile playing on his lips. It had been a clever thing, taking the women from the crowd, and all but one of them had followed her into the Keep. Who was the father? The girl displayed a prickly intelligence that could never have come from Elyssa. Poor Elyssa, who had needed most of her brains to decide which dress to wear in the morning. The girl was worth ten of her.

Beside the moat, the children's cage flamed, a towering pyre in the dusk. One of the Queen's Guard had been left behind to fire the rest of the cages, but the people (and several soldiers) were far ahead of him. One by one, each cage went up in a gust of flame. people shouted for the Queen, and the air remained thick with the sound of weeping.

The Fetch shook his head in admiration. "Bravo, Tear Queen."

The Census table looked like an anthill that some cruel child had stirred with a stick. Officials hurried back and forth, their movements frenzied by panic; they'd quickly grasped the consequences of this day. Arlen Thorne had disappeared. He would be out for the girl's blood, and he was a much cannier adversary than her idiot uncle. The Fetch frowned, deliberating for a moment before speaking over his shoulder. "Alain."

"Sir?"

"Something is already brewing in Thorne's mind. Go find out what it is."

"Yes, sir."

Lear spurred his horse forward until he was abreast of the Fetch. Lear was in a bad mood, and no wonder. When they went about undisguised, it was Lear's black skin that caught the world's attention. He loved to have people stare at him, riveted, while he spun his tales, but he hated to be an object of curiosity.

"Thorne may not accept him," Lear muttered. "And even if he does, Alain's anonymity will be compromised forever. Is the girl really worth it?"

"Don't underestimate her, Lear. I certainly don't."

"Can we dispatch the Regent?" Morgan asked.

"The Regent is mine, and unless I've misjudged the girl, I'll have him shortly. Luck to you, Alain."

Alain turned his horse without a word and rode back into the city. As he disappeared into the crowd, the Fetch closed his eyes and bowed his head.

So much now depends on one young girl, he thought grimly. *God plays at hazard with us.*

BOOK II

CHAPTER 6

THE MARKED QUEEN

When I was five years old, my grandmother took me for an outing. As her namesake, I was Gran's favorite, very proud to be in my new dress and holding her hand out on the city streets while my siblings were left behind.

We had a picnic in the great park in the center of the city. Gran bought me a book at Varling's Bookshop, which carried the first books with colored pictures. We saw a puppet show in the theatre district, and in a shodder on the Lady's Approach, Gran also purchased me my first grown-up pair of shoes with laces that tied. It was a fine day.

Near the hour to go home for supper, Gran took me to the Glynn Queen's memorial, a statue of a faceless woman on a granite throne, situated at the entrance to the Keep Lawn. We looked at the statue for a very long time, and I was silent because of the silence of my grandmother. She chattered incessantly, Gran did, so that sometimes we had to shush her when company came. But now she stood in the front of the Glynn Queen's memorial for a solid ten minutes, her head bent, saying nothing. Eventually I became bored and began to squirm, and finally asked, "Gran, what are we waiting for?"

She tugged gently at my braid, signaling me to be silent, then

gestured toward the memorial and said, "But for this woman,
you would never have been born."
        —*The Legacy of the Glynn Queen,* GLEE DELAMERE

Kelsea woke in a deep, soft bed hung with a light blue canopy. Her first thought was a trivial one: the bed had too many pillows. Her bed in Barty and Carlin's cottage had been small, but clean and comfortable, with a single serviceable pillow. This bed was comfortable as well, but it was an ostentatious sort of comfort. The bed could easily have held four people, its sheets were pear-colored silk, and an endless vista of small, frilly white pillows stretched across the blue damask coverlet.

My mother's bed, and just what I should have expected.

She rolled over and saw Mace in the corner, curled up in an armchair, asleep.

Sitting up as quietly as she could, Kelsea examined the room: satisfactory at first glance but filled with disturbing touches upon a closer look. It was a high-ceilinged affair with light blue hangings to match the bed. One wall was lined with bookcases, empty save for a few trinkets scattered among several shelves, covered in dust. Someone had made sure that her mother's chamber remained untouched. Mace? Probably not. It seemed more like Carroll's doing. Mace had betrayed fleeting touches of disloyalty to her mother. Carroll had shown none.

To Kelsea's left was a doorway that led to a bathroom; she could see half of an enormous marble bathtub. Beside the doorway was a dressing table with a large, jewel-encrusted mirror. She caught a glimpse of her reflection and winced; she looked like a goblin, her hair wild, her face streaked with dirt. She lay back down and stared at the canopy over her head, her mind wandering. How could so much have changed in a single day?

She suddenly recalled being nine and taking one of Carlin's fancy dresses out of Barty and Carlin's closet. Carlin had never expressly forbidden the dresses, but that was only a loophole to be exploited if Kelsea was caught; she knew that she was doing wrong. After donning the dress, she also put on a homemade crown of flowers. The dress was too long and the crown kept falling off, but still Kelsea felt very grown-up, very queenly. She was in the middle of parading up and down the room when Carlin walked in.

"What are you doing?" Carlin asked. Her voice had sunk to its lowest note, the one that meant trouble. Kelsea trembled as she tried to explain. "I was practicing being a queen. Like my mother."

Carlin moved forward so quickly that Kelsea didn't even have time to step backward. There were only Carlin's burning eyes and then the crack of a slap across Kelsea's face. It barely hurt, but Kelsea burst into tears all the same; Carlin had never hit her before. Carlin grabbed the dress by the back and yanked sharply, ripping it down the front and sending small buttons scattering across the room.

Kelsea fell to the floor, crying harder now, but her tears didn't move Carlin; they never did. She left the room and didn't speak to Kelsea for days, even after Kelsea had washed and ironed the dress herself and put it back in Carlin's closet. Barty crept around the cottage that week with reddened eyes, miserable, sneaking Kelsea extra sweets when Carlin couldn't see. After several days, Carlin finally returned to normal, but when Kelsea looked in Carlin's closet the next week, all of the fancy gowns were gone.

Kelsea had always thought that Carlin had been angry at her for borrowing the dress without asking. But now, looking around the room, she saw a different story. Empty bookshelves. An enormous oak wardrobe that took up nearly the entire wall opposite. A mirror big enough to fit several reflections. Golden fixtures. This bed, draped in yards and yards of costly materials. In her mind, Kelsea could see the people out on the Keep Lawn, their underfed frames and gaunt faces. Carlin had known plenty. Kelsea wanted to scream her rage into the silence of the chamber. And what if there were more happy revelations still to come? She had always assumed that her mother had sent her away for her own protection. But maybe that wasn't it at all. Maybe Kelsea had simply been sent away. She kicked her feet angrily, digging her heels into the soft feather mattress. Childish, but effective; after two minutes of furious kicking, she knew that the time for sleep was done.

The queenship she'd inherited, problematic enough in the abstract, now appeared insurmountable. But of course, she had already known the road would be difficult. Carlin had told her so obliquely, through years spent studying the troubled nations and kingdoms of the past. Carlin's library, filled with books . . . Kelsea suddenly felt the last of her anger at Carlin slide away. She missed them both, Barty *and* Carlin. Everything around her was so strange, and she missed the easy familiarity of the two people she knew well. Would Carlin approve of what she'd done yesterday?

Kelsea sat up, pulled back the covers and dangled her feet from the edge of the bed. The necklace had become stuck in her hair while she slept, and she spent a minute untangling it. She should have braided her hair and taken a bath last night, but it had all been a blur; she'd been hurried through torch-lit corridors, with nothing but Mace's hissed commands in her ear. Someone had carried her up a seemingly endless staircase, and Kelsea had been so tired that she fell asleep in the clothes from the Fetch. The garments were so filthy now that she could actually smell their sweaty, salted odor. She should throw them away, but she knew she wouldn't. The Fetch's face had been the last thing in her mind before she dropped off into unconsciousness, and she was sure that she'd dreamed about him as well, though she couldn't remember the dream. He had given her a test, all right, and he would kill her if she failed, Kelsea had no doubt. But his threats occupied only a very small corner of her thoughts. She allowed herself the luxury of daydreaming about him for a few more minutes before turning her mind back to the real world.

She needed to see a copy of the Mort Treaty as soon as possible. The thought galvanized Kelsea, and she hopped out of the bed and tiptoed over to Mace in his chair. He'd grown a few days' worth of beard stubble, brown salted with grey. The lines seemed to have etched themselves even more deeply into his face. His head was tipped back in the chair, and every few seconds he emitted a very light snore.

"So you do sleep."

"I do not," Mace retorted. "I doze."

He stretched until his spine cracked, and then pushed himself up from the armchair. "Had there been a single wrong breath of air in this room, I would have known."

"Is this place safe?"

"Yes, Lady. We're in the Queen's Wing, which is never left unguarded. Carroll went over every detail of this room before we left, and six days isn't enough time for your uncle to accomplish anything elaborate. Today someone will inspect it more thoroughly while you're gone, just in case."

"While I'm gone?"

"I informed your uncle that you'd be crowned today, at your leisure. He didn't take it well."

Kelsea opened a drawer and saw a comb and brush set that looked like pure gold. She slammed the drawer shut. "My mother was a vain woman."

"Yes. Will the room suit?"

"Let's get rid of these stupid pillows," Kelsea reached out and swept several of them from the bed. "What in God's name is the point of—"

"Much to do today, Majesty."

Kelsea sighed. "First I need breakfast and a hot bath. Something to wear to my crowning."

"You know you'll need to be crowned by a priest of God's Church."

Kelsea looked up. "I didn't know that."

"Even if I could dragoon your uncle's house priest into the task, he's not the man we want. I'll have to fetch another priest from the Arvath, and I may be gone for an hour or so."

"No chance of legitimacy without a priest?"

"None, Lady."

Kelsea drew an exasperated breath. She'd never discussed her actual coronation with Carlin, since it seemed so abstract. But the language of the ceremony would undoubtedly be infused with religious vows. That was how the Church kept the wallet open. "Fine, go. But if possible, get a timid priest."

"Done, Lady. Keep your knife about you while I'm gone."

"How did you know about my knife?"

Mace gave her a speaking glance. "Wait a moment, and I'll

bring your dame of chamber." He opened the door, letting in a brief babble of voices, and then closed it behind him. Kelsea stood in the center of the empty chamber, feeling a subtle sense of relief steal over her. She had missed being alone. But now there was no time to enjoy it.

"So much to do," she whispered, rubbing lightly at the stitches on her neck. Her gaze roved over the tall ceilings, the blue hangings, the bed with its endless, infuriating rows of pillows, and worst of all, the long wall of empty book-shelves. Something seemed to boil over inside her, angry tears coming to her eyes.

"Look at you," she hissed at the empty room. "Look what you've left here for me."

"Lady?" Mace knocked briefly at the door and entered. A tall, slim woman trailed silently behind him, nearly hidden by his bulk, but Kelsea already knew who it was. The woman had none of her children with her now, and without them she seemed younger, only a few years older than Kelsea herself. She wore a simple, cream-colored wool dress, and her long, dark hair had been combed and pulled into a tight knot on her head. The bruise on her cheek was the only blemish. She stood in front of Kelsea with a quality of waiting, but there was nothing subservient in her manner; indeed, after a few seconds Kelsea felt so intimidated that she was compelled to speak.

"You're welcome to have your little one in here, if she's too young to be left alone."

"She's in good hands, Lady."

"Leave us alone, please, Lazarus."

To her surprise, Mace immediately turned and left, closing the door behind him.

"Sit, please." Kelsea indicated the chair that sat in front

of the vanity table. The woman placed the stool in front of Kelsea and sat down in a single graceful movement.

"What's your name?"

"Andalie."

Kelsea blinked. "Of Mort origin?"

"My mother was Mort, my father Tear."

Kelsea wondered if Mace had elicited that information. Of course he had. "And which are you?"

Andalie stared at her until Kelsea wished that she could take the question back. The woman's eyes were a cold, piercing grey. "I'm Tear, Majesty. My children are Tear, through their worthless father, and I can't discard the children along with the man, can I?"

"No . . . no, I suppose not."

"If you question my motives, I came to serve Your Majesty mostly for my children's sake. Yours was a powerful offer for a woman with as many children as I have, and the opportunity to remove them from their father's reach was a godsend."

"Mostly for your children's sake?"

"Mostly, yes."

Kelsea was unnerved. The Tearling took in Mort emigrants out of necessity for the skills the Tear lacked, particularly ironwork, medicine, and masonry. The Mort commanded a high price for their services, and there were a fair number of Mort salted around Tear villages, particularly in the more tolerant south. But even Carlin, who prided herself on her open mind, didn't really trust the Mort. According to Carlin, even the lowest Mort carried the strain of arrogance, a conqueror's mentality that had been drilled into them over time.

But Andalie's background was only part of the problem.

The woman was too educated for her station in life: married to a laborer, with too many children. She carried herself with an air of inscrutability, and Kelsea would wager that this had driven Andalie's husband as red to a bull. She was entirely detached. Only when she spoke of her children did she display warmth. Kelsea had to trust Mace's judgment; without him, she would already be dead. But what had made him choose this woman?

"Lazarus elects you to be my dame of chamber. Is this agreeable to you?"

"If special provision can be made when my youngest is ill or difficult with others."

"Of course."

Andalie gestured toward the dreadful vanity table. "My qualifications, Lady—"

Kelsea waved her off. "Anything you claim, I'm sure you can do. May I call you Andalie?"

"What else would you call me, Lady?"

"I'm told that many women at court like to have titles and such. Lady of the Chamber, that sort of thing."

"I'm no court woman. My own name will do."

"Of course." Kelsea smiled regretfully. "If only I could shed my own court titles so easily."

"Simple people need their symbols, Lady."

Kelsea stared at her. Carlin had said the same thing many times, and the echo was unwelcome now, when Kelsea thought she had escaped the schoolroom forever. "May I ask you an unpleasant question?"

"By all means."

"The night before your daughter was to go to Mortmesne, what did you do?"

Andalie pursed her lips, and again Kelsea felt a fierceness

that was entirely lacking on other topics. "I'm not a religious woman, Lady. I'm sorry if it pains you, but I believe in no god, and even less do I believe in any church. But two nights ago, I came as close to prayer as I've ever come. I had the worst of all visions: my child lying dead, and I powerless to prevent it." Andalie took a deep breath before continuing. "She would have died before long, you know. The girls die much more rapidly than the boys. Used for menial labor until she was old enough to be sold for pleasure. That is, if she was fortunate enough not to be bought by a child rapist upon arrival." Andalie bared her teeth in a grim, pained smile. "Mortmesne condones many things."

Kelsea tried to reply, but failed, unable to speak or even move in the face of Andalie's sudden anger.

"Borwen, my husband, said that we would have to let her go. He was quite . . . forceful about it. I planned to run, but I underestimated him. He knows me, you see. He took Glee while I slept and gave her to his friends for safekeeping. I woke to find her gone, and no matter where I looked I could only see her body . . . red, all red."

Kelsea jumped in her seat, then flexed her leg, as though it had cramped. Andalie didn't seem to notice. Her hands had hooked into claws now, and Kelsea saw that three of her fingernails were ripped down to the quick.

"After despairing for some hours, Lady, I had no choice but to beg for help from every god I could think of. I don't know that you could truly call it praying, since I believed in none of those gods at that moment and believe in none of them now. But I begged help from every source I know, even a few I shouldn't mention in the light of day.

"When I came to the Keep Lawn, my Glee was already in the cage and lost to me. My next thought was to send my other children away and go after the shipment, but only after I'd killed my husband. I was considering all the ways I might watch him die, Lady, when I heard your voice."

Andalie stood without warning. "Your Majesty needs a bath, I believe, and clothing and food?"

Kelsea nodded mutely.

"I'll see to it."

When the door closed, Kelsea drew a shaking breath, rubbing gooseflesh from her arms. It had been like being in the room with a vengeful ghost, and Kelsea still felt Andalie's eyes on her, long after the woman herself had gone.

Did she tell you she was part Mort?"

"She did."

"And it bothered you not at all?"

"It might have been cause for concern in someone else."

"What does that mean?"

Mace fiddled with the short knife strapped to his forearm. "I have only a few gifts, Lady, but they're a strange, powerful few. Had there been danger to Your Majesty in the deepest part of any of these people, I'd have ferreted it out and they wouldn't be here."

"She's not a danger to me, I agree, not now. But she could be, Lazarus. To anyone who threatened her children, she could be."

"Ah, but Lady, you saved her youngest child. I think you'll find that anyone who threatens *you* faces grave danger from her."

"She's cold, Lazarus. She'll serve me only so long as it serves her children."

Mace considered for a moment, and then shrugged. "I'm sorry, Lady. I think you're simply wrong. And even if you're right, you're currently serving her children infinitely better than she could with that jackal of a husband, or even on her own. Why be gloomy?"

"If Andalie should become a danger to me, would you know it?"

Mace nodded, a gesture with so many years of certainty behind it that Kelsea let the matter drop. "Is my crowning arranged?"

"The Regent knows you're coming during his audience. I didn't specify a time; may as well not make things too easy for him."

"Will he try to kill me?"

"Likely, Lady. The Regent doesn't have a subtle bone in his body, and he'll do anything to keep the crown off your head."

Kelsea inspected her neck in the mirror. Mace had restitched the wound, but his work wasn't as neat as that of the Fetch. The gash would leave a noticeable scar.

Andalie had found a plain black velvet dress that hung straight to the floor. Kelsea guessed that sleeveless dresses were the fashion; many of the women she'd seen in the city had displayed their bare arms. But Kelsea was self-conscious about her arms, something Andalie seemed to understand without being told. The dress's loose sleeves concealed Kelsea's arms, while the neckline was just low enough to allow the sapphire to hang against her bare skin. Andalie had done an excellent job with Kelsea's thick, heavy hair as well, wrestling it into a braid and then pinning it high on her head. The woman was a monument to competence, but still, black couldn't conceal all flaws. Kelsea looked at herself in the mirror for a moment, trying to project more confidence than she felt. Some ancestor of hers, her mother's grandmother or great-grandmother, had been known as the Beautiful Queen, the first in a line of several Raleigh women renowned for fairness. The Fetch's face surfaced in her mind, and Kelsea smiled sadly at her reflection, then turned away and shrugged.

I'll be more than that.

"I need to see a copy of the Mort Treaty as soon as possible."

"We have one here somewhere."

Kelsea thought she heard disapproval in his tone. "Did I do the wrong thing yesterday?"

"Right versus wrong is a moot point, Lady. It's done, and now we'll all face the consequences. The shipment is due in seven days. You'll need to make some fast decisions."

"I want to read the treaty first. There must be some loophole."

Mace shook his head. "If so, Lady, others would have found it."

"Didn't you think I would need to know, Lazarus? Why keep it from me?"

"Please, Lady. How could any of us tell you something like that, when your own foster parents had kept it secret from you all your life? You might not even have believed me. It seemed better to let you see for yourself."

"I need to understand this system, this lottery. Who was that man in charge on the lawn yesterday?"

"Arlen Thorne," Mace said, his face furrowing. "The Overseer of the Census."

"A census only counts the population."

"Not in this kingdom, Lady. The Census is a powerful arm of your government. It controls all aspects of the shipment, from lottery to transport."

"How did this Arlen Thorne merit his position?"

"By being extremely clever, Lady. Once he nearly out-smarted me."

"Surely not you."

Mace opened his mouth to argue, but then he saw Kelsea's face in the mirror. "Hilarious, Majesty."

"Don't you ever make mistakes?"

"People who make mistakes rarely live through them, Lady."

She turned from the mirror. "How on earth did you become what you are, Lazarus?"

"Don't mistake our relationship, Lady. You're my employer. I don't confess to you."

Kelsea looked down, feeling thoroughly rebuffed. She *had* forgotten who he was for a moment; it had been like talking to Barty. Mace held up the breastplate from Pen's armor, and she shook her head. "No."

"Lady, you need it."

"Not today, Lazarus. It sends a poor signal."

"So will your dead body."

"Doesn't Pen need his armor back?"

"He has more than one set."

"I won't wear it."

Mace stared at her stonily. "You're not a child. Stop behaving like one."

"Or what?"

"Or I bring several more guards in here and they hold you down while I strap this armor on you forcibly. Is that really what you want?"

Kelsea knew he was right. She didn't know why she kept arguing. She *was* acting like a child; she remembered similar fights with Carlin over cleaning her room in the cottage. "I don't do well being ordered around, Lazarus. I never have."

"You don't say." Mace shook the armor again, his expression implacable. "Hold out your arms."

Kelsea did, grimacing. "I need my own armor, and soon. A silly queen I'll look when I've been slowly flattened into a man."

Mace grinned. "You wouldn't be the first queen of this kingdom to be mistaken for a king."

"God granted me a small enough helping of femininity. I'd like to keep what I have."

"Later, Lady, I'll introduce you to Venner and Fell, your arms masters. Women's armor is an odd order, but I'm sure they can fill it. They're good at their jobs. Until then, any time we leave the Queen's Wing, you wear Pen's armor."

"Wonderful." Kelsea sucked in a breath as he tightened a strap around her arm. "It doesn't even cover my back."

"I cover your back."

"How many people are in the Queen's Wing?"

"Twenty-four all told, Lady: thirteen Queen's Guards, three women, and their seven children. And of course, your own helpful self."

"Piss off," Kelsea muttered. She'd heard the phrase during the Fetch's poker game, and it seemed to fit her mood perfectly, though she wasn't sure she'd used it right. "How big can we grow in here?"

"Considerably bigger, and we will," Mace replied. "Three of the guards have families in a safe house. As soon as we're settled, I'll send them one at a time to bring back their kin."

Kelsea turned away and found herself staring at her mother's bookshelves again. They bothered her more every moment. Bookshelves weren't meant to be empty. "Is there a library in the city?"

"A what?"

"A library. A public library."

Mace looked up at her, incredulous. "Books?"

"Books."

"Lady," Mace said, in the slow, patient tones one would use with a young child, "there hasn't been a working printing press in this kingdom since the Landing era."

"I know," Kelsea snapped. "That's not what I asked. I asked if there was a library."

"Books are hard to come by, Lady. A curiosity at best. Who would have enough books for a library?"

"Nobles. Surely some of them still have some hoarded books."

Mace shrugged. "Never heard of such a thing. But even if they did, they wouldn't open them to the public."

"Why not?"

"Lady, try to take away even the most resilient weed in a nobleman's garden, and watch him scream trespass. I'm sure most of them don't read any books they might have, but all the same, they would never give them away."

"Can we buy books on the black market?"

"We could, Lady, if anyone valued them enough. But books aren't contraband. The black market deals in vice for value. The Tear market has high-value weapons from Mortmesne, some sex traffic, rare animals, drugs . . ."

Kelsea wasn't interested in the workings of the black market; in every society, they were always the same. She let Mace keep going while she stared despondently at the empty bookshelves, thinking of Carlin's library: three long walls full of leather-bound volumes, non-fiction on the left and fiction on the right. There was a certain patch of sunlight that came through the front window and remained until early afternoon, and Kelsea had liked to curl up in this patch every

Sunday morning to read. One Christmas, when she was eight or nine, she had come downstairs and found Barty's present: a large built-in chair constructed squarely in the patch of sunlight, a chair with deep pillows and "Kelsea's Patch" carved into the left arm. The happy memory of collapsing into that chair was so strong that Kelsea could actually smell cinnamon bread baking in the kitchen and hear the grackles around the cottage working their way into their usual morning frenzy.

Barty, she thought, and felt tears well in her eyes. It seemed very important that Mace not see; she widened her eyes to keep the tears from falling and stared resolutely at the empty bookshelves, thinking hard. How *had* Carlin acquired all of her books? Paper books had been at a premium long before the Crossing; the transition to electronic books had decimated the publishing industry, and in the last two decades before the Crossing, many printed books had been destroyed altogether. According to Carlin, William Tear had only allowed his utopians to bring ten books apiece. Two thousand people with ten books each made twenty thousand books, and at least two thousand now stood on Carlin's shelves. Kelsea had spent her entire life with Carlin's library at her fingertips, taking it for granted, never understanding that it was invaluable in a world without books. Vandals might find the cottage, or even children searching for firewood. That was what had happened to most of the books that originally came over in the British-American Crossing: the desperate had burned them for fuel or warmth. Kelsea had always thought of Carlin's library as a set piece, unified and immovable, but it wasn't. Books could be moved.

"I want all of the books from Barty and Carlin's cottage brought here."

Mace rolled his eyes. "No."

"It might take a week, perhaps two if it rains."

He finished buckling the heavy piece of steel to her forearm. "The Caden likely burned that cottage down days ago. You have a limited number of loyal people, Lady; do you really want to throw them away on a fool's errand like this?"

"Books may have been a fool's errand in my mother's kingdom, Lazarus, but they won't be in mine. Do you understand?"

"I understand that you're young and likely to overreach, Lady. You can't do all things at once. Power dispersed has a way of scattering altogether in the wind."

Unable to debate that point, Kelsea turned back to the mirror. Thinking of the cottage had reminded her of something Barty had said, one week and a lifetime ago. "Where does my food come from?"

"The food's secure, Lady. Carroll didn't trust the Keep kitchens, and he had a kitchen specially constructed out there." Mace gestured toward the door. "One of the women we brought in is a tiny thing named Milla. She made breakfast for everyone this morning."

"It was good," Kelsea remarked. It *had* been good . . . griddle cakes and mixed fruit in some sort of cream, and Kelsea had eaten for at least two.

"Milla's already staked out the kitchen as her province, and she means business; I hardly dare go in there without her permission."

"Where do we get the actual food from?"

"Don't worry. It's secure."

"Do the women seem scared?"

Mace shook his head. "Mildly concerned about their

children, perhaps. One of the babies has some sort of retching sickness; I already sent for a doctor."

"A doctor?" Kelsea asked, surprised.

"I know of two Mort doctors operating in the city. One we've used before; he's greedy but not dishonest."

"Why only two?"

"The city won't support more. It's rare that a Mort doctor emigrates, and the rates they charge are so exorbitant that few can afford them."

"What about in Bolton? Or Lewiston?"

"Bolton has one doctor that I know of. I don't think Lewiston has any at all."

"Is there a way to tempt more doctors from Mortmesne?"

"Doubtful, Lady. The Red Queen discourages defection, but some still make the attempt. But professionals have a comfortable life in Mortmesne. Only the very greedy come to the Tear."

"Only two doctors," Kelsea repeated, shaking her head. "There's a lot to do, isn't there? I don't even know where to start."

"Start by getting the crown on your head." Mace tightened a final strap on her arm and stepped back. "We're done. Let's go."

Kelsea took a deep breath and followed him out the door. They emerged into a large room, perhaps two hundred feet from end to end, with a high ceiling like her mother's chamber. The floor and walls were blocks of the same grey stone as the exterior of the Keep. There were no windows; the only light came from torches mounted in brackets on the walls. The left wall of the chamber was interrupted by a door-filled hallway that stretched for perhaps fifty yards and ended in another door.

"Quarters, Lady," Mace murmured beside her.

On her right, the wall opened into what was clearly a kitchen; Kelsea could hear the clang of pans being washed. Carroll's idea, Mace had said, and it was a good one; according to Barty, the Keep kitchens, some ten floors below, had over thirty staff and multiple entrances and exits. There was no way to secure them.

"Do you think Carroll is dead?"

"Yes," Mace replied, his face crossed by a momentary shadow. "He always said that he'd die bringing you back, and I never believed him."

"His wife and children. I made a promise in that clearing."

"Worry later, Lady." Mace turned and began to bark orders at the guards stationed on the walls. More guards emerged from the quarters at the end of the hall. Men surrounded Kelsea until she could see nothing but armor and shoulders. Most of her guards seemed to have bathed recently, but there was still an overwhelming man-smell, horses and musk and sweat, which made Kelsea feel as though she was in the wrong place. Barty and Carlin's cottage had always smelled like lavender, Carlin's favorite scent, and although Kelsea had hated the cloying smell, at least she had always known where she was.

Mhurn crowded behind her, boxing her in. Kelsea thought about greeting him and decided not to; Mhurn looked as though he hadn't slept in days, his face far too white and his eyes rimmed in red. To her right was Dyer, his expression hard and truculent behind his red beard. Pen was on her left, and Kelsea smiled, relieved to see him unharmed. "Hello, Pen."

"Lady."

"Thanks for the loan of your horse; I'll return your armor as soon as may be."

"Keep it, Lady. It was a good thing you did yesterday."

"It probably won't make any difference. I've doomed myself."

"You've doomed us all with you, Lady," Dyer remarked.

"Stuff that, Dyer!" Pen snapped.

"You stuff it, runt. The very moment that shipment doesn't arrive, the Mort army begins to mobilize. You're fucked as well."

"We're all fucked," Elston rumbled behind her. His voice came thickly through his broken teeth, but he didn't seem so hard to understand now. "Don't listen to Dyer, Lady. We've watched this kingdom sink into the mud for years. You might've come too late to save it, but it's a good thing, all the same, to try to stop the slide."

"Aye," someone joined in behind her. Kelsea blushed, but was spared from replying by Mace, who shoved his way through the group of guards to station himself on her right.

"Tighten it up, men," he growled. "If I could get through, so could anyone else."

The journey to the Great Hall was an ordeal of low grey hallways cut by torchlight. Kelsea suspected that Mace was taking a roundabout route, but still she was daunted by the endless corridors and staircases and tunnels. She hoped there was a map of the Keep somewhere, or she would never dare to venture outside her own wing.

They passed many men and women dressed in white, with hoods drawn low over their foreheads. From Carlin's descriptions, Kelsea knew that these must be Keep servants. The Keep had its housekeepers and plumbers, but it was also stuffed to bursting with unnecessary services: bartenders, hairdressers, masseuses, all of them on the Crown's payroll. Keep servants were supposed to remain inconspicuous when they weren't needed, and they drew out of Kelsea's way to hug the wall as she passed. After passing perhaps the twentieth servant, Kelsea felt her temper beginning to unravel, and no amount of gnawing on the inside of her cheek could bring it back into line. This was where her treasury had been going for the past two decades: into luxury and cages.

At last they crossed a small antechamber toward massive double doors made of some sort of oak. It didn't look like Tearling oak, though. The grain was too even, and the doors were covered in elaborate carvings of what appeared to be zodiacal signs. Tearling oak didn't carve well; Kelsea had tried to whittle it with her knife as a child, only to find the wood chipping away in chunks and splinters. She tried to get a better look at the doors, but had no time; at her approach, they opened as if by magic, and the tide of guards pushed her through.

To her left, a herald shouted, "The Princess Apparent!" Kelsea grimaced, but quickly found other things to focus on. She was in a room of greater size than she had ever imagined, with ceilings at least a good two hundred feet high and the far wall so distant that she couldn't clearly see the faces of those who stood there. The floor had been assembled from enormous tiles of dark red stone, each some thirty feet square, and the room was interspersed with massive white pillars that could only be Cadarese marble. Several skylights had been carved into the ceiling, allowing random shafts of bright sunlight to arrow down to the floor. It was eerie, the enormous torch-lit room broken by those random scatterings of white-hot light. As Kelsea and her guards passed through one beam, she felt momentary heat on her arm, then it was gone.

But for the shuffling and clinking as they moved forward down the aisle, the great room was silent. Kelsea's guard had loosened up a bit, allowing her to peek at the crowd, ranks of men and women whom Kelsea thought must be nobles. Velvet garb predominated, rich velvet in scarlet and black and royal blue. Velvet was a Callaen specialty, and there was no way to get it without going through Mort trading controls. Were all of these people doing business with Mortmesne?

Everywhere Kelsea looked were faces, both male and female, enhanced with cosmetics: dark-smudged eyes, lined and rouged lips, even one lord who appeared to have powdered his skin. Many of them displayed elaborate hair-styles that must have taken hours to create. One woman had bound her hair into a large spiral, something like the arc of a leaping fish, which ascended from one side of her head and landed on the other. Around the entire construction rested a silver tiara interspersed with amethysts, a really beautiful piece of metalwork even to Kelsea's untrained eye. Yet the woman's face had a pinched look that suggested she was prepared to be displeased with anything and everything that might occur, including her own hairstyle.

Laughter threatened to bubble up in Kelsea's throat, laughter that came from a dark well of anger. The noble-woman's hairstyle wasn't even the most ridiculous thing in the crowd. Hats seemed to be everywhere: huge and ostentatious hats with wide brims and pointed crowns in every color of the rainbow. Most were decorated with jewels or gold and elaborated with feathers. On a few hats, Kelsea even saw peacock feathers from Cadare, another luxury surely confined to the black market. Some of the hats were so wide that they took up more space than their occupants; Kelsea spotted a husband and wife with matching designs on their blue cloaks whose hats forced them to stand more than two feet apart. Noticing her stare, the couple gave a shallow curtsy, both smiling. Kelsea ignored them and turned away.

Mace's eyes were fixed on the narrow gallery that ran the length of the left wall above their heads. Following his gaze, Kelsea saw that this gallery was also crammed with people, but they weren't nobles; their clothing was plain and dark, with only a random glitter of gold here and there. Merchants, Kelsea guessed, important enough to gain entrance to the Keep but not wealthy enough to be allowed down on the floor. There were no poor in this throng, none of the gaunt people she'd seen in the fields of the Almont or out on the Keep Lawn.

Hundreds of eyes were upon her. Kelsea could feel their weight, but thousands of miles seemed to exist between her and the crowd. Had Queen Elyssa felt equally alone in this enormous room? But Kelsea turned away from that idea, furious that any part of her mind would try to relate to her mother.

At the end of the hall was a great raised dais, in the very center of which sat a throne, brilliant even in torchlight. It had been forged from pure silver, formed and shaped into a great flowing seat whose various parts simply melted one into the next, arms to back to base. The high, arched back of the throne was at least ten feet tall and carved in an aquatic relief depicting various scenes from the Crossing. It was an extraordinary piece of art, but as with so many relics of the Tear dynasty, no one knew who'd done the work, and now the throne was only a mute reminder of a time long gone.

By all rights, no one should have sat on this throne since the day her mother had died, but Kelsea wasn't surprised to see a man seated there. Her uncle was a short man with dark hair and a curling beard, a fashion that Kelsea had observed many times on her journey through the city and one to which she'd taken an instant dislike. The Regent fidgeted with the beard as Kelsea approached, wrapping it in tight coils around his index finger. He wore a tight-fitting purple jumpsuit that hid nothing. His face was pale and bloated, with deep-set eyes, and Kelsea read signs of dissipation in the broken veins of his large nose and sagging cheeks. Alcoholism, if not something more exotic; Kelsea suddenly knew, the knowledge coming from nowhere, that if there was an expensive vice out there, her uncle had tried it. He watched her with an indifferent stare, one hand hooked into his beard, the fingers of the other tapping idly on the arm of the throne. He was cunning, Kelsea could see, but not brave. Here was a man who'd been trying to kill her for years, yet she didn't fear him.

At the Regent's feet sat a red-haired woman, perched motionless on the top step of the dais, staring at nothing, extraordinarily beautiful despite her vacant stare. Her face was a perfect oval, utterly symmetrical, with a fine upturned nose and wide, sensual mouth. She was dressed in soft blue gauze, a garment of so few layers that it was nearly transparent, revealing a figure that was both willowy and voluptuous. The gauze did nothing to hide her nipples, deep pink points that poked out against the fabric. Kelsea wondered what sort of man paid for his women to dress like whores, but then the redhead looked up and Kelsea's breath hissed through her teeth. A yoke had been tied around the woman's throat, and not loosely either; puffy, welted flesh showed where the rope had abraded her skin. The other end of the rope snaked upward, over the steps of the dais, to rest in the Regent's hand.

At Mace's word, Kelsea's guard halted in front of the dais. Her uncle was surrounded by his own guard, but one glance could chart the difference between a true guard and a bunch of mercenaries. Her uncle's men wore voluminous, impractical uniforms of midnight blue, and their posture was as insolent and lazy as his. When her uncle met her gaze, Kelsea saw with some surprise that he had the same deep green, almond-shaped eyes as her own. A true blood relation, and the only one she had left . . . the thought made Kelsea pause. It seemed like blood should matter. But then her eyes returned to the roped woman huddled on the floor, and an insistent beat began in Kelsea's temples. This man wasn't a relation, her mind insisted, not if she didn't want him to be. She unclenched her fists and gentled her voice to disciplined reason. "Greetings, Uncle. I come to be crowned today."

"Welcome to the Princess Apparent," her uncle replied in a pinched, nasal voice. "We require the proof, of course."

Kelsea reached up to take off the necklace. On the Keep Lawn the day before, she had noticed that it came off rather unhappily, with a prickly feeling that seemed to tug at her skin. Today was worse; she seemed to feel the silver chain pulling at her flesh, a sensation like ants crawling beneath the surface. She held the necklace high for her uncle's inspection, and once he nodded, she turned and displayed it to the enormous company gathered in the hall.

"Where's the companion jewel?" her uncle asked.

"That's not your concern, Uncle. I have the jewel I was sent away with, and that's the proof required."

He waved a hand. "Of course, of course. The brand?"

Kelsea smiled, baring her teeth, as she pulled up the sleeve of her dress and turned her forearm to the light. The burn scar didn't look as ugly in torchlight, but it was clear all the same: someone had laid a white-hot knife against her forearm. For a moment, Kelsea could almost picture the scene: the dark room, the fire, the outraged screams of a baby who had just felt real pain for the first time in her life.

Who did this to me? she wondered. *Who would have been able to do it?*

At the sight of the scar, the Regent seemed to relax, relief settling over his shoulders. Kelsea was amazed at how easily she could read him. Was it because they were related? More likely it was merely that her uncle was fairly simple, greed and gluttony rolled together. He didn't like uncertainty, even when it worked to his advantage.

"My identity is true," Kelsea announced. "I will be crowned now. Where's the priest?"

"Here, Lady," a thin voice quavered behind her. Kelsea turned to see a tall, gaunt man of perhaps sixty approaching from the nearest pillar. He wore a loose white robe with no decoration, the uniform clothing of an ordained priest who hadn't advanced in the hierarchy. His face was that of an ascetic, drawn and pale, and his hair and eyebrows were likewise a faded, colorless blond, as though life had leached the very pigment from him. He shuffled forward with nervous, uncertain steps.

"Well done, Lazarus," Kelsea murmured.

The priest halted some ten feet from Kelsea's guard and bowed. "Lady, I'm Father Tyler. It will be my honor to administer your coronation. Where is the crown, please?"

"Ah," the Regent replied, "that has been a difficulty. Before her death, my sister hid the crown for safekeeping. We haven't been able to locate it."

"Of course you haven't," Kelsea replied, fuming inside. She should have expected some cheap nonsense like this. The crown was a symbolic instrument, but it was an important one all the same, so important that Kelsea had never heard of anyone becoming a monarch without some overdone piece of jewelry placed on his head. Her uncle probably had made an extraordinary effort to find the crown, so that he could wear it himself. If he hadn't found the thing, it was unlikely to be found.

The priest appeared to be near tears. He looked back and forth between Kelsea and the Regent, wringing his hands. "Well, it's difficult, Your Highness. I . . . I don't see how I can perform the ceremony without a crown."

The crowd was beginning to shift restlessly. Kelsea heard the strange susurration of innumerable voices murmuring in an enormous room. On impulse, she craned her neck over the priest and scanned the throng. The woman she was seeking wasn't difficult to find; her spiraled hair towered at least a foot over those around her. "Lazarus. The woman with the hideous hair. I want her tiara."

Mace peered into the crowd, his face bewildered. "What's a tiara?"

"The silver thing in her hair. Didn't you ever read fairy tales?"

Mace snapped his fingers. "Coryn. Tell Lady Andrews the Crown will reimburse her."

Coryn went swiftly down the steps, and Kelsea turned back to the priest. "Will that do, Father, until the true crown can be found?"

Father Tyler nodded, his Adam's apple working nervously. It occurred to Kelsea that for all the priest knew, she could have been raised to the Church's teachings, could even be truly devout. As the priest took another cautious step forward, Kelsea broadened her smile in slow degrees until it felt genuine. "We're honored by your presence, Father."

"The honor is mine, Lady," the priest replied, but Kelsea sensed a broad vein of anxiety beneath his placid expression. Did he fear the wrath of his superiors? Carlin's warnings about the power of the Arvath resurfaced in Kelsea's mind, and she watched the pale man with distrust.

"How dare you!" a woman shouted, the words followed by the clear crack of a slap. Kelsea peered between Elston and Dyer and saw that there was quite a tussle going on; as the crowd shifted, she caught a quick glimpse of Coryn, his hands buried in a nest of thick, dark hair. Then he disappeared again.

Elston was shaking, and when Kelsea looked up, she found him red with bottled-up laughter. He wasn't the only one; all around her, Kelsea heard quiet snickers. Mhurn, standing just behind her on the left, was openly giggling, and it had brought some color to his pallid face. Even Mace had clamped his jaw shut tight, though his lips continued to twitch. Kelsea had never seen Mace laugh, but after a moment, his mouth relaxed and he resumed scanning the gallery.

Coryn finally emerged from the crowd, tiara in hand. He looked like he'd been through a raspberry thicket; one side of his face bore a long, ugly scratch, the other was bright red, and his shirtsleeve was torn. Behind him, Kelsea could see the noblewoman progressing with sorry dignity toward the door, her elaborate hairstyle in tatters.

"Well, you've lost Lady Andrews," Pen murmured.

"I didn't need her," Kelsea replied, her temples throbbing with sudden anger. "I don't need anyone with hair like that."

Coryn handed the tiara to the priest and took his place at the front of Kelsea's guard.

"Let's do this as fast as possible, Father," Kelsea announced. "I'd hate to endanger your life any further."

The words had the desired effect; Father Tyler paled and darted a wary glance over his shoulder. Kelsea felt a moment's pity, wondering how often he was allowed to leave the Arvath. Carlin had told her that some priests, particularly those who joined young, lived their entire lives in the white tower, only leaving in a box.

The company of guards shifted now, allowing Kelsea to kneel at the foot of the dais, facing the throne. The stone floor was cold and jagged, digging into her kneecaps, and she wondered how long she would have to kneel. Her guard closed in around her, half of them facing the Regent and his guards, half directing their attention into the crowd. Father Tyler moved as close as Coryn would allow him, some five feet away.

Mhurn stood just behind her right shoulder, Mace beside him. When Kelsea twisted around to peer up at Mace, she saw that he had his sword raised in one hand, his mace in the other. The ball of the mace was still crusted with dried blood. Mace's expression was one of dangerous serenity: a man so casual and comfortable with death that he begged it to come forward and make its presence known. But the rest of the guards were so on edge that half of them drew their swords when a woman in the crowd sneezed.

Kelsea's sapphire began to burn against her skin, and she fought the urge to look down at her chest. The jewel had flared into an inferno on the Keep Lawn, but when Kelsea inspected her skin this morning, there hadn't even been the faintest hint of a mark. She had many questions about the sapphire, but the strength it provided seemed more important than her questions, more important than wonder.

If she looked down, she knew she would see the jewel gleaming against her chest, a bright, healthy blue of warning. Something was going to happen here.

Father Tyler began to mutter in tones so low that Kelsea didn't think the audience could hear him. He appeared to be settling in for some kind of soliloquy on the grace of God and His relationship to the monarchy. Kelsea ceased to pay attention. She peeked over her shoulder, but no one was moving in the crowd. Near the back, almost hidden beside one of the pillars, she glimpsed Arlen Thorne's unmistakably skeletal body in its tight blue uniform. He looked like a praying mantis leaning against the wall. A businessman, by Mace's account, but that made him even more dangerous. When Thorne noticed Kelsea watching him, he turned away.

The priest produced an aged Bible from the folds of his robe and began to read something about the ascendancy of King David. Kelsea clamped her jaws shut over a yawn. She had read the Bible from cover to cover; it had some good stories, and King David was one of the most compelling. But stories were only stories. Still, Kelsea couldn't help but admire the ancient Bible in the priest's hands, its pages as delicate as the priest himself.

Father Tyler came within two feet of Kelsea, one hand clutching the crown. She felt her guard edge up on their toes, heard the dry rasp of a sword being drawn to her right. The priest looked over her shoulder and flinched – the expression on Mace's face must be dreadful – then lost his place in his book and looked down for a moment, fumbling.

Several things happened all at once. A man shouted behind her, and Kelsea felt a knifing pain in her left shoulder. Mace shoved her flat to the floor and crouched above her, shielding her with his body. A woman screamed in the audience, an entire world away.

Swords clashed all around them. Kelsea scrabbled beneath the cover of Mace's frame, trying to get her knife from her boot. Exploring with her free hand, she found a knife handle protruding just above her shoulder blade. When her fingers brushed it, a bolt of pain arrowed all the way down to her toes.

Stabbed, she thought, dazed. *Mace didn't cover my back after all.*

"Galen! The gallery! The gallery!" Mace roared. "Get up there and clear it out!" Then he was jerked away from Kelsea. She scrambled to her feet, knife in hand. All around her, men were fighting, three of them attempting to skewer Mace with long swords. Her uncle's men, the deep blue uniforms swirling around them as they fought.

A breath of air came from behind her and Kelsea whirled to find a sword coming for her neck. She ducked, slid under her attacker's arm, and shoved her knife upward between his ribs. Warm wetness splattered her face, and she closed her eyes, blinded by red. The dead man fell on top of her, crushing her to the ground with a pure, bright explosion of pain as the knife in her shoulder hit the floor. Kelsea's teeth clenched on a scream, but she shoved the man off, wiping her eyes with the sleeve of her dress. She ignored the blood trickling down her face, pulled her knife from her attacker's rib cage, and hauled herself to her feet. Her vision was clouded by red gauze that seemed to cover everything. Someone grabbed her uninjured shoulder and she sliced savagely at the hand.

"Me, Lady, me!"

"Lazarus," she panted.

"Back to back." Mace pushed her behind him, and Kelsea

planted herself against his back, hunching forward to protect her shoulder as she faced the audience. To her surprise, none of the nobles appeared to have fled; they remained in orderly rows behind the pillars at the foot of the steps, and Kelsea wanted to shout at them. Why didn't they help? But many, the men in particular, weren't watching Kelsea. They were watching the fighting behind her, their eyes darting avidly between combatants.

Sport, Kelsea realized, sickened. She held her knife up toward the crowd in as threatening a gesture as she could muster, longing for a sword, though she had no idea how to use one. The blade dripped crimson, slippery in her blood-coated hand. She remembered when Barty had given her that knife, on her tenth birthday, in a gold-painted box with a small silver key. The box must still be in her saddlebags, somewhere upstairs. She had finally used her knife on a man, and she wished she could tell Barty. A wave of darkness crashed across her vision.

Pen had stationed himself in front of her now, a sword in each hand. When one of the Regent's guards broke forward, trying to push through, Pen sidestepped him neatly and chopped off his arm at the biceps, burying a sword in his rib cage. The man screamed, a high, thin shrieking that seemed to go on and on as his severed arm landed several feet away on the flagstones. He dropped to the ground and Pen resumed his waiting posture, unfazed by the blood dripping down his sword arm. Mhurn joined him a moment later, his blond hair streaked with crimson and his face whiter than ever now, as if he were on the edge of fainting.

Two men appeared on her periphery and Kelsea swung that way, trying to tighten her grip on the slippery knife. But it was only Elston and Kibb, planting themselves on either side of her, their swords dripping blood. Kibb had taken a wound to the hand, a deep gash that looked like an animal bite, but otherwise they appeared unharmed. The clang of swords came more slowly now, the fighting dying down. When Kelsea looked out into the crowd, she saw that Arlen Thorne had disappeared. The priest, Father Tyler, was crouched against the nearest of the massive pillars, hugging his Bible to his chest, staring at a blue-clad corpse that lay bleeding at the foot of the dais. The priest looked as though he might faint, and in spite of her distrust, Kelsea felt a brief flash of pity for him. He didn't seem the sort who'd ever been strong, even as a young man, and he wasn't young.

He needs to recover, another, colder voice snapped in her mind. *Quickly*. Kelsea, brought back to herself by the steel in that voice, nodded in agreement. It was extraordinary, how a coronation could mean so little and yet so much. Her legs gave way and she stumbled against Mace, hissing as pain dug into her back like a burrowing insect.

Women scream when they're hurt, Barty's voice echoed in her head. *Men scream when they're dying.*

I'm not going to scream, either way.

"Lazarus, you have to hold me up."

Mace got an arm beneath hers and firmed it up, giving her something to lean on. "We need to get that knife out, Lady."

"Not yet."

"You're losing blood."

"I'll lose more when the knife is pulled. First this."

Mace inspected the wound in a cursory way. The color drained from his face.

"What?"

"Nothing, Lady."

"*What?*"

"It's a grave wound. Sooner or later you're going to pass out."

"Then hit me and wake me up."

"I was set to guard your life, Lady."

"My life and that throne are one," Kelsea replied hoarsely. It was true, though she hadn't fully realized until she said it. She reached up to clutch Mace's shoulder, pointing to the sapphire on her chest. "I'm nothing now but this. You see?"

Mace turned and shouted to Galen in the gallery. Two bodies clad in blue tumbled over the wall and landed with a wet thud on the flagstones. The foremost members of the audience cried out and drew back several feet.

"Wary now!" Mace barked. "Eyes on the crowd! Kibb, you need a doctor?"

"Fuck you," Kibb replied in a good-natured tone, though his face was white and he was clutching his hand in a death grip. "I'm a medic."

Many of her uncle's guard were dead on the dais. Several of her own guards were sporting wounds, but she could see no grey-clad bodies on the floor. Who had thrown the knife?

The Regent remained seated, his manner still unconcerned despite the blood that spattered his face and the four Queen's Guards who had him at sword point. But a thin layer of sweat gleamed on his upper lip now, and his eyes twitched continuously toward the crowd. Considering the lax skills of his guard, it had been a fool's attempt on Kelsea's life. A delaying tactic; her uncle knew the importance of this crowning as well as Kelsea did. An entirely new landscape of pain had begun to radiate outward from her shoulder, and blood was pooling in the small of her back. She sensed that she had very little time. She reached out and grabbed one of her guards, a young one whose name she didn't know. "Get the priest."

With a doubtful glance, the guard went and hauled Father Tyler back up to the dais, where he blanched at the pile of dead bodies strewn across the floor. Kelsea opened her mouth and that cold voice emerged, a tone of command that didn't seem entirely her own. "We'll continue now, Father. Stick to the essential language."

He nodded, producing the tiara in one shaking hand. With Mace's help, Kelsea knelt back down on the floor. Father Tyler opened his Bible again and began to read in a quavering voice, the words running together in Kelsea's ears. Beyond the priest, she saw the beautiful redhead, still as stone on the top step of the dais, her body streaked and smeared with blood. It had painted her face and soaked through the blue gauze of her clothing. She hadn't moved an inch, but she was alive; her grey eyes stared at the same fixed point on the floor. Kelsea closed her eyes for a moment, and then she was looking up at the ceiling, an enormous vaulted expanse, revolving above her.

Mace's boot landed in the small of her back, and Kelsea bit her tongue against a scream. Her vision cleared slightly, and she saw the priest advancing upon her, Bible closed, tiara in hand. Her guard tensed up around her. Father Tyler leaned down, his eyes wide, his face drained of all blood, and Kelsea felt her earlier suspicions inexplicably vanish. She wished that she could comfort him, tell him that his part in this business was almost done.

But it isn't, another voice whispered, quiet but sure in her mind. *Not even close.*

"Your Highness," he asked, his tone almost apologetic, "do you swear to act for this kingdom, for this people, under the laws of God's Church?"

Kelsea drew a hoarse breath, feeling something rattle in her chest, and whispered, "I swear to act for this kingdom and for this people, under the law."

Father Tyler paused. Kelsea tried to draw another breath and felt herself fading, drifting to the left. Mace kicked her again, and this time she couldn't stop the small screech that escaped her lips. Even Barty would have understood. "You'll watch out for your church, Father, and I'll watch out for this kingdom and its people. My vow."

Father Tyler hesitated a moment longer, then tucked his Bible into the fold of his robes. His face was a mask of resignation and regret, as though he could see into the future, the many possible consequences of this moment. Perhaps he could. He reached out and set the tiara on Kelsea's head with both hands. "I crown you Queen Kelsea Raleigh of the Tearling. Long be your reign, Majesty."

Kelsea shut her eyes, her throat choked with a relief so great that it bordered on ecstasy. "Lazarus, help me up."

Mace hauled her to her feet, and her legs promptly gave way. His arms wrapped around her from behind, holding her up like a rag doll, pitching her torso forward to avoid the knife hilt buried in her shoulder.

"The Regent."

Mace swung her carefully around and Kelsea faced her uncle, finding his eyes bright with stupid desperation. Slowly, deliberately, she leaned back against Mace until the hilt of the knife bumped his chest. The pain jolted her awake, but not much; darkness was closing in now, a blackening border around the edge of her vision.

"Get off my throne."

Her uncle didn't move. Kelsea leaned forward, summoning all of her strength, her breath rasping loudly in the vast, echoing chamber. "You have one month to be gone from this Keep, Uncle. After that . . . ten thousand pounds on your head."

A woman behind Kelsea gasped, and muttering began to spread throughout the crowd. Her uncle's panicked eyes darted behind her.

"You can't place a bounty on a member of the royal family."

The voice behind her was an oily baritone that Kelsea already recognized: Thorne. She ignored him, forcing words out in thin wheezes of breath. "I've given you . . . a running start, Uncle. Get off my throne right now, or Lazarus will throw you out of the Keep. How long . . . do you think you'll last?"

Her uncle blinked slowly. After several seconds he rose from the throne, his stomach ballooning as he stood upright. *Too much ale*, Kelsea thought vaguely, followed by: *My god, he's shorter than I am!* Her vision doubled, then tripled. She nudged Mace with one elbow, and he understood, for he hauled her forward and eased her onto the throne. It was like sitting on a freezing cold rock. Kelsea swayed against the icy metal, shut her eyes, and opened them again. There was something else she had to do, but what?

In front of her, Kelsea spotted the redhead, still covered in blood. Her uncle stumbled down the steps of the dais, the slack in the rope pulling tighter as he went.

"Drop the rope," Kelsea whispered.

"Drop the rope," Mace repeated.

Her uncle whirled around, and for the first time, Kelsea saw naked fury in his eyes. "The woman's mine! She was a gift."

"Too bad."

Her uncle looked around for reinforcements, but most of his guards were dead. Only three of them followed at his heels, and even these remaining men seemed reluctant to meet his eye. Her uncle's face was white with anger, but Kelsea saw something worse written in his expression: aggrieved bewilderment, the look of a man who didn't know why so many terrible things should happen to him when he had meant so well. After another moment's deliberation, he dropped the rope and scuttled backward.

"She's mine," he repeated plaintively.

"She goes with us. Elston – see to it."

"Majesty."

"Take me out, Lazarus, please," Kelsea rasped. Drawing breath was an exercise in agony. Mace and Pen debated for a moment, and then each of them stooped down and got an arm beneath her, forming a chair. Kelsea was dimly grateful; it was a more dignified way to leave the room than being slung around like a sack. Her guard quickly reformed around her, then made their way off the dais and down the center aisle. The crowd blurred past. Kelsea wished they hadn't first seen her this way, bloody and weakened. At some point they passed a noblewoman in a red velvet dress, the color brilliant in the darkness. Carlin had always liked to wear that same deep, rich red at home, and Kelsea reached out a hand to the woman, whispering, "It will be a hard road." But she was too far away to touch. Many faces streaked by; for a moment, Kelsea thought she saw the Fetch, but that was madness. Still she reached out again, grasping helplessly.

"Sir, we need to hurry," Pen muttered. Mace grunted assent, and their progress quickened, through the enormous double doors and out into the broad entry passage. Kelsea could smell her own blood now, impossibly vivid. All of her senses were in riot. Each torch was as bright as the sun, but when she squinted at Mace, she found his face shrouded in darkness. The guards muttered to each other, their whispers deafening, but Kelsea couldn't understand a single word. The tiara was slipping from her head.

"My crown is falling off."

Mace tightened the arm that supported her back. Reaching for a wall, he touched something invisible to Kelsea's eyes, and to her astonishment, a hidden door swung open into darkness. "Not if I can help it, Lady."

"Nor I," echoed Pen. As they went through the darkened doorway, Kelsea felt a careful hand secure the crown on her head.

CHAPTER 7
RIPPLES IN THE POND

In the wake of her crowning, the Glynn Queen was not seen in the Keep for five days. She was unconscious for much of that time, having taken a knife wound that bled her close to death. For the rest of her life, she would carry the scar on her back; it was this scar, and not, as popularly supposed, the burn on her arm, that earned her the designation "The Marked Queen."

But the world didn't stop moving while the Queen slept.

— The Early History of the Tearling,
AS TOLD BY MERWINIAN

When Thomas woke the next morning, he hoped the coronation had been a bad dream. He clung to that, clung hard, even though part of his mind already knew that it wasn't so. Something had gone wrong.

The first clue was Anne, who slept beside him with her manicured hands curled around her pillow. Only Marguerite ever slept beside him. Anne was a poor substitute, with a shorter, pudgier body and red hair that frizzed while Marguerite's flowed like a river of amber. Anne had a better mouth, but she was no Marguerite. Thomas's head throbbed, the beginnings of a hangover waiting to assert itself. Marguerite was definitely part of the problem.

He rolled over and buried his head in the pillow, trying to drown out the noise beyond his chamber. It sounded as if someone was moving boxes, a combination of shuffling and thumping that made it impossible to get back to sleep. But the pillow only made his head throb harder, and he finally took it off, cursing fluently under his breath, rang for Pine, and then pulled the coverlet back over his head. Pine would stop the noise.

The girl had taken Marguerite, he remembered now. The girl had fixed on the one thing he couldn't bear to lose, and that was what she'd taken. There had been one brief moment of hope when the guard managed to knife the girl and she went down, but then Thomas had watched her drag herself from the floor and complete her crowning while her life's blood ran out, an act of absolute will. She'd taken Marguerite for her own and now she would go to bed with Marguerite every night and oh how his head throbbed, it was like a bellows inside.

Still, perhaps some hope remained. The girl *had* lost a lot of blood.

It had been several minutes, and no Pine. Thomas pulled the coverlet off his head and rang again, feeling Anne stir beside him. The racket was pretty bad if it had woken her as well; they had put away three bottles of wine last night, and Anne had no head for wine at all.

Pine wasn't coming.

Thomas sat up and flung off the covers, snarling another curse. More than once, he'd gifted Pine with the use of one of his women for the night, but Pine wasn't the sort to stop at what was offered. If Thomas found him in bed with Sophie, he would skin Pine alive.

Thomas finally located his robe beneath a pile of clothes in the corner, but the silk tie was stuck and yanked right out of its loops. Thomas cursed again, louder this time, and looked toward Anne, who merely rolled over and put her own head back under a pillow. He wrapped the robe around his body, holding the front closed. If Pine had bothered to actually hang up the clothes, this wouldn't have happened. When Thomas found him, it would be time for a serious discussion. Failure to answer the bell, piles of dirty laundry everywhere ... and hadn't they run out of rum a few days ago? The entire place was falling apart, and at absolutely the worst time. He pictured the girl's face, that round face that would have been right at home on any peasant in the streets of New London. But her eyes were the same cat-green as his own, and they had pinned him like a dart.

She sees me, he'd thought helplessly. *She sees everything.*

Of course she couldn't see everything. She might guess, but she couldn't know. Arlen Thorne, who always prepared for every eventuality, would already have one of his many backup plans in motion; he had just as much to lose if the shipment failed. Thorne had never bothered to hide his contempt for Thomas, telling him only what he needed to know to play his part. But only now did Thomas see how well Thorne had planned things, absolving himself of all risk. It had been Thorne's scheme, but none of the Census people had been involved. Thomas's guards had been the ones to create the diversion. No one could implicate Thorne but Thomas himself, Thomas who was now surely suspect.

His stomach had swelled again; the robe was barely large enough to wrap around it. The best Thomas could do was to hold it closed in two places, over his stomach and his groin.

Six months ago, when the robe was ordered, he hadn't been this fat. But he'd been eating more and drinking more heavily as he slowly realized that no one was going to be able to find and kill the girl in time . . . not even the Caden, who had never failed to hunt down anything.

Thomas headed for the door. Even if Pine was ignoring the bell, a good shout would bring him running; the Regent's quarters weren't as large or luxurious as the Queen's Wing, and sound carried well. Years ago Thomas had tried to move into the Queen's Wing, but both Carroll and the Mace had stopped him short, and that was when Thomas had realized that they were all there, the Queen's Guard, still living in the guard quarters, still waiting in the vain hope that the Queen would appear someday. Worse yet, they were recruiting. The Mace had reached into that dim heart of the Tearling that only he could navigate and produced Pen Alcott, who was good enough with a sword to be one of the Caden, but had chosen to be a Queen's Guard at half the pay. Thomas himself had tried several times to recruit Alcott, along with other members of the Queen's Guard, but they'd never wanted to ally with him, and he hadn't understood why until the girl's crowning. She wasn't like him at all, nor, for that matter, was she anything like Elyssa.

Her father's child, Thomas thought bitterly. They'd had to arrange three abortions for Elyssa (that Thomas knew of, anyway); she was as absentminded about taking her damned syrup as she was about everything else. But Thomas hadn't been able to talk her into the last abortion, the one he most needed her to have. She'd been terrified of the doctor in those last years, seeing him as a potential assassin. Even Thomas had to admit that it would probably be very easy to kill a woman during the procedure, but that knowledge only increased his bitterness. How like Elyssa, to jettison three pregnancies without a thought and then decide, for all the wrong reasons, to bear this particular child, the one who would make things difficult. Pine had told him yesterday that the girl was already installed in the Queen's Wing, with guards surrounding her and the great doors locked. Any hope Thomas had ever had of moving into Elyssa's chambers was now gone.

Still, it could be worse. His own quarters were comfortable; there was room enough for his own personal guard and all of the women, as well as several body servants. It had been a drab place when Thomas had first moved in, but he'd dressed it up with a number of pictures by his favorite artist, Powell. Pine had also found some thick gold paint, which seemed a good, cheap way to make everything look regal. Once Thomas had received the patronage of the Red Queen, she sent better and more expensive presents, and these littered his quarters: a solid silver statue of a naked woman, deep red velvet drapes, and a set of real gold dishes set with rubies. This last gift had pleased Thomas most of all, so much so that he ate dinner off the dishes every night. From time to time, the unpleasant realization surfaced that the Red Queen was using him, much as the Tear nobility used their overseers; Thomas was a buffer, a necessary conduit standing between the one who had all the power and those who had none. He was the one the Tear hated; Elyssa was gone, and so there was only him. If the Tear poor ever rebelled, his was the head they would want, and the Red Queen would undoubtedly sacrifice him, just as the Tear nobles would undoubtedly barricade themselves up high and leave their overseers to the mob. This, too, was unpleasant knowledge that could not always be ignored . . . but the idea of the Tear poor rebelling against anyone was so remote as to be laughable. They were too busy trying to find their next meal.

Light blinded Thomas as soon as he opened the door. Even as he squinted, trying to adjust, the scene in the common room stopped him short. The first thing he saw were his gold-and-ruby dishes, being loaded none too carefully into an oakwood box by a manservant in the white dress of the Keep. Keep servants were never allowed in the Regent's private quarters; they would steal anything that wasn't nailed down. But now one of them was here, and he was busy. He lifted gold plates one stack at a time and piled them into the box with a resounding crash that made Thomas shudder.

Other changes caught his eye. His red velvet drapes were gone, pulled down from their place on the east wall. The windows were wide open, and sunlight streamed in. Both of his good statues, which had graced the far corners of the room, were gone. On the north side of the room, stacked in the corner, were some twenty kegs of beer, and beside them crates and crates of Mort wine. Another Keep servant was lining up bottles of whiskey (some of it very good stuff too, stuff Thomas had purchased himself at the Whiskey Festival that was held every July in the streets of New London). Next to the kegs was a large wagon, its function clear: they were going to cart out his entire supply of liquor as well.

Thomas tightened his grip on the robe, whose edges were still trying to escape, and stormed over to the servant handling his gold dishes. "What do you think you're doing?"

The servant cocked a thumb over his shoulder without meeting Thomas's eye. Looking beyond him, Thomas felt his heart sink further; Coryn stood behind the pile of beer kegs, making notations on a piece of paper. He wasn't wearing his grey cloak, but he didn't need to. The Keep servants were doing his bidding all the same.

"Oi! Queen's Guard!" Thomas shouted. He wished he could snap his fingers, but he didn't dare, lest his robe fall open. "What is all this?"

Coryn tucked his pen and paper away. "Queen's orders. All of these items are Crown property, and they go today."

"What Crown property? It's *my* property. I bought it."

"Then you shouldn't have kept it in the Keep. Anything in the Keep is subject to seizure by the Crown."

"I didn't . . ." Thomas pondered this assertion, sure there must be a loophole for the royal family. He'd never really studied the Tearling's laws, even when he was a child and required to study; government wasn't interesting. But hell, Elyssa hadn't studied either, and she was the firstborn. He cast around for another argument and spotted his gold dishes in the box. "Those! Those were a gift!"

"A gift from whom?"

Thomas clamped his jaw shut. His robe threatened to come loose again, and he gathered a great fold of fabric in one hand, miserably aware that he was giving Coryn a glimpse of his puffy white stomach.

"Your personal items, clothing and shoe leather, are yours, as well as any weapons you might have," Coryn told him, his blue eyes infuriatingly impassive. "But the Crown will no longer fund your lifestyle."

"How am I to live then?"

"The Queen has decreed that you have one month to vacate the Keep."

"What of my women?"

Coryn's face remained businesslike, but Thomas could feel waves of contempt coming off the man like heat. "Your women are free to do what they like. They may keep their clothing, but their jewelry has already been confiscated. If any of them are willing to leave with you, they're welcome."

Thomas glared at him, trying to think of a way to explain things, how the women would otherwise have spent their lives in the most acute poverty imaginable, how they had acquiesced to the bargain – well, all of them except Marguerite, who was simply difficult. But the sun was too bright, and it made thinking hard. When was the last time he'd actually opened those curtains? Years, it had to be years. Sunlight washed the room, turning it white instead of grey, revealing cracks that had never been repaired; wine and food stains on the carpets; even a jack of diamonds that lay alone in the corner, like a raft set adrift on God's Ocean.

Christ, how many games did I play without that in the deck?

"I never hit any of my women," he told Coryn. "Not once."

"Well done."

"Sir!" a Keep servant called. "We're ready to load the liquor!"

"Proceed!" Coryn tipped his head at Thomas. "Any other questions?"

He turned away without waiting for an answer and began to nail one of the boxes closed.

"Where's Pine?"

"If you mean your manservant, I've seen no sign of him for a while. Perhaps he had other things to do."

"Yes," Thomas replied, nodding. "Yes, he did. I sent him down to the market early this morning."

Coryn murmured something noncommittal.

"Where are my women now?"

"I've no idea. They didn't take well to losing their jewelry."

212

Thomas winced; of course they didn't. He ran his hands through his hair, forgetting about his robe, which billowed open. He snatched it closed. One of the Keep servants snickered, but when he looked around, they were all going about their assigned tasks.

"I'll call on the Queen as soon as I have the free time," he told Coryn. "It may be several days."

"Yes, it may be."

Thomas hesitated, trying to decide if there'd been any sort of threat in the statement, then turned and trudged toward the women's quarters, trying to think of what to say to them. Petra and Lily might go elsewhere; they'd always been the most rebellious after Marguerite. But the rest could be persuaded. Of course, he would need to find money somewhere. But he had many noble friends who would probably help him, and in the meantime, he could go and stay in the Arvath. The Holy Father wouldn't dare turn him away, not after all the gold Thomas had given him over the years. Even the Red Queen might be willing to fund Thomas, if he could convince her that he'd be back on the throne before long. But he shuddered at the thought of asking.

Food and paper littered the common room of the women's quarters. The cupboards had been left open, the drawers yanked from their chests, and clothing was strewn everywhere. How long had Coryn been at work in here? He must have come in early this morning, perhaps just after Thomas had gone to bed.

Pine let him in, Thomas realized. *Pine sold me out.*

Only Anne was in the women's quarters. She'd apparently gotten up while he was talking to Coryn, and now she was nearly dressed, her frizzy red curls pinned neatly on top of her head.

"Where are the others?" he asked.

Anne shrugged, reaching around behind herself and lacing up her own dress with quick, clever fingers. Thomas felt cheated: why had he been paying all those professional dressers? "What does that mean?"

"It means I haven't seen any of them." Anne produced a trunk and began to pack.

"What are you doing?"

"Packing. But someone moved my jewelry."

"It's gone," Thomas replied slowly. "The Queen took it." He sat down on the nearest sofa, staring at her. "What are you doing? None of you have anywhere else to go."

"Of course we do." She turned, and Thomas saw a hint of the same contempt in her eyes that he'd seen in Coryn's. A memory rippled in his mind, but he forced it away; he sensed that it was something from childhood, and very few things from childhood had been good.

"Where will you go?"

"To Lord Perkins."

"Why?"

"Why do you think? He made me an offer, months ago."

The betrayal! Thomas played poker with Lord Perkins, invited him to dinner once a month. The man was old enough to be Anne's father.

"What sort of offer?"

"That's between me and him."

"Is that where the rest of them went?"

"Not to Perkins." A note of pride entered Anne's voice. "He only offered for me."

"This is only temporary. A few months, and I'll be back on the throne. Then you can all come back."

Anne stared at him as though he were a roach in the

kitchen. Memory was thrashing its way to the surface now. Thomas fought it, but suddenly it was there: Queen Arla had looked at him in exactly the same way. Thomas and Elyssa had been schooled together, and learning had always been hard for both of them, but Elyssa had understood more, so she had continued to work with the governess while Thomas simply stopped after his twelfth year. For a while, Mum had tried to talk to him about politics, the state of the kingdom, dealings with Mortmesne. But Thomas had never been able to grasp the things that he was supposed to intuitively understand, and that look in Mum's eyes had grown stronger and stronger. Eventually the conversations stopped, and Thomas saw very little of Mum after that. He was allowed to do what he had always wanted to do in the first place: sleep all afternoon and go hellraising around the Gut at night. It had been years since anyone had dared to look at him with open contempt, but now here he was again, feeling just as small as he'd felt when he was young.

"You really don't understand, do you?" Anne asked. "She's set us free, Thomas. Maybe you'll be back on the throne, maybe not; I wouldn't know about that. But none of us will be back."

"You weren't slaves! You had the best of everything! I treated you like noblewomen. You never had to work."

Anne's eyebrows lifted higher, her face darkening, and now her voice nearly thundered. "Never had to work? Pine wakes me up at three in the morning and tells me you're ready for me. I go to your chamber and get to lick Petra's cunt for your pleasure."

"I paid you," the Regent whispered.

"You paid my *parents*. You paid my parents a tidy sum when I was fourteen years old and too young to know anything about anything."

"I paid for your food, your clothing. Good clothing! And I gave you jewelry!"

Now she looked straight through him. He remembered this too; this was how Queen Arla the Just had looked at him for the last ten years of her life, and nothing he could say or do had ever caused her to see him again. He had turned invisible.

"You should leave the Tearling," Anne remarked. "It's not safe for you."

"What do you mean?"

"The Mace is her Captain of Guard, and you tried to have her killed. If I were you, I would leave the country."

"This is *all temporary*." Why could no one see this but him? The girl had already made enemies of both Thorne and Mortmesne. Thomas hated government, but even he'd read the Mort Treaty. The default clause would trigger in seven days. If the shipment failed to arrive in Demesne ... he couldn't even imagine it. No one had ever seen the Red Queen in a rage, but in her silences one could feel the world beginning to end. A picture suddenly popped into Thomas's mind, eerie in its realism: the Keep, surrounded by Mort hawks wheeling and plunging around its many turrets, hunting, always hunting. "Her head will be hanging on the walls of Demesne by the end of the month."

Anne shrugged. "If you say so."

She crossed the room and took another pile of dresses from the chest of drawers, then picked up a hairbrush from the floor, commonplace movements that dismissed Thomas. He saw the meaning of the open chests of drawers: they'd all abandoned him and taken the clothes!

Perhaps Anne was right. He could conceivably go to Mortmesne and beg the Red Queen for clemency. But she had tired of him long ago. She might just as easily decide to hand him over to an executioner. And how could he leave the Keep, even to make the journey? The Fetch was out there, the Fetch who seemed to know everything and anticipate everything. The stone bulwark was scant protection against him, for the Fetch could enter the Keep like a ghost, but it was better than nothing, better than being out in the open. If Thomas tried to make for the Mort border, the Fetch would find out, Thomas knew that as well as he knew his own name, and no matter how many guards he took with him, one night he would open his eyes and see that face above him, that dreadful mask.

If he even had any guards left. More than half of his force had been slaughtered in the attempt on the girl. No one had come to arrest Thomas yet, which had seemed an extraordinary stroke of good fortune; perhaps they thought his guards had hatched the plot on their own. But now, remembering the utter lack of concern in Coryn's voice, Thomas realized that maybe that wasn't it at all. Maybe they knew and just didn't care.

Anne snapped the clasps on her trunk and went to check herself in the mirror. To Thomas, she looked somewhat bare without any jewelry, but she seemed pleased enough; after tucking one wild lock of hair back behind her ear, she smiled, grabbed hold of the trunk, and turned to him. Her eyes seemed to burn right through him, and Thomas wondered why he'd never noticed them before; they were a warm, brilliant blue.

"I never hit you," he reminded her. "Not even one time."

Anne smiled, a friendly grin that failed to conceal something unpleasant lurking at the corners of her mouth. "Clothing, jewelry, food, and gold, and you think you paid, Thomas. You didn't, not even close. But I think you will."

Father Tyler finished the last bit of his chicken, then set his fork down with an unsteady hand. He was frightened. The summons had come just as he was sitting down to his lunch, a simple bit of fowl that had been boiled to blandness. Tyler had never had much taste for food anyway, but in the past two days he'd eaten as an act of utter mechanics, tasting only dust.

At first he was elated. He'd been a bit player in one of the great events of his time. There hadn't been many great events in Tyler's life. He'd grown up a farmer's son in the Almont Plain, one of seven children, and when he was eight years old, his father had given him to the local priest in place of tithing. Tyler never resented his father's decision, not even then; he had been one child among too many, and there was never enough to eat.

The parish priest, Father Alan, was a good man. He needed an assistant, for he suffered from severe gout. He taught Tyler how to read and gave him his first Bible. By the time Tyler was thirteen, he was helping Father Alan write his sermons. The parish congregation was not large, perhaps thirty families, but the Father couldn't get to them all. As his gout worsened, Tyler began to make the Father's rounds, visiting families and hearing their troubles. When those too old or sick to reach the church wanted to confess, Tyler took their confessions, even though he hadn't been ordained yet. He supposed it was technically a sin, but he also didn't think God would mind, particularly not for those who were dying.

When Father Alan was summoned to New London for promotion, he took Tyler with him, and Tyler finished his training in the Arvath and became ordained at the age of seventeen. He might have had his own parish, but his supervisors had already realized that Tyler was ill suited to minister to the public. He liked research more than people, liked to work with paper and ink, and so he became one of the Arvath's thirty bookkeepers, recording tithes and tributes from the surrounding parishes. It was relaxing work; once in a while a cardinal would attempt to pad his own lifestyle by hiding his parishes' income, and there would be some excitement for a month or so, but most of the time bookkeeping was a quiet job, leaving plenty of time to think and read.

Tyler stared at his books, spread over ten shelves of good Tearling oak that had cost most of one year's stipend. The first five books had come to him from a parishioner, a woman who'd died and left them to the Church with a small bequest. Cardinal Carlyle had taken the bequest and made it disappear, but he'd had no use for the books, so he dumped them on young Father Tyler's desk, saying, "You're her priest. Figure it out."

Tyler had been twenty-three. He'd read the Bible through many times, but secular books were a novelty, so he opened one and began reading, idly at first, then turning one page after another with the amazed, fortunate feeling of a man who finds money on the ground. He had become an academic that day, though he wouldn't know it for many years.

He could no longer delay the inevitable. Tyler left his small room and shuffled down the hallway. He had suffered from arthritis in his left hip for some seven or eight years now, but his slow gait was less the effect of pain than of reluctance. He was a good bookkeeper, and life in the Arvath had been a comfortable, inexorable march of time . . . until four days ago, when everything changed.

He'd conducted the coronation in a state of near terror, wondering what perverse twist of fate had guided the Mace to his door. Tyler was a devout priest, an ascetic, a believer in the great work of God that had brought humanity through the Crossing. But he was no performer. He'd stopped giving sermons decades before, and each year he retreated further into the world of books, of the past. He would have been the Holy Father's last choice to perform the crowning, but the Mace had knocked on his door and Tyler had gone.

I am part of God's great work. The thought darted in from nowhere and disappeared with the same blinding speed. He knew the history of the Tearling monarchs in detail. The great socialist vision of William Tear had eroded after the Landing, dying in increments until it ended in bloody disaster with the assassination of Jonathan Tear. The Raleigh line had taken over the throne, but the Raleighs were not the Tears, never had been. By now they had become as fatuous and sickened as any royal line of pre-Crossing Europe. Too much intermarriage and too little education. Too little understanding of humanity's tendency to repeat its own mistakes, over and over again. But Tyler knew that history was everything. The future was only the disasters of the past, waiting to happen anew.

At the time of the crowning, he hadn't yet heard the story of what had happened on the Keep Lawn; the price for his seclusion and study was a woeful ignorance of current events. But in the days since, his brother priests had refused to leave him alone. They knocked on his door constantly, ostensibly for clarification of some point of theology or history, but none would leave without hearing some version of the Queen's crowning. In return, they told Tyler of the freeing of the allotted, and the burning of the cages.

This morning Father Wyde had come in, fresh from handing out bread to the beggars who lined the steps of the Arvath. According to Wyde, the beggars were calling her the True Queen. Tyler knew the term: it was a female variant on the pre-Crossing Arthurian legend, the Queen who would save the land from terrible peril and usher in a golden age. The True Queen was a fairy tale, a balm for childless mothers. Yet Tyler's heart had leaped at Wyde's words, and he'd been forced to look out the window to conceal eyes suddenly bright with tears.

I am part of God's great work.

He didn't know what to say to the Holy Father. The Queen had refused to swear allegiance to God's Church, and even Tyler knew the importance of that vow. The Regent, despite a complete lack of personal morality, had remained firmly under the Holy Father's control, donating vast sums of money to the Church and allowing construction of a private chapel inside the Keep. Should an itinerant friar come along, preaching the ancient beliefs of Luther to an ever more enthusiastic audience, the friar would disappear and never be heard from again. No one spoke of these things, but Tyler was a perceptive man, and he knew the sickness of his church. Over the years he had chosen seclusion, loving God with his whole heart, intending to die quietly someday in the small room, surrounded by his books. But now he'd been inexplicably drawn into the great events of the world.

Tyler's heart thumped in the narrow cage of his chest as he trudged up the enormous marble staircase toward the Holy Father's audience room. He was getting old, yes, but he was also frightened. His private conversation with the Holy

Father had been limited to a few words of congratulation upon Tyler's ordination. How long ago had that been? Some fifty years gone. The Holy Father had aged, just as Tyler had, and was now nearing his hundredth year. Even in the Tearling, where the wealthy lived long, the Holy Father's life span was impressive. But illness plagued him: pneumonia, fevers, and some sort of digestive ailment that reportedly prohibited him from eating meat. However, his mind had remained sharp as his body dwindled, and he'd managed the Regent so adroitly that the Arvath now had a steeple of pure gold, a luxury unheard of since the pre-Crossing. Even the Cadarese, with their enormous supply of underground riches, didn't confer so much wealth upon their temples.

Tyler shook his head. The Holy Father was an idolater. Perhaps they all were. When the girl refused to take the vow, Tyler had made an immediate decision, perhaps the first of his entire life. The Tearling did not need the Queen to be loyal to the Church, with its infection of greed. The Tearling simply needed a queen.

Two acolytes were stationed outside the door to the audience room. Despite their shaven heads and eyebrows, they shared the narrow weasel's look of all the Holy Father's attendants. Both of them smirked as they unbolted the doors and tugged them open, the message clear: *You're in trouble.*

I know, Tyler thought. *Better than anyone.*

He crossed the threshold, making a special point of keeping his gaze down. The Holy Father was rumored to become difficult when people failed to pay him proper respect. The walls and floor of the audience chamber were constructed of quarried stone that had been washed so white by the passage of water that the room actually seemed to glow under the skylight. It was extremely warm; with the skylight glassed in, there was nowhere for the heat to go. After his many bouts with pneumonia, the Holy Father reportedly liked the excessive warmth. His oakwood throne sat atop the dais in the center of the room, but Tyler halted at the foot of the dais and waited, keeping his head carefully lowered.

"Ah, Tyler. Come here."

Tyler mounted the steps of the dais and reached automatically for the Holy Father's outstretched hand, kissing the ruby ring, then retreated to the second riser and knelt. His left hip began to throb immediately; kneeling always played hell with his arthritis.

When he looked up, Tyler felt a small stirring of pity. The Holy Father had once been a well-built middle-aged man, but now one arm was withered and useless from the stroke he'd suffered several years ago, and his face was likewise lopsided; the right side sagged like a sail that had lost its wind. For the past few months, the Arvath had quaked with rumors that the Holy Father was dying, and Tyler thought this was probably the truth. His skin was as transparent as parchment; actual bone seemed to poke through his bald head. He had not aged so much as shriveled, and now he seemed almost the size of a child, nearly lost in the folds of his white velvet robes. He gave Tyler a benevolent smile that put Tyler immediately on his guard, dissolving the pity like sugar.

Beside the Holy Father, just as Tyler had feared, was Cardinal Anders, stately in his voluminous robes of scarlet silk. Cardinals' robes had once been nearly orange due to the imperfect red that dyers produced in the Tearling, but Anders's robes were true red, a clear sign that the Church, like everyone else, was getting Callaen dyes off the black market out of Mortmesne. In addition to the robes, Anders wore a small gold pin in the shape of a hammer, a memento of his time spent on the Regent's antisodomy squads. Anders's hatred of homosexuals was well known, exceptional even for the Arvath, and rumor said he was the one who had originally suggested the idea of a special law enforcement contingent to the Regent. But then, several years ago, he had gone a step further, volunteering for duty in his free hours. It had made for quite the scandal, a sitting cardinal working for law enforcement, but Anders had refused to quit and stayed with the squads for several years. Tyler wondered why the Holy Father still allowed Anders to wear the pin on top of his robes, now, when Anders had finally ended his involvement.

Cardinal Anders's presence at this meeting meant trouble. He was the Holy Father's clear choice as successor, even though he was only forty-three, over twenty years younger than Tyler. Anders had first come to the Arvath at the young age of six; his parents were devout nobles, and they'd intended him for the priesthood since birth. Smart and unscrupulous, he had risen through the ranks with extraordinary speed; at the age of twenty-one, he'd been the youngest priest ever promoted to the bishopric of New London, and he'd been named a cardinal only a few short years afterward. In all that time, his face never seemed to change; it was a slab of wood, heavy features pitted with scars that suggested adolescent acne, and eyes so black that Tyler couldn't distinguish iris from pupil. Watching him was like staring at a Tearling oak. Tyler had met greedy priests, venal priests, even priests tormented by hidden, twisted sexual desires that were repugnant to the Church. But whenever he saw that wooden face, the face of the next Holy Father, which would look on God's work and the devil's horrors with the same clinical detachment, Tyler felt profoundly uneasy. He didn't like or trust the Holy Father, never had, but the Holy Father at least was a predictable blend of religion and expedience; one could work with the man. Cardinal Anders was another matter altogether; Tyler had no idea what he might be capable of without restraint. The Holy Father was a weak check only, a check that would soon be gone.

"What service can I do Your Holiness?"

The Holy Father chuckled. "You think I've brought you here to consult your specialized knowledge of history, Tyler? Indeed, no. You've been bound up in extraordinary events lately."

Tyler nodded, hating his own eager, servile tone. "I was summoned by Lazarus of the Mace, Your Holiness. He made it clear that I was wanted immediately, or I would have sent for another priest."

"The Mace is a fearsome visitor, to be sure," replied the Holy Father smoothly. "And how did you find our new Queen?"

"Surely there isn't a soul left in the Tear who hasn't heard the story by now, Your Holiness."

"I know the events of the crowning well, Tyler. I've heard the tale from many sources. Now I wish to hear it from you."

Tyler repeated the Queen's words, watching the Holy Father's face darken. He leaned back in his chair, his gaze speculative. "She refused to make the vow."

"She did."

Anders broke in. "And yet you took it upon yourself to complete the crowning."

"It was unprecedented, Your Eminence. I didn't know what to do. There are no rules set down . . . there was no time . . . it seemed best for the kingdom."

"Your primary concern is not the health of this kingdom,

but the health of God's Church," Anders replied. "This kingdom and its people are the concern of its ruler."

Tyler stared at him. The statement was nearly identical to the new Queen's words at her crowning, yet the meaning was so far distant that Anders might as well have spoken in an unknown language. "I know that, Your Eminence, but I had no time to reflect and I had to choose."

The two senior priests regarded him narrowly for a moment longer. Then the Holy Father shrugged and smiled, a smile so wide that Tyler wished he could retreat down the steps. "Well, it couldn't be helped then. Most unfortunate that you were thrust into such a situation."

"Yes, Your Holiness," Tyler replied. His hip was throbbing in earnest now, with that particular delight that arthritis seemed to take in its own doings. He considered asking the Holy Father if he might stand, and then dismissed the idea. It would be a mistake to show weakness in front of either of these men.

"The Queen will need a new Keep priest, Tyler. Father Timpany was the Regent's man, and she will distrust him, wisely so."

"Yes, Your Holiness."

"Because of your role in her coronation, you're the logical choice."

The statement meant nothing to Tyler. He waited.

"She'll trust you, Tyler," the Holy Father continued, "certainly more than she'll trust any of us, precisely because you crowned her without the vow."

Realizing that the Holy Father was serious, Tyler stammered, "Wouldn't the Church prefer someone else in that role, Your Holiness? Someone more worldly?"

Again, it was Anders who replied. "We're all men of God

here, Father. Devotion to your God and your church is more important than your understanding of the things of Caesar."

Tyler looked down at his sandals, his stomach roiling with nausea, the sensation that a nightmare had come to life all around him. He had come here expecting to be censured, perhaps even to have his duties altered for a time; priests who committed a small infraction typically had to spend a period down in the kitchens, washing dishes or hauling garbage. But for a priest who wanted only to be left alone in his room with his books and thoughts, an appointment to the royal court was infinitely worse, perhaps the worst thing that could happen.

Perhaps she won't have a Keep priest. Perhaps she'll boot the lot of us from the Keep and that godless chapel can molder to dust.

"We must have eyes and ears on this throne, Tyler," the Holy Father continued, his tone still deceptively mild. "She hasn't given the vow, and that puts the life of God's Church at great hazard under her rule."

"Yes, Your Holiness."

"You'll give periodic reports directly to me."

Directly to the Holy Father? Tyler's anxiety deepened. Anders was the one who buffered dealings between the Holy Father and the rest of the Church, the rest of the kingdom. Why not Anders? The simple answer came immediately: the Holy Father had handpicked Anders as his successor, but even he didn't trust the man.

I'm in a nest of wasps, Tyler thought miserably.

"What shall I report on, Your Holiness?"

"Those things occurring within the Keep that concern the Church."

"But Your Holiness, she'll know! She's no fool."

The Holy Father's eyes bored into him. "Your loyalty to this church will be measured by the detail imparted in these reports. Do you understand?"

Tyler understood. He would be a spy. He thought again with longing of his room, the rows of books there, all of them utterly vulnerable to the Holy Father's heavy hand.

"Tyler? Do you understand?"

Tyler nodded, thinking: *I am part of God's great work.*

"Good," the Holy Father remarked softly.

Javel crept down the Butcher's Staircase, shrouded in a grey cloak. If anyone saw him, they would take him for a Queen's Guard, which was the idea. He'd actually tried to become a Queen's Guard long ago, at the beginning of his career. They hadn't accepted him, so he'd been relegated to guarding the Keep Gate. But the grey cloak still retained as much power over him as ever; with every man who drew aside in the street, or gave him a shallow bow, Javel felt himself stand taller, straighter. Illusion was better than nothing.

At the end of the staircase he found himself in a tight alley, a curtain of mist hanging just above his head, and he crept along with his hand on his knife. The streetlamps in this part of the Gut had been broken for years, and moonlight shone only briefly through the mist, bathing the alley in dim blue effulgence that did nothing to reveal potential predators. Javel carried no gold, but the cutthroats in this area wouldn't bother to ascertain that before they rushed him, and they were likely to stick a knife into his ribs for good measure.

Two dogs snarled from a doorway. They might as well have announced his presence, but Javel was only wary, not frightened. He'd been a Gate Guard forever, but like most of the outer guards, he never penetrated further into the Keep than the gatehouse. The Keep was a mystery. Javel's environs were here: the Gut, a labyrinth of echoing alleys and darkness and bolt-holes that he knew almost as well as the shape of his own hands. The entire sector was buried in the depression between foothills; mist always seemed to collect there, as did people with business to hide.

At last Javel came to the paint-chipped door of the Back End. He glanced behind him to see if he'd picked up any tails, but apparently the grey cloak had done its work again. No one wanted to give a Queen's Guard any trouble, particularly not now, when the poor had taken on the new Queen as their champion. Even to someone like Javel, who had little interest in the mood of the people, the transformation was extraordinary. Already, songs for the Queen were beginning to circulate through the city. Mobs of idle poor roamed the boulevards shouting the Queen's name, and those who didn't join in risked a beating. The city people were like every drunkard Javel had ever known, including himself, enjoying the slide of a long, oblivious night with no thought toward the next morning. They would sober up soon, though. Even now, the Mort would be mobilizing, their soldiers preparing to march, their foundries working overtime in the production of steel. Thinking of Mortmesne made Javel think of Allie, her long blonde hair hiding her face as she disappeared. Every day it was something different about Allie, some feature that jumped up and bit him on the ass and wouldn't let go. Today it had been Allie's hair, a curtain of blonde that looked amber indoors and gold outdoors. Javel's fingers shook as he opened the door of the pub. Inside would be whiskey, but also Arlen Thorne.

The Back End was a drunkard's pub, a tiny, windowless hovel with cheap wooden floors soaked in years' worth of beer. The entire place smelled like a vat of yeast. It wasn't one of Javel's favorite haunts, but beggars couldn't choose. The better areas of New London observed a closing time of one in the morning; the Gut was the place to go if you wanted to keep drinking until sunup. But now the pub was nearly deserted; it was almost four in the morning and even the day laborers had dragged themselves home. Only someone with a serious drinking problem or truly bad business would still be awake. Javel suspected he had both. A feeling of doom hung over him, a premonition of dark work that would not be shaken.

The note had come from Arlen Thorne just as Javel was getting off shift at midnight, and it told Javel nothing. Whatever else Thorne might be, he was a slippery bastard, certainly not fool enough to put anything incriminating in writing. Javel had never spoken to Thorne in his life before, but there had been no question of refusing the note; when Thorne demanded your presence, you went. Javel didn't have any relatives left to be shipped off to Mortmesne, but he didn't underestimate Thorne's ability to think of something equally vile. Allie's hair surfaced again in his mind. Ever since that day on the Keep Lawn, all the whiskey in the world couldn't keep her at bay.

Still, I'm ready to try again, Javel thought miserably.

Thorne sat at a table in the corner of the pub, his back against both walls, sipping from a cup that almost certainly contained water. It was a well-known fact that Thorne didn't drink. Early in his career his sobriety, combined with his tall, thin frame and delicate features, had made Thorne a prime target for the Regent's antisodomy hooligans. He had taken several beatings at their hands before he'd begun to move up in the Census. Were any of those men still walking around breathing? Javel doubted it.

Vil, who dealt directly with Thorne from time to time, said that Thorne didn't drink for the obvious reason: he didn't like to be out of control for even a single second. Javel thought this assessment was probably correct. The pub was nearly empty, but still Thorne's eyes marked Javel, dismissed him in the same second, and then continued around the room, clocking who was there to notice him, who might see that the Overseer of the Census was meeting with a Gate Guard, who might care.

Seated beside Thorne was the woman, Brenna. Javel had never seen her before, but he knew her instantly. Her skin was a deep, translucent pearl, so milky white that Javel could see the blue veins running up and down her arms. She was ageless, her hair a thinning blonde cap around her face. Javel, along with everyone else in the Tear, had heard of her, but few ever saw her, for she could only go out at night.

Dark work, Javel thought again, and ordered two whiskeys at the bar. The second was for pleasure; the first was an absolute requirement for him to be able to sit down at the table with Arlen Thorne, who had pulled Allie's name from the lot with his own hand. When the shots came, Javel nearly threw the first down his throat. But he held on to the second, staring down at the bar, trying to linger there as long as he could.

Three stools down was an aging whore with a transparent white blouse and blonde hair that was almost certainly dyed. She leaned back against the bar in a contortionist's pose, one that allowed her to poke her breasts out two inches farther than nature had ever intended, and looked Javel over with a businesslike gaze. "Queen's Guard, are you?"

Javel nodded shortly.

"Five for a fuck, ten for the works."

Javel closed his eyes. He'd tried to go to a whore once, three years ago, but he hadn't been able to get it up, and had ended up weeping. The woman had been very kind and understanding, but it had been a surface sort of understanding, and Javel could sense her eagerness to get him gone so that she could move on to the next customer. Business was business.

"No, thanks," he muttered.

The whore shrugged, taking a deep breath and thrusting forward again as two more men entered the pub. "Your loss."

"Javel." Thorne's low, unctuous voice carried across the pub with perfect clarity. "Join me."

Javel carried his whiskey across the room and sat down. Thorne leaned across the table, crossing his long, thin arms. Every time Javel saw Thorne, he seemed to have too many limbs. Javel turned away and found the woman Brenna staring at him, though rumor had it she was stone-blind. Her milky eyes had the distinctive pink cast of the albino. If Javel had to guess what sort of woman Thorne would pick for a captive, this was exactly what he would come up with: shunned, blind, and dependent. Vil said that she had always been with Thorne, a tag-along remnant of his childhood in the Gut, that she was the only thing on God's earth that Thorne cared about. But that was just a tale begun by some idiot storyteller who needed to rehabilitate even the likes of Arlen Thorne. Javel wondered what services Brenna had to perform for Thorne's patronage, but his mind shied away from the question.

"She doesn't like it when you stare."

Javel glanced away quickly and met Thorne's eyes.

"You're a Gate Guard, Javel."

"Yes."

"And are you happy in your work?"

"My work's fine."

"Really?"

"It's an honest job," Javel replied, trying not to sound self-righteous. There were probably those in the Tear who would call Thorne's current job honest, but they were a rarefied group who had never had to watch their wife's blonde hair disappear over the Pike Hill.

"Your wife was shipped six years ago."

"My wife is none of your business."

"Everything shipped is my business." Thorne's eyes lingered on Javel's clenched fist, his smile widening. Men like Thorne were built to notice what others tried to keep hidden. Javel glanced at Brenna out of the corner of his eye, unable to avoid rogue thoughts about the life she must lead. Thorne reached for his cup of water, and Javel watched with sickly fascination.

That hand put Allie in the cage. One inch to the left, and it would have been someone else's wife.

"My wife wasn't a thing."

"Cargo," Thorne replied dismissively. "Most people are cargo, and they're content to be cargo. I'm content to facilitate the shipment."

That was certainly true. Even before the Mort shipment legitimized the practice, the Tearling had had a thriving underground slave trade, and Thorne had been right in the middle of it. Even after Thorne became Overseer of the Census, he was still the man to see if you wanted something more exotic, a child or a redhead, even a black woman out of Cadare. As Javel sat there, wondering what he was doing with this flesh peddler who had sent his wife to Demesne, an idea began to occur to him, an idea that improved as the whiskey spread along his veins. Javel didn't know why he hadn't thought of it before.

Each Gate Guard carried two weapons: a short sword and a knife. The knife was tucked into Javel's waistband right now; he could feel the uncomfortable weight of the hilt pressing into his left ribs. He was no great fighter, but he was very quick. If he pulled the knife now, he could chop off Thorne's right hand, that hand that had reached to the left when it might have reached right and changed everything. If he could take Thorne's good hand, he could probably take a considerable portion of the rest of the man too; Thorne was rumored to be quick himself, but he'd come here without a guard. He obviously didn't consider Javel a threat.

Javel grasped the second shot and downed it in a fiery gulp, judging the distance between Thorne's hand and the knife. He'd been afraid of Thorne a few minutes ago, but all the punishment in the world suddenly seemed less important than what could be accomplished here. The Census Bureau wouldn't crumble without Thorne; it was too regimented for that. But the loss would be a crippling blow. Thorne ruled his bureaucracy by fear, and fear only worked from the top down. Javel had no time to grab the knife with his stronger hand; he'd have to draw with his weak hand and hope for the best. He glanced between Thorne's hand and his own, calculating the distance.

"You'd never make it."

Javel looked up and saw that Thorne was smiling again, tight-lipped and coldly amused. "And even if you did make it, you'd die all the same."

Javel stared blankly. Beside Thorne, the woman, Brenna, let out a high-pitched, squealing laugh, a sound like rusted hinges.

"I dosed your shot, Gate Guard. If you don't get the antidote from me in about ten minutes, you'll die in agony."

Javel looked down at his empty shot glass. Could Thorne have slipped something in there? Yes, while Javel was busy staring at the cursed albino. Thorne wasn't lying; one only had to look into his eyes, blue ocean rimmed with ice, to know he was telling the truth. Javel glanced at the albino and found that she was gazing adoringly at Thorne, her opaque pink eyes locked on his face.

"You know the worst thing about having my job?" Thorne asked. "No one understands that it's business. That's all it is. Fifteen times in my memory, people have tried to ambush the shipment somewhere between New London and the Mort border. They usually try it just after the end of the Crithe, where there's nothing but grassland for about a million miles around and you could hide an entire army in the wheat. And you know, ten of those times I've been able to simply talk them out of their foolishness. It was easy to do, and I didn't punish them."

"Right," Javel muttered. His heart was thudding uncomfortably now. He thought he'd felt a small twinge in his gut, just below his navel. He couldn't convince himself that it was his imagination, and couldn't convince himself that it wasn't. He should try to attack Thorne now, before whatever was in his innards came to fruition. But Thorne was ready for him; Javel would have no advantage.

"I *didn't* punish them," Thorne repeated. "I simply explained the situation to them and let them go. Because it was business. They were misguided, but they didn't harm my cages, only frightened the horses, and that's easily repaired. The delay was no more than five or ten minutes. I don't punish mistakes, at least not first mistakes.

"But the other five—"

Thorne leaned forward, his eyes glowing with an unpleasant righteousness, and Javel felt the poison for certain: a clenching sensation deep inside his stomach, something like indigestion. Merely uncomfortable, but Javel sensed its potential to become much more, and fast.

"The other five weren't interested in talking. I looked those people in the eye and knew that I could talk rings around them forever and they'd still keep coming for my cages. Some people don't know or care when they've played their hand and lost."

Javel hated himself for asking, but couldn't help it. "What did you do to them?"

"I made them into an object lesson," Thorne replied. "Some people can't do the math, but an object lesson teaches them very quickly. I regretted that it was necessary, of course—"

I bet you did, motherfucker, Javel thought. *I just bet.*

"—but it *was* necessary. And you'd be astounded at how quickly my lessons make people fall in line. Take yourself, for example—"

Thorne's slow, patient voice was unbearable. Javel felt as though he were trapped in a schoolroom again, an experience he hadn't missed since running away from home at the age of twelve. He glanced over at the albino, found her sightless eyes staring directly at him, and quickly looked away.

"You had a notion that you could grab your knife and put me away. As though I wasn't ready for you yesterday. The day before that. As though I haven't been ready for you since the day I was born."

Javel recalled a rumor he'd heard once: that Thorne's mother had been a prostitute in the Gut, that she had sold

Thorne to a slave trader when he was only a few hours old. Javel's stomach twisted again, more sharply now, as though someone had reached in through his navel, grabbed a handful of moving parts, and squeezed until something popped. He leaned back, breathing slowly, trying to remember the plan, but pain had cut right through the bravery of the whiskey. Javel had always been a baby about pain.

"So now, Javel, the question is: do you want to keep coming at me, or do you want to talk business?"

"Talk business," Javel gasped. Thoughts of his knife were gone; all he could think of was the antidote. So many nights he had gone home, so stuffed to the gills with whiskey that he could barely clamber down off his horse, and thought about ending it all. Now he was surprised by how badly he still wanted to live.

"Good. Let's talk about your wife."

"What about her?"

"She's alive."

"Bullshit!" Javel snarled.

"She is. She's alive and well in Mortmesne." Thorne tilted his head in acknowledgment of some distinction before remarking, "Fairly well."

Javel winced. "How would you know?"

"I know. I even know where she is."

"Where?"

"Ah, that would be giving away the store, wouldn't it? It doesn't concern you at this point, Gate Guard. What concerns you is that I know exactly where she is, and what's more, I can get her back."

Javel stared at Thorne, dumbfounded. His mind dug deep and came out with the last thing he wanted: one of Allie's birthdays, some nine or ten years ago. Allie had mentioned that she wanted a loom, so Javel went to a women's shop and bought a pair of looms that seemed well made for a reasonable price. Allie had seemed delighted, but in the months that followed, the two looms stayed in her sewing basket. Javel never saw her weave, not once, and he'd been too puzzled and hurt to ask her why. It wasn't like Allie, who admitted herself that she was the sort of child who always wanted to play with new things the very instant she got them home.

But then, about six months after her birthday, Allie had taken the looms out and begun working with them, creating hats and gloves and scarves, and later sweaters and blankets. Javel's salary wasn't enormous, but it was enough to keep Allie supplied in wool, and by the time her lottery tile had come, she'd been weaving most of their winter clothing, clothing that was warm and comfortable. After Allie had gone to Mortmesne, Javel had never quite been able to pack up her things; Allie's sewing basket still sat beside their fireplace, the looms holding half of a hat. Javel liked seeing the basket there, full of unfinished projects, as though Allie had only gone to visit her parents and would be back any day. Sometimes, after a particularly bad drunk, he would even sit in front of the fireplace, holding the basket in his lap. That wasn't something he could ever tell anyone about, but it helped him to fall asleep.

Still, that six months worried him. After Allie had gone, Javel found a woman to clean the house and do the laundry, and after several weeks, he picked up the sewing basket and showed the cleaning woman the looms, asked if there was anything wrong with them. That was how Javel found out that he hadn't bought Allie looms at all, but knitting needles. Weaving and knitting were two different things; even Javel knew that, though how they were different he really couldn't say. And Allie, who usually didn't hesitate to tell him when he'd done something wrong, had never said a word, spending six months learning to knit while he was at work. Javel had many regrets about Allie, and new ones seemed to show up every day, but one of the greatest and oddest was that he hadn't found out about the knitting needles before she'd gone. Some mornings, when he woke up in their bed (still on the same side; he could no more sleep on Allie's side of the bed than he could breathe underwater), he thought that he would give anything for Allie to know that he understood about the knitting needles. It seemed vitally important, for her to know that he knew.

"How do I know you can bring her back?"

"I can," Thorne replied. "And I will."

Another spasm punched Javel in the stomach, and he doubled over, trying to compress his midsection into the smallest ball possible. It didn't stop the pain, didn't even come close. Eventually, little by little, the spasm lessened, the fist in his belly unclenching, and when Javel looked up, he found Thorne watching him with a clinical detachment. "You should trust me, Javel. I don't break my word."

Javel considered this statement, one hand on his stomach in preparation for the next assault. The city was full of information about Thorne, some true and some apocryphal. Javel had heard plenty of stories that could curdle the blood, but he had never heard that Thorne had broken his word.

Beside Thorne, the albino began to breathe in quick, shallow pants, almost as though she were approaching hyperventilation. Her eyes were closed as though in ecstasy. She reached up and began to tweak her own nipple, lightly and tenderly, through the thin fabric of her pink shirt.

"Calm yourself, Bren," Thorne murmured. "Our business here is almost concluded."

The woman subsided, placing her hand back in her lap. Javel's flesh crawled. "What do you want?"

Thorne nodded in approval. "I need to get something inside the Keep. I want a man on the Keep Gate to conveniently fail to ask difficult questions."

"When?"

"When I say."

Javel stared at Thorne, understanding dawning in his mind. "You're going to kill the Queen."

Thorne merely looked at Javel, that cold gaze never wavering. Javel thought of the vision he had seen on the Keep Lawn: the tall woman, older and hardened, with the crown on her head. The Queen *had* been crowned, Javel knew, two days ago; Vil, who always got information first, told them that the Regent had tried to ambush her during the coronation itself, but had failed. When Javel rode through the streets at dusk, he'd passed through the usual cacophony of vendors closing up shop, yelling and gossiping and trading news, and heard them call her the True Queen. Javel didn't know the phrase, but there was no mistaking the sentiment: it was the name for the tall, grave woman he'd seen on the Keep Lawn, the one who didn't exist yet.

But she could, Javel thought. *Someday she could.* And although he hadn't been to church, hadn't even believed in God since the day Allie had vanished into Mortmesne, he suddenly felt damnation hanging over his head, damnation and history like two hands waiting to grab him and squeeze. The men who'd assassinated Jonathan the Good had never been caught, but theirs were the blackest pages in the history of the Tearling. Whoever they were, Javel had no doubt that they had been damned for their crimes. But he couldn't articulate any of these fears to Thorne. He could only say, "She's the Queen. You can't kill the Queen."

"There's no proof that she's the actual Queen, Javel. She's only a girl with a burn scar and a necklace."

But Thorne's eyes shifted away, and in a sudden flash of intuition, Javel knew: Thorne had seen that tall, regal woman on the Keep Lawn too. He'd seen her, and the sight had scared him so badly that he'd conceived this course. Thorne had never seemed so much like a spider as he did at that moment; he'd crept out from a corner to repair his web, and soon he would scuttle back into his dark crack to scheme, to wait with an endless, malevolent patience for some helpless thing caught and thrashing.

Javel looked around the pub, seeing it with fresh eyes: the dirt that had grimed into the floorboards; the cheap tallow that dripped from the torches to harden on the walls; the whore who smiled desperately at every man who walked in. Most of all, the smell of beer and whiskey mingled, a mist so pervasive that it might as well precipitate out of the air. Javel loved that smell, and hated it, and he knew somehow that the love/hate tangle in his mind was the reason Thorne had chosen him. Javel was weak, and his weakness probably smelled just as good to Thorne as whiskey did to Javel.

This is the dark crack, Javel finally realized. *This right here.*

He doubled over again; some small animal had awakened inside his stomach, shredding pink meat with jagged claws and teeth like needles. He was walking a tightrope; the distance was short, but below him lay infinite darkness. And what would he see on the way down?

"What if your plan fails?" he gasped. "What guarantee do I have?"

"You have no guarantees," Thorne replied. "But you needn't worry. Only a fool keeps all of his eggs in one basket. I have many baskets. If one idea fails, we move to another, and eventually we succeed."

Thorne reached into his shirt and pulled out a vial of amber-colored liquid. He offered it to Javel, who grabbed for it, only to close his fingers on empty air.

"I'd estimate you have only a minute, maybe two, before this won't help you. So, Gate Guard, I have only one question: can you do the math?"

I can't win, Javel thought, clutching his stomach. There was a dark, sneaking comfort in the knowledge. Because once you couldn't win, it wasn't your fault, no matter what course you chose.

The shipment was late.

The Queen of Mortmesne had not been able to forget this fact, not today, not yesterday, not the day before. She tried to concentrate as her Auctioneer gave her the figures from last month's auction. February had been good; the crown had cleared well over fifty thousand marks. Typically, when the shipment came in, the Queen cherry-picked the best merchandise, either for her own use or to give as gifts. But most of the slaves went at auction, to Mort nobles or wealthy entrepreneurs who would resell the slaves for higher prices in the northern cities and outlying towns. The auction always produced a good profit, but February's high sales were not enough to distract the Queen from the nagging sense of disruption, the feeling that a problem was developing just out of her reach. The girl had turned nineteen, she had not been found, and now the shipment was late. What did that mean?

Without a doubt, the Tear Regent had botched things. He had allowed Elyssa to smuggle the girl into exile in the first place (although even the Queen herself hadn't foreseen that particular move . . . who would have thought Elyssa had even an ounce of guile?). But after eighteen years, the girl should have been found. At the Queen's urging, the Regent had finally hired the Caden several months ago, but she'd known somehow that it was already too late.

"That's all, Majesty." Broussard, her Auctioneer, tucked his papers away into his case.

"Good."

Broussard remained standing below, his case clutched in both hands.

"Yes?"

"Any word on the new shipment, Majesty?"

Even her own people wouldn't allow her to forget.

"When I know, you'll know, Broussard. Go prepare for your auction. And remember to weed out the vermin this time."

Broussard colored, his jaw clenching beneath his beard. He was good at his job, with an instinctive ability to monetize flesh. Years ago, when the auction had still been a novelty, the Queen had enjoyed sitting on a low balcony on the tenth of every month, watching Broussard wring the last possible profit from each pound of humanity. It satisfied something deep inside her, to see the Tear go on the block. But there had been one month, some four or five years ago, when one of Broussard's handlers had been lax in the delousing process, and soon the Palais and several noble homes were crawling with lice. The Queen had kept the whole mess from going public by offering a free slave to each offended party, taking the loss from Broussard's pay. The lice had been bad, but in retrospect, she was glad the incident had happened. It was good to have a failure to dangle in front of Broussard at moments like this, moments when he forgot that he was only a flesh peddler, and that without the Queen there would be no auction at all.

Broussard left, holding his case as though it were his only child, and the Queen was pleased to see the stiff, offended set of his shoulders. But it didn't still the whispering of her mind, the quiet question that had been nagging at her for days now: *where was the shipment?* Four days in good weather, five days in bad. It had never come any later than the fifth of the month. Now it was the sixth of March. If there had been a problem, either the Regent or Thorne should have informed her by now. The Queen pressed one palm to her forehead, feeling the beginning of a headache developing behind her temples. Her physiology had progressed so far that she hardly ever got sick anymore. The only exception was the headaches, which came from nowhere, had no medical cause, and disappeared just as quickly.

What if the shipment doesn't come at all?

She jumped in her seat, as though someone had pinched her through her dress. The flow of human traffic had become a crucial part of the Mort economy, as regular and expected as the tides. Callae and Cadare sent slaves as well, but even their combined tribute didn't equal half of the Tear shipment. Affordable slaves kept her factories running, her nobles happy, her treasury full. Any snag in the process created a loss.

The Queen suddenly found herself missing Liriane. Like all of the Queen's servants, Liriane had aged while the Queen remained young, and several years ago she'd been laid in her grave. Liriane's had been the true sight, an ability to see not only the future but the present and past as well. She would have been able to see what had happened in the Tear. Try as the Queen might to convince herself otherwise, she couldn't escape a nagging suspicion that whatever had gone wrong must have something to do with the girl. Unless they'd killed her en route, she would have reached the Keep by now. Had Thorne managed to take care of it yet? The Regent was incompetence personified, but Thorne was quite the opposite. If Thorne failed, what was the next step? To haul out the treaty and go to war? The Queen had never wanted to invade the Tearling in the first place. Holding a foreign territory took money, equipment, trouble. The shipment was cleaner, an elegant solution.

Still, she realized, it might not be the worst thing in the world to mobilize her army. Her soldiers hadn't had to go to war since the last Tear invasion. There were no threats on the Mort border. There hadn't even been any fighting since the Exiled had hatched their conspiracy. Even on its worst day, her army was still more than a match for the Tear's, but it wasn't beyond possibility that they had grown soft during the caesura. It might be good to get them into shape now. Just in case. But at the thought, her headache seemed to double in amplitude, a steady incoming tide against the walls of her skull.

Some sort of commotion had begun brewing outside her audience chamber. The Queen looked up and saw Beryll, her chamberlain, striding off toward the great doors. He would handle it. Now that Liriane was dead, Beryll was her oldest and most trusted servant, so attuned to her wishes that the Queen rarely even had to interest herself in the everyday doings of the castle anymore. She looked down at her watch and decided to retire to her room. An early dinner, and then she would have one of her slaves. The tall one she'd taken from the last Tear delivery, a muscular man with thick black hair and beard and the look of a blacksmith. Only in the Tearling did men grow so tall.

The Queen signaled Eve, one of her pages, and whispered for her to remove the man to her chamber after the performance. Eve listened with as bright an expression as she could muster, which the Queen appreciated. Her pages hated this duty; the men weren't always cooperative. Eve would drug him and feed him a constrictive, and then the Queen could have him hard enough to escape the dream. The drug wasn't necessary anymore, of course; by now the Queen's transformation had progressed so far that she wasn't even sure she *could* be hurt. But she had never told her pages, and today she was glad. With a headache coming on, she wanted the man pliant. She swept out of the audience chamber, through her private entrance behind the throne and down a long hallway to her apartments.

The hallway was lined with guards, all of whom kept their eyes prudently on the ground. At the sight of them, some of the Queen's ebullience faded. The Regent's last report had informed her that most of Elyssa's guards had departed the castle to search for the girl. Carroll, the Mace, Elston . . . these were names the Queen knew, men she had learned to take into consideration. If she had found the Mace before Elyssa had, things might have been so different. The Tear sapphires had disappeared, seemingly into thin air, a development that reeked of the Mace's guile. If only the Queen had been able to get hold of the jewels before Elyssa died! She probably wouldn't even have headaches anymore, much less need medicine.

But now everything would be righted. She would have the

sapphires, and when the shipment came, she could probably even charge the Regent a hefty late fee. He would whine and complain, but he would pay, and the thought of his white, upset face made the Queen smile as she took off her clothes, anticipating the slave's arrival. Her pages were very quick; she had been in her apartments for no more than five minutes when the knock came on her door.

"Come!" she snapped, annoyed to find that her headache was worsening. The kitchen might create a powder for her to take, but the powder would delay sleep long after the slave had ceased to perform, and sleep was at a premium these days.

The door opened. She turned to see Beryll, and began to ask him for a headache powder. But the request caught in her throat. Beryll's face was white, his eyes socketed with deep fear. He clutched a scroll of paper in one shaking hand.

"Lady," he quavered.

CHAPTER 8
THE QUEEN'S WING

It's easy to forget that a monarchy is more than just the monarch. The successful reign is a complex animal, with countless individual pieces working in concert. Looking closely at the Glynn Queen, we find many moving parts, but one cannot overestimate the importance of Lazarus of the Mace, the Queen's Captain of Guard and Chief Assassin. Remove him, and the entire structure collapses.

—*The Tearling as a Military Nation*, CALLOW THE MARTYR

Upon waking, Kelsea was pleased to find that all of the decorative pillows had been removed from her mother's bed. *Her* bed; it was all hers now, and that thought brought her less pleasure. Her back was a mess of bandaging. When she ran a hand through her hair, it came away slicked with oil. She'd been asleep for some time. Mace wasn't in the corner armchair, and there was no one else in the room.

It took a few minutes for Kelsea to raise herself to a sitting position; she felt no bleeding on her shoulder, but the wound pulled with every movement of her torso. Someone, undoubtedly Andalie, had placed a pitcher of water on the small table beside her bed, along with an empty glass. Kelsea drank and splashed some on her face. Andalie must have washed the blood from Kelsea as well, for which she was grateful. She thought of the man she'd killed, and was relieved to feel nothing.

She hauled herself to her feet and walked around the room, testing the wound. In her circuit, she discovered that a long rope now hung on the far side of her bed; it stretched to the ceiling, where it threaded through several hooks and then disappeared through a small opening carved in the antechamber wall. Kelsea smiled, tugging gently on the rope, and heard the muted sounds of a bell.

Mace opened the door. Seeing her standing beside the bed, he nodded in approval. "Good. The doctor said you were to stay in bed for at least another day, but I knew he was coddling you."

"What doctor?" She'd assumed that Mace had patched her wounds.

"The doctor I got for the sick baby. I dislike doctors, but he's a competent man, and it's likely due to him that you haven't taken infection. He said your shoulder will heal slowly, but clean."

"Another scar." Kelsea rubbed her neck gingerly. "Soon I'll be a bundle of them. How's the baby?"

"She fares better. The doctor gave the mother some medicine that seems to have quieted the baby's stomach, though it cost the damned moon and stars. She'll likely need more later."

"I hope you paid him well."

"Very well, Lady. But we can't use him forever, nor the other doctor I know. Neither is trustworthy."

"Then what do we do?"

"I don't know yet." Mace rubbed his forehead with his thumb. "I'm thinking on it."

"How are the guards who were injured?"

"They're fine. A couple will need to limit their duties for a time."

"I want to see them."

"I wouldn't, Lady."

"Why not?"

"A Queen's Guard is a very proud creature. The men who took wounds won't want you to notice."

"Me?" Kelsea asked, puzzled. "I don't even know how to hold a sword."

"That's not how we think, Lady. We just want to do our jobs well."

"Well, what am I to do? Pretend they weren't even injured?"

"Yes."

Kelsea shook her head. "Barty always used to say there were three things men were stupid about: their beer, their cocks, and their pride."

"That sounds like Barty."

"I thought pride was the one he might be wrong about."

"It's not."

"Speaking of pride, who threw the knife?"

Mace's jaw clenched. "I apologize, Lady. It was my failure of security, and I take full responsibility. I thought we had you sufficiently covered."

Kelsea didn't know what to say. Mace was looking very hard at the ground, his lined face twisted up as though he were waiting for a lash to fall on his shoulders. Being caught off guard was intolerable to him. He'd told her that he'd never been a child, but Kelsea had her doubts; this particular effect looked like the result of some fairly harsh parenting.

Kelsea wondered if she looked just as pained when she didn't know the answer. Mace's voice echoed in her head again: she was his employer, not his confessor. "You're working on finding out, I trust?"

"I am."

"Then let's move on."

Mace looked up, visibly relieved. "Typically, the first thing a new ruler would do is hold an audience, but I'd like to put that off for a week or two, Lady. You're in no shape, and there's plenty to do here."

Kelsea picked up her tiara from the gaudy vanity table and considered it thoughtfully. It was a beautiful piece of jewelry, but flimsy, too feminine for her taste. "We need to find the real crown."

"That'll be difficult. Your mother set Carroll the task of hiding it, and believe me, he was clever that way."

"Well, let's make sure to pay that hussy for this thing."

Mace cleared his throat. "There's much to do today. Let's get Andalie in here to fix your appearance."

"How rude."

"Forgive me, Lady, but you've looked better."

A thud came against the outer wall, the impact so hard that it rattled the hangings on Kelsea's bed. "What's going on out there?"

"Siege supplies."

"*Siege?* Are we expecting one?"

"Today is March the sixth, Lady. There are only two days left until the treaty deadline."

"I won't change my mind, Lazarus. That deadline means nothing to me."

"I'm not sure you fully understand the consequences of your own actions, Lady."

She narrowed her eyes. "I'm not sure you fully understand me, Lazarus. I know what I've loosed here. Who commands my army?"

"General Bermond, Lady."

"Well, let's bring him here."

"I've already sent for him. It might take him another few days to return; he's been on the southern border, inspecting garrisons, and he doesn't ride that well."

"The general of my army doesn't ride well?"

"He's lame, Lady: a wound he took defending the Keep from an attempted coup ten years ago."

"Oh," Kelsea murmured, embarrassed.

"I warn you, Lady: Bermond will be difficult. Your mother always left him to his own judgment, and the Regent hasn't bothered him for years. He's gotten used to having his own way. He'll also loathe discussing military strategy with any woman, even a Queen."

"Too bad. Where's the Mort Treaty?"

"Outside, waiting for your inspection. But I think you will have to reconcile yourself."

"To what?"

"War," Mace replied flatly. "You've effectively declared war on Mortmesne, Lady, and believe me, the Red Queen will be coming."

"It's a gamble, Lazarus, I know."

"Just remember, Lady: you're not the only one gambling. You're playing hazard with an entire kingdom. High dice, and you'd better be prepared to lose."

He left to fetch Andalie, and Kelsea sat down on the bed, her stomach sinking. Mace was clearly beginning to understand her, for he'd thrust the sword right where it would have the most impact. She closed her eyes, and behind them she saw Mortmesne, a vast dark land in her imagination, awakened from long slumber, looming like a shadow over everything she wanted to build.

Carlin, what can I do?

But Carlin's voice had fallen silent in her mind, and there was no reply.

The Mort Treaty had been spread out on the large dining table that stood at one end of Kelsea's audience chamber. It was short for such a document, only several sheets of thick vellum that had browned slightly with age. Kelsea touched the sheets gingerly, fascinated to see her mother's initials, ER, scrawled messily in black at the bottom left of each page. On the right was a separate set of initials, scrawled in dark red ink: QM. The final page of the document contained two signatures: on one line, "Elyssa Raleigh," the handwriting almost illegible, and on the other, "Queen of Mortmesne," neatly written in the same bloodred ink.

She truly doesn't want anyone to know her real name, Kelsea realized, her intuition flickering. *It's desperately important to her that no one finds out who she really is. But why?*

Kelsea was disappointed to find the language of the treaty as straightforward as Mace had claimed. The Tearling was obligated to provide three thousand slaves per year, divided into twelve equal shipments. At least five hundred of them needed to be children, at least two hundred of each gender. Why so many children? Mortmesne took a quota of slave children from Callae and Cadare as well, but children weren't much use for hard industrial labor or mining, and Mortmesne had few farms. Even if there were a disproportionately high number of pedophiles in the market, they couldn't go through children so quickly. Why so many?

The terse, mechanical language of the treaty provided her with no answers. If any individual shipment failed to reach Demesne by the eighth day of the month, the treaty granted Mortmesne the right to immediately enter the Tearling and satisfy its quota by right of capture. But, Kelsea noticed, the document placed no limits on the length of that entry, nor did it include any requirement of withdrawal when conditions were met. Reluctantly, she was forced to admit that Mace was right: by stopping the shipment, Kelsea had given the Red Queen an umbrella grant to invade. What had possessed her mother to sign such a one-sided document?

Be fair, a new voice cautioned in her mind. The voice was neither Carlin's nor Barty's; Kelsea couldn't identify it, and distrusted its pragmatism. *What would you have done, with the enemy at the very gates?*

Again, Kelsea had no answer. She gathered the pages of the treaty together into a neat sheaf and straightened them, feeling sick. A new idea occurred to her, one that would have been unthinkable a few weeks ago, but Kelsea had already found her mind trying to insulate itself from further disaster by imagining the worst. She turned to Mace. "Was my mother assassinated?"

"There were several attempts," Mace replied indifferently, though Kelsea thought his indifference feigned. "She nearly died of nightshade poisoning when someone got it into her food. That was when she decided to send you away for fostering."

"So she did send me away to protect me?"

Mace's brow furrowed. "Why else?"

"Never mind." Kelsea looked back down at the table, the treaty in front of her. "There's no mention of a lottery in here."

"The lottery is an internal matter. At first, your mother simply sent convicts and the mentally ill. But such people make poor slaves, and the arrangement didn't satisfy the Red Queen for long. The Census Bureau was your uncle's answer."

"Is no one exempt?"

"Churchmen. But otherwise, no. Even the babies are taken; their names go into the lot as soon as they're weaned. They say the Red Queen uses them as gifts for barren families. For a while women got around it by nursing their children well beyond the weaning age, but Thorne's on to that trick. His people are in every village in the kingdom, and there's little they don't know."

"Is he loyal to my uncle?"

"Thorne's a businessman, Lady. He'll go whichever way the wind is blowing."

"And which way is it blowing now?"

"Toward Mortmesne."

"We should keep an eye on him then."

"I always have at least one eye on Arlen Thorne, Lady."

"How did my mother actually die? Carlin would never tell me."

"They say it was the poison, Lady. That it gradually weakened her heart until she died a few years later."

"They say that. What do *you* say, Lazarus?"

He stared at her without expression. "I say nothing, Lady. That's why I'm a Queen's Guard."

Frustrated, Kelsea spent the rest of the day inspecting the Queen's Wing and meeting various people. They began with her new cook: Milla, a blonde so petite that Kelsea didn't even want to think about how she'd borne her four-year-old son. Kelsea gathered that Milla had been doing something unpleasant to make ends meet; when told that her only job would be cooking, even for the twenty-odd people who now crowded the Queen's Wing, she became so violently happy that Kelsea had to tuck her own hands into the folds of her dress, terrified that the woman would try to kiss them.

The other woman who'd come in with them, Carlotta, was older and round-faced, with bright red cheeks. She seemed frightened, but after a few repeated questions admitted that she could sew passably well. Kelsea asked her for more black dresses, and Carlotta agreed that she could make them.

"Though I would do better if I took your measurements, Majesty," she ventured, looking terrified at the very idea. Kelsea found the idea of being measured nearly as terrifying, but she nodded and smiled, trying to put the woman at ease.

She met several guards who hadn't been with them on their journey: Caelan, a thuggish-looking man whom everyone simply called Cae; and Tom and Wellmer, both archers. Wellmer seemed too young to be a Queen's Guard. He was doing his best to appear as stoic as the older men, but he was clearly fidgety; every few seconds he switched his weight between feet.

"How old is that boy?" Kelsea whispered to Mace.

"Wellmer? He's twenty."

"What did you do, pick him from a nursery?"

"Most of us were barely teenagers when we were recruited, Lady. Don't worry about Wellmer. Give him a bow, and he could pick out your left eye from here, even in torchlight."

Kelsea tried to reconcile this description with the nervous, white-faced boy in front of her, but gave up. After the guards went back to their posts, she followed Mace down the corridor to one of the first rooms, which had been hastily converted into a nursery. The room was a good choice; it was one of the few chambers with a window, so that light spilled in and made it seem brighter and cheerier than it really was. All of the furniture had been cleared to the walls, and the floor was littered with makeshift toys: dolls made of cloth and stuffed with straw that leaked from every patch, toy swords, and a wooden shopkeeper's stall shrunken to child size.

Kelsea saw a number of children seated in a half-circle in the middle of the nursery, their focus entirely on a beautiful woman with auburn hair whom Kelsea hadn't seen before. She was telling the children a story, something about a girl with extraordinarily long hair imprisoned in a tower, and Kelsea leaned against the doorway, unnoticed, to listen. The woman spoke with a pronounced Mort accent, but she had a good power of voice and she told her story well. When the prince was injured by the guile of a witch, the corners of the woman's mouth went down, her face transformed into grief. And then Kelsea knew her, and turned to Mace, astonished.

He motioned Kelsea away from the door, speaking in a low voice. "She's been a wonder with the children. The women are content to leave their little ones with her while they work, even Andalie. It's an unexpected gift; otherwise we'd have children underfoot everywhere."

"The women don't mind that she's Mort?"

"Apparently not."

Kelsea peered around the doorway again. The redhead was pantomiming now, showing the healing of the prince's eyes, and she was radiant in the candlelight, a world apart from the miserable creature Kelsea had seen huddled in front of the throne.

"What happened to her?"

"I didn't question her about her life with the Regent, Lady, deeming that her affair. But if I had to hazard a guess . . ." He lowered his voice even further. "She was the Regent's favorite plaything. He wouldn't let her conceive, lest it ruin his sport."

"I beg your pardon?"

Mace splayed his hands. "She made no secret of her wish for a child, Lady, even one by the Regent. The rest of your uncle's women took contraceptives willingly, but not this one. They say he had to lace her food. But he also promised to kill any child she bore; I heard that threat myself."

"I see." Kelsea nodded calmly, though she was fuming inside. She took a last look at the woman, at the group of children. "What's her name?"

"Marguerite."

"How did my uncle get hold of a Mort slave?"

"Redheads are even more of a curiosity in Mortmesne than in the Tearling. Marguerite was a gift to your uncle from the Red Queen several years ago, a sign of great favor."

Kelsea tipped her head back against the passageway wall. Her shoulder was beginning to throb. "This place is a festering sore, Lazarus."

"Leadership was needed, Lady. There was none."

"Not even you?"

"Certainly not." Mace gestured toward the open doorway. "I would have let your uncle keep his toy. I would have come to an agreement with the Red Queen before stopping the shipment."

"I heard what you said earlier."

"I know you did. Don't misunderstand me, Lady. I don't say that your choices are right or wrong, only that you were needed to do the things you've done, and you were not here."

There was no tone of reproach in his voice. Kelsea's irritation quieted, but her shoulder gave another throb, stronger now, and she wondered how on earth simply standing there could have aggravated it. "I need to sit down."

Within five minutes her guards had moved the large, comfortable armchair out of Kelsea's bedchamber and into the audience chamber, where they settled the chair securely against a wall.

"My throne," Kelsea murmured.

"We can't secure the throne room at present, Lady," Mace replied. "It has too many entrances, and that twice-damned gallery is simply impossible to cover without more guards. But we could have the throne itself moved in here for the time being."

"That seems fairly pointless."

"Maybe, maybe not. The crown on your head is a bit pointless as well, but I know you recognize its value. Perhaps a throne serves the same purpose."

Kelsea tilted her head, considering. "I'll need to hold audience, you said."

"Yes."

"I suppose I can't do that in my armchair."

"You could," Mace replied, the hint of a smile at the corner of his mouth. "It would be an unusual development for the Raleigh monarchy. But whatever chair you sit in, this room is much easier to defend and control. There's only one public entrance to the Queen's Wing, a long passageway with no openings. You saw it when we came in."

"I don't remember that at all."

"Understandable. You were half-conscious both times we dragged you through. There are many hidden ways in and out of this wing, but they're well guarded, and only I know them all. The passage outside gives us good control of the regular traffic."

"All right." Kelsea lowered herself gingerly into the armchair. "Have I begun to bleed again?" She leaned forward and let Mace peek under the bandage that swaddled her shoulder blade.

"No blood."

"I feel like I should sleep again soon."

"Not yet, Lady. Meet everyone at the same time, so no one feels snubbed." Mace crooked his finger at Mhurn, who was stationed at the opening to the hallway. "Get me Venner and Fell."

Mhurn disappeared, and Kelsea relaxed into the armchair. Andalie took a place against the wall, apparently meaning to stay. Kelsea thought Mace might object, but he ignored Andalie entirely, and Kelsea understood that she was supposed to do the same. After years when there had only been Carlin and Barty in her life, she now had so many people around her that some of them were supposed to be invisible. "When can we bring Barty and Carlin here?"

Mace shrugged. "A few weeks, perhaps. It'll take time to find them."

"They're in a village called Petaluma, near the Cadarese border."

"Well, that simplifies things."

"I want them," Kelsea told him. And she did; she hadn't realized how badly until this moment. She felt a sudden, fierce longing for Barty, for his clean, leathery smell and the crinkle of his eyebrows when he smiled. Carlin ... well, she didn't precisely long for Carlin. In fact, she dreaded the moment when she would need to stand before Carlin and account for her deeds. But Carlin and

Barty were a package. "I want them as soon as possible."

"Dyer's the best man for such jobs, Lady. We'll arrange it when he comes back."

"Back from where?"

"I've already sent him on an errand."

"What errand?"

Mace sighed and shut his eyes. "Do me a favor, Majesty: let me do my job in peace."

Kelsea bit back another question, annoyed at being silenced, and peeked at the four guards who stood against the walls of the chamber. One of them was Galen, whom Kelsea had never seen before without a helmet. His hair was a shock of grey, and strangely, the lines in his face were even more prominent in torchlight than they'd been out in the forest. Five and forty, at least; he must have been with her mother's Guard for many years. Kelsea turned this fact over in her mind for a moment before tucking it away.

The other three were Elston, Kibb, and Coryn, men she'd also met on the journey. These three weren't quite as old as Galen, but they were still many years beyond Kelsea herself. Kelsea wished more of her guards were younger; her youth only served to increase her isolation here. All four guards kept their eyes resolutely away from Kelsea, a practice she assumed was standard but also found demeaning. After a minute, she grew so tired of not being looked at that she called across the room, "Kibb, how's your hand?"

He turned to face her, eyes down, refusing to meet her gaze. "Fine, Lady."

"Leave him alone," Mace muttered.

Footsteps rapped up the corridor and two men emerged, both dressed in the grey of the Guard. One was tall and thin, the other short and husky, but both moved with the easy, silent grace that Kelsea associated with trained fighters, especially Mace himself. The way they walked together told Kelsea that they were accustomed to moving as a pair. When they bowed low before her, it seemed a choreographed gesture. Kelsea might have thought they were fraternal twins, except that the tall man was at least ten years older than the short one.

Mhurn followed the two men out of the hallway and stationed himself again at the entrance to the corridor. It had been more than a week since they'd arrived back at the Keep, but Kelsea noticed with some concern that Mhurn looked no more rested than he had out in the countryside. His face was still a pale oval in the torchlight, and she could see the dark sockets around his eyes from here. Why didn't he sleep?

"Venner and Fell, Lady," Mace announced, bringing her attention back to the two men in front of her. "Your arms masters."

Once they straightened, Kelsea reached out to shake their hands. They reacted with some surprise, but shook. Fell, the shorter one, had a nasty scar down his cheekbone; the wound had been poorly stitched, or not at all. Kelsea thought of her own wound, Mace's clumsy stitches in her neck, and shook her head to clear the unwanted thought. Her shoulder was throbbing steadily now, reminding her that it was time to go back to sleep.

Mace expects me to stay awake, she thought stubbornly. *And I will.*

"Well, arms masters, what exactly do you do?"

The two men looked at each other, but it was Fell who answered first. "I oversee weapons and garrison for Your Majesty's guard."

"I oversee training," Venner added.

"Could you get me a sword?"

"We have several swords for you to choose from, Majesty," replied Fell.

"No, not a ceremonial sword, though I know I must have one of those as well. A sword fitted to my build, to wield."

Both men gaped at her, then looked instinctively to Mace, which irritated Kelsea so much that she dug her nails into the soft fabric of the armchair. But Mace merely shrugged.

"To wield, Majesty?"

Kelsea thought of Carlin, the hard disappointment in her face whenever Kelsea lost her temper. She bit down, hard, on the inside of her cheek. "I'll need a sword and armor made to my build. And I want to be trained as well."

"To swordfight, Majesty?" asked Venner, clearly horrified.

"Yes, Venner, to swordfight. I've learned to defend myself with a knife, but I know little of swords."

She looked to Mace to see how he was taking the idea and found him nodding, a thin smile creasing his face. His approval soothed Kelsea's anger, and she softened her tone. "I won't ask men to die for me while I sit and do nothing. Why shouldn't I learn to fight as well?"

Both men opened their mouths to reply and then stopped. Kelsea gestured for them to continue, and Fell finally spoke. "Only appearance, Lady, but appearance in a queen is important. For you to wield a sword, it's . . . not queenly."

"I can't be queenly when I'm dead. And I've had to defend myself too often lately to be content with only my knife."

"You'll need to be measured, Lady," Fell replied grudgingly. "And it might take a while to find a blacksmith who'll make armor for a woman."

"Search fast, then. You're dismissed."

Both men nodded, bowed, and headed down the hallway,

Venner muttering something to Fell as they went. Mace snorted as they disappeared around the corner.

"What was that?"

"He said you couldn't be less like your mother."

Kelsea smiled, but it was a tired smile. "I suppose we'll find out. Who's left?"

"Arliss, your Treasurer. The Regent has also put in a standing order to speak with you. A nuisance, but it would be good to get him out of the way."

Kelsea sighed, thinking of her soft bed, of a hot mug of tea with cream. She jerked awake and realized she had begun to nod off in her chair; Andalie was no longer beside her, and Mace was still waiting. Straightening up, she rubbed her eyes. "Let's have the Regent first, then the Treasurer."

Mace snapped his fingers at Coryn, who nodded and slipped into the kitchen.

"Speaking of your uncle, I should tell you that he finds himself in greatly reduced circumstances in the last few days."

"My heart bleeds."

Andalie silently reappeared and handed Kelsea a steaming mug of milky liquid. Taking a cautious sniff, Kelsea smelled black tea, laced with cream. She looked up in surprise at Andalie, who had stationed herself against the wall again, her serene gaze aimed far away.

"What I mean is," Mace continued, "I believe the Regent feels ill treated by my decisions. I confiscated most of his property."

"In my name?"

"You were asleep."

"Still, it's my name. Maybe you could wait for me to wake up next time."

Mace looked at her, and Kelsea realized that he considered this a dolls-and-dresses moment. She sighed. "What property did you confiscate?"

"Jewelry, some liquor and tasteless statuary. Some spectacularly bad paintings, gold plate—"

"Fine, Lazarus, I'll leave you to do your job in peace, just as you wanted." She peeked up at him. "You should thank me for that."

Mace bowed. "My most humble thanks, your most illustrious—"

"Stuff it."

He grinned, then resumed waiting in silence until a hollow boom echoed through the audience chamber from the double doors on the west wall. These doors stretched nearly twenty feet high and were not only locked but bolted with heavy slabs of oak at the height of a man's knees and head. Kibb opened a small peephole in the right-hand door while Elston rapped twice on the left. Three answering knocks came from outside, echoing off the east wall and back again, and Elston answered in kind.

Kelsea found this system fascinating. Elston murmured something, apparently satisfied, and he and Kibb laid hold of the bolts and pulled them back. It was a struggle; even from the other end of the room, Kelsea could see the veins standing out in Elston's enormous forearms.

"A good system," she told Mace. "Yours, I'm guessing?"

"The details are mine, but the original idea was Carroll's. We change the knocks every day."

"It seems a bit labor-intensive for just one visitor. Why don't they bring him in the same way Coryn left?"

Mace gave her one of his speaking glances.

"Oh."

"A few people know some of these passageways, Lady, but I'd be shocked if the Regent's ever dragged himself out of bed long enough to discover even a quarter of what I know."

"I see. Someone should shut the door to the nursery. I don't want Marguerite to hear this."

Mace snapped his fingers at Mhurn, who went. Kelsea would have found the constant snapping demeaning, but the guards clearly didn't mind; they even seemed to take pride in the fact that Mace didn't issue them specific orders. Elston and Kibb laid their shoulders into the doors now, pushing them outward, and Kelsea saw a broad tunnel, lit by many torches, which stretched downward on a gentle slope for several hundred feet before disappearing around a corner. She remembered this tunnel, but she hadn't been walking, had she? No, that's right; Mace had finally been forced to physically drag her up the slope. Why would anyone create an artificial hill inside a building?

For defense, of course, Carlin replied. *Think, Kelsea. For the day when they come to the Keep with pitchforks to take your head.*

"Cheery," Kelsea murmured. "Thank you."

"What, Lady?"

"Nothing."

Through the doors came the Regent, escorted by Coryn. Kelsea read everything she needed to in the laxness of Coryn's posture: he didn't expect the Regent to give him any trouble. He hadn't even put his hand to his sword.

The Regent's face was drawn and pinched, and he wore a shirt and matching trousers of the same hideous purple as before. As he approached, Kelsea became more and more certain that she was looking at clothing that hadn't been washed for some time; dried food was crusted on the shirt where her uncle's puffy stomach began to slope downward, and several drops of what looked like wine were splattered across his chest. But he'd clearly taken considerable trouble with his beard, for it still bushed out in the same unnatural curls, an effect that could only have been achieved with a hot iron.

When they were fifteen feet from the armchair, Coryn reached out and grabbed the Regent's upper arm. "Not one step closer, understand?"

The Regent nodded. Kelsea remembered suddenly that his given name was Thomas, but she couldn't attach that name to the man who stood before her. Thomas was a name for choirs and angels, a biblical name. Not for her uncle, who had a ratty gleam in his eye. Clearly, he'd come here with a plan.

When Kelsea was fourteen, Carlin had ordered her, with no warning or explanation, to suspend her other homework and read the Bible. This surprised Kelsea; Carlin made no secret of her contempt for the Church, and there were no other religious symbols in their home. But it was a school assignment, and so Kelsea dutifully read through the thick, dusty King James volume that usually resided in the topmost corner of the last bookshelf. It took her five days to finish, and she assumed that she was done with the heavy book, but she was wrong. Carlin spent the rest of that week (forever known as Bible Week in Kelsea's mind) quizzing her on the Bible, its characters and events and morals, and was forced to pull the thing back down from the bookshelf not just once but many times. Finally, after three or four days of solid Bible work, they were done, and Carlin told Kelsea that she could put the book away for good.

"Why do you have such a nice Bible?" Kelsea asked.

"The Bible is a book, Kelsea, a book that has influenced mankind for thousands of years. It deserves to be preserved in a good edition, just like any other important book."

"Do you believe it's true?"

"No."

"Then why did I have to read it?" Kelsea demanded, feeling resentful. It hadn't been a particularly good book, and it was *heavy*; she had hauled the damned thing from room to room for days. "What was the point?"

"To know your enemy, Kelsea. Even a book can be dangerous in the wrong hands, and when that happens, you blame the hands, but you also read the book."

Kelsea hadn't understood what Carlin meant at the time, but after getting a look at the golden cross on top of the Arvath, she was starting to form a better picture. She doubted her uncle had ever read a Bible in his life, but as she stared at him now, she remembered something else from Bible Week: Thomas was not only Thomas the Apostle but also Thomas the Doubter. Perhaps Queen Arla had looked at him when they first put him into her hands and seen exactly what Kelsea saw now: weakness, all the more dangerous for being combined with a sense of entitlement.

He's your last living relative, a voice protested inside. But the voice was swept aside by a sudden wave of fury that dwarfed family loyalty, dwarfed curiosity. Kelsea had done the math. Her mother had died sixteen years ago, and her uncle had been in charge ever since. Sixteen years times three thousand equaled forty-eight thousand Tear citizens that her uncle had shipped off to save his own hide. She saw no remorse in his face, no lingering regret of any kind, only the bewildered look of a man wronged. He was worth so little, but he was certain that the world owed it to him to make up the slack.

How can I see so much? Kelsea wondered. As if in response, her sapphire gave a tremor, a tiny throb of heat that seemed to ripple through her chest. Kelsea was startled, but much less jolted than she had been on the Keep Lawn the other day. Perhaps she was only deluding herself, but she felt that she was coming to understand the jewel, if only a little bit. Several times now, she had noticed it responding to her moods, but sometimes it also seemed to demand her attention as well. Now, she could have sworn the thing was telling her to keep her mind on business.

"What do you want, Uncle?"

"I come to petition Your Majesty to let me remain in the Keep," the Regent replied, his nasal voice echoing around the chamber in what was clearly a prepared speech. The four guards, though they still held their positions against the wall, were no longer looking away; Mhurn in particular was watching the Regent with the narrow, waiting expression of a hungry dog. "I feel that my banishment was both unfair and ill advised. Furthermore, the confiscation of my belongings was carried out in a clandestine manner, so that I had no chance to present my case."

Kelsea raised her eyebrows, surprised at his vocabulary, and leaned toward Mace. "How do I handle this?"

"However you like, Lady. God knows I need the entertainment."

She turned back to her uncle. "What's your case?"

"What?"

"You said you had no chance to present your case. What is your case?"

"Many of the items your guard removed from my quarters were gifts. Personal gifts."

"So?"

269

"So they weren't Crown property. The Crown had no right to them."

Mace interrupted. "The Crown has a right to confiscate anything that comes into the Keep."

Kelsea nodded in agreement, though this rule was news to her. "He's right, Uncle. That includes your trinkets from Mortmesne."

"They weren't just trinkets, niece. You took my best woman as well."

"Marguerite's under my protection now."

"She was a gift, and a valuable one."

"I agree," Kelsea replied, widening her smile. "She's very valuable. I'm sure she'll serve me fine."

Red began to creep up the Regent's neck now, working its way steadily toward his chin. Carlin always said that most men were dogs, and Kelsea had never taken her seriously; there were too many good books written by men. But now she saw that Carlin hadn't been entirely wrong either. "Perhaps when I tire of Marguerite, I'll set her free. But at the moment she's happy here."

The Regent looked up, his face incredulous. "Bullshit!"

"I assure you, she's quite content," Kelsea replied blithely. "Why, I don't even need to keep her tied up!"

Elston and Kibb snickered on their adjacent walls.

"That bitch wouldn't be happy anywhere!" the Regent snarled, tiny darts of spittle spraying from his lips.

"Watch your language in front of the Queen," Mace growled. "Or I'll tie a big red bow around you and throw you out of the Keep right now. The Fetch can use your bones for silverware."

Kelsea cut him off. "I assume that Marguerite's the only issue you came here to raise? Because no one would be willing to argue over that pile of spectacularly bad art."

The Regent's mouth dropped open. "My paintings are by Powell!"

"Who's Powell?" Kelsea asked, throwing the question out to the room.

No one answered.

"He's a well-known painter in Jenner," the Regent insisted. "I had to *collect* those paintings."

"Well, perhaps we'll allow you to bid on the ones we can't sell."

"What about my statues?"

Coryn spoke up. "The statues will sell, Majesty. Most of them are pretty bad, but the materials are costly. I suspect someone could melt them down."

The Regent looked injured. "I was assured that those statues would only appreciate in value."

"Assured by whom?" Kelsea asked. "The seller?"

The Regent opened his mouth, and nothing came out. Kelsea shifted impatiently; there was no sport in this anymore, and she was getting tired again. Still, it had amused her guard for a while, and that was something. Elston and Kibb were grinning broadly, Coryn was trying to hide a smirk, and even Mhurn looked wide-awake for the first time.

"I'm keeping your pile of junk, Uncle. I can't imagine what argument you'd raise on being banished, but if you have one, I'm listening."

"I can be very useful to you, niece," the Regent replied, shifting gears so quickly that Kelsea had to wonder if he'd only been dancing around the real matter all along.

"Useful how?"

"I know a lot of things you'd like to know."

"This is getting tedious, Majesty," Mace interrupted. "Just let me throw him out of the Keep."

"Wait." Kelsea held up a hand. "What do you know, Uncle?"

"I know who your father is."

"He knows nothing, Lady," Mace growled.

"Of course I know, niece. And I know plenty more about your mother that would interest you. This lot won't tell you. They took vows. But I'm not a Queen's Guard. I know everything about Queen Elyssa that you'd ever want to know, and I can tell it all to you."

Had her guards' eyes been swords, her uncle would have been run through. Kelsea turned to Mace and found his face stricken, a terrible sight.

I do want to know. She desperately wanted to know which of her mother's apparently infinite men had actually fathered her; she wanted to know what her mother had really been like. Perhaps everything was not as it appeared. She grasped at the idea, wondering if there were redeeming qualities in her mother, things that no one else knew. But there were hidden dangers as well. Kelsea gave her uncle a cold stare. "What exactly are you asking for, Scheherazade? Asylum in the Keep?"

"No, I want to be involved. I want to contribute and govern. I also have considerable information on the Red Queen."

"Are we really going to play this game? You tried to have me killed, Uncle. It didn't work, so I forgive you, but it doesn't incline me toward you either."

"Where's the proof?"

Mace stepped forward. "Two of your own guard already confessed and implicated you, jackass."

The Regent's eyes widened, but Mace wasn't done. "That

doesn't even include the Caden you engaged to hunt the Queen down three months ago."

"The Caden never reveal their employers."

"Of course they do, you miserable whelp. You just have to catch the right one in the right mood and feed him enough ale. I have all the proof I need. Consider yourself fortunate that you're still standing here."

"Why *am* I standing here, then?"

Mace began to answer, but Kelsea waved him to silence, her heart sinking. No matter how badly she wanted her uncle's knowledge, she couldn't take his offer. He would never stop trying to take back what he'd lost; it was clear in the way he darted glances around the room. She didn't know the man at all, but she recognized his character well. He would never stop plotting. He could never be trusted.

"The truth is, Uncle, I don't consider you important enough to imprison." Kelsea pointed at Coryn. "Take Coryn here."

The Regent turned to Coryn in surprise, as though he'd forgotten that Coryn was standing beside him. Coryn himself looked taken aback.

"I could take away everything Coryn owns, clothing and money and weapons and any women he might have stashed somewhere—"

"Plenty," Coryn remarked cheerfully.

Kelsea smiled indulgently before continuing. "And he would still be Coryn, an extremely honorable and useful man." She paused. "But look at you, Uncle. Divested of your clothing and women and guard, you're just a traitor with his crimes laid bare for the world to see. Putting you in my dungeons would be a waste of a cell. You're nothing."

The Regent whirled away, a movement so sudden that

Mace sprang in front of Kelsea, his hand going to his sword. But the Regent only stood there for a moment with his back to them, his shoulders heaving.

"My judgment stands, Uncle. You now have twenty-five days to clear the Keep. Coryn, escort him back."

"I don't need your escort!" the Regent snarled, turning around to face her. His eyes were wide with fury, but there was pain there too, deeper pain than Kelsea had intended. She felt a sudden, absurd urge to apologize, but it faded quickly as he continued. "You're adrift in deep waters, girl. I don't think even your Mace understands how deep they are. The Red Queen knows what you've done; I sent the messenger myself. You've interfered with the Mort slave trade, and believe me, she's going to come and gut this country like a hog at slaughter."

He glanced behind Kelsea and fell suddenly silent, eyes wide and terrified.

Kelsea turned and saw Marguerite standing behind her. Her neck hadn't healed; the welts had faded to a deep purple, visible even in torchlight. She wore a shapeless brown dress, but here was indisputable proof that clothes didn't make the woman: Marguerite was Helen of Troy, tall and imposing, her hair deep flame in the torchlight, staring at the Regent in a way that made Kelsea's skin prickle in gooseflesh.

"Marguerite?" the Regent asked. All of his previous bluster was gone; he gazed at Marguerite with a stark longing that made him look like a calf. "I've missed you."

"I don't know how you have the balls to speak to her," Kelsea snapped, "but you certainly won't do it again without my permission."

The Regent's face darkened, but he held silent, his eyes pinned on Marguerite. She stared back at him for a moment

274

longer, then darted forward, prompting both Mace and Coryn to put hands on their swords. But Marguerite ignored them entirely, walked right up to Kelsea's armchair, and sat down at Kelsea's feet.

The Regent stared at this development for a moment, his face frozen in shock. Then it contorted with hatred. "What did you give her?"

"Nothing."

"How did you buy her?"

"For starters, I don't keep a rope around her neck."

"Well, enjoy it. That bitch would as soon cut your throat as smile at you." He glared at Marguerite. "Damn you, you Mort whore."

"No one fears your curses, Tearling pig," Marguerite replied in Mort. "You have damned yourself."

The Regent stared at Marguerite with a bewildered expression, and Kelsea shook her head, disgusted; he didn't even speak Mort. "We have nothing further to say, Uncle. Get out, and best of luck in your trek across the countryside."

The Regent gave Marguerite one final, agonized look, then turned and stormed away, Coryn right behind him. Elston and Kibb opened the doors just wide enough for the Regent to pass through, and Marguerite waited until they closed before she scrambled up, speaking in rapid Mort. "I must get back to the children, Majesty."

Kelsea nodded. She had questions for Marguerite, but this wasn't the time; she watched the woman retreat down the hallway before relaxing into her armchair. "Tell me that's everything."

"Your Treasurer, Lady." Mace reminded her. "You promised to meet him."

"You're quite the taskmaster, Lazarus."

"Fetch Arliss!" Mace called. "Just for a few minutes, Majesty. It's important. Personal connections create loyalty, you know."

"How can we trust my uncle's Treasurer?"

"Please, Lady. Your uncle never had a Treasurer, just a bunch of vault-keepers who were usually drunk on their own watch."

"So who's this Arliss?"

"I picked him for the job."

"Who is he?"

Mace's eyes shifted away from her. "A local businessman, very good with money."

"What kind of businessman?"

Mace crossed his arms, a fairly prissy gesture for him. "If you must know, Lady, he's a bookmaker."

"A bookmaker?" Kelsea was momentarily bewildered, but her confusion quickly gave way to excitement. "But you said there was no printing press. How does he make books? By hand?"

Mace stared at her for a moment and then burst out laughing. Kelsea knew now why he didn't laugh often: it was a hyena sound, the screech of an animal. Mace clapped a hand over his mouth, but the damage was done, and Kelsea felt a hot blush spreading over her cheeks.

I'm not used to being laughed at, she realized, and rearranged her mouth into something that felt almost like a smile. "What did I say?"

"Not a book publisher, Lady. A bookmaker. A bookie."

"A bookie?" Kelsea asked, forgetting her embarrassment. "You want me to hand the treasury keys to a professional gambler?"

"You have a better idea?"

"There must be someone else."

"No one else as good with money, I can tell you that. In fact, I had to give Arliss the hard sell to get him in here, so you should be nice to him. He has a pre-Crossing calculator in his head, and he positively loathes your uncle. I thought that was a good place to start."

"How can you be sure he'll be honest?"

"I won't," croaked a hoarse voice, and around the corner came a wizened old man, his frame shrunken and hunched. His left leg must have been lame, for he moved his right side first and then dragged the left to match. But even so, he moved so fast that Kibb, behind him, had to hurry to keep up. Arliss's left arm appeared to be lame as well; despite the fact that a sheaf of papers was clamped in his armpit, he held the forearm cupped in against his rib cage like a child. What was left of his white hair sprouted up in tufted patches over his ears (and, Kelsea noticed as he got closer, from inside his ears as well). His old eyes were yellowed, the lower lids drooping to show flesh that wasn't even red anymore; age seemed to have leached it of all but the barest pink. He was the ugliest creature Kelsea had ever seen in her life.

Finally, she thought, regretting her own unkindness even as it crossed her mind, *someone who makes me look beautiful*.

The old man held out his good hand for her to shake, and Kelsea did so gently. His hand felt like paper: smooth, cool, and lifeless. He smelled terrible, a thick, acrid smell that Kelsea took for the scent of old age.

"I'm not honest," the old man wheezed. Kelsea didn't recognize his accent, which wasn't pure Tear; it managed to be both broad and nasal at the same time. "But I can be trusted."

"Contradictory statements," Kelsea replied.

Arliss's eyes gleamed at her. "Still and all, here I am."

"Arliss *can* be trusted, Lady," Mace told her. "And I think–"

"First things first," Arliss interrupted. "Who's your father, Queenie?"

"I don't know."

"Crap. The Mace here won't tell me, and I'm going to clean up when that comes out." Arliss leaned forward, staring at her chest. "Marvelous."

Kelsea reared back indignantly, but then she realized that he was inspecting her sapphire, eyeing it with a greedy collector's eye. "I take it it's real?"

"Real enough, Majesty. Pure emerald-cut sapphire, no flaws, absolutely beautiful. The setting's not bad, either, but the jewel . . . I could fetch you a hell of a price."

Kelsea leaned forward, her exhaustion suddenly forgotten. "Do you know anything about where it came from?"

"Just rumors, Queenie. No way to know what's true. They say William Tear made the king's necklace just after the Crossing. But Jonathan Tear wasn't content with that, and he had his people create the Heir's Jewel as well. Much good it did him; poor bastard was assassinated only a couple years later."

"Where did they get the jewels from?"

"Cadare, most likely. No jewels that fine in the Tear or Mortmesne. Maybe that's why she wants 'em so badly."

"Who?"

"The Red Queen, Lady. My sources say she wants your jewels just as badly as she wants you."

"Surely she can get all the jewels she wants in tribute from Cadare."

"Maybe." Arliss gave her a sideways glance from beneath

his bushy eyebrows. "These sapphires were rumored to be magic, a long time ago."

"Unlikely," Mace rumbled. "They never did anything for Queen Elyssa."

"Where's the other one at?"

"Weren't we talking about the treasury, Arliss?"

"Ah, yes." Arliss changed gears immediately, pulling the sheaf of papers from his left armpit. He performed a neat trick, holding the papers with his teeth, riffling through them until he found the page he wanted and jerked it from the pile. "I've inventoried your uncle's possessions, Queenie. I know good places to sell the expensive, and good fools to pawn the worthless. You can clean up at least fifty thousand on all the shit your uncle thought was art, and the whores' jewelry is worth twice that on the open market—"

"Watch your language, Arliss."

"Sorry, sorry." Arliss waved away the reprimand as though it didn't matter, and Kelsea found that it didn't. She liked his profanity; it suited him. "I ain't been through the vault yet; believe it or not, I'm still trying to find someone who actually has a key. But I've a pretty good idea of what I'll find there. By the way, you'll need new vault-keepers."

"Apparently," Kelsea replied. Her shoulder was screeching now, but she ignored it, slightly overwhelmed by the old man's enormous energy.

"After the Census chews off its piece of graft, the Tear takes in about fifty thousand in taxes. Your uncle's spent well over a million pounds since your mother died. I'm going to guess, and I ain't usually wrong about these things, that there's a hundred thousand sitting in the treasury, no more. In other words, you're broke."

"Wonderful."

"Now," Arliss continued with a gleam in his eye, "I've some good ideas on how to increase revenue."

"What ideas?"

"Depends, Majesty. Am I hired? I don't do nothing for free."

Kelsea looked a mute appeal at Mace, but he merely raised his eyebrows in an expressive gesture that dared her to say no. "You're not honest, but you can be trusted?"

"That's right."

"I think you're more than a bookmaker."

Arliss grinned, his pointy hair sticking straight up over his head as though he'd taken a bolt of lightning. "I might be."

"Why do you *want* to work for me? I assume that whatever we might pay you, it's not what you make at night."

Arliss chuckled, a tiny wheeze like a deflated accordion. "Matter of fact, Queenie, I'm probably richer than you are."

"So why do you want this job?"

The little man's face sobered, and he gave Kelsea an evaluating look. "They're singing about you in the streets, you know that? Absolutely petrified of invasion, the entire city, but still they're making songs about you. Calling you the True Queen."

Kelsea gave Mace a questioning glance, and he nodded.

"I don't know whether it's true, but I hedge my bets," Arliss continued. "Always good to be on the winning side."

"What if I'm not what they say?"

"Then I've got enough money to buy myself out of trouble."

"What do you want to be paid?"

"The Mace and I already dealt with the details. You can afford me, Queenie. You just have to say yes."

"Would you expect me to turn a blind eye to your other dealings?"

"We can deal with that as it comes up."

Slippery, Kelsea thought. She appealed to Mace again. "Lazarus?"

"You won't find a better money man in the Tear, Lady, and that's not the least of his skills. It's going to take a lot of work to repair your uncle's damage. This is the man I'd choose for the job. Although," he growled, bending a hard gaze toward Arliss, "he'll have to learn to speak to you with some respect."

Arliss grinned, showing a mouthful of crooked yellow teeth.

Kelsea sighed, feeling a mantle of inevitability settle over her, understanding that this would be the first of many compromises. It was an uneasy feeling, like getting into a boat on a wild river with no possibility of portage. "Fine, you're hired. Prepare me some sort of accounting, if you would.

The old man bowed and began to walk-drag himself backward from the armchair. "We'll talk again, Queenie, at your leisure. Meanwhile, do I have your permission to inspect the vault?"

Kelsea smiled, feeling a sickly film of sweat on her forehead. "I doubt you need my permission, Arliss. But yes, you have it."

She leaned back against the armchair, but her shoulder rebelled, making her jerk forward again. "Lazarus, I need to rest now."

Mace nodded and gestured for Arliss to go. The Treasurer did his odd crab-walk back toward the hallway, and Mace and Andalie each got an arm beneath Kelsea and physically hauled her from the armchair, then lifted and dragged her back into her chamber.

"Will Arliss live here with us?" Kelsea asked.

"I don't know," Mace replied. "He's been in the Keep for a couple of days now, but that's only to inspect all of your uncle's things. He has bolt-holes all over the city. I'm guessing he'll come and go as he pleases."

"What exactly is his business?"

"Black marketeering."

"Be more specific, Lazarus."

"Let's just say procurement of exotic items, Lady, and leave it at that."

"People?"

"Absolutely not, Lady. I knew you wouldn't accept that." Mace turned away so that Andalie could help Kelsea undress, and walked around the room extinguishing torches. "What did you think of Venner and Fell?"

Who? Kelsea thought, and then she remembered the two arms masters. "They'll train me to fight, or I'll make them regret it."

"They're good men. Be patient with them. Your mother didn't even like the sight of weapons."

Kelsea grimaced, thinking again of Carlin, of that day with the dresses. "My mother was a vain fool."

"And yet her legacy lies all around you here," Andalie murmured unexpectedly, pulling pins from Kelsea's hair. Once Andalie had finally completed the messy business of getting the dress off without aggravating Kelsea's wound, Kelsea climbed into bed, so tired that she barely registered the cool softness of clean sheets.

How did they change my sheets so fast? she wondered sleepily. Somehow, this seemed more magical than anything else so far. She turned her head to say good night to Mace and Andalie and found that they'd already disappeared and shut the door.

Kelsea couldn't lie on her back; she shifted slowly in the bed, trying to find a comfortable position. Finally she relaxed on her side, facing the empty bookshelves, exhausted. There was so much to be done.

You've done plenty already, Barty's voice whispered in her mind.

A panoply of images poured from Kelsea's memory. The cages burning. Marguerite, tied before her uncle's throne. The old woman in the crowd who'd wept on the ground. Andalie, shrieking in front of the cage. The row of children seated in the nursery. Kelsea shifted beneath the sheets, trying to feel comforted, but she couldn't. She sensed her kingdom around her, beneath her, stretching for miles in all directions, its people in extraordinary danger from the Mort cloud on the horizon, and she knew that her first feeling was true.

It's not enough, she thought bleakly. *Not nearly enough.*

CHAPTER 9

THE JEWEL

So many forces were at work against the Glynn Queen that she might have been a rock outcropping in God's Ocean, worn down by the inexorable tide. Instead, as history shows, she shaped herself.

—*The Glynn Queen: A Portrait*, KARN HOPLEY

"Faster, Lady! Move faster!" Venner barked.

Kelsea danced backward, trying to remember the careful footwork Venner had taught her.

"Keep the sword up!"

Kelsea raised the sword, feeling her shoulder protest. The thing was incredibly heavy.

"You need to move quicker," Venner told her. "Your feet must be faster than your opponent's. Even a clumsy swordsman could outmaneuver you at this point."

Kelsea nodded, blushing slightly, and readjusted her grip. Being quick with a knife was very different from being quick with a sword. The width of her body, combined with the unwieldy appendage of the sword itself, was a hindrance. When Kelsea twisted around, she found her own limbs blocking her passage. Venner refused to let her work against anyone but himself until she moved faster, and Kelsea knew he was right.

"Again."

Kelsea readied herself, cursing inside. They hadn't even gotten to what she was supposed to do with the sword; her job right now was to keep it raised in front of her. Between her shoulder wound, her lack of muscle tone, and Pen's heavy armor, holding the weapon was a daunting task in itself, and remembering the intricate footwork at the same time was nearly impossible. But Venner was a demanding teacher, and he wanted his full hour. He would doubtless keep her working for the remaining fifteen minutes. She raised the sword, sweat running down her cheeks.

"Dance, Lady, dance!"

She stepped backward, then forward, anticipating an imaginary opponent. She didn't stumble this time, an improvement, but she could tell from Venner's sigh that she'd moved no faster. She turned to him, panting, and raised the sword helplessly. "Well, what more am I to do?"

Venner shifted from one foot to another.

"What?"

"You require conditioning, Lady. You'll never be as lithe as a dancer, but you'd move faster if you carried less weight."

Kelsea flushed and quickly turned away. She knew she was heavier than she should be, but there was a big difference between knowing something and hearing it spoken out loud. Venner was old enough to be her father, but she didn't like hearing criticism from him. If Mace was in the room, she knew, he would never have let Venner get away with it. But she also knew that she invited impertinence by her casual manner, her refusal to punish anyone for speech.

Erika Johansen

"I'll speak to Milla about it," she replied after a long moment. "Maybe she can change my diet."

"I meant no disrespect, Lady."

Kelsea gestured him to silence, hearing a soft movement outside the door. "Lazarus, is that you?"

Mace entered with a perfunctory rap on the door frame. "Majesty."

"Are you spying on my lessons?"

"Not spying, Lady. Merely protecting an interest."

"So say all spies." Kelsea took a small cloth from the bench and wiped the worst of the sweat from her face. "Venner, I believe we're done."

"We've ten more minutes to go."

"We're done."

Venner put his sword back in its scabbard, his face disgruntled.

"Only three days till you can torment me further, arms master."

"I torment you for your own good, Lady."

"Tell Fell I'll expect a report tomorrow on my armor."

Venner nodded, visibly uncomfortable. "I apologize for the delay, Lady."

"You may also tell Fell that if there's been no demonstrable progress by tomorrow, I may have only one arms master from now on. A man who can't procure a suit of armor after two weeks can hardly be trusted with anything else."

"One man can't adequately cover everything, Lady."

"Then make him understand, and quickly. I'm tired of his delays."

Venner departed, his face troubled. With Mace's help, Kelsea began to remove Pen's breastplate from her sweaty torso, breath hissing through her teeth as it came loose. Her breasts ached while she had the thing on, but they ached even worse when she took it off.

"He's right, Majesty," Mace told her, laying the breastplate on the bench. "You need two arms masters; that's how it's always been. One for training, one for procurement."

"Well, neither of mine will be this slow." Kelsea fiddled with the buckles that held armor to her calf. The things had clearly been made for men, men with short fingernails. Tugging against the thin leather, Kelsea felt the nail of her index finger bend back, and snarled under her breath.

"The Regent left the Keep this morning."

"Really? Before the deadline?"

"I believe he means to avoid pursuit."

"Where will he go?"

"Mortmesne, perhaps. Though I doubt he'll get the sort of welcome he expects." Mace leaned back against the wall, inspecting Pen's breastplate. "But really, who cares?"

"You came to talk to me about something else, Lazarus. Let's hear it."

The ghost of a smile crossed Mace's face. "I need to change your guard, Lady."

"Change it how?"

"In our present position, I can't see to everything and be a shield to Your Majesty as well. You need an actual body-guard, a protector constantly at your side."

"Why is this only coming up now?"

"No reason."

"Lazarus."

Mace sighed, his face tightening. "Lady, I have been over and over what happened at your crowning. I've discussed it with the others. They were placed to guard you from every angle."

"Someone shouted. I heard it right before the knife hit."

"To create a distraction, Lady. But we're all too well trained for that. A Queen's Guard might turn his head, but he wouldn't move."

"Someone in the crowd, then? Arlen Thorne?"

"Possible, Lady, but I don't think so. You were covered from a straight assault. The knife could have come from the gallery above us, but . . ."

"What?"

Mace shook his head. "Nothing, Majesty. I'm still uncertain, that's the point. You need a close guard, one whose loyalty is beyond question. Then I can be free to investigate this matter, to do other things."

"What things?"

"Things Your Majesty doesn't wish to know about."

Kelsea looked sharply at him. "What does that mean?"

"You don't need to know every detail of how we defend your life."

"I don't want my own Ducarte."

Mace looked surprised, and Kelsea felt a small glow of triumph; she rarely surprised Mace in anything.

"Who told you about Ducarte?"

"Carlin told me he was the Mort chief of police, but he really has an umbrella license for torture and murder. Carlin says everything done by a chief of police reflects on the ruler he serves."

"Ducarte's actual title is Chief of Internal Security, Lady. And like so many treasures from the Lady Glynn, that statement sounds remarkably naive in this day and age."

"The Lady Glynn?" Kelsea forgot all about Ducarte. "Carlin was a noble?"

"She was."

"How did you know her?"

Mace raised his eyebrows in mild surprise. "Did she never tell you, Lady? She was your mother's governess. We all knew her, perhaps better than we'd wish to."

A governess! Kelsea considered this for a moment, picturing Carlin here, in the Queen's Wing, teaching a child Elyssa. It was surprisingly easy. "How does a noblewoman become a governess?"

"Lady Glynn was one of your grandmother's closest friends, Lady. I'd imagine it was a favor. Queen Arla considered Lady Glynn extremely clever, and she did have a lot of books."

"But why did my mother give me to Carlin? Were they friends?"

Mace's jaw firmed in a mulish way that Kelsea knew well by now. "We were speaking of a bodyguard for you, Lady."

Kelsea glared at him for a moment before returning to her armor. She ran over the list of guards in her mind. "Pen. Can I have Pen?"

"Christ, what a relief. Pen wants the job so badly that I don't know what I'd do with him otherwise."

"Is he the best choice?"

"Yes. If you can't have me, you want Pen's sword." He picked up the breastplate and carried it to the door, then paused. "The priest who conducted your coronation, Father Tyler. He requested a private audience with you."

"Why?"

"My guess is the Arvath wants to keep an eye on you. The Holy Father's a crafty old man."

Kelsea thought of the Bible in the priest's hand, impossibly ancient. "Bring him on Sunday; the Church should like that. And extend him every courtesy. Don't frighten him."

"Why?"

"I think the Church must have books."

"So?"

"So I want them."

"You know, Majesty, there are places down in the Gut that cater to all tastes."

"I don't know what that means."

"It means a fetish is a fetish."

"You really don't see any value in books?"

"None."

"Then we're different. I want all the books we can put our hands on, and that priest might be useful."

Mace gave her an exasperated look, but picked up her armor and carried it out the door. Kelsea sat back down on the bench, exhausted. Her mind returned to Venner's words, and she found herself blushing again. She was carrying too much weight, she could feel it. She'd always been thick, but now she'd been indoors too long, and between that and her injuries, whatever physical condition she might have had was gone. No queen in a storybook ever had to deal with such a problem. She would speak to Milla, but tomorrow, when she didn't feel so sweaty and wretched. Besides, after Venner's workout she needed a good meal.

She gave a nod to Cae, who was stationed on the door to one of the rooms along the corridor. This room was a security concern, for it gave access to a wide balcony with a magnificent panoramic view of the city and the Almont Plain beyond. Kelsea had taken to going out there whenever she missed the outdoors, but it wasn't at all the same as the forest, and sometimes Kelsea felt a rogue urge to run a long way, to be under trees and sky.

This is how women are trained to stay indoors, she

thought, the idea echoing in her mind like a gravesong. *This is how women are trained not to act.*

She plodded down the hallway and into the audience chamber, where the guards on duty stood at respectful attention. Today it was Pen, Kibb, Mhurn, and a new man whom Kelsea had never seen before. From overheard conversations, she understood that they'd picked up a few more recruits; these men faced a truly fearsome interrogation from Mace upon volunteering, but once they passed, they took vows and became Queen's Guards for life. The annoying practice of refusing to meet her eyes continued, but today Kelsea was grateful for it. She knew she looked a mess, and she felt too tired to maintain anything resembling a conversation. All she wanted was a hot bath.

Andalie stood in her accustomed spot at the door of Kelsea's chamber, holding out a clean towel. Kelsea had made it clear that she didn't require help with her bath (her mind boggled at the sort of woman who would), but still, Andalie always seemed to know when to have things ready. Kelsea took the towel, meaning to head on into her chamber, but then stopped. Something in Andalie's face was different, not her normal inscrutable expression. Her brow was furrowed, and her hands betrayed a slight flutter.

"What is it, Andalie?"

Andalie opened her mouth and then closed it. "Nothing, Lady."

"Has something happened?"

Andalie shook her head, her forehead wrinkling further in frustration. Looking closely, Kelsea saw that there was a burning whiteness about Andalie's face, bright circles around her eyes. "Something's wrong."

"Yes, Lady, but I don't know what it is."

Kelsea stared at her in confusion, but Andalie didn't elaborate, so Kelsea gave up and went into her chamber, breathing a sigh of relief when the door was shut. Her bath was ready; tendrils of steam rose from the tub and obscured the mirror. Kelsea left a trail of damp clothes behind her and climbed into the hot water. Tipping her head back against the rim of the tub with a contented sigh, she shut her eyes. She meant to relax and think of nothing, but her restless mind returned to Andalie, Andalie who knew things without being told. If Andalie was worried, Kelsea knew she needed to worry as well.

Arliss and Mace made an efficient machine. They'd already managed to suborn someone in the Census Bureau, and information was beginning to trickle into the Queen's Wing. Even these isolated facts were frightening: the average Tear family had seven children. God's Church railed against contraception, and the Regent had backed this view, his own quiet use of contraceptives notwithstanding. Charges of abortion, once proven, carried a death sentence for both mother and surgeon. The wealthy could buy their way around these rules, as always, but the poor were stuck, and it aggregated into an old problem: there were simply too many poor children. When the current generation grew to adulthood, it would further strain the resources of the kingdom.

If any of them even lived to adulthood. The lack of affordable doctors was a problem with no clear solution. Pre-Crossing America had reached a height of medical miracle that the world was unlikely to see again, not after the disaster of the White Ship. Now the Tear's poor died regularly from botched appendectomies conducted at home.

But water filtration, even of the most subtle impurities, was gradually being perfected. Hat making continued to advance, and agricultural traditions remained strong. Kelsea supposed these were portable skills. She washed her arms, her eyes on the ceiling. Andalie had found her some good soap, of a light vanilla scent rather than the heavy florals apparently favored by the rich. Andalie at least had the good fortune to be able to go down to the market every day, although she went always with the same heavy guard of five. Kelsea hadn't forgotten about Andalie's burly husband, and she didn't trust him not to snatch Andalie right off the streets of the city. That would be a disaster. Kelsea could no longer deny that Andalie was worth her weight in gold, for Kelsea had only to think of something she wanted and Andalie would have it there at hand. Pen said that Andalie's quality of anticipation was the mark of a seer, and Kelsea was sure he was right.

Her sapphire had begun to burn against her chest. She lifted it, dripping, and found that it was glowing again, a bright blue gleam that reflected off the sides of the bathtub. The jewel was magical, all right, but what purpose did it really serve? Kelsea made a face at it, dropped it back against her chest, and sank deeper into the vanilla-scented water, her mind skipping onward to bigger issues.

After medicine, education was another problem. More than two decades had passed since children were last required to attend school in the Tearling. Even before the entire literate population had been conscripted into the Census, the state's interest in education had been steadily diminishing. And who had finally repealed mandatory schooling? The illustrious Queen Elyssa, of course. Even Mace had looked ashamed when he admitted this fact. It was an excellent system to increase productivity: allow children to stay home so they could learn to work in the fields for nobles. Every day Kelsea seemed to learn something new about her mother's government, and each revelation was worse than the last.

The heat from the sapphire flared suddenly, searing her chest. Kelsea's body jerked and her eyes flew open.

A man stood over her, less than a foot away.

He was dressed all in black, masked but for his eyes. He wore thick leather gloves and held a long, tapered knife. Perhaps he was Caden, perhaps not, but the figure he cut was unmistakable: an executioner. Before Kelsea could draw breath, he placed the knife against her throat. "Not a sound, or you die."

Kelsea looked around the room, but there was no help. The door, which she never locked behind her, was locked now. If she screamed, they would come, but not in time.

"Out of the tub."

Grasping the sides, Kelsea hauled herself up, splattering water to the floor. The assassin backed up slightly, allowing her to climb out, but the knife never left her throat. She stood shivering beside the tub, dripping water on the cold stone. She flushed at her own nakedness, and then stuffed that impulse. A voice spoke up in her head; she didn't know if it was Barty or Mace.

Think.

The assassin took the knife from her throat and placed the tip of it against her left breast.

"Move very slowly." The cloth of the mask muffled his voice, but Kelsea thought he must be fairly young. She shivered more violently now, and the tip of the knife pricked her, hard.

"Reach up with your right hand, take off your necklace, and hand it to me."

Kelsea stared at him, bewildered, though she could see nothing but a shadowed pair of eyes behind the black mask. Why not just kill her and take the necklace himself? He meant to kill her anyway, no doubt of that.

He can't take the necklace off himself. Or at least he thinks he can't.

"It takes both hands to remove it," Kelsea replied carefully. "There's a clasp."

Three hard knocks sounded on the door, making Kelsea jump. Even the assassin was startled; the knife dug deeper into Kelsea's breast, and she hissed with pain, feeling a trickle of blood work its slow way toward her nipple.

"Answer very carefully," the assassin whispered. His eyes were cold pinpoints of light.

"Yes?"

"Lady?" It was Andalie. "Are you all right?"

"I'm fine," Kelsea replied easily, steeling herself to feel the knife go in. "I'll ring when it's time to wash my hair."

The assassin's eyes glinted behind the mask, and Kelsea worked to keep her face expressionless. The pause outside the door seemed very long.

"Yes, Lady," Andalie replied. Then there was silence.

The assassin listened for perhaps a minute, but there was no sound from outside. Finally he relaxed, easing the pressure of the knife. "The necklace. You can use both hands, but slow. Take it off and hand it to me."

Kelsea reached up, so slowly that she felt as though she were engaged in some sort of performance. She grabbed the clasp of the necklace and pretended to work at it, knowing that if she took it off, she was dead. Looking past the man in front of her, she saw that one of the flagstones had been lifted up and out of its groove so that a square of darkness broke the smooth pattern of the floor. Time, she needed time.

"Please don't kill me."

"The necklace. Now."

"Why?" From the corner of her eye, Kelsea saw movement at the door, the lock, but kept her gaze on his mask. "Why can't you simply take it?"

"Who knows? But I get less money for the necklace than I do for cutting your throat, so don't play with me. Take it off."

The lock clicked.

At the sound, the assassin whirled, a graceful movement of feet and limbs. He materialized behind her, pressing an arm to her waist and his knife hand against her throat, so quickly that Kelsea was helpless in front of him before the door even opened.

Mace moved slowly into the room. Kelsea glimpsed some ten guards behind him, peering in, then the assassin dug the knife against her throat and her vision blurred.

"No closer, or she dies."

Mace paused. His face and eyes were wide, disingenuous, almost blank.

"Close and lock the door."

Mace reached behind him, never taking his eyes from the assassin, and closed the door gently, leaving the rest of the guards outside. He flipped the lock.

"You may reach me, Queen's Guard," the assassin continued in a low, almost conversational tone, "but not before she dies. Remain where you are, answer my questions, and you prolong her life. Understand?"

Mace nodded. He didn't even look at Kelsea, who gritted her teeth. The assassin took a step backward, pulling her with him, the knife digging deeper into her throat.

"Where's the companion necklace?"

"Only Carroll knew."

"You lie." Another step backward. "Both necklaces went with the girl. We know that."

"Then you know more than me." Mace splayed his hands. "I delivered the baby with only one necklace on her."

"Where's the crown?"

"Same answer. Only Carroll knew."

Another step backward.

The hole in the floor, Kelsea thought. Did he mean to take her with him? Of course not; they couldn't both fit in there. He meant to cut her throat and then escape. Mace had clearly arrived at the same conclusion, for his eyes flickered between the assassin and the hole in the floor with increasing speed. "You can't hope to escape."

"Why?"

"I know every hidden passage through this wing."

"Apparently not."

Beyond the wall, Kelsea heard the rumble of many voices, the ring of weapons. But they might as well have been a world away. In here, there was only the cool whistling of the man's breath in her ear, shallow and even, without even a hint of anxiety.

"This is your last chance to take off the necklace," he murmured, digging the knife farther into her throat, forcing her to back up against him. "I might let you live."

"Piss off," Kelsea snarled. But beneath her anger she felt a deep throb of despair; had she really gone through everything only to be taken naked and defenseless like this? Was this how history would say she'd died?

The assassin tugged at the sapphire pendant between her breasts, but the chain refused to give. He pulled harder and the chain bit into the back of Kelsea's neck. Kelsea stiffened, fury blooming from nowhere. It was a gift; her fear melted quickly and silently away. She could feel the sapphire now, a throbbing pressure that burned like a pulse inside her mind. With every jerk on the chain, Kelsea became angrier. The sapphire didn't want to be removed.

Why not? she asked. And although she had not expected an answer, one came smoothly, bubbling up from some dark place inside her mind. *Because I have so much to show you, child.*

The voice was alien, incredibly far away. It seemed to be coming to her from a place beyond distance. Kelsea blinked in surprise. The chain wasn't cooperating, and the assassin began to exert more force. His attention was divided now, and Mace knew it; he'd begun circling to the left, his flat gaze moving swiftly between Kelsea, her captor, and the hole in the floor. Kelsea's midriff was smeared with blood, and the arms around her felt like they might have some give. But the knife at her throat remained steady, and Mace was still ten feet away. She didn't dare try to break free.

The assassin gave a tremendous yank at the sapphire now, so hard that the clasp bit cleanly through the flesh at the nape of Kelsea's neck. Her temper snapped and something seemed to break open inside her; heat welled up in her chest, a small explosion of force that pushed her backward. Mace drew his sword with a dry rasp, but he seemed miles away, not a part of this at all. The assassin gave a grunt and the arm around her loosened; a moment later, she heard his body crash to the floor.

"Lady!"

Mace grabbed her, kept her from falling. She opened her eyes and found his face inches away.

"I'm fine, Lazarus. Only a few pinpricks."

The assassin lay motionless on his back, his limbs sprawled out wildly. Mace let her go and dropped to a crouch over the assassin's body, moving carefully in case of a trick. When he pulled the knife from the man's clenched hand, the fingers didn't even twitch. Kelsea couldn't see a wound, but she knew he was dead. She'd killed him . . . the jewel had killed him. Or was it both? "What happened?"

"Blue light, Lady, from your jewel. I'd never have believed it unless I saw it myself."

Kelsea suddenly realized that she was stark naked, and Mace seemed to notice only a moment later, tossing her the large white towel that hung beside the bathtub. Kelsea wrapped it around her, ignoring the blood that began to soak through from her left breast, and studied her sapphire. The heat that had flared so suddenly was gone and now the jewel merely hung there, sparkling, a low, deep blue.

Contented with itself, Kelsea thought.

Mace had bent to the assassin again. He seemed to have no natural revulsion for the corpse, his hands moving over the body, testing, checking for a pulse. "Dead, Lady. Not a mark on him, either."

Fumbling at the man's neck, he pulled off the black mask to reveal a dark-haired young man with an aristocratic profile and deep red lips. With an inarticulate mutter, Mace rolled the body over, produced a knife from his belt, and cut through the corpse's clothing, ripping the fabric off to reveal a mark branded into the shoulder blade: a hound, its legs outstretched as though running. With a shudder, Kelsea realized that the mark was in the exact same location as her own wound.

"Caden," Mace muttered.

The din outside had grown louder, and they both seemed to notice it at once; Mace popped up from his crouch and went to the door, knocking softly. "It's Mace. Hold your weapons."

Opening the door slowly, he beckoned Elston into the room. More guards followed, swords drawn, staring first at Kelsea and then at the man on the floor. Coryn came running in with his kit, but Mace held up his hands. "The Queen's only scratched."

Kelsea made a face. She *was* only scratched, but her wounds were starting to hurt badly now that the adrenaline was leaving her body. The skin above her nipple felt rubbed raw by the rough material of the towel. She touched an exploratory hand to her throat and it came away smeared with crimson. Resigned, she watched Coryn pull out a thin white strip of cloth and soak it with disinfectant. She wished he would let her get dressed first. She didn't want all of these men to see her bare arms and legs. Then she felt even worse. Vanity. Her mother's hallmark, and Kelsea wanted nothing of her mother. For one wild moment, she thought of simply dropping the towel, just to make the point. But she didn't have the courage.

Mace was staring down at the hole in the floor. Kelsea couldn't see his face, but the set of his shoulders spoke volumes. Before she could say a word, he drew his sword, leaped into the hole, and disappeared from sight. No one seemed to find this odd. Several of her guards surrounded the assassin's corpse, staring at it like doctors preparing to diagnose.

"Traitors all, God help us," Galen muttered, and the men around him nodded.

"The Regent?" Cae asked.

"Not a chance. This is Thorne."

"We'll never prove it," Mhurn said, shaking his head.

"Who is this man?" Kelsea asked, clutching the towel tightly around her. Coryn pressed the cloth to her neck, and she hissed and bit down on her lip. Whatever his disinfectant was, it stung like a bastard.

"A lord of the Graham house, Lady," a new guard told her. "We thought them loyal to your mother."

Kelsea didn't recognize the guard, but she knew his voice. After a moment she realized, bemused, that it was Dyer. He'd shaved his red beard. "Dyer, is that your face under there?"

Dyer flushed bright red. Pen snorted gleefully, and Kibb clapped Dyer on the back. "I told him, Lady . . . now we can see every time he blushes."

"Where have you been, Dyer?"

The door to the chamber slammed back against the wall. All of them whirled around, Kelsea with a small shriek, as Mace stormed in. His cheeks were stained wine-red and his dark eyes burned so fiercely that Kelsea almost expected them to throw sparks. Mace's voice was the bellow of a wrathful God. "PEN!"

Pen darted forward. "Sir."

"From now on, you'll be the Queen's close guard. You won't leave her side for a moment, do you understand? Not for a moment, not ever."

"Lazarus," Kelsea interrupted, as gently as she could, "this isn't your fault."

Mace's teeth clenched, his eyes darting desperately, like caged things. Kelsea was suddenly afraid that he might strike her.

"Not for a moment, sir," Pen replied, and went to stand in front of Kelsea, pointedly shielding her from the rest of the guard.

Mace turned back to the room at large, pointing at the hole in the floor. "That's a tunnel, lads. I knew about it, but I wasn't concerned. You know why? Because it runs beneath three chambers and comes out in one of the empty ones down the hall."

Her guards exchanged shocked looks. Elston took an involuntary step back. Mhurn had turned white as a sheet.

"Anyone not see what that means?"

All of them stood there as though waiting for a storm to break.

"It means," Mace roared, "that we have a traitor here!"

In one seamless movement, he picked up the chair from the vanity table and hurled it at the far wall, where it shattered into several jagged lumps of wood. "Someone let this pile of shit in! Someone who either guarded one of the tunnels or knew the knocks. One of you is a lying fuck, and when I find you—"

"Sir," Galen interrupted quietly, his hands up in a placating gesture.

"What?"

"It takes more than one traitor to smuggle an assassin in here. It would take a Gate Guard as well."

Several of the guards nodded, murmuring agreement.

"I don't care about the Gate Guard," Mace hissed. "They're worthless, that's why they guard the gate."

He stood there for a moment, breathing hard. Kelsea thought of storm clouds, clouds that could either blow themselves out or touch down in a funnel that would blast the land. She shivered, suddenly freezing, and a small, selfish part of her wondered when this scene would end so that she could put some clothes on.

"What I care about," Mace continued, his voice a low

threat caged in violence, "is that someone here broke his vow. I'll warrant it's the same someone who managed to stick a knife into the Queen during her crowning. And I'm going to find him; he's a fool if he thinks I won't."

Breathing heavily, he fell silent. Kelsea looked at the rest of her guard, those men who had surrounded her at her coronation. Elston, Kibb, Pen, Coryn, Mhurn, Dyer, Cae, Galen, Wellmer . . . all of them had been close enough to throw the knife, and only Pen was apparently above suspicion. Mace had pulled the knife from his belt, and now he stared at each of them in turn, his eyes cold. Kelsea wanted to say something, but the silence of the rest of the Guard told her that nothing she might say would do much good. She tried to wrap her mind around the idea that one or more of these men had broken vows. She had thought that she was making progress with them, but once again she had been naive.

After a moment, Mace seemed to come back to them a bit; he tucked his knife away and pointed to the body on the floor. "Get that pile of shit out of here!"

Several men sprang forward, and Kelsea almost did so herself.

"We need something to cover him," Kibb murmured. "The children don't need to see the blood."

Elston hoisted the corpse into a sitting position. "There's no blood."

"Broken neck?"

"No."

"Then how'd he die?" Mhurn asked from the far wall, his blue gaze pinned on Kelsea.

"Move along!" Mace barked. Elston and Kibb hoisted the body, and the rest of her guards followed them from the room in a murmuring herd, sneaking puzzled glances at Kelsea as they went.

Mace turned to Pen. "I'll spell you out; you get two weekends off each month. But the rest of the time, I don't want to see you more than ten feet from the Queen, understand? Take one of the bedrooms with an antechamber. You can sleep there, and the Queen can have her privacy."

"Some privacy," Kelsea murmured. Mace's large, dark eyes turned to her, and she raised her hands in a gesture of surrender. "Fine, fine."

He whirled and strode from the room.

"He'll be all right, Lady," Pen assured her. "We've seen him like this before. He only needs to go off and kill someone and he'll be right as rain."

Kelsea smiled uneasily, not sure whether he was joking. Although she didn't feel cold, she was shivering, and her legs wobbled beneath her. Andalie appeared out of nowhere, carrying a stack of clean clothes. "You're covered in blood, Majesty. You should get back into the bath."

Pen gave her an apologetic grin. "I'm not supposed to leave you alone, Lady. How about if I face the wall?"

Kelsea shook her head, chuckling without humor. "Privacy."

Pen turned and faced the doorway. After a moment, seeing no alternative, Kelsea took off her towel and climbed back into the tub, grimacing as the water turned a dull pink around her. She began to wash, trying and utterly failing to forget that Pen was in the room

Oh, who cares? They've all seen me naked now. The idea was awful, so mortifying that Kelsea found herself giggling helplessly. There was nothing else. Andalie, busy jerking Kelsea's unruly wet hair up into a knot on her head and fastening it with a silver pin, appeared not to notice. Her face was immobile, fazed by nothing, and it struck Kelsea for the first time, though not nearly the last, that some fateful mistake had been made. Andalie should have been the Queen.

"Cup of tea, Lady?"

"Please."

On the threshold, Andalie paused and spoke without turning around. "Forgive me, Lady. I saw it coming, but not the shape it would take. I couldn't see the man or the room."

Kelsea blinked, but Andalie had already left, closing the door behind her.

The Mort deadline came and went, but Mace did not reappear. Kelsea was briefly alarmed until she realized that the rest of her guards took his absence as a matter of course. Pen explained that Mace had a habit of going off on his own errands from time to time, leaving without warning and returning the same way. And Pen was right, for on the third day Mace did return; Kelsea found him sitting at the table, freshly showered, when she came out for lunch. She demanded to know where he'd been, and Mace, being Mace, refused to tell.

Her guards had taken the assassin's body to the plaza at the center of New London and (by custom, Kelsea was appalled to discover) spitted his corpse on a sharpened pole, leaving it there to rot. If Arliss was to be believed, word was running like quicksilver through the city that the Queen had killed a Caden herself, that she'd used magic. There wasn't a mark on the young Lord Graham, but he was dead as a doornail all the same.

Several times a day, Kelsea pulled the sapphire from her dress and stared at it, willing it to speak to her again, to do anything out of the ordinary. But nothing happened. She felt like a fraud.

Mace didn't share her concern. "Just as useful as if you'd done it on purpose, Lady, so who cares?"

Kelsea was perched over the dining room table, looking at a map of the Mort border. Mace had pinned its four corners down with tea mugs to keep it from rolling up. "I care, Lazarus. I've no idea what happened or how to repeat it."

"Yes, but only you and I know that, Lady. It's a boon, believe me. They'll think twice before trying a direct attack on you again."

Kelsea lowered her voice, mindful of the guards stationed on the walls. "What of our traitor?"

Mace frowned and pointed to a space on the map, lowering his voice as well. "I've made some progress, Lady. Nothing concrete to place before you yet."

"What progress?"

"A theory, nothing more."

"That's not much."

"My theories are rarely wrong, Majesty."

"Should I be worried?"

"Only if Pen gets caught off guard, Lady. I'm more worried about the sun rising westerly." The map suddenly escaped from one of its corners and Mace cursed, unrolled it, and slammed the mug back down to hold it in place.

"What's eating at you, Lazarus?"

"Whoever this man is, Majesty, he should never have gotten so far. Treachery leaves a smell; a stench really, and I've never before failed to sniff it out."

Kelsea smiled, poking him in his bicep. "Perhaps this is a healthy test of your complacency." But then, seeing that his pride was really injured, she sobered and clasped his shoulder. "You'll find him, Lazarus. I wouldn't be that traitor for all the steel in Mortmesne."

"Majesty?" Dyer had emerged from the hallway.

"Yes?"

"We've something to show you."

"Now?" Kelsea straightened and saw an odd phenomenon: Dyer was grinning. Mace waved a hand to indicate that she should go, and she followed Dyer down the corridor with Pen's soft tread just behind her. Tom and Wellmer were waiting two doors down from her new bedchamber, both grinning as well, and Kelsea approached cautiously. Maybe she had been too casual with them all. Was she about to become the subject of a practical joke?

"Go on, Lady," Wellmer told her, gesturing her inside. In his excitement, he seemed even younger than usual, hopping from foot to foot like a small boy on Christmas, or at least a small boy who had a dire need for the bathroom.

Kelsea turned into the chamber, a cozy space with low ceilings and no windows. Five armchairs and two sofas had been scattered around, and several of these contained children. Andalie's, Kelsea thought, but she couldn't be sure. She turned a questioning glance to Dyer, and he gestured toward the far wall.

She recognized the bookshelves; she'd been looking at them in her mother's chamber, hating their emptiness, for the past two weeks. But now the shelves were full. Kelsea moved further into the room, staring at the books as though hypnotized. She recognized all of the titles, but it was only when she saw the enormous brown leather volume of Shakespeare, Carlin's pride and joy, that she knew what Mace had done.

"Dyer, is this where you've been?"

"Aye, Lady," he replied. "Mace was determined to make it a surprise."

Kelsea inspected the books closely. They looked just as she remembered them in Carlin's library. Someone had even gone to the trouble to alphabetize them all by author. They'd left the fiction intermingled with the nonfiction; Carlin would have screamed bloody murder. But Kelsea was touched by the effort.

"We didn't lose a single book, Majesty. We covered the wagon well, but it didn't even rain. I don't think they took any damage."

Kelsea stared at the shelves for a moment longer, and then turned back to him, her vision blurred with sudden tears. "Thank you."

Dyer looked away. Kelsea turned her attention to the children perched on the furniture: two adolescent boys, a girl of perhaps eleven or twelve, and a younger girl, eight or so. "You're Andalie's children, aren't you?"

The older three remained silent, but the youngest girl nodded her head vigorously and exclaimed, "We helped alphabet the books! We stayed up late!"

"They're Andalie's, Lady," Dyer informed her.

"You did a very good job," Kelsea told them. "Thank you."

The boys and the younger girl smiled timidly, but the oldest girl merely sat there, staring at Kelsea with sullen eyes. Kelsea was puzzled. She'd never spoken to the girl before, barely even recognized her. Of all of the children on the sofa, this one looked the most like Andalie's husband; her mouth was naturally downturned at the corners, her eyes dark-socketed and suspicious. After a moment she turned away, and Kelsea was reassured; the girl might look like her father, but the dismissal in the gesture was pure Andalie.

Kelsea looked around for Mace, but he wasn't there. "Where's Lazarus?"

She found him back at the dining table, still bent over the enormous map of the New World. "Thank you for the surprise."

Mace shrugged. "I could tell you wouldn't be able to focus on anything until we got you some books."

"It means the world to me."

"I don't understand your fascination with the damned things. They don't feed or protect you. They don't keep you alive. But I see that they're important to you."

"If there's ever something I can do for you in return, you've only to name it."

Mace raised his eyebrows. "Be careful about making open-ended promises, Lady. I know all about those, believe me; they bite you in the ass when you least expect it."

"Even so, I mean it: if there's ever anything I can do for you, it's yours."

"Fine. Put all of those books in a pile, and set them on fire."

"What?"

"There's your open-ended promise."

Kelsea's stomach clenched in knots. Mace watched her with an interested gaze for a moment before he chuckled. "Relax, Lady. The debt of a queen is a valuable commodity; I wouldn't waste it. Your books are harmless enough, at least from a defensive standpoint."

"You're a piece of work, Lazarus."

"Indeed."

"Honestly, thank you."

He shrugged. "You earned it, Lady. It's twice as easy to guard a tough customer."

Kelsea bit back a smile, then sobered. "Any word on Barty and Carlin?"

"Nothing yet."

Kelsea frowned. Lately, she was surprised to find that she wanted to see not only Barty but Carlin as well. She had many things to say to Carlin. It would be a relief to be able to talk to Carlin about her mother, about the state of the kingdom, the true state of the kingdom, the one Carlin had never been allowed to broach. It would also be a relief, Kelsea thought guiltily, to tell Carlin that she had been right, that day when she'd torn the dress from Kelsea's body. So much of her resentment over that day seemed to have melted away now.

Don't deceive yourself, her mind whispered. *Nothing has melted away. It's just found a better target.*

"Are they no longer in Petaluma?"

"When I know, Lady, you'll know."

"All right." She stood up, nearly bumping into Pen, who put a hand on her back. "Sorry, Lady."

"How's it working out between the two of you?" Mace asked, his attention on the map.

Kelsea looked at Pen in surprise. He smiled and shrugged. "Fine, I suppose. Though Pen snores like a bellows."

"To be fair, Lady, Mace knew that before."

"Honestly, you're like a foundry in there. If only you produced Mort steel, you'd be an invaluable resource."

"He is an invaluable resource," Mace replied absently. He'd produced a pen from his shirt, and now began to draw a thick, dark line down the Mort border. "Snoring and all."

"I'd agree."

"Arliss!" Mace shouted toward the corridor. "We're ready for you now!"

310

Arliss had clearly been eavesdropping; he emerged from the hallway almost immediately, walking with his familiar crablike gait, one leg dragging the other along behind it. Kelsea made a face at his approach. She'd been planning to go and spend several hours, or perhaps a year, looking over Carlin's books before dinner, though it would mean skipping her usual lesson with Venner. But the military men would be here in a few days' time, and her first audience would take place on Saturday; she was supposed to spend several hours in conference with Arliss to prepare for both. All of the information that Carlin had never given her now needed to be crammed into the space of one week, and the schedule was exhausting.

"Nice collection you've got in there, Queenie," Arliss remarked as he approached the table. "There's a few odd duck book collectors salted around the Tearling. I could probably get you a damn good price."

"What collectors?"

"I don't reveal my clients. Want to sell?"

"Not a chance. I'd give up my crown first."

"Could probably get you a good price on that as well." Arliss sat down, grabbing the fabric of his trousers to drag his lame leg onto the chair. "But then, the market can always change."

Kelsea wasn't the only one pleased with her library. Queen's Guards had to be able to read and write, and whenever Kelsea wandered in, she found off-duty guards lying on sofas or curled up in armchairs with one of her books. There seemed to be something for everyone.

Almost everyone. Mace avoided the library entirely. There were so many books there that he would have loved, but he clearly felt that reading was only good for messages and bills and pronouncements, nothing that wasn't of the moment. Kelsea found his disinterest maddening.

Milla's son and Carlotta's baby were too young for books, but all of Andalie's children – except Glee, the toddler – knew how to read, and they seemed to live in the library while their mother was on duty. Kelsea didn't mind having them there as long as they were quiet. And they were quiet. They had found the seven volumes of Rowling with no help at all, but there was no squabbling. To Kelsea's private amusement, the oldest boy, Wen, sat the other three down, and they drew straws, very diplomatically, with four twigs broken from the library's firewood. Matthew, who was thirteen, won the right to the first book, and the other three were left to look over the shelves for alternatives. Wen found a book on anatomy and opened it unerringly to the drawings that had caused such trouble for Leonardo da Vinci. Morryn, who was eight and a girl's girl, seemed entirely disgusted with the choices. All of the romances were too old for her, and Carlin had never collected what she called "women's literature." Finally, Kelsea reached up to a high shelf and produced a book of Grimm's fairy tales. Although the stories weren't particularly feminine, Kelsea hoped the princesses might placate the girl. Morryn stalked off to a chair, staring at the cover with deep distrust.

But it was the eleven-year-old girl, Aisa, whom Kelsea watched most closely. Aisa picked up and put down many of the reading staples of Kelsea's childhood, but none of them seemed to meet with her approval. Watching the girl, Kelsea realized that her sullen expression was partly a result of the construction of her face: masculine, snub-nosed, and heavy-browed. The mouth went down, the eyebrows went up, and the result conveyed belligerence.

Summoning her courage (for some reason, she found this girl nearly as intimidating as Andalie herself), Kelsea moved closer and ventured, "I might be able to recommend something, if you can tell me what you're looking for."

Aisa turned. Her black eyes were her father's, but the expression in them belonged entirely to Andalie. "I want something with adventure."

Kelsea nodded, reading much from this statement. She scanned the bookshelves, but deep down she knew that she had no real adventure stories with a female hero. She ran a finger down a lower shelf until she found a green leather-bound volume with gold filigree on the spine. She pulled out the book and handed it to Aisa. "There's no girl in this one. But if you like it, the sequel has a heroine."

"Why can't I simply read the sequel?" Aisa asked, her expression retreating into sullen anger again. Kelsea found herself fascinated by the change in the girl's face; it was like watching a trap snap shut. Kelsea's first instinct was to answer sharply, but winning over Andalie's children seemed nearly as important as winning over Andalie herself. Instead, Kelsea modulated her voice to be as gentle as possible. "No. You have to read this first, or the sequel won't mean as much to you. Treat it well; it's one of my favorites."

Aisa walked away with *The Hobbit* under her arm. Kelsea stood looking after her, torn between wanting to watch the children and wanting to read *The Lord of the Rings* all over again. She didn't really have time for either. In ten minutes she would need to be dressed and ready for Venner's torment. She nodded to Pen, grabbed her own books and papers from her desk, and headed for the door.

On her way out, she took a last look at the four children, each curled up very comfortably. Galen, too, was sprawled out on a couch against the wall, one leg dangling over the armrest, reading a book covered in blue leather. Kelsea thought of how much Carlin would like to see this: her library in use by a community of readers, an oasis in an entire nation starved for books.

No, not even starved, Kelsea thought grimly. The Tearling was like a man who hadn't eaten in so long that he didn't even remember what it was like to be hungry anymore. The spark of an idea ignited in her mind, then danced away.

Pen was waiting for her to clear the doorway; Kelsea gave him an apologetic smile and headed down the hall. On impulse, she stopped in the balcony room, as everyone now called it. Mhurn was on the door today, and he bowed as Kelsea approached. He was the only one besides Pen who bowed regularly, though Kelsea didn't really worry about formalities. Bowing would have seemed unnatural from most of the others, especially Dyer, who was just as likely to offer a sarcastic remark. Mhurn still didn't look like he was getting any sleep; by now Kelsea wondered if he had chronic insomnia, if he was one of those unfortunate souls who simply couldn't sleep no matter what the circumstance. She felt a twinge of pity, and smiled at him as she passed. But then she remembered that night in her chamber – the man who had pulled her from the bathtub, the overturned flagstone in the floor – and the memory made the smile freeze on her face. Mace thought it could be any one of them.

The balcony ran the length of the room, perhaps thirty feet from edge to edge, bordered by a waist-high parapet. It was a crisp March afternoon, just beginning to darken to night; beneath the deep blue sky, an icy wind blew across the front of the Keep, moaning hollowly as it passed beneath the eaves and through the many battlements. Kelsea leaned against the parapet and looked out, beyond the cluttered half-lit mosaic of New London, to where the Almont Plain rolled toward the horizon in mottled shades of brown and yellow green, its expanse only broken by the twin curves of the Caddell and Crithe Rivers stretching into the distance. Her kingdom was beautiful, but daunting. So much land, so many people, and all of their lives now balanced on the edge of a blade. The army men were coming tomorrow, and it was a conference that Kelsea dreaded. From what Arliss and Mace had told her, she wasn't going to like General Bermond one bit. She stared out over her kingdom, worrying. She wished that she could see all the way to Mortmesne, that she could know exactly what was coming.

Darkness descended over her vision, instantly, like a curtain dropping. Kelsea stumbled, clutching the parapet for balance, only dimly aware of herself as a physical creature still standing on the balcony. The rest of her was rushing through a high, cold night sky, freezing wind screaming in her ears.

Looking down, she saw a vast land covered in deep pine forest. This land was crisscrossed with roads: not dust roads like those of the Tearling, but real roads that had been paved with some sort of stone, roads made for moving large quantities of goods in wagons and caravans. On the northern horizon she saw high hills, almost mountains, dotted with pits: mining facilities. There were no farms here; rather, there were factories, piles of brick emitting great gouts of smoke and ash into the air. Was it day? Night? Kelsea couldn't tell. The entire world was painted in a blue twilight.

"Lady?" From a great distance away, Kelsea heard Pen's voice. She shook her head, silently begging him not to intrude. She was frightened, she hated heights, but oh . . . she wanted so badly to see.

Ahead was an enormous city, far larger than New London, built on a stone plateau that rose above the level of the pines. A palace thrust upward from the center of the city, dwarfing the buildings around it, not so tall as the Keep but elegant, symmetrical in a way the Keep was not. At the very top of the tallest tower, a blood-red flag snapped in the wind. Kelsea's vision lingered on this for a moment before dropping again to the ground. A tall wooden wall encircled the city, and a wide road emerged from the front gate, its edges dotted with tall sticks. Streetlamps? No, for as Kelsea's vision swooped closer, she saw that each stick had a small, oblong object at its top – human heads, some weathered away to skulls, some still in the freshest stages of decay, their features still visible, caked with mold.

The Pike Hill, Kelsea realized. *Demesne, it must be.* Looking down to the left of the city, she saw a huge black mass dotted with firelights. She needed to move closer, and did so, swooping downward, the way a bird might when it dropped from the sky to attack.

"Lady?"

An army lay beneath her, a massive army that covered the ground for several square miles: tents and campfires, men and horses and wagons filled with extra ordnance, knives and swords, bows and arrows and pikes. At the rear were several pieces of massive wooden equipment that Kelsea recognized from descriptions in books: siege towers, each of them at least twenty yards long, laid flat on their sides for transport. She splayed her arms in desperation, feeling wings flap around her, her feathers ruffling in icy air.

Wheeling around, she swooped back for another pass,

soaring over the camped battalions. Dawn was far away; the soldiers were preparing to sleep. She heard snatches of song, smelled roasting cow meat, even the tang of ale. She could see every detail on the ground, infinitely clearer than her vision had ever been in her life, and longing lanced her, some part of her knowing even now that she would have to return to her human eyes, that this clarity couldn't last.

Passing over the east side of the encampment, Kelsea saw something unfamiliar: the sheen of a sizable piece of metal, gleaming in the firelight. She tucked her wings and dove closer until she was right over the camp. The repugnant stench of many people crowded together filled her head, but she continued, even lower now. Soaring right over the eastern edge of the encampment, she saw a row of squat metal objects, each in its own wagon, neatly lined up like soldiers for march. It took several passes to understand what she was seeing, and when she did, her desperation turned to despair.

Cannons.

Impossible! There's no gunpowder, not even in Mortmesne!

The cannons gleamed beneath her, silently mocking. There were ten of them, built of steel, and all looked new. She couldn't even smell rust.

The Tearling!

She wheeled around, determined to return, to warn someone. There was no hope here, no victory, only a metal smell of carnage and death.

Her chest exploded. Below her, she heard a man's roar of triumph. Something pierced deep into her right breast, a flaming spear that crushed her heart.

"Mhurn! Medic!" Pen shouted, his voice dull to Kelsea, as if heard through water. "Get Coryn now!"

Kelsea fought desperately to stay aloft, but her wings no longer worked. She was screaming, she realized, though she could barely hear her own voice. She fell gracelessly, dropping like a rock through the blue world, and didn't even feel it when her body hit the ground.

You don't understand," Kelsea repeated, for perhaps the seventh time that day. "The Mort army is already mobilized."

General Bermond smiled at her from his end of the table. "I'm sure you believe that, Majesty. But it doesn't mean we can't still make peace."

Kelsea glared at him. The meeting had been a contentious one so far, and she was developing a low headache. General Bermond was probably no more than fifty years old, but to Kelsea he seemed more ancient than the hills, his head as bald as a pin and face wrinkled from long exposure to the sun. He had sewn his uniform sleeve to cover his lame arm.

Beside Bermond sat his second-in-command, Colonel Hall, who was perhaps fifteen years younger, thick and heavyset with a square jaw. Hall didn't say much, but his grey eyes missed nothing. Both men had presented themselves in full army uniform, probably to intimidate Kelsea, and she was annoyed to find that it was working.

Pen sat beside her, quiet as a statue. Kelsea liked having him there. Being followed around by guards was irritating, but Pen was different somehow; he knew how to keep himself from being intrusive. Although it was an unkind comparison, Kelsea thought of a faithful dog, one with a light tread. Pen was vigilant, but he would never wear her out with his constant presence, as Mace undoubtedly would have. Mace himself sat on her right, and every few minutes Kelsea would look over at him, trying to make a decision. News had arrived at the Keep yesterday: a stronghold of the Graham house, some fifty miles south of the Keep, had been gutted by fire.

Kelsea had spent the past day thinking hard about this turn of events. The stronghold had been a gift to the youngest Lord Graham upon his christening; it was difficult to reconcile that baby with the man in the black mask who'd tried to steal her sapphire and cut her throat. An assassination attempt on the Queen rendered all of the assassin's lands forfeit, but there had been men and women in that fortress, noncombatants, and with no warning given, several of them had burned along with the garrison. Kelsea had no doubt that the fire was Mace's doing, no doubt at all, and now she knew that a part of him was essentially beyond her control. It was a new thought, like living with a rogue dog that might slip its lead at any moment, and she wasn't sure what to do about it.

Mace's map of the border lay open on the table in front of them, along with a copy of the Mort Treaty. The latter offered no options, so Kelsea focused on the map. It was very old, drawn and inked in a careful hand long before Kelsea was born. The thickness of the paper, perhaps an eighth of an inch, betrayed an earlier stage in the pulping process of Mortmesne's mills. But the land was fundamentally the same, and Kelsea found her attention drawn to the Mort Road, the route the shipment had taken for the past seventeen years. The Mort Road led almost directly to the Argive Pass. Beyond the Tear border, the Argive Pass ended and sank in a steep decline, the Mort Road turning into the Pike Road, a wide boulevard, surrounded by forest, which led all the way to the walls of Demesne.

Just as I dreamed it, Kelsea thought, rubbing her forehead. But it hadn't been a dream. It had been too clear, too real, for that. When Coryn and Mace had rushed out to join Pen on the balcony, they found her unconscious. They couldn't wake her up; Coryn had tried every trick he knew. The rise and fall of her stomach was the only real sign of life. They thought she was dying.

But I wasn't.

Pen told her that before she fell, her sapphire had been glowing so brightly that it lit the entire balcony in the night. Kelsea still had no idea what had happened. Somehow the jewel had shown her something she needed to see. She slept for several hours, then woke up ravenous, and if that was the price of seeing, she could live with it.

"Majesty?" Bermond was still waiting for a response.

"There will be no peace, General. I've made my decision."

"I'm not sure you understand the consequences of your decision, Majesty." Bermond turned to Mace. "Certainly, sir, you can advise the Queen on this matter."

Mace held up his hands. "I guard the Queen's life, Bermond. I don't make her decisions."

Bermond looked shocked. "But surely, Captain, you see that there can be no victory here! You can tell her! The Mort army is—"

"I'm right here, General. Why don't you talk to *me*?"

"Forgive me, Majesty. But as I told your mother many times, women haven't the gift for military planning. She always left these matters to us."

"I'm sure she did." Kelsea glanced left and found Colonel Hall watching her, measuring. "But you'll find I'm a very different queen."

Bermond's eyes glinted with anger. "Then, once again, I

320

think your best option is to send emissaries to Mortmesne. Genot's no fool; he knows this would be a difficult kingdom to hold. He won't be anxious to invade, but believe me, if he chooses to do so, he will succeed."

"General Genot is not the king of Mortmesne, any more than you are the king of the Tearling, Bermond. What makes you think he's the one I would have to convince?"

"Offer a reduced shipment, Majesty. Buy them off."

"You are very anxious to offer other people as collateral, Bermond. What if I offered them you?"

"The Tear *are* collateral now, Lady. I would consider that a great service to my country."

Kelsea gritted her teeth, feeling her headache deepen. "I will ship no more slaves, not even you. Resign yourself to that fact, and let's move forward."

"Then I return to what I said before. You've put us in an impossible position. The Tear cannot repel the Mort army. And if, as you seem to think, they've somehow rediscovered gunpowder and mounted cannons, the situation becomes even more hopeless. You open the door to wholesale slaughter."

"Be careful, Bermond," Mace said quietly. Bermond swallowed and looked away, his jaw flexing.

"If the Mort had recovered the secret of gunpowder, surely we would've seen it flood the black market," Colonel Hall mused.

"Probably," Mace agreed. "I've heard no such report."

"Perhaps they've been keeping it to themselves?" Kelsea asked.

"The Mort have poor control of their weapons, Lady. After they perfected hawk training, it seemed like there were hundreds of hawks on the market within weeks."

"But hawks need a handler, food, space," Pen argued. "Without a handler, they're worthless. Gunpowder would be easier to ship in secret."

Kelsea turned to Arliss, who had been silent for a few minutes now. He would know, better than anyone, what might have found its way onto the black market. But he had dozed off. The sagging side of his mouth gaped open, a line of drool working its way down his chin. When he had arrived at the Keep that morning, he had a long, thin, papery object clamped in his teeth. Kelsea, who hadn't wanted to look silly for asking, had studied him covertly for a few minutes before she saw him exhale a stream of smoke and realized that he was smoking a cigarette. She hadn't even known that cigarettes existed anymore. They must be another black market item out of Mortmesne, but if there was tobacco production in the Tearling, Kelsea had a whole new set of problems. She arched her back, stretching, and felt her shoulder throb in warning. Today was the first day they'd left off the gauze. "Could they have a supply of old weapons from the pre-Crossing?"

Bermond shook his head. "All of the gunpowder that came over in the Crossing went bad."

"Even if they found some preserved under ideal conditions," Hall added, "it would never have lasted more than a century."

"To power a cannon, they would have had to synthesize it, or some substitute."

"That's not beyond all possibility, sir. Who knows what the Mort may have dug out of their mines?"

Bermond frowned at Hall, who fell silent. Kelsea considered waking Arliss to ask his opinion, then abandoned the idea. He would only exacerbate the contention at the table.

He clearly held the military men in small esteem; before falling into his doze, he'd taken several opportunities to bring up the army's old failures during the Mort invasion, harping on them so gleefully that Kelsea wondered whether he'd lost money on the outcome.

"So what will the Red Queen do first?" she asked.

"Invade our borders."

"Full invasion?"

"No. A few villages only, at first."

"What's the point of that?"

Bermond sighed in exasperation. "Majesty, put it this way. You don't throw yourself off a cliff hoping that the water is deep enough. If you're the Red Queen, you throw stones at the water, because you can afford to; you have all the time in the world and no shortage of stones. The Red Queen may not consider you a real threat, but she won't act in ignorance of the facts either."

"But why raid us? Why not simply send spies?"

"To demoralize the populace, Lady." Bermond pulled out a small dagger, one of the seemingly infinite number of weapons that hung on his person, and made a slashing motion in the air. "See? I cut off your pinky finger. You don't need your pinky, but I've made you bleed. Moreover, I've shown that I may violate your person at any time."

Kelsea thought this further evidence that conquering was an incredibly stupid business, but she closed her mouth before she said something regrettable. Beside her, Arliss emitted a light, slurping snore. "Arliss! Do you agree with this assessment?"

"I do, Majesty," he croaked, jerking to attention. "But don't fool yourself; the Tearling's already infested with spies as well."

Mace nodded agreement, and Kelsea turned back to Bermond. "Will they invade by the Mort Road?"

"Doubtful, Majesty. The Mort Road sends them through the Argive Pass, and no army wants to come down switchbacks out of the mountains; it leaves them wide open. We will still need to blockade the road, though, to prevent them from using it as a supply route." Bermond leaned over the map, shaking his head. "It's a pity the Argive Tower is gone."

Kelsea looked a question at Mace, who replied, "Once, Lady, there was a fortress built at the mouth of the Argive Pass. The Mort army tore it down as part of their retreat, and now it's only a bunch of stones littering the floor of the pass."

Bermond traced a finger over the northern Mort border, where the mountains fell into hills. "Here is where I'd come, if I were Genot. That's craggy hill country, and the terrain will slow them down, but there's plenty of forest cover, and a sizable force can spread wide, rather than bottlenecking at any one point."

"What's our best option to repel such an attack?"

"You can't."

"Your helpful attitude overwhelms me, General."

"Majesty—"

"Colonel Hall, what do you think?" Kelsea asked, turning to the second-in-command.

"I'm forced to agree with the General, Lady. There's no hope for ultimate victory here."

"Wonderful."

Hall held up a hand. "But you could slow them down. Considerably."

"Explain."

Hall leaned forward, ignoring Bermond's deepening frown beside him. "Our only option seems to be delaying tactics, Lady, a campaign designed to hinder and slow the main bulk of the Mort army. That means guerrilla warfare."

"To what end?" asked Bermond, throwing up his hands. "They will take the country regardless, quick or slow."

"Yes, sir, but it extends the time during which the Queen might make peace, or explore other options."

Kelsea nodded, pleased. Hall, at least, was capable of thinking creatively. Bermond was glaring at him openly now, but Hall seemed determined not to notice as he continued. "The possibilities are even better if they try to move their army as the General has indicated. I grew up in Idyllwild, Majesty. I know that part of the border like the back of my hand."

"What of the border villages?"

"Evacuate them, Majesty. They're vulnerable, and the Mort army comes for plunder as well as territory. Let them find a bunch of empty villages, and it will at least give them pause."

"Majesty, that wouldn't be a wise use of resources," Bermond announced fretfully. "Evacuation takes a lot of manpower. Those soldiers would be better stationed back from the border in case the Mort reach the Almont."

"Have you heard nothing I've said, Bermond? The Mort army is already assembled, and you yourself just said they'll begin by invading the villages on the border. Those people are in immediate danger."

"They chose to live on the border, Majesty. They knew the risks."

Kelsea opened her mouth to snap back, but Mace jumped in ahead of her. "An evacuation would burden the interior with a flood of refugees, Lady. Refugees must be fed and housed."

"So we feed and house them."

"Where?"

"I'm sure you'll figure it out, Lazarus."

"What if they refuse to come?" Bermond asked.

"Then we leave them out there, if that's their choice. We're not talking about internment." Kelsea smiled pleasantly at Bermond. "But I'm sure you're capable of explaining it to them in just the right way."

"Me?"

"You, General. You will take a good chunk of the army, as many as you deem necessary, and go out to evacuate and secure the border and the Mort Road."

Bermond turned to Hall. "Evacuation will be your responsibility."

"Just a moment," Kelsea interrupted. She dug in her memory for what Arliss had told her of military structure. "Hall, being a colonel, I assume you command your own battalion?"

"I do, Lady. The left flank."

"Good. Your battalion will separate from the main army and undertake a guerrilla operation along the lines you mentioned."

"Majesty!" Bermond snapped, his face reddening. "I deploy my own troops."

"No, General. This is the Crown's operation, and I'm conscripting a battalion of your army for other work."

"And my executive officer as well!"

"Yes, him too."

Arliss snorted. Kelsea glanced at him and found him grinning around a newly lit cigarette. It smelled just as terrible as before, but Kelsea said nothing. It was Arliss who had informed her of the obscure right of the Crown to take direct military action, an old remnant of powers granted to the American executive. When she met his eye, he gave her a wink.

Looking around the table, she found both Pen and Mace glaring at Bermond, who was staring daggers at Hall. But Hall was still watching Kelsea. The flare of ambition in his eyes was easy to see, but there was something more, something she couldn't identify but liked nonetheless.

If this one wasn't built to be a soldier, I'd have him in my Guard tomorrow.

"Of particular concern to me are the cannons," Kelsea told Hall. "I saw ten of them, but there may be more. I couldn't tell whether they were iron or steel. Your first task will be to disable them."

"Understood, Majesty."

"Cannons," Bermond scoffed, and turned to Mace again. "There's no gunpowder. Are we really to base military strategy on a girl's fever dreams?"

Mace began to reply, but Kelsea cut him off. "That's the second time you've failed to speak directly to me, General. And if you value your career, all your years of service, as much as I do, it'll be the last."

"This plan is not tenable, Majesty!" Bermond snarled. "It's a waste of good people!"

"So is the lottery!" Kelsea snapped back. "I don't suppose any of *your* loved ones have ever been shipped, General?"

Pen grasped her elbow in a gentle squeeze.

"Not mine." Bermond's eyes flicked toward Hall.

Pen leaned in close to Kelsea and murmured, "Hall's brother, Lady. They were close."

"I apologize, Colonel Hall."

Hall waved her away. He didn't seem offended; his

eyebrows were lowered in thought, his mind clearly already far away, out on the border. Kelsea couldn't tell whether he believed her about the cannons or not, but it didn't matter. All that mattered was that he'd said yes.

"Is there anything else?"

Neither of the army men said anything. Bermond looked as though he had swallowed something distasteful. Kelsea wondered briefly whether she should be concerned about Bermond's loyalty, but dismissed the thought from her mind. He didn't seem the type to try to stage a coup, even if he'd been twenty years younger. He simply wasn't imaginative enough.

"We're done then," Mace announced. Bermond and Hall stood quickly, startling Kelsea.

"Thank you," she told them. "In a week, I'd like a progress report from each of you."

"Majesty," they murmured, and remained standing, staring at her for so long that Kelsea wondered if something was wrong with her appearance. She was on the verge of asking when she finally realized what they were waiting for.

"Dismissed."

They bowed and left.

CHAPTER 10
THE FATE OF
THOMAS RALEIGH

It's difficult to analyze the motivations of a traitor. Some betray their country for money, some for revenge. Some do so in order to satisfy a feeling of true alienation from their country's values. Some betray when they have no choice. Often these reasons will blur; treachery is hardly a one-size-fits-all proposition. Indeed, one of the most famous traitors in Tear history sold his country for the most basic motive of all: because he didn't know why he shouldn't.

—*The Early History of the Tearling,*
AS TOLD BY MERWINIAN

I should have known, Javel thought, both at that moment and many more times that day. *I should have known that this is where things would end.*

He didn't know why he still listened to Arlen Thorne. In hindsight, he could see what a stupid plan it had been: Thorne had engaged a single Caden to assassinate the Queen, and not even one of the famous ones ... Lord Graham the younger, who was barely more than a boy.

Rumors quickly flooded the city that the new Queen had actually killed the assassin herself, but that was bullshit. The Mace had killed him, then killed his retinue, and burned down his entire household for good measure. Graham had failed spectacularly, and worse, publicly; his body had hung in the center of the city for less than an hour before the crowd tore it from its post and ripped it to pieces. Javel had resolved never to lift a finger for Thorne again. But of course, the summons had inevitably come, and now here he was.

They met in a large warehouse out on the eastern outskirts of New London. Javel knew the place; at one point it had been used to house lumber before sale or transport to Crossing's End. But Thorne had apparently taken it over for his own dark work. One of his innumerable Census thugs met Javel at the door, looked him over for a moment, and then waved him inside. Javel found himself in a small antechamber, lit by a weak fire, surrounded by men who looked just as angry and confused as himself.

Thorne hadn't arrived yet, but looking around the room, Javel began to understand what was driving this entire endeavor: money. He felt a fool for not seeing it before, but of course he had been thinking only of Allie. He hadn't considered the enormous amount of wealth at stake in the shipment, how much some people had to lose.

Lord Tare leaned against the far wall, his ridiculous purple hat taking up more space than the rest of him. The Tares held lands in the east, fields of wheat stretching for miles across the Almont Plain, and they took toll from the Mort Road. In fact, Javel remembered hearing of some contention at one point: Lord Tare liked to charge toll by the head, while the Regent wanted him to charge by the conveyance. But the Regent hadn't been strong enough to force such a change, and if Lord Tare was still charging by the head, then the shipment represented a monthly gold mine.

Two Caden, the Baedencourt brothers, were seated in front of the fire. They were nearly twins, blond-haired and blue-eyed, with flowing beards that reached all the way to their considerable guts. No one would dare plot against the Queen without consulting the Caden, but Javel wasn't even sure that the Baedencourts were empowered to negotiate for the rest. They were simply the easiest Caden to get hold of, since they could usually be found drunk and whoring in the New Globe.

The Caden had their own problems now. It was common knowledge in the Gut that the Regent had offered them an exorbitant bonus to find and kill the princess, and they had committed the bulk of their resources to that endeavor, ignoring the everyday jobs – guarding nobles under threat, collecting bounties, and escorting valuable deliveries – that were their bread and butter. For the past few months the Caden had bled money, expending an enormous amount of manpower for nothing, and at any rate the royal treasury was now closed to them. Their failure to find the princess had also cost them a considerable amount of prestige, which further cut into business. It had always been standard practice for nine or ten Caden to join each shipment when it left New London; there was no better deterrent to would-be vigilantes. Escorting the shipment was understood to be fairly soft duty for Caden, but it still constituted a significant piece of their collective income each month. Now that was gone as well.

In the past month, Javel had heard rumors of Caden taking freelance jobs to make ends meet: manual labor, highway robbery, teaching swordsmanship or archery to nobles' sons. One handsome Caden named Ennis had even been hired as the escort to a noble's homely daughter, taking her to dances and reading her poetry and God knew what else. Even to Javel, who had no great love for the assassins, this was a sorry state of affairs. He wondered how the Caden themselves must feel, after being steeped for so long in arrogance and exclusivity, and couldn't quite imagine. Either way, it seemed more than likely that the Baedencourts were freelancing here, and so Javel didn't trust them, didn't trust their commitment to the enterprise.

Four more men, none of whom Javel knew, were seated near the fire. One of them was a young, weaselly looking priest, which gave Javel pause; he wouldn't guess that God's Church would involve itself directly in something like this. The priest's shaved head and thin white hands marked him as an ascetic, and given his youth, Javel thought he was probably one of the Holy Father's stable of personal aides. Beside the priest was a scruffy blond creature who looked as though he'd crawled from the gutter. A thief, or even a simple pickpocket, probably looking for a quick pound.

Money, Javel thought. *It's all about money for all of them. For everyone but me.*

And what is it about for you? a voice, thin and cold, hissed deep inside him. Thorne's voice, Javel realized, horrified, as though he'd somehow allowed Thorne to worm his way even into the darkest corner of his own mind.

It's about getting Allie back, he replied angrily. *That's all it's ever been about.*

No answer. Thorne was gone. But the question had been asked, and Javel sensed that real damage had been done. He was working to free a slave, surely a noble endeavor if there ever was one. But Allie was only one slave . . . one of tens of thousands who had gone the same way. Javel had no thought of the rest; he was only trying to get his own. And did that make him any better than these men?

I am better, he insisted to himself. *I know I am.*

But now, peering into the darkest corner of the room, he saw the worst development of all: Keller, his fellow Gate Guard, lounging against the wall with crossed arms and a satisfied expression. Javel remembered a night, several years ago, when Vil had quietly sent several of them off the gate and down to the Cat's Paw to fetch Keller, who had gotten himself into real trouble this time. There had been problems before; Keller had once flung a woman through a wall, and there had been several rape accusations, one of which had required a direct appeal to the Regent before it disappeared. But even Javel had been unprepared for what met them at the Cat's Paw, where they found Keller drunk off his ass, one blood-covered hand still clutching a straight razor. He'd beaten the whore within an inch of her life before slicing up her face and tits. Javel could still see the girl weeping in the corner, blood pouring from the razor slashes that criss-crossed her upper body. She couldn't have been more than fourteen. Javel had gone home at dawn and drunk himself to blackout, thanking God that he was alone, that Allie couldn't see him. Now here he was again, tangled in bad business, staring at Keller across a shadowy room.

Thorne came in, clad in a deep blue cloak that swirled around his insectile body. Javel was relieved to see that Brenna was not with him this time; there were still two hours of daylight left outside. Thorne's bright blue eyes marked each of them in turn before he turned to take off his cloak, and Javel watched him curiously, wondering what Thorne's real game was here. He ran the Census, but that was a day job at government pay. By night, Thorne was a king on the black market, and even if the shipment disappeared forever, his income wouldn't suffer that much. Of course Overseer of the Census was a useful post, one that allowed him to lean on many people, but someone as slick as Thorne always had other ways of applying leverage.

What are you really after, Arlen? Javel wondered, staring at him. *What drives a creature like you?*

The answer came easily: clout. Thorne was not greedy; it was well known that he lived modestly. He had no taste for gold or gambling or whores, no vices at all beyond his fixation on the albino. What Thorne valued was the freedom to continue doing whatever he wished, without restraint. With the official slave trade gone, it seemed a likely bet that the Queen would turn her attention to the black market next. Traffic in weapons, narcotics, children . . . the new Queen was not the Regent, she'd proved that already; she cared about the low as well as the great. That was why Thorne had decreed that she had to go.

"Well, we're all here," Thorne announced. "Let's get down to it."

"Yes, let's," Lord Tare snarled. "You fucked up, you miserable bureaucrat. It's only God's luck the Mace didn't take the boy alive; he could've implicated us all."

Thorne tipped his head at Lord Tare, then looked around the room, as though for confirmation.

"I agree," announced the priest, though his tone was more conciliatory. "I convey the Holy Father's disappointment at the amateur nature of the attempt as well as its failure."

"I promised eventual success," Thorne replied mildly. "Not success on the first try."

"Pretty words, ferret," Arne Baedencourt sneered. He

sounded as though he was fighting with his own tongue.

Why, he's drunk! Javel realized, appalled. *Even I knew enough to sober up for business this black.*

"Why didn't you engage one of the real Caden?" Lord Tare asked angrily. "Dwyne, or Merritt? A professional killer wouldn't have failed."

"Every Caden is a real Caden!" Hugo Baedencourt barked. Compared to his brother, he sounded mercifully sober. "The Graham boy was tested just as the rest of us were. Do not sully his memory by implying otherwise."

Lord Tare splayed his hands outward in apology, though his glare never wavered from Thorne.

Thorne shrugged. "I do not concede that the plan was doomed to fail. The boy got very close; my source tells me that he had a knife to the Queen's throat. However, I do admit to underestimating the Queen's Guard, and the Mace in particular. My man got through so easily at the crowning . . . I assumed the Mace had grown soft over the years."

"Only a fool would ever underestimate the Mace," Hugo Baedencourt remarked gloomily. "We think he slew four of ours on the banks of the Crithe."

"Well, rest assured, it's not a mistake I'll make again," Thorne replied, in a tone that precluded further discussion. "At any rate, it's pointless to hash over the past. What matters is the future."

"The past *is* the future, Thorne," the priest disagreed quietly. "What guarantee does my master have that you won't fumble the next attempt as well?"

Javel was impressed. Few men, nobles aside, would dare to speak so to Thorne, even with the might of the Arvath behind them. And the priest had expressed Javel's own doubts precisely. Looking forward, he could see an endless corridor of failed attempts on the Queen's life. He couldn't face that, not even for Allie; his own courage didn't stretch so far. He wanted to be out of this, his life no longer beholden to secret plots and the constant fear that each fist hammering on the door would be the Mace, come to take him for interrogation.

"I guarantee nothing," Thorne replied coldly. "I never have. And while killing the Queen would solve many problems, I concede that it may simply be beyond our capacity at the moment."

"What of your Queen's Guard?" Lord Tare asked. "Can't he simply do the job?"

"What Queen's Guard?" the scruffy blond man asked.

Thorne shook his head. "He's unwilling to risk his neck so far. The Mace is already aware of a traitor; he's tightened security around the Queen and installed Pen Alcott as her close guard. My man is frightened, and I can't say I blame him. Even if he succeeded, there's no corner of the New World in which the Mace wouldn't find him."

Or us, Javel murmured to himself.

"You've turned a Queen's Guard?" the blond man asked again.

"Not your concern, little one," Thorne replied. "Remember your place here."

The pickpocket shrank back into his chair, and Javel shook his head. How had Thorne managed to suborn a Queen's Guard? They were unflinchingly loyal, even more steeped in their pride and traditions than the Caden were. So far as Javel knew, no royal guard had ever gone traitor.

But if anyone could do it, he thought in disgust, *it would be Thorne.*

"Pen Alcott is a gifted swordsman," Hugo Baedencourt

remarked, staring thoughtfully into the fire. "Few of us would dare to challenge him. Merritt perhaps, but you'll never get him to come in on this business."

"No matter," Thorne said. "I've had a better idea, one that serves all of our purposes. Alain, here" – he gestured toward the pickpocket – "has given me information vital to its success."

The scruffy pickpocket smiled wide, happy as a dog that had pleased its master. Javel began to wonder if he was right in the head.

"I would say that we can't fail," Thorne continued, "but such arrogance would be unproductive."

"Fail at what?" Hugo asked.

"In one form or another, you all need money."

Javel opened his mouth to disagree, then thought better of it.

"Money will no longer come to you from the Keep. The Queen will not support the shipment, not now and not ever."

"You've had conference with her?" Lord Tare asked.

"No need. The signs are clear. She met with General Bermond three days ago, and they've begun plans for initial deployment of more than half of the Tear army to the Mort border. The Queen's Wing is stocked with siege supplies. I tell you, she prepares for war, and without swift action on our part, the Mort will be coming."

Javel's mouth dropped open in horror. A Mort invasion . . . he had never seriously considered it. Even after the Queen had set the cages on fire, he'd always assumed that they would sign a new treaty, or that Thorne would sort it out, that something else would intervene. He thought of the wise, sad woman he'd seen on the Keep Lawn . . . despite Thorne's maneuverings, Javel had been certain that she would some-how save them all.

"God help us," Alain murmured.

"I assume that you would all like to avoid such an invasion. My plan will kill two birds with one stone."

Without warning, Thorne popped to his feet. Javel recoiled as he passed, not wanting to feel even the brush of those skeletal limbs. Thorne's tone was positively enthusiastic. "Come with me!"

They followed him through a door that led farther into the warehouse, into what had once been an office. Desks and chairs stood empty, coated with a thick layer of dust. Wall-mounted torches provided the light, since the windows had been blocked with black paint. Above one desk, a portrait of a dumpy-looking woman had been stuck to the plaster. Beyond the office wall, Javel could hear thudding blows, the muted sounds of someone hammering. Sawing as well; these were the sounds of serious construction, but this lumber company had gone out of business long since.

They reached the end of the offices, and Thorne led them through another door into the warehouse itself. It was a dank, cavernous space, lit by only the dimmest torchlight. The smell of old, dry sawdust made Javel's nostrils twitch. All around were enormous rectangular piles of ancient lumber, some nearly twenty feet high, covered with thick green canvas. Like all such abandoned buildings, the warehouse struck Javel as ghostly, dead space haunted by activity that had long since ceased.

"Come along," Thorne commanded, and the men followed him toward the far end of the huge space. The hammering grew louder as they neared, and when they rounded the last corner Javel saw a man stationed between two sawhorses, busily sawing oakwood. Planks of the stuff, each about ten feet long, were piled neatly and symmetrically beside him.

"Liam!" Thorne shouted.

"Aye!" A voice echoed from behind one of the lumber piles.

"Out here, please!"

A gnome of a man emerged from behind the tarp, wiping his hands on his trousers. He was covered from head to foot in a thin layer of sawdust, and Javel was suddenly assaulted by the certainty that he was having the most vivid yet of his Allie nightmares; any moment now, the warehouse around him would disappear and he would be standing at the edge of the Argive Pass, watching her disappear over the Pike Hill.

"This is Liam Bannaker," Thorne introduced the gnome. "I assume you've heard of him."

Indeed Javel had. Liam Bannaker was one of the best carpenters in the Tearling, and good with brick and stone as well. The wealthy of New London often engaged him to build their houses, and even nobles had been known to hire him from time to time, when they had broken stonework or foundations on their castles. But the man didn't look like a builder; he was short and skinny, with delicate-looking arms. The other carpenter, the man with the saw, was ignoring them entirely; Javel began to wonder if he was deaf.

"You'll be wanting a demonstration, I suppose?" Bannaker asked Thorne. His voice was also gnome-like, high and tinny, buzzing unpleasantly in Javel's ears.

"It would help."

"Lucky for you, three of them are all ready to go." Bannaker shoved through the group and hurried over to one of the covered piles of lumber. "A quick demonstration only, though. We're a bit behind schedule since Philip got the flu."

He grabbed one end of the green canvas tarp and gave it a jerk. Even as the tarp fell, Javel was assailed by a premonition of horror, something even worse than his nightmares, and he wanted to close his eyes. But it was too late, the tarp had already fallen, and his first thought was *I should have known*.

It was a cage, wide and squat, some thirty feet long and fifteen feet wide. A door stood at one end, just tall enough to admit a single man. The bars weren't steel; the entire cage, floors and bars and wheels, looked to be Tearling oak. It was not as well built as the cages Javel had seen once a month for his entire adult life, but it looked sturdy, sturdy enough to do the job.

"I sure as hell didn't sign on for *this*," Arne Baedencourt grumbled, and Javel nodded numbly. Looking to his right, he found Thorne staring raptly at the cage, the way a loving parent would gaze at his child.

Thorne shrugged. "What you signed on for is a moot point. You're all implicated now. Each of us is a danger to the other. But cheer up! I've already completed negotiations with Mortmesne. Each of you will get his original reward, as promised."

"And what's your reward, Arlen?" the priest asked, his weasel's eyes fixed distrustfully on Thorne. "What is it that you hope to gain from this?"

"That's no concern of yours." Thorne continued to stare at his cage with bright eyes. "Your master will be content when he gets his price."

"How many to each cage?"

"Twenty-five, perhaps thirty. More if they're children."

The priest bowed his head, his lips moving soundlessly. Javel thought he understood: the priest feared damnation. So

340

did Javel. He looked around the enormous warehouse, the tarp-covered piles that he had assumed were lumber, and counted a total of eight. He had never been good at math, but it took him only a moment to estimate this particular product.

At least two hundred people, he thought, his skin crawling. *Maybe as many as three.* Eight cages, and Allie's face seemed to peer through the bars of each one.

For perhaps the hundredth time since leaving the Keep, Thomas cursed the rain. The skies had opened as he crossed the New London Bridge, and now it had been pouring steadily for three days. It was March, the season for rain, but Thomas still felt as though the rainstorm had been sent to torment him. Perhaps the girl had conjured a storm on purpose with her damned jewel, or perhaps it was God's punishment. Either way, he was soaked through. He hadn't ridden a horse in at least a year, and his riding outfit turned out to be much too small; the wet fabric of the trousers had already rubbed his thighs raw, causing pain with every stride. The world had become nothing but these things: the cold, the wet, the chafing, and the endless splash of the horses' hooves through puddles and mud.

His men weren't complaining, but they weren't exactly cheerful either. Only three had agreed to come along; he'd promised them rewards once they reached Mortmesne, and these three had been stupid enough to believe him. He had never found Pine, a fact he regretted bitterly. Worse, not one of the Caden had agreed to come with him, not even after he promised to pay them double once they reached Mortmesne. One couldn't expect loyalty from mercenaries, certainly, but he had believed he might convince at least one.

But he had managed to grab Keever, and that was something. Keever had the brains of a block of stone, but he'd been in his family's business of shipping produce to Mortmesne, and he knew the Mort Road. The plan had been to leave the road once New London was behind them, but the weather precluded that idea, and perhaps it was for the best. On the road, superior skill in the wild would count for less, and Thomas didn't deceive himself; when it came to navigating the woods, Keever was outmatched. They all were.

But the road brought its own problems. The mud was so thick that Thomas could feel his horse panting with the effort of hauling its hooves from the mire. Every time they heard a party larger than their own approaching, they had to leave the road and hide in the undergrowth until it was clear. Thomas had planned to make the journey to Demesne in a straight three days, but that was never going to happen now. It would take five days, perhaps six, and the longer he was in the open, the more he could sense death near him, closing in. His guards gave him uncertain glances from time to time, and in these glances Thomas could feel the heavy hand of history. The girl had called him nothing, and somehow he knew that nothing was what he would become. Dimly, from the years when he was still in school, he remembered the tiny star and the note at the bottom of a book's page. A footnote . . . that's what he would become. In the stories, the mythology that the Tearling passed down from generation to generation, he would be an afterthought. Even if he reached the Mort border alive, the Red Queen would likely kill him for his failure.

It wasn't my fault.

She wouldn't care.

"Let's stop for the night," he suggested.

"We don't want to stop here," Keever replied. "Much too open. We should keep going until dark."

Thomas nodded and looked resentfully at the dusky grey sky. Although it was darkening fast, they hadn't even reached the end of the Caddell. Even if the weather cleared, it would take at least two more days of hard riding to reach the border. His thighs felt as though they had no skin left at all, and with each of his horse's strides, he felt fluid ooze from the raw flesh. His men must be suffering similar pains, but of course they never said anything, and the more furiously he wished for them to complain, the more certain he became that they wouldn't.

Thomas heard something.

He drew his horse to a halt and turned around, listening. But he couldn't hear anything over the rain. An enormous boulder hid the road behind them.

"What is it?" asked Keever. He'd taken on the role of unofficial leader on this journey, though the old Regent's Guard wouldn't have let Keever lead an expedition to the market.

"Quiet!" Thomas snapped. He'd always liked the way his voice sounded when he gave commands; it brooked no refusal, and Keever fell obediently silent.

Now he heard the sound again, even over the rain: hooves, perhaps a hundred meters back, around the bend.

"Riders," Arvis announced.

Keever listened for a moment. "They're moving at a good clip. Let's get into the woods over there."

Thomas nodded, and the four men picked their way off the road and into the woods, which were so shadowed that Thomas could barely guide his stallion. They moved far enough into the trees to block the view of the road, halting in a tiny copse. A steady hiss of rain fell on the leaves over their heads, but Thomas could still hear the approaching horses. Sudden dread coiled around his heart. Perhaps it was only a party returning from a hunt, or a gang of black marketeers who didn't want their doings observed, but the noose tightening inside Thomas didn't think so. He sensed eyes on him, deep black eyes that somehow saw every dreadful thing he'd ever done.

When the hoofbeats were perhaps fifty yards away, they ceased.

Thomas looked around at his men, and they looked blankly back at him, their eyes seeking answers, but Thomas had none. Riding farther into the woods was out of the question; it was nearly black in there, and being caught in darkness by what was after them would be even worse than being caught in this half-light.

Thomas was arrested suddenly by an old memory, a game he used to play with himself when he was a child: Queen's Guard. Perhaps once a month, he would wake up feeling inexplicably brave. There was never any particular reason, just a mood he woke up in; the world would seem a brighter, better place, and for that entire day, he would try to live life as a Queen's Guard, doing honorable deeds. He wouldn't pull Elyssa's hair or steal her dolls or lie to the governess about nicking things from the kitchen. He would make his bed and clean up his toys in the nursery and even do his homework. And oddly enough, either Mum or the governess would usually notice, giving him a compliment and something extra at bedtime, a small piece of chocolate or a new toy. But those days became fewer and fewer as time went on, as he realized that he would never be anything but a younger son, a spare. Sometime around thirteen, the Queen's Guard days vanished for good.

If only I had woken up that way every morning, Thomas thought, the idea awakening a deep and hopeless longing. *If I could have been a Queen's Guard every day of my life, things might have turned out so differently.*

Now the sound of rain was broken by singing, a man's sonorous baritone echoing through the woods behind them. The tone was mocking, but carried such an undercurrent of violence that Thomas's stomach clenched. He heard this voice often in dreams, and each time he woke before its owner could kill him. But now he was wide-awake.

> *The shipment nears, the cages fill,*
> *A voice rings out across the Tear,*
> *The cages burn, the Keep Lawn still,*
> *The Tearling weeps, the Queen is here.*

The singing stopped as suddenly as it had begun. Thomas squinted into the dusk. He could see nothing, but he didn't deceive himself that the blindness was mutual; that bastard had cat's eyes. Thomas's guards surrounded him, each of them peering into the foliage, swords drawn. He thought of telling them to save the effort, but remained silent. If they wanted to die bravely, it wasn't his business to tell them otherwise. They knew the identity of the singer, of course they did. The rain poured down even harder, the world narrowing to all of them standing there into the stillness. Thomas called out, "Let my men pass!"

Laughter echoed from multiple directions.

"These men who follow you to swear allegiance to the Mort bitch?" the Fetch called from his invisible vantage. "I'd sooner allow a pack of rogue dogs to live. Cowards and traitors, all of you!"

He broke into song again.

The Queen concealed now reappears,
The knife is thrown, the girl struck down,
Still she rises, eighteen long years,
Our Queen, and we care not which crown.

"They're singing it in every corner of the city!" the Fetch shouted, anger biting through the mockery now. "Who will ever compose a ballad for you, Thomas Raleigh? Who will extol your greatness?"

Tears filled Thomas's eyes, but in front of his men he didn't dare dash them away. He suddenly understood why, despite so many opportunities, the Fetch had never killed him before. The Fetch had been waiting for the girl, waiting for her to come out of hiding.

"I won't beg!" Thomas cried.

"I've heard you beg enough."

On Thomas's left, Keever went down with a horrible gurgling sound, a knife protruding from his throat. Arvis and Cowell crumpled next, pierced with arrows in their chests and heads. Thomas looked up and saw a monstrous black shape against the trees, descending on him from above. He shrieked in terror, but his voice cut off as the thing landed on him, knocking him from his horse. He hit his head, hard, on the ground and lay momentarily stunned, rocks digging into his back, the air full of his stallion's outraged scream, hooves tearing away through the woods.

When he opened his eyes, he was looking up at the Fetch, who perched like a giant bat on his chest, pinning him to the ground. The Fetch wore the same mask he donned each time he entered the Keep: a harlequin, designed for masquerades. Such masks could be bought at many shops in the city, but Thomas had never seen the like of this one anywhere else: the red-smudged mouth drawn up into a sneer and the eyes deep-socketed in black. Once, Thomas had woken deep within the womb of his quilts to find that face leaning over him, and he'd wet himself like a baby. The Fetch had waltzed out of his chamber and disappeared from the Keep like smoke, and Thomas had been so ashamed that he had never told anyone about the incident. It was almost possible to believe the Fetch an illusion until he inevitably reappeared, utterly substantial, always wearing his dreadful mask.

"Well, false prince?" The Fetch grabbed Thomas by the shoulders and shook him as a dog would a bone, slamming his head repeatedly against the ground. Thomas felt his teeth rattle. "No bribes to offer, Thomas? And where's your puppeteer? Hasn't she sorcery enough to get you out of this?"

Thomas remained mute. He had tried to argue with the Fetch before and found that he only made himself more vulnerable. The man was devilishly clever with words, and Thomas had thanked God more than once that the Fetch was forced to remain anonymous. As a public orator, he would have been devastating.

Then again, if he were a public orator, we could've taken and killed him long ago.

"The Census Bureau is in shambles," the Fetch whispered silkily. "They may construct new cages, but no one will forget what became of the old. If the girl lives, she'll undo much of your harm."

Thomas shook his head. "The Red Queen is coming. She'll

level the kingdom before the girl can accomplish anything."

The Fetch leaned closer, until he was only inches away. "The Mort bitch never cared for you, you know."

"I know," Thomas replied, and then clamped his mouth shut, wondering for perhaps the thousandth time at the source of the Fetch's information. His raids on Tear nobles had caused endless trouble, for the Fetch always seemed to know how taxes had been paid, where the money was stored, when the delivery would depart. Angry nobles came to the Keep to demand redress and Thomas had been forced to pay out large bribes in lieu of security, which made him even more despised with the peasantry. And where were those nobles now? Snug in their own castles while he was evicted from his, stuck in the forest with this blood-mad lunatic.

"Did you throw the knife?"

"What?"

The Fetch slapped him across the face. "Did you throw the knife at the girl?"

"No! Not me."

"Who?"

"I don't know! It was Thorne's plan. Some agent."

"What agent?"

"I don't know. My men were only to provide the diversion, I swear!"

The Fetch pressed both thumbs against Thomas's eyes and ground down until Thomas shrieked helplessly, but the sound vanished into the pouring rain without so much as an echo.

"What agent, Thomas?" the Fetch asked relentlessly. His thumbs jammed down harder and Thomas felt his left eye fill with hot liquid. "I'll begin cutting you next. Don't even kid yourself that I won't. A Mort agent?"

"I don't know!" Thomas cried, sobbing. "Thorne wouldn't tell me."

"That's right, Thomas, and do you know why? Because he knew you'd fuck it all up."

"It wasn't my fault!"

"You'd better think of something useful to tell me."

"Thorne has a backup plan!"

"I know of Thorne's backup plan, you miserable shit. I knew of it before he conceived it himself."

"Then what do you want?"

"Information, Thomas. Information about the Red Queen. You slept with her, this entire kingdom knows it. You must know something useful."

Thomas's eyes popped open. He tried to keep his face expressionless, but it clearly betrayed him, for the Fetch leaned forward again, his eyes gleaming behind the mask, so close that Thomas could smell horses and smoke and something else, a cloying scent that he felt he should recognize.

Fifteen years ago, he was in bed with her, the air still reeking of sex, and he had asked her what she wanted with him. Even back then, he hadn't been able to deceive himself that she cared about him. She fucked automatically, impersonally; he'd gotten better mechanics from mid-priced whores in the Gut. And yet he couldn't be free of her; she'd grown like a disease in his mind.

"Tell me something useful, and I will end your life without pain, Thomas. I swear it."

"Who is the father?" the Red Queen asked. When she turned to him in the dark, her eyes were glowing, a bright vulpine red. Thomas had reared back, scrambling to get out of bed, and she laughed, that deep bedroom chuckle that got him hard all on its own.

His eyes ached; he could see nothing but a haze of red from the left. The burning in his thighs was worse. But physical pain paled in comparison to the wave of self-loathing that swept him. The Fetch would have the information; it wouldn't even take very long.

"What d'you want to know for?" he asked thickly. She could do that, make him feel as drunk as though he'd put away eight pints of ale. "Elyssa's dead. What could it possibly matter now?"

"It doesn't," she replied with a smile. And Thomas, who could never tell what she was thinking, nevertheless saw that it did matter, that it mattered a great deal. She wanted to know, badly, and she knew that he had the answer. It was the only leverage he had ever held, and he had never deceived himself. If he told her, she might kill him.

"I don't know," he replied.

The light in her eyes faded then, and suddenly she was just a beautiful woman in bed with him, grabbing at his cock as though it were a toy. He had kept the one secret, but all other bulwarks had fallen; she'd stretched out before him and he'd agreed to find and murder Elyssa's daughter, his niece. He even remembered entering her and gasping, "Fuck you," to a different queen, one who'd been laid in her grave years before. But the Red Queen understood. She always understood, and she had given him what he needed.

"Well, Thomas?"

Thomas looked up at the Fetch, seeing him through a wash of tears. Time stretched years back and years forward, but nothing that came afterward ever had the power to wash away what came before. This order of things seemed monstrously unfair, even now when Thomas knew that he had only moments left. He gathered the remaining pieces of his courage. "If you take off the mask, I'll tell you everything I know about her."

The Fetch turned and took a quick survey of the action behind him. Squinting, his good eye blurry with moisture, Thomas saw that all three of his men were dead. Keever was the worst; he'd fallen with his throat gashed wide open, and now lay in a pool of his own blood, staring without sight.

Three men, masked and dressed in black, were crouched in the copse. They watched Thomas with a predatory, waiting quality, like dogs that had brought something to bay. But still he feared them less than he did their master. The Fetch was intelligent, diabolically so, and intelligent people devised intelligent cruelties. That was where the Red Queen had always excelled.

When he looked back up at the Fetch, the mask was gone, the man's face plain in the dying light. Thomas dashed the tears from his right eye and stared for a long minute, his mind blank. "But you're dead."

"Only on the inside."

"Is it magic?"

"The darkest kind, false prince. Now speak."

Thomas spoke. The words came slowly at first, caught in his throat, but then they became easier. The Fetch listened carefully, even sympathetically, asking occasional questions, and soon it seemed perfectly rational for the two of them to be sitting here together, telling tales while the night fell. Thomas told the Fetch the entire story, the story he had never told to anyone, each word easier than the last. Telling the truth was what a Queen's Guard would do, he realized, and that seemed so much the crux of the matter that he found himself repeating important points carefully, desperate to make the Fetch understand. He told all that he could remember, and when there was no more, he stopped.

The Fetch straightened and called out, "Bring an axe!"

Thomas clutched the Fetch's arm. "Won't you forgive me?"

"I will not, Thomas. I'll keep my word, and that's all."

Thomas closed his eyes. *Mortmesne, Mortmesne, burning bright*, he thought inexplicably. The Fetch would take his head, and Thomas found that he didn't begrudge him. Thomas thought of the Red Queen, the first time he'd ever seen her, a moment of such mixed terror and longing that it still had the power to freeze his heart. Then he thought of the girl, dragging herself from the floor with the knife in her back. Perhaps she could do it, extricate them all from the quagmire they'd created. Stranger things had happened in the history of the Tearling. Perhaps she was even the True Queen. Perhaps.

CHAPTER 11

THE APOSTATE

God's Church was a strange marriage of the hierarchy of pre-Crossing Catholicism and the beliefs of a particular sect of Protestantism that emerged in the early aftermath of the Landing. This sect was less concerned with the moral salvation of souls than with the biological salvation of the human race, a salvation viewed as God's great plan in raising the New World out of the sea.

This strange mixture of disparate elements was both a marriage of necessity and a harbinger of things to come. God's Church became a realist's religion, its interpretation of the gospels riddled with pragmatic holes, the influence of the pre-Crossing Bible limited to what would serve. Ecclesiastical discontent was inevitable; many priests, faced with the increasingly brutal political realities of theology in the Tearling, needed only the slightest touch and they were ready to topple.

—Religious Dimensions of the Tearling:
AN ESSAY, FATHER ANSELM

When Father Tyler entered the audience chamber, Kelsea's first impression was that he carried a great burden. The priest she remembered had been timid, not saturnine. He still moved cautiously, but now his shoulders sagged. This weight on him was new.

"Father," she greeted him. Father Tyler looked up toward the throne, his blue eyes flickering to meet hers and then darting away. Years of Carlin's tutelage had prepared Kelsea to find all priests either bombasts or zealots, but Father Tyler seemed neither. She wondered about his function in the Church. With such a quiet demeanor, he couldn't be a ceremonial priest. There were weak priests, certainly; Carlin had covered that territory extensively. But only a fool mistook caution for weakness.

"You're welcome here, Father. Please." She indicated the chair on her left.

Father Tyler hesitated, and no wonder; Mace was stationed behind the proffered chair. The priest approached as toward a chopping block, his white robe trailing behind him up the steps to the dais. He sat down without meeting Mace's eyes, but when he finally turned to Kelsea, his gaze was clear and direct.

More afraid of Mace than of me, Kelsea thought ruefully. Well, he wasn't the only one.

"Majesty," the priest opened, in a voice as thin as paper. "The Church, and the Holy Father in particular, send greetings and wishes for Your Majesty's health."

Kelsea nodded, keeping her expression pleasant. Mace had informed her that the Holy Father had entertained many Tear nobles in the Arvath over the past week. Mace had great respect for the guile of the Holy Father, and so Kelsea did not underestimate it either; the question was whether that guile extended to this junior priest, who stared at her expectantly.

Everyone is waiting for something from me, Kelsea thought tiredly. Her shoulder, which hadn't troubled her for at least several days, gave an answering throb. "Daylight runs, Father. What can I do for you?"

"The Church wishes to consult you about the matter of your Keep Priest, Majesty."

"I understood that a Keep Priest was a discretionary matter."

"Yes, well . . ." Father Tyler glanced around, as though looking for his next words on the floor. "The Holy Father requests a report on what your discretion has dictated."

"Which priest would they give me?"

His face twitched, betraying anxiety. "That matter hasn't been decided yet, Majesty."

"Of course it has, Father, or you wouldn't be here." Kelsea smiled. "You're no card player."

Father Tyler gave a surprised huff of laughter. "I've never played cards in my life."

"Are you close to the Holy Father?"

"I've met him personally twice, Lady."

"In the past two weeks, I'll wager. What are you really doing here, Father?"

"Just what I said, Majesty. I've come to consult you about appointment of your Keep Priest."

"And who would you recommend?"

"Me." The priest stared at her defiantly, his eyes full of a bitterness that seemed entirely impersonal. "I present myself and my spiritual knowledge for Your Majesty's service."

No one would ever know the courage it took Tyler to drag himself to the Keep on his devil's errand. If he succeeded, he would become a loathsome creature, an agent of duplicity. If he failed, the Holy Father would have his revenge on Tyler's library. For years, the Church had turned a blind eye to the growing collection of secular books in Tyler's quarters. The senior priests thought his hobby odd but harmless. Ascetics had few enough pleasures, and no one had a burning interest in pre-Crossing history anyway. Upon Tyler's death, his room would be cleaned out and all of his books would belong to the Church. No harm done.

But if the question were put to him, Tyler would be forced to admit that he wasn't a true ascetic. His love of the things of this world was as strong as anyone's. Wine, food, women, Tyler had let them all go easily. But his books . . .

The Holy Father wasn't a stupid man, and neither was Cardinal Anders. Two days ago, Tyler had awakened from the most vivid yet of his nightmares, in which he failed in his errand and returned to the Arvath to find his room locked from the inside, smoke pouring from beneath the door. Tyler knew it was a dream, for he was wearing robes of grey, and no priest of God's Church wore grey. But the knowledge that he was dreaming didn't change the horror. Tyler clawed at the doorknob, then tried to break the door down, until both of his thin shoulders were battered and he was screaming. When he finally gave up, he turned and found Cardinal Anders behind him, holding a copy of the Bible, his red robes aflame. He held the Bible out to Tyler, intoning solemnly, "You are part of God's great work."

For the past two days, Tyler had slept for only a few minutes at a time.

He thought that the Queen might burst out laughing when he finally got around to the real subject of his visit, but she didn't. She stared at him, and Tyler began to glimpse, if only dimly, how this girl could command such a fearsome character as the Mace. One could watch the Queen and almost see her thinking, a series of rapid and complex calculations. It made Tyler think of pre-Crossing computers, machines whose great value had essentially been the ability to do many things at once. He felt that hundreds of small variables went into the Queen's deliberation, and wondered what sort of variable he was.

"Accepted, with conditions."

Tyler struggled to hide his surprise. "Yes?"

"The Keep chapel will be converted into a school."

She watched him narrowly, clearly expecting an outburst, but Tyler said nothing. As far as he was concerned, God had never lived in that chapel. The Holy Father would rant and rave, but Tyler couldn't worry about that now. He was focused on the exact task he'd been given.

"You are not, at any time, to attempt to proselytize *me*," the Queen continued. "I'll have none of it. I won't silence you when you speak to others, but I may debate you to the best of my ability. If you can tolerate my arguments, you're free to minister to or convert any other occupant of this Keep, not excepting the pigs and chickens."

"You make sport of my religion, Lady," replied Tyler, but his words were automatic, without rancor. He had long outgrown the period of his life when atheism could rouse his temper.

"I make sport of all things inconsistent, Father."

Tyler's attention was drawn to the silver tiara on her head, the tiara that he had held in his hand. Again he was arrested by the revolving nature of history; it repeated itself in such extraordinary and unexpected ways. There had been another monarch, a pre-Crossing monarch, crowned amid bloodshed, never meant to ascend the throne. Where had it been . . . France? England?

The Holy Father won't care about the pre-Crossing, his mind whispered, and Tyler shook himself from such thoughts. "If there's no chapel in the Keep, Majesty, and you yourself reject the word of God, what exactly am I to do here?"

"You're an academic, I'm told, Father. What is your area of expertise?"

"History."

"Ah, good. That will be your use to me. I've read many works of history, but I've missed many also."

Tyler blinked. "What works of history?"

"Works mostly of the pre-Crossing. I flatter myself that I have a good knowledge of pre-Crossing history, but I'm poorly informed about early Tear history, and particularly the Crossing itself."

Tyler stuck on one piece of information. "What works of the pre-Crossing?"

The Queen smiled, slightly smug, the corners of her mouth tucking downward. "Come with me, Father."

The Queen's wound must have been well on the way to healing, for she rose from the throne without assistance. Tyler made no sudden moves as he followed her down the steps, avoiding the guards who shifted themselves expertly to follow her progress and block him off. He could sense the Mace right behind him, and resolved not to turn around.

The Queen walked in a purposeful way that many would describe as mannish. No one had taught her the graceful little steps that Tyler had observed in women born ladies. The Queen moved in great strides, so great that Tyler, whose arthritic hip never really quieted these days, was hard-pressed to keep up. He sensed again that he was in the middle of something extraordinary, and didn't know whether to thank God or not.

Pen Alcott walked a few feet ahead of Tyler, right on the Queen's heels, his hand on his sword. Tyler had assumed that the Mace would be her close guard; no doubt the whole kingdom had thought so. But the Mace had other business several days ago, in the south of the kingdom. News of the fire that destroyed the southern Graham stronghold had run like quicksilver through the Arvath. The Grahams were generous donors, and the senior Lord Graham was one of the Holy Father's old friends. The Holy Father had made it clear that Tyler should call the Mace and his mistress to account.

Later, Tyler thought. *For now, the exact task I was given.*

The Queen led Tyler down a long corridor behind the throne, a corridor with at least thirty doors. It was a servant's wing, Tyler realized with astonishment. Could anyone, even a queen, need that many servants?

Only a few of the doors were guarded. When the Queen approached one of them, the guard opened the door and then stood aside. Tyler found himself in a small chamber that was nearly empty, save for a desk and a few armchairs and sofas. It seemed an odd use of space. But then he halted just inside the threshold, dumbfounded.

The far wall was covered with books, beautiful leather-bound volumes in the rich hues that had been used before the Crossing: red, blue, and most astonishing of all, purple. Tyler had never seen purple leather, hadn't even known it was possible. Whatever the dye was, the formula had been lost.

At a gesture of invitation from the Queen, Tyler ventured closer, assessing the quality of the books with a collector's eye. His own collection was much smaller; many of his volumes were as ancient as these, but most were bound in cloth or paper, and required great care and constant treatment with fixatives to keep them from falling to pieces. Someone had taken equally conscientious care of these books. Their leather bindings appeared to be intact. There had to be well over a thousand, but Tyler noted – with some satisfaction – that he had many titles that the Queen's collection was lacking. His fingers itched to touch the books, but he didn't dare without her permission.

"You may, Father." When he looked up, he found her watching him with clear amusement, her mouth curled as if at a private joke. "I told you that you were no card player."

Tyler turned eagerly to the shelf. Several authors' names immediately leaped out at him. He took down a Tuchman book and opened it gently, grinning with delight. Most of his own books had been treated with an imperfect fixative, leaving their pages wrinkled and discolored. This book's pages were crisp yet soft, nearly white. There were also several inset pages of photographs, and these he perused closely, almost unaware that he was speaking at the same time. "I have several Tuchman books, but this one I've never seen. What's the subject?"

"Several eras of pre-Crossing history," the Queen replied, "used to illustrate the fact that folly inherently pervades government."

Despite his fascination with the book, something in the Queen's tone made Tyler close the cover. Turning, he found her staring at her books with utter devotion, like a lover. Or a priest.

"The Tearling is in crisis, Father."

Tyler nodded.

"The Arvath gave its blessing to the lottery."

Tyler nodded again, his face coloring. The shipment had rolled right past the Arvath for years, and even from his small window, Tyler had always been able to hear the tide of misery below. Father Wyde said that sometimes the families followed the shipment for miles; rumor had it that one family had even walked behind the cages all the way to the foothills of Mount Willingham. As far as Tyler knew, Father Timpany had given the Regent absolution for his sins with the sanction of the Holy Father. It was so much easier for Tyler to ignore these matters in his room, with his mind wrapped in his studies, his bookkeeping. But here, with the Queen staring at him, her expression demanding explanation, the things Tyler knew deep down couldn't be so easily dismissed.

"So what do you think?" the Queen asked. "Have I pursued folly since taking the throne?"

The question seemed academic, but Tyler understood that it wasn't. It hit him suddenly that the Queen was only nineteen years old, and that she had cheated death for years. And yet her first act upon arrival had been to poke a stick at a hornets' nest.

Why, she's frightened, he realized. He would never have considered the possibility, but of course she would be. He could see that she had already taken responsibility for her actions, that consequences already sat on her shoulders. Tyler wanted to say something reassuring but found that he couldn't, for he didn't know her. "I can't speak to political salvation, Majesty. I'm a spiritual adviser."

"No one needs spiritual advice right now."

Tyler spoke more sharply than he intended. "Those who cease to worry about their souls often find them difficult to reclaim later, Majesty. God doesn't make such distinctions."

"How do you expect anyone to believe in your God in these times?"

"I believe in my God, Majesty."

"Then you're a fool."

Tyler straightened and spoke coldly. "You're welcome to believe what you like, and think what you like of my church, but don't malign my faith. Not in front of me."

"You don't give the Queen orders!" the Mace snarled.

Tyler cringed; he had forgotten that the Mace was there. But the Mace fell silent as suddenly as he'd begun, and when Tyler turned back to the Queen, he found her wearing an odd smile, both rueful and satisfied.

"You are genuine," she murmured. "Forgive me, but I had to know. There must be so few of you living over in that golden nightmare."

"That's unfair, Majesty. I know many good and devout men in the Arvath."

"Was it a good and devout man who sent you to keep an eye on me, Father?"

Tyler couldn't answer.

"Will you live in here with us?"

Thinking of his books, he shook his head. "I'd prefer to remain in the Arvath."

"Then I propose an exchange," the Queen replied briskly. "You take the book in your hand and borrow it for a week. Next Sunday, you'll return it to me, at which time you may borrow another. But you'll also bring me one of your own books, one I don't have."

"A library system," Tyler replied with a smile.

"Not exactly, Father. Clerks are already at work copying my own books, several at a time. When you loan me a book, they'll copy it as well."

"To what purpose?"

"I'll hold master copies here in the Keep, but sooner or later, I'll find someone who can construct a printing press."

Tyler inhaled sharply. "A press?"

"I see this land flowing with books, Father. Widespread literacy. Books everywhere, as common as they used to be in circulation before the Crossing, affordable even for the poor."

Tyler stared at her, shocked. The necklace on her chest twinkled; he could have sworn it had winked at him.

"Can't you see it?"

And after another moment, Tyler could. The idea was staggering. Printing presses meant bookshops and libraries. New stories transcribed. New histories.

Later, Tyler would realize that his decision was made then, that there was never any other path for him. But in the moment, he felt only shock. He stumbled away from the bookshelves and came face-to-face with the Mace, whose face had darkened. Tyler hoped the man's anger wasn't directed toward himself, for he found the Mace terrifying. But no, the Mace was looking at the books.

An extraordinary certainty dawned in Tyler's mind. He tried to dismiss it, but the thought persisted: the Mace could not read. Tyler felt a stab of pity, but turned quickly away before it showed on his face. "Well, it's quite a dream, Majesty."

Her face hardened, the corners of her mouth tucking in. The Mace gave a quiet grunt of satisfaction, which only seemed to irritate the Queen further. Her voice, when she spoke, was businesslike, all passion vanished. "Sunday next, I'll expect you. But you're welcome in my court anytime, Father."

Tyler bowed, feeling as though someone had grabbed him and shaken him hard. *This is why I never leave my room*, he thought. *So much safer there.*

He turned and trudged back toward the audience chamber, clutching the book in his hand, nearly oblivious to the three guards who followed him. The Holy Father would undoubtedly want an immediate report, but Tyler could sneak into the Arvath through the tradesmen's entrance. It was Tuesday, and Brother Emory would be on duty; he was young and lazy, and often forgot to report arrivals. Tyler might read well over a hundred pages before the Holy Father knew he'd returned.

"And Father?"

Tyler turned and found the Queen seated on her throne, her chin propped on one hand. The Mace stood beside her, as forbidding as ever, his hand on his sword.

"Majesty?"

She grinned impishly, looking her true age for the first time since Tyler had seen her. "Don't forget to bring me a book."

On Monday Kelsea sat on her throne, biting relentlessly at the inside of her cheek. Technically, she was holding audience, but what she was really doing was allowing various interested parties to have a look at her, and looking at them in turn. After the incident with the assassin, she'd thought that Mace might cancel this event, but now he seemed to consider it even more important that Kelsea show her face. Her first audience went ahead on schedule, although the entire Queen's Guard had been stationed in the audience chamber, even those who usually worked the night and slept during the day.

True to his word, Mace had moved the great silver throne, along with its dais, into the Queen's Wing. After perhaps an hour perched on the throne, Kelsea discovered that silver was hard, and worse, it was *cold*. She longed for the comfort of her old, worn armchair. She couldn't even slouch; there were too many eyes on her. A crowd of nobles thronged the room, many of them the same people who had attended her crowning. She saw the same clothing, the same hairstyles, and the same excess.

Kelsea had spent long hours preparing for this audience with Mace and Arliss, as well as with Marguerite, who had a surprising amount of information to share about the Regent's allies in the nobility. The Regent had kept her nearby at all times, even while doing business. This further evidence of her uncle's poor judgment came as no surprise to Kelsea, but it made her feel despondent all the same.

"Are you happy here?" Kelsea had asked Marguerite, when they finished talking for the night.

"Yes," replied Marguerite, so quickly that Kelsea didn't think she understood the question. Marguerite knew a fair amount of Tear, but she'd been delighted to find that Kelsea spoke good Mort, so they spoke in that language. Kelsea tried her question again, making sure she was using the correct words.

"I understand that you were delivered here, against your will, from Mortmesne. Don't you want to go home?"

"No. I like taking care of the children, and there's nothing for me in Mortmesne."

"Why?" Kelsea asked, confused. She found Marguerite to be both educated and intelligent, and when it came to human nature the woman was smart as a whip. Kelsea had been pondering what to do about the rest of the Regent's women; she had no urge to have them all invade the Queen's Wing, nor could she offer them any sort of gainful employment. But she thought they deserved *something* from the Crown, since their lives couldn't have been easy.

Marguerite had assured Kelsea that the other women would be snapped up quickly as paid companions by nobles, most of whom had cast a jealous eye on the Regent's women for years. This was useful information, if an extremely unwelcome insight into the male psyche, and Marguerite had been right; when Coryn went to make sure that the Regent had cleared out, the women and their belongings were gone as well.

"Because of this," Marguerite replied, running an explanatory hand up her body and circling it around her face. "This determines what I am."

"Being beautiful?"

"Yes."

Kelsea stared at her, bewildered. She would give anything to look like Marguerite. The Fetch's voice echoed in her head, always within cutting reach: *Far too plain for my taste.* She had already noticed how, on those rare occasions when Marguerite emerged from the nursery, the guards' eyes followed her across the room. There was no overtly boorish behavior, nothing for which Kelsea could take them to task, but sometimes she wanted to reach out and slap them, scream in their faces: *Look at me! I'm valuable too!* Eyes followed Kelsea across the room as well, but it wasn't the same at all.

If I looked like Marguerite, the Fetch would worship at my feet.

Some of this must have shown on Kelsea's face, for Marguerite smiled sadly. "You think of beauty only as a blessing, Majesty, but it brings its own punishments. Believe me."

Kelsea nodded, trying to look sympathetic, but in truth she was skeptical. Beauty was currency. For every man who valued Marguerite less because of her beauty, there would be a hundred men, and many women as well, who automatically valued her more. But Kelsea liked Marguerite's grave intelligence, so she tried to curb her resentment, though something inside told her that it would be a constant struggle, to look at this woman every day without jealousy.

"What's Mortmesne like?"

"Different from the Tearling, Majesty. At first glance, better. Not so many poor and hungry. Order in the streets. But look long enough, and you will notice that all eyes are afraid."

"Afraid of what?"

"Of her."

"They're afraid here, too, but not of me. Of the lottery."

"Once, perhaps, Majesty."

The people in the audience chamber certainly weren't afraid of Kelsea. Some of them looked at her wistfully, some with suspicion. Mace, not liking the pockets of shadow created by the crowd, had ordered the walls hung with extra torches for the audience, and he had also produced a herald from somewhere, a thin, harmless boy-man named Jordan with an extraordinarily deep, clear voice, who announced each personage before the throne. Those who wanted to have private speech with Kelsea came forward only after being searched for weapons and cleared by Mhurn. Some had come simply to swear fealty, perhaps in the hope of gaining access to the treasury or putting Kelsea off her guard. Many of them tried to kiss her hand; one noble, Lord Perkins, even succeeded in planting a moist, sticky patch on her knuckle before Kelsea could yank free. She tucked both hands inside the black folds of her skirt to keep them safe.

Andalie sat on a chair to Kelsea's right, the seat several inches lower so that she appeared shorter than Kelsea. Kelsea had argued against this arrangement, but Andalie and Mace had overruled her. As Lord Perkins and his retinue left the dais, Andalie offered a cup of water, which Kelsea accepted gratefully. Her wound was healing well, and she could sit up for longer periods now, but she had been exchanging pleasantries more or less nonstop for two hours and her voice was becoming unwieldy.

A noble named Killian came forward with his wife. Kelsea searched through the files in her mind and placed the man: Marguerite had told her that Lord Killian liked to gamble at cards and that he had once knifed another noble over a disputed hand of poker. None of his four children had ever run afoul of the lottery. The Killians looked more like twins than husband and wife; both had round, well-fed faces, and both eyed her with the same expression Kelsea had seen on the faces of many nobles over the course of the day: smiles on top and craft underneath. She exchanged pleasantries with the pair and accepted a beautiful tapestry that the wife assured her had been woven by her own hands. Kelsea very much doubted this; the era in which noblewomen actually had to do their own handwork was long gone, and the tapestry bespoke considerable skill.

When the Killians' audience was over, Kelsea watched the pair retreat. She hadn't liked most of the nobles she'd met today. They were dangerously complacent. Even the inadequate old concept of noblesse oblige had fallen by the wayside in this kingdom, and the privileged refused to look beyond their own walls and gardens. It was a problem that had contributed greatly to the Crossing; Kelsea could almost feel Carlin hovering somewhere close by, her face pinched in its old disapproval as she spoke of the ruling classes of times long gone.

Mace was peering toward the end of the hall, and as the Killians disappeared and Kelsea's guard began to relax, he called a sharp command to remain at attention. A solitary man was trudging toward the throne, his face nearly hidden under a thick black beard. At the edge of Kelsea's vision, Andalie made an involuntary movement, her hands stiffening.

Kelsea tapped her fingers on the silver arm of her throne, debating, while the man was searched. She looked to Andalie, who was staring at her husband with deep, dark eyes, her hands clenched tightly in her lap.

Mace had descended to the foot of the dais and taken up what Kelsea thought of as his ready pose, a stance so casual that one who didn't know Mace might think him lounging. But if Andalie's husband should move a muscle in the wrong direction, Mace would have him down. The husband seemed to know as well; his eyes twitched toward Mace and he halted of his own volition, announcing, "I am Borwen! I come to demand the return of my wife and children!"

"You demand nothing here," Kelsea replied.

He glowered at her for a moment. "Ask, then."

"You'll address the Queen properly," Mace growled, "or you'll be removed from this hall."

Borwen took several deep breaths, his right hand creeping to his left bicep and feeling it gently, as though for comfort. "I ask Your Majesty for the return of my wife and children."

"Your wife is free to leave, of her own volition, at any

time," Kelsea replied. "But if you wish to ask her anything here, you'll first account for the marks on her skin."

Borwen hesitated, and Kelsea could see countless excuses tumbling through his head. He mumbled a reply.

"Repeat!"

"Majesty, she wasn't an obedient wife."

Andalie snickered softly. Kelsea shrank from the sound, which held murder. "Borwen, are you a believer in God's Church?"

"I go every Sunday, Majesty."

"A wife is to be obedient to the husband, yes?"

"Such is the word of God."

"I see." Kelsea leaned back, studying him. How on earth had Andalie ended up wed to this creature? It would have taken a braver woman than Kelsea to ask her. "And did your manner of correction make her obedient?"

"I was within my rights."

Kelsea opened her mouth, not knowing what would come out, but fortunately she was stalled by Andalie, who stood to her full height and said, "Majesty, I pray you, do not place myself or any of my children under this man's dominion."

Kelsea reached out and clasped her wrist. "You know I wouldn't."

Andalie looked down, and Kelsea thought she saw a flash of warmth in those grey eyes. Then she was simply Andalie again, her face blank and cold. "I know it."

"What would you have me do here?" Kelsea asked.

"I care little, so long as he never comes near my children again."

Andalie's tone was as flat as her expression. Kelsea stared at her for a moment, a terrible picture forming in her mind, but before it could take shape, she whipped back to Borwen.

"Denied. On the day your wife wishes, she can return to you with my blessing. But I won't compel it."

Borwen's black eyes blazed, and a strange, feral sound emerged from his beard. "Is Your Majesty ignorant of the word of God?"

Kelsea frowned. The crowd, which had seemed sleepy, was fully awake now, looking between her and Borwen as though the conversation were a tennis volley. Any reply she made would get back to the Church, and she couldn't lie; there were too many people in this hall. She arranged her words carefully before speaking. "History is full of failed kingdoms that purported to be ruled solely by the word of God. The Tearling is not a theocracy, and I must look to more sources than the Bible." She felt her voice sharpening, but couldn't stop it. "The word of God aside, Borwen, it seems to me that if you truly deserved the sort of obedience you crave, you would be able to compel it with some lever besides your fists."

Color rose in Borwen's face, and his eyes squinted down to black slits. Dyer, at the foot of the dais, advanced a few steps to stand in his path, one hand on his sword.

"Is there a recorder here?" Kelsea asked Mace.

"Somewhere. I sent him into the crowd, but he should be listening."

Kelsea raised her voice and spoke over the hall. "My throne won't tolerate abuse, no matter what God says about it. Husband, wife, child, it makes no matter; the one who lays violent hands on the other will account for it."

She focused on Borwen again. "You, Borwen, as the first offender before me, won't be punished. You provide the example around which I structure my law. But if you ever come before me again, or before any member of my judiciary, on a similar charge, the law will deal heavily with you."

"I've been charged with nothing!" Borwen shouted, his heavy face crimson with rage. "I come to reclaim my stolen wife and children, and find myself put upon! It's no justice!"

"Have you ever heard of the equitable doctrine of clean hands, Borwen?"

"No, and I care not!" he snarled. "I'm a man robbed, and I'll say so before all the Tearling, if I must, to gain justice!"

Mace moved forward, but Kelsea snapped her fingers. "No."

"But Lady—"

"I don't know what's gone on here in the past, Lazarus, but we don't punish people for words. We'll ask him to leave, and if he doesn't, you can remove him as you like."

Borwen was breathing hard now, great hoarse gasps; the sound reminded Kelsea of a slumbering brown bear that she and Barty had once come upon in the woods. Barty had given Kelsea a signal, and they had quietly reversed their steps. But the man in front of Kelsea was something entirely different, and she thought suddenly that she would enjoy fighting him, even with her bare hands, even if she took a beating for it.

I have too much anger in me, Kelsea realized. But the thought was a proud one: whatever her other failings, she knew that the anger would always be there, a deep and tappable well of force. Carlin would be disappointed, but Kelsea was the Queen now, not a frightened child, and she had learned much since leaving the cottage. She would be able to stand before Carlin and account for herself ... not without fear, perhaps, but at least without the debilitating certainty that Carlin always knew best. Carlin had been right about many things, but even she had limitations; Kelsea saw them clearly now, outlined in bright colors. Carlin was without passion, without imagination, and Kelsea had plenty of both. Looking at the man below her, she saw an easy way out.

"Borwen, you've taken too much of my time with this nonsense, and you'll leave my hall now. You're free to charge my throne with any sort of injustice, but know that I will match it with your wife's account of you. The choice is yours."

Borwen's mouth worked, but words had deserted him. His black eyes rolled like those of a cornered animal, and he slammed one large fist into his other hand, glaring up at Andalie. "Still haughty as ever, aren't we? Does she know where you were raised? Does she know you have Mort blood?"

"Enough!" Kelsea pushed herself up from the throne, ignoring the protest from her shoulder. Her sapphire had come roaring to life; she felt it, a small, violent animal beneath her dress. "You've reached the end of my patience. You'll leave this hall immediately, or I'll allow Lazarus to remove you by any means he likes."

Borwen backed away, smiling triumphantly. "Mort she is! Infected!"

"Lazarus, go."

Mace leaped toward Borwen, who turned tail and sprinted toward the doors. Appreciative laughter rippled from the crowd as he fled up the aisle. Andalie reseated herself beside Kelsea, her face as blank as ever. Once Borwen disappeared, Mace stopped his halfhearted pursuit and returned, his eyes sparkling with mirth. But Kelsea rubbed her own eyes wearily. What next?

"Lady Andrews, Majesty!" the herald cried.

A woman stormed toward the throne. Today her hair was covered by an elaborate hat, bright purple velvet decorated with purple silk ribbons and peacock feathers. But Kelsea recognized that pinched, displeased mouth with no difficulty at all.

"Oh, for God's sake," she muttered to Mace. "Didn't we pay her for the damned tiara?"

"We did, Lady. Overpaid, actually. The Andrews are a house of chiselers, and Arliss didn't want them to have any cause for complaint."

Lady Andrews halted at the foot of the steps. She was much older than she'd seemed in the dim light of the throne room, perhaps as old as forty, and her face appeared to have been pulled unnaturally taut. Cosmetic surgery? There were no plastic surgeons in the Tearling, but it was rumored that Mortmesne had revived the practice. Tear nobles might dare the journey, particularly nobles like this one. Lady Andrews wore a saccharine smile, but her eyes said it all.

She hates me, Kelsea realized with some bemusement. Didn't the woman have anything to worry about besides her hair?

"I've come to swear fealty before Your Majesty," Lady Andrews announced. She had a distinctive voice, so raspy and hoarse that Kelsea wondered if she was a smoker, like Arliss. Or perhaps it was merely excessive drink.

"I'm honored."

"I bring Your Majesty a gift, a gown of Callaen silk."

The gown was beautiful, made of a bright royal blue silk that gleamed in the torchlight. But when Lady Andrews held it up, Kelsea saw that it was perhaps three sizes too small, tailored for a tall, slender woman like Lady Andrews herself. After considering it for a moment, Kelsea decided that the woman had sized the gown deliberately out of spite, just for the joy of having it be too small when Kelsea tried it on.

"Thank you," Kelsea replied, feeling a small smile play on her lips. "How kind."

Arliss took the dress and placed it among the steadily growing stack of gifts. Some of them were truly dreadful, given by people who apparently had the same taste in art as the Regent. But all of the gifts were at least valuable in materials; no one was quite brave enough to give Kelsea something that was junk. She had already decided to sell most of them, but Arliss was well ahead of her. He eyed the blue gown with a calculating gaze for a moment before making a note in his little book.

"I've also come to ask what Your Majesty means to do about Mortmesne."

"I beg your pardon?"

Lady Andrews smiled, that deceptively sweet smile that seemed built to hide gnashing teeth. "You've violated the Mort Treaty, Majesty. I own lands toward the end of the Crithe, in the eastern Almont. I have much to lose."

Kelsea snuck a glance at Mace and found him staring out across the crowd. "I have more to lose than you, Lady Andrews. More land, and my life as well. So why don't you let me worry about it?"

"My tenants are alarmed, Majesty. I can't say I blame them. They stand right in the path to New London, and they suffered cruelly in the last invasion."

"I'm sure you cared deeply then as well," Kelsea murmured. Her sapphire gave a sharp burn against her chest, and she suddenly saw a picture in her mind: a tall tower, its doors closed, its gates barricaded. "Did you and your guard go out to defend them?"

Lady Andrews opened her mouth, then paused.

"You didn't, did you? You remained in your tower and left them to their own devices."

The older woman's face stiffened. "I saw no point in dying with them."

"I'm sure you didn't."

"What is your grievance with the shipment, Majesty?"

"My grievance?"

"It's a fair system. We owe Mortmesne."

Kelsea leaned forward. "Do you have children, Lady Andrews?"

"No, Majesty."

Of course not, Kelsea thought. Children conceived by this woman would only be cannibalized by her womb. She raised her voice. "Then you don't risk much in the lottery, do you? You have no children, you don't look strong enough for labor, and you're really too old to appeal to anyone for sex."

Lady Andrews's eyes widened in fury. Several feminine giggles echoed across the hall behind her.

"I'll listen to complaints about Mortmesne and the lottery from people who actually have something to lose," Kelsea announced to the hall. "People with a stake in the shipment can come and raise this issue with me any time I hold audience."

She turned back to Lady Andrews. "But not you."

Lady Andrews's hands had clutched into claws. The nails were long hooks, manicured a bright purple. Deep pockets of red had emerged in the fleshless crescents beneath her eyes. Kelsea wondered if the woman would actually try to strike with her bare hands; it seemed unlikely, but Kelsea wasn't sure. Neither was Mace; he'd moved a few inches closer, and now he stared at Lady Andrews with his most forbidding expression.

What does she see when she looks in the mirror? Kelsea wondered. How could a woman who looked so old still place so much importance on being attractive? She had read about this particular delusion in books many times, but it was different to see it in practice. And for all the anguish that Kelsea's own reflection had caused her lately, she saw now that there was something far worse than being ugly: being ugly and thinking you were beautiful.

Lady Andrews recovered quickly, though her low voice still shook with anger. "And what have you to lose, Majesty? You spent your childhood in hiding. Has your name ever gone into the lot?"

Kelsea flushed, surprised into silence; this was something she'd never even considered. Of course her Glynn name had never been in the lottery, since no one knew that Kelsea Glynn existed. But was there even a lottery marker for Kelsea Raleigh? Of course not, no more than there had been a marker for Elyssa Raleigh or Thomas Raleigh or any of the countless parade of nobles who could afford to buy their way free of the lot.

Lady Andrews took another step forward now, undaunted by the proximity of Mace, her smile pure spite. "In fact, Majesty, you risk less than any of us, don't you? If she invades again, you merely barricade yourself in your own tower, just as I did. Only your tower is even taller."

Kelsea colored, thinking of the several rooms down the hallway filled with siege supplies: provisions and weapons, torches and barrels of oil. What could she do, promise to fight alongside the populace of New London? Seconds passed, and the people in the hall began to whisper. She looked to Mace and Pen, but found them stumped as well. Lady Andrews was grinning, the grin of a hunter with cornered prey, all perfectly shaped fangs. The thought of being cornered by this woman made Kelsea die inside, in some deep, dark place where none of Carlin's lessons had penetrated.

In desperation, Kelsea grabbed her necklace and drew the sapphire out, clutching it tightly in one hand. She would take any answer it had, but the jewel gave her nothing, not even a hint of heat. The murmuring grew louder, echoing off the walls. Any moment now, someone would begin to laugh, and this creature would win.

"I was one of your villagers, Lady."

Kelsea looked past Lady Andrews and saw that Mhurn had stepped forward. His face was white as ever, his bloodshot eyes pinned on Lady Andrews, but for once, his pallor was not from sleeplessness. It was from fury.

"Who the fuck are you?" Lady Andrews snarled at him. "A guard who dares to address a noble direct? You'd be whipped for that in my audience chamber."

Mhurn ignored her. "We tried, you know. My wife had never learned to ride, and my daughter was ill. We had no chance to outrun the Mort on the horizon. We went to the gate of the castle and begged for shelter, and I saw you up at the window, staring down at us. You had all those rooms, yet you refused to give us even a single one."

Kelsea was suddenly overcome with memory: the day in the Almont, the farmers working in the fields and the tall tower of brick. Lady Andrews had begun to back away, but Mhurn advanced, and Kelsea saw the glint of tears in his eyes. "I've known the Queen barely a month, but I promise you, when the Mort come, she will try to cram the entire Tearling into this Keep, and she won't care how recently they've bathed or how poor they are. She'll make room for all."

Lady Andrews stared at him, her mouth open wide, utterly speechless. Mace went to Mhurn and spoke to him in a low voice. Mhurn nodded and walked quickly behind the throne toward the guard quarters. Kelsea remembered the day, earlier this week, when she had passed Mhurn to go out on the balcony and been overwhelmed by suspicion. She looked around at the other guards stationed on the chamber, nineteen of them now, their faces hard. Did they all have similar stories? She felt suddenly wretched. Even if one of them was guilty, how could she suspect any of them?

"I demand punishment, Majesty!" Lady Andrews had recovered her voice. "Give me that guard!"

Kelsea burst out laughing, true laughter that rang across the audience chamber. It felt wonderful, more so as Lady Andrews's face turned a bright, choleric purple.

"I'll tell you what you do, Lady Andrews. You take your dress and get the hell out of my Keep."

Lady Andrews opened her mouth, but for a moment nothing came out. In the space of seconds, a thousand tiny lines seemed to have sprung up in the taut skin of her face. Arliss had produced the dress and now offered it to Lady Andrews, though his lowered brows told Kelsea that they'd be discussing it later.

Lady Andrews snatched the dress back and stomped away with her neck hunched into her shoulders, her gait showing her age. As she went up the aisle, many in the crowd gave her disgusted glances, but Kelsea was unimpressed; they'd likely behaved no better during the last invasion. As on the day of her crowning, there were no poor here. She would have to change that. Next week when she held audience, she would tell Mace to throw the doors open to the first few hundred who came.

"Are there any more?" she asked Mace.

"Don't think so, Lady." Mace raised his eyebrows toward the herald, who shook his head. Mace made a cutting motion, and the herald announced, "This audience is concluded! Please proceed in an orderly fashion through the doors!"

"He's good, that herald," Kelsea remarked. "Hard to believe that much sound could come from such a slight boy."

"Thin men always make the best heralds, Lady, don't ask me why. I'll let him know you were pleased."

Kelsea sank back against the throne, wishing again that it were her armchair. Leaning back in this thing was like reclining against a rock. She decided to pile it with cushions when there was no one around.

Orderly fashion was a bit much to hope for; the crowd had bottlenecked at the door, each of them apparently feeling that he deserved to go through first.

"God, what a scrum," Pen remarked, chuckling. Kelsea took the opportunity to scratch her nose, which had been itching madly for some time, then beckoned Andalie. "I'm fine for the night, Andalie. You're off duty."

"Thank you, Lady," Andalie replied, and left the dais.

When the crowd had finally disappeared and her guard had begun to bolt the doors, Kelsea asked, "So what do you think Lady Andrews was trying to do?"

"Ah, she was set up to it," Mace replied. "Just making trouble."

Arliss, who'd been listening from his place at the foot of the dais, nodded. "Scene had Thorne all over it, but he wasn't stupid enough to show up today."

Kelsea frowned. Thanks to Mace and Arliss, she now understood much more about Thorne's Census Bureau.

Although it had originally been created as a tool of the Crown, it had taken on a terrible life of its own, becoming such a power in the Tearling that it rivaled God's Church. The Census was too big to be shut down wholesale; it would need to be dismantled piece by piece, and the biggest piece was Thorne himself. "I won't have Thorne sabotage what we build. He needs to go, with a decent pension."

"The Census Bureau has most of the educated men in the kingdom, Lady," Mace cautioned. "If you try to break it up, you'll have to find them all gainful employment."

"Perhaps they could become teachers. Or tax collectors, I don't know."

She would have to wait to see what they thought of this idea, for Wellmer's stomach suddenly gurgled quite loudly in the silence, prompting muted laughter from the group of guards. Milla was cooking dinner now, and the scent of garlic permeated the hall. Wellmer turned tomato-red, but Kelsea smiled and said, "We're done. I'll eat in my chamber tonight; you're welcome to the table. Someone bring Mhurn some food and force him to eat."

They bowed in unison, and several guards headed off to the kitchen while the rest disappeared down the corridor to their families and the guard quarters. Milla had put her foot down and declared that she wouldn't have twenty guards invade her kitchen every mealtime, so now several of the guards worked as servers for the rest of the families at each meal. They'd created some sort of system very diplomatically among themselves, and Mace hadn't needed to intervene. A minor detail, but Kelsea felt that it was a positive note, a sign of community.

"Lazarus, wait a moment."

Mace leaned down to her. "Lady?"

381

"Any progress on locating Barty and Carlin?"

Mace straightened. "Not yet, Lady."

Kelsea gritted her teeth. She didn't want to hassle him, but she wanted Barty, wanted to see his crinkle-eyed smile more than ever. The urge to see Carlin was even more urgent somehow. "Did you search the village?"

"There has been a lot to do, Majesty. I will move on it shortly."

Kelsea narrowed her eyes. "Lazarus, you're lying to me."

Mace stared at her without expression.

"Why are you lying?"

"Lady!" Venner called to her from the hallway. "Your armor is ready!"

Kelsea turned, irritated. "Why are you telling me this, Venner?"

"Fell's been down sick."

Another lie. She imagined that Venner had finally been forced to procure the armor himself. But her appetite for conflict was dwindling apace with her growing desire for whatever Milla was preparing in the kitchen. "We'll take a look at it during tomorrow's shaming exercise."

Venner's mouth twitched, and he went on to the kitchen. Kelsea turned back to continue with Mace and found him gone, vanished from the audience chamber like smoke.

"Sneaky bastard," she muttered. What had happened to Barty and Carlin? Had they fallen ill? It was a long journey south for two old people during the winter. Had the Caden found them? No, Barty knew how to cover his tracks. But something was wrong. She could see it on Mace's face.

She descended the dais, Pen in tow. The smell of garlic made her stomach rumble, and Kelsea fought back a giggle of bitter amusement; even anxiety couldn't dull her appetite. She looked for Mace in the hallway, but he'd hidden himself somewhere. Kelsea thought about demanding his whereabouts from Coryn, who was on duty at the balcony room, but that seemed childish, so she went on down the hallway with a heavy tread.

At the door of her chamber, Kelsea heard Andalie speak her name in the next room over and halted automatically, Pen following suit behind.

"I assure you, the Queen is afraid."

"She doesn't look afraid." That was Andalie's oldest girl, Aisa, her voice easily recognizable, right on the cusp of deepening and full of discontent.

"But she is, love," Andalie replied. "She hides her fear in order to lessen ours."

Kelsea leaned against the wall, knowing that eavesdropping was rude but unable to walk away. Andalie remained a mystery. Even Mace could find nothing of her ancestry or history beyond the fact that she was half Mort, and Andalie had disclosed that fact herself. It was as if she'd dropped from the sky at the age of fifteen and married her worthless husband; all before that was dark.

"This kingdom hasn't seen anything extraordinary, or even particularly good, in a long time," Andalie continued. "The Tearling needs a queen. A True Queen. And if she lives, Queen Kelsea will be exactly that. Maybe even a queen of legend."

Kelsea's eyes widened and she turned to Pen, who placed a finger to his lips.

"I'd like to be part of a legend, Maman."

"That's why we stay." Andalie's voice shifted, moving closer now. Kelsea crooked a finger at Pen and they slipped into Kelsea's chamber. Pen closed the door behind them, muttering, "I told you she had the sight."

"And I agreed with you. Still, it's a mistake to put too much stock in visions."

Here in the antechamber, Pen had set up his own bed, a messy affair of thrown-together sheets and blankets that didn't match. Dirty clothes were strewn across the floor, and Pen did his best to kick them under the bed. A knock came at the door, and he opened it to admit Milla, carrying two trays of what looked like beef stew. Milla had already staked out her right to bring Kelsea's food personally; according to Mace, she also tasted every dish of Kelsea's food before it left the kitchen. This was something of an empty gesture, since so many poisons came with a time delay, but Kelsea had been moved nonetheless.

"Want to eat with me?" she asked Pen.

"All right." He followed her through the archway into her chamber, where Mace had set up a small table for the nights when Kelsea wanted to eat alone. Milla set the two trays on the table, bowed to Kelsea, and vanished.

Kelsea dug into the stew. It was as good as everything Milla cooked, but tonight Kelsea ate automatically, her mind on Andalie's oldest girl. If she understood right, some or all of Andalie's children had been subjected to abuse, and such treatment always left scars. The girl was also entering adolescence, and Kelsea remembered *that* transition well enough: the feeling of helplessness, and most of all the quick anger at adults' failure to understand what was important. One day, when Kelsea was perhaps twelve or thirteen, she had found herself screaming at Barty for moving something on her desk.

She looked up and found Pen watching her, his gaze speculative. "What?"

"I enjoy watching you think. It's like watching two dogs fight in a pen."

"You watch dogfighting?"

"Not by choice. It's a vile sport. But my father ran dogpen fights when I was growing up. That's how I got my name."

"Where was this?"

Pen shook his head. "When we join the Queen's Guard, we earn the right to leave our past behind. Besides, you're just crusader enough to imprison my father."

"Maybe I should. He sounds like a butcher."

Kelsea regretted the statement as soon as it came out of her mouth. But Pen only considered her words for a moment before replying mildly, "Perhaps he was once. But now he's only a blind old man, unable to harm anyone. There's danger in a system of justice that makes no allowance for circumstance."

"I agree."

Pen went back to his stew, and Kelsea to hers. But after another moment, she put down her spoon. "I'm worried about that girl."

"Andalie's oldest?"

"Yes."

"She's troubled, Lady. We found no information on Andalie before her marriage, and believe me, Mace and I looked hard. But their family life was a different matter."

"Different how?"

Pen paused for a moment, and Kelsea could see him framing his answer. "Lady, it was common knowledge in their neighborhood that Andalie's husband had a taste for young girls. His daughters were the worst case, but not the only ones."

Kelsea swallowed her revulsion, striving for a businesslike

tone. "Carlin told me that with no real courts, communities typically take care of these problems themselves. Why didn't they deal with him?"

"Because Andalie forbade it."

"That makes no sense. I would expect Andalie to kill her husband herself, before anyone else had a chance."

"Me as well, Lady, but for that riddle I could find no answer. The neighbors were happy enough to talk about Borwen, but not about Andalie. They thought her a witch."

"Why?"

"No one would say. Perhaps it's just her way of looking through you. *I* fear Andalie, Lady, for all that I fear no man with a sword."

"I do too."

Pen took another spoonful of his stew, and his lack of curiosity allowed Kelsea to bring out the heart of her fear. "Andalie should have been the Queen, Pen. Not me. She looks like a queen and talks like a queen, and she inspires dread."

Pen thought for a minute before answering. This quality of pensiveness was something Kelsea liked about him, that he didn't seek to fill empty silence with meaningless words. He swallowed two more mouthfuls of stew before replying. "What you've just given, Lady, is a perfect description of the Queen of Mortmesne. Andalie may be part Tear, but the essential core of her is Mort. She'd make an ideal queen in that kingdom. But you seek to create another type of queenship entirely, one not built on fear."

"What's mine built on?"

"Justice, Lady. Listening. Whether it'll succeed, none of us know; it's certainly easier to hold power through fear. But there's something hard in Andalie, something without mercy, and while it might create a certain advantage, I don't know that I'd call it strength."

Kelsea smiled as she turned back to her stew. Justice and listening. Even Carlin would have to be pleased with that.

Kelsea sat up in the dark. She'd heard a child scream in pain, somewhere beyond her own walls. She looked automatically to the left, searching for her fire, but there was nothing, not even the glowing hint of ashes. It must be almost dawn.

She reached to her bedside table for the candle that always stood there, but her fingers closed on nothing. Fear broke over her in a wave, sharp fear with no clear source. She groped, frantically now, and found that even the bedside table was gone.

A woman shrieked outside, her voice escalating until it cut off in a short, choked grunt.

Kelsea threw off her covers and jumped to the ground. Her feet landed not on the cold stone floor of her room but on what felt like hard-packed dirt. She rushed toward the door, not left across her own chamber, but ten feet to the right, through the kitchen area, steps she knew as well as her own name.

Throwing open the door, she cringed at the bitter cold of the night air. The village was still bathed in darkness, only a trace of dawn visible on the horizon. But she could hear pounding feet, the sound of many people running.

"Raiders! Raiders!" a woman shouted from one of the houses behind her. "They're—"

Her voice cut off without a trace.

Terrified, Kelsea shut the door and threw the bolt down. She groped on the kitchen table until she found a candle and matches, then lit a single weak flame, cupping it with her fingers to hide the light. Jonarl had made their house well, out of hard-baked mud leavened with small stones. He'd even given her a couple of windows, made of broken glass that he'd salvaged on several trips into the city. The house had been a lovely wedding present, but the windows made it difficult to shield light from the outside.

When she went back into the bedroom, she found William sitting up in bed, blinking sleepily, looking so much like Jonarl that her heart nearly broke at the sight. Jeffrey was still mercifully asleep in his crib, and she scooped him into her arms, keeping him wrapped in his blanket, and held out a hand to William. "It's all right, love. Up now; I need you to walk. Can you walk for Mummy?"

William climbed out of bed, his toddler's legs dangling for a moment before he dropped to the ground. He reached up and took her hand.

Booted feet pounded through the street outside. *Male feet*, she thought automatically. But all of the men were off in the city, trading wheat. Panic was trying to dig into her mind like a fever; where could they go? The house didn't even have a basement to hide in. She shifted Jeffrey to her other arm and dug in the corner for her cloak and shoes.

"Can you find your jacket and shoes, William? Let's see who can find their jacket first."

William stared up at her, bewildered. After a moment he began digging through the pile of outer clothes and blankets. Kelsea moved a stack of quilts and found Jonarl's winter cloak, still sitting there neatly folded. That was the closest she came to crying, right then, with her dead husband's cloak staring up at her from the ground. Nausea rose in her throat, good old morning sickness, which always picked the worst possible time to show up.

The front door burst open, the flimsy wood bar shattering into two pieces, which landed on either side of the kitchen. Kelsea cupped one protective hand around Jeffrey's downy head, then grabbed William and shoved him behind her with the other.

Standing in the doorway were two men, their faces blackened with soot. One of them had a bright red cloak, and even Kelsea knew what that meant. *Caden? Here?* she thought wildly, before he moved forward and laid hold of Jeffrey where he slept in her arms. The baby woke up and immediately began to scream.

"No!" she cried. He shoved her backward and tore Jeffrey free. Kelsea collapsed into the corner, grabbing the table leg to keep from falling directly on William. Her hip hit the wall with bruising force, and she groaned.

"Get the boy," the Caden told the other man, then disappeared out the door with Jeffrey. Kelsea shrieked, feeling something pull loose inside her. This was a nightmare, it had to be, but when she looked down she saw that her left foot had landed in her own right shoe as she fell, and now the shoe stuck up at a crazy angle. This detail alone precluded the comfort of nightmare. She grabbed William and shoved him behind her again, holding up her hands to ward off the man standing over her.

"Please," he said, leaning down to extend a hand. "Please come with me. I don't want to hurt you or the boy."

Even beneath the soot, Kelsea could see that his face was pale and drawn. He looked about Jonarl's age, maybe a bit older . . . the greying hair made it difficult to tell. He had a knife in the hand at his side, but she didn't think he meant to use it; he looked as though he'd forgotten about it himself.

"Where is he taking my son?"

"Please," he repeated. "Come quietly."

"What the fuck is taking so long, Gate Guard?" a hoarse voice barked outside.

"I'm coming!"

He turned back to Kelsea, his face twisting. "Please, for the last time. There's no other option."

"William needs his cloak."

"Quickly, then."

She looked down at William and saw that he had slipped on his own shoes, and held his cloak in one hand. She knelt in front of him and helped him put it on, doing the buttons with shaking fingers. "Weren't you smart, William? You beat Mummy."

But William was staring up at the man with the knife.

"Come now, please."

She took William's hand and followed the man out the front door. Briefly she cursed Jonarl for dying, for leaving them alone this way. But of course, it wouldn't have made any difference. It was the middle of March, and all of the men in Haven had gone to trade wheat in New London, as they did every year at this time, leaving the village defenseless. Kelsea had never thought about it before. The village had never faced this sort of trouble, not since the invasion; they were too far from the Mort border to worry about raiders.

Outside, she was relieved to see the big Caden with Jeffrey carefully balanced on one hip. Jeffrey had quieted a bit, but that wouldn't last long; he was emitting little snuffles, rooting around on the front of the man's cloak for a breast. When he didn't find it, the screaming would begin.

"Come along," the Caden told her.

"Let me carry my son."

"No."

She opened her mouth to protest, but the other man, the shorter one, grabbed her arm and squeezed it gently, warning. She took William's small hand and followed the Caden down the street toward the outskirts of the village. The horizon was lightening now, and she could see the vague outlines of houses and stables around her. Other groups joined them as they went, more women and children. Allison and her daughters emerged from their house, and Kelsea saw that Allison had a red slash down her arm, that her hands were bound.

She was braver than I was, Kelsea thought unhappily. But most of the women looked like Kelsea herself, dazed, their faces as bewildered as though they'd just awakened from a dream. She stumbled along, dragging William beside her, not understanding where they were going, only knowing that something terrible was happening. Her chest burned, but when she looked down, there was nothing there.

It was only when she rounded the corner of John Taylor's house, now empty and darkened, that she understood everything, the meaning of all these men, the women and children dragged from their homes. The cage stood high and stark against the lightening horizon, a symmetrical black silhouette with several human shapes moving inside. Another empty cage stood beside it, surrounded by mules. Looking away from the village, Kelsea saw several more of them, lined up perhaps several miles distant, in the direction of the Mort Road.

This is the punishment, Kelsea realized. She could recall two occasions when one of Haven's villagers had been pulled from the lot. The village treated the allotted as dead, holding a wake and speaking of them in doleful tones of grief. They'd all watched the shipment go by on the Mort Road many times, and each time Kelsea had been secretly thankful in her heart that it wasn't her, wasn't her husband or children.

This is the punishment for my relief.

The grey-haired man turned to her. "I must have your son now."

"No."

"Please don't make this difficult. I don't want them to think you a troublemaker."

"What will you do with him?"

He pointed to the second cage. "He'll go in there, with the other children."

"Can't I keep him with me?"

"No."

"Why not?"

"That's enough," a new voice rasped. Out of the darkness came a tall, skeletal man in a blue cloak, his gaunt face pitiless in the grey dawn light. Kelsea knew him, but did not know him, and she recoiled instinctively, trying to shield her son as he approached. "We're not here to debate with these people, Gate Guard. Time is of the essence. Split them up and put them in."

The Gate Guard reached out and grasped William's wrist, and William yelled indignantly. Hearing his brother's shouts, Jeffrey began to scream as well, beating tiny, angry fists against the Caden's cloak. Kelsea grabbed William's arm, trying to keep him close, but the man was too strong for her, and William was screaming in pain; if she didn't let him go, he would be pulled apart. She forced herself to release his wrist, and now she was screaming herself.

"Lady! Lady, wake up!"

Someone grabbed her shoulders and shook her, but she strained toward William, who was being hustled away toward the cage. It was a cage built for children, she saw now, filled with small, crying forms. The big Caden turned and strode off in that direction as well, taking Jeffrey, and Kelsea screamed without words, helpless to stop. She had a strong, clear voice, often chosen to sing solos at church, and now scream after scream pealed forth, terrible screams that echoed across the Almont Plain.

"Kelsea!"

A slap cracked across her face, and Kelsea blinked, her screams cutting off as sharply as they'd begun. When she looked up, Pen was there, perched on the bed, his hands resting on either side of her, surrounded by the familiar comfort and firelight of her chamber. Pen's dark hair was rumpled from sleep, and he wasn't wearing a shirt. Seeing his chest, muscular and well proportioned, with only the lightest dusting of hair, Kelsea felt a sudden, unaccountable urge to run her fingers across it. Something was burning her.

The cages!

Her eyes widened, and she sat up quickly. "Oh, God."

Mace bolted into the chamber, his sword in one hand. "What the hell?"

"It's nothing, sir. She had a nightmare."

But Kelsea was already shaking her head as he spoke. "Lazarus. Wake everyone up."

"Why?"

Kelsea shoved Pen to one side, threw off the covers, and hopped out of bed. Her sapphire popped loose from her nightgown, blazing blue light across the room. "Wake them up *now*. We have to leave within the hour."

"And go where, pray tell?"

"To the Almont Plain. A village called Haven. Maybe all the way to the Mort border, I don't know. But there's no time to lose."

"What the hell are you talking about? It's four in the morning."

"Thorne. He's made a deal behind my back, and he's on the way to Mortmesne with a shipment of Tear."

"How do you know?"

One of the switches on Kelsea's temper went, just like that. It didn't feel as though there were many more to flip. "Dammit, Lazarus, I *know*!"

"Lady, you had a nightmare," Pen insisted. "Maybe you should get back into bed and—"

Kelsea took off her nightgown, and had the small, spiteful satisfaction of seeing Pen's cheeks redden before he whirled around to face the wall. She turned to her chest of drawers and found Andalie already standing there, holding out a pair of black trousers.

"Lady," Mace said, in the slow, logical voice one would use with a child, "it's the middle of the night. You can't go anywhere now."

Another switch flipped. "Don't even think about trying to stop me, Lazarus."

"It was a *dream*."

Andalie spoke up in a quiet, firm tone. "The Queen has to go."

"Have you both gone mad? What the fuck are you talking about?"

"She has to go. I see it. There's no other way."

Kelsea finished dressing herself and found that her sapphire had already sprung free again, its light glaring across the room. Mace and Pen hissed and raised hands to shield their eyes, but Kelsea didn't even need to blink. Holding the sapphire up, she realized suddenly that she could see a face within its depths: a beautiful woman with dark hair and sharp, cold eyes. Her cheekbones were high and curving, the angles of her face cruel. She smiled at Kelsea and then vanished, leaving the jewel a bright, blank gleam of aquamarine in the torchlight.

For a moment, Kelsea wondered if she really was mad. But that seemed too easy a solution; if she'd gone mad, the real world wouldn't seem nearly so important. That day in front of the Keep had been her entire foothold, and if a shipment managed to make it to Mortmesne in spite of her decree, she was finished. She would be a paper ruler, and anything else that she tried to accomplish would be doomed to fail.

"Andalie's right, Lazarus. I have to go."

Mace swung back to Andalie, his tone disgusted. "Well done."

"You're welcome." Kelsea was surprised to hear the faint trace of a Mort accent, something she'd never heard before in Andalie's voice. "You make no allowance for gifts beyond your own."

"Your sort of gift has never been consistent. Not even the Red Queen's seer could foretell everything."

"Foretell this, Captain."

"Shut *up*!" Kelsea shouted. "We're all going to go. Pick a couple of guards to stay here with the women and children."

"No one's going anywhere," Mace growled. He took her arm, roughly. "You had a bad dream, Majesty."

"He's right, Lady," Pen told her. "Why don't you just go back to sleep? By morning you'll have forgotten all about it."

Mace was nodding agreement, his face arranged in a

solicitous expression that made Kelsea want to smack him. She bared her teeth. "Lazarus, this is a direct order from your Queen. We're leaving."

She went for the door again, and this time they both grabbed her, Mace by the arm and Pen around her waist. Kelsea's temper gave, pulling wide open, a seamless implosion inside her head, and she shoved out at both of them with her anger, feeling it depart her body like a current. Both men flew backward, Pen landing in a huddle at the foot of the bed and Mace bouncing off the far wall to crash on the floor. She hadn't shoved them very hard, and they recovered easily, each sitting up to stare at her, their faces bathed in blue light. Andalie had backed up to press against the vanity table.

"No one has to come with me," Kelsea told them, relieved to find that her voice was steady. "But don't try to stop me. I don't want to hurt either of you, but I will."

Mace and Pen looked at each other for a moment, their faces blank. What would they have done if she hadn't had her sapphire? Locked her in her chamber, she supposed, and allowed her to cry herself out, just as Carlin had always done when Kelsea was a child. She searched for that reserve of anger inside herself and found it, banked but still full. Had she ever been ashamed of her anger? Now it was a gift, somehow reflected through the jewel. It had the potential to be dangerous, certainly . . . if she'd been even a little angrier, Pen and Mace could have been seriously hurt.

Pen recovered first. "If you mean to do it, Lady, we shouldn't go as the Queen's Guard. We should dress as army. You'll want the outfit of a low-ranking officer."

Mace nodded slowly. "You'll also have to cut your hair, Majesty. All of it, right down to the nape."

Kelsea breathed a hidden sigh of relief; she needed Mace's support, at least. She didn't even know where her horse was kept, where to find supplies. Andalie crossed the room and went out the door.

"Without your hair," Mace continued, his tone tinged with malice, "you should have no trouble passing as a man."

"Of course," Kelsea replied. *A test*, she remembered, with a touch of nostalgia. *It's all a test*. "Anything else?"

"No, Lady." He left the room, closing the door behind him, and began firing orders left and right. Kelsea could hear his deep, angry voice even through the thick walls of the chamber.

Pen settled himself in the corner, ignoring her glare. She could see their perspective, and yet . . . they didn't trust her to know the difference between a nightmare and what she had seen, which had been a vision far more real than any dream. She'd even felt the prickle of goose bumps on her arms in the morning air. Was it a real woman, out there on the Almont Plain? A real bird flying over the Mort army? Kelsea had no proof, but she trusted the visions implicitly; she felt as though she had no choice. She supposed she could see Pen's side, but she didn't want to.

You should have believed me, she thought, staring at him from beneath lowered brows. *My word should have been enough for you*.

Andalie returned with a small towel and a pair of sewing shears. Kelsea reached for the tiara on the vanity table, then drew her hand back. Fake crown or not, she felt real attachment to the thing. But she would have to leave it here.

"Sit, Lady."

Kelsea sat, and Andalie began shearing the top of Kelsea's

head in great chunks. "I've been cutting my children's hair for years. We couldn't afford a dresser."

"Why'd you marry him, Andalie?"

"We don't always make these choices ourselves."

"Did someone force you?"

Andalie shook her head, chuckling mirthlessly, then leaned down and murmured in Kelsea's ear. "Who's the man, Majesty? I've seen his face in your mind many times. The dark-haired man with the snake-charmer's smile."

Kelsea blushed. "No one."

"Not no one." Andalie grabbed a hank of hair over Kelsea's left ear and sheared straight through it. "He means very much to you, this man, and I see shame covering all of those feelings."

"So?"

"Did you *choose* to feel this way for this man?"

"No," Kelsea admitted.

"One of the worst choices you could have made, no?"

Kelsea nodded, defeated.

"We don't always choose, Majesty. We simply make the best choices we can once the deed is done."

Rather than being comforting, this statement made Kelsea feel utterly hopeless. She sat in silence while Andalie finished, staring bleakly at the growing pile of dark hair on the floor. She meant nothing to the Fetch, she knew, but remote possibility had kept her going. The act of cutting her hair seemed to cross a final bridge into a land where there was no possibility at all.

A guard knocked at the door and, at Pen's summons, brought in a black Tearling army uniform, dumping it on the bed. His eyes widened at the sight of Kelsea, but when she glared back, he ducked out, closing the door behind him.

Pen returned to his armchair, apparently determined not to meet Kelsea's eye. Andalie finished and motioned for Kelsea to lean over, then quickly combed out the last of her long hair and cut. Levering Kelsea back upright, Andalie surveyed her work. "It'll do, Lady. A professional dresser can clean it up later."

Kelsea's head felt light, almost buoyant. Gathering her courage, she looked in the mirror. Andalie had given her a good haircut, almost the duplicate of Coryn's, a tight cap of hair around her head. Another woman, one with a perfect elfin face, might even have looked good with such hair, but Kelsea felt like crying. A boy stared back at her from the mirror, a boy with full lips and fine green eyes, but a boy all the same.

"Shit," she muttered. She'd heard the word from her guard many times, but only now did she understand the real use of profanity. That one word said exactly what she was feeling, said it better than a hundred other words could have done.

"Come, Lady. Clothes next." Andalie's blank gaze held a trace of pity.

"Will we succeed, Andalie?"

"I can't know, Lady. But you have to go, all the same."

BOOK III

CHAPTER 12
THE SHIPMENT

Question: What is an exiled girl with a false crown?
Answer: A True Queen.

—The Tear Book of Riddles

They left the Queen's Wing at dawn by one of Mace's tunnels, through a passage in darkness and then down a square staircase that seemed to descend forever. Kelsea moved along half in a dream, for the jewel wouldn't let her think clearly. She saw many faces in her mind now: Arlen Thorne; the Fetch; the cold-eyed woman with the high cheekbones. By the time they crossed the drawbridge, Kelsea was certain that this woman was the Red Queen of Mortmesne. She couldn't say how she knew.

She had expected to be overjoyed at being outside again, but the jewel wouldn't let her enjoy the outdoors either. Once they cleared New London, apparently free of pursuit, the sapphire began to pull Kelsea along. There was no other way to describe it; the thing exerted physical force, as though a string were tied beneath her rib cage. She was being hauled in a nearly straight line east, and if she tried to go in a different direction, the jewel flared into unbearable heat and Kelsea's stomach was racked with nausea, so much so that she could barely stay on her mount.

She couldn't keep this state of affairs secret from Pen for long, and Pen insisted on telling Mace. The troop had stopped to water the horses on the shores of the Crithe, on a low knoll that sloped down to the edge of the river. Except for Galen and Cae, whom Mace had left behind to guard the Queen's Wing, Kelsea's entire Guard was here, standing or crouching on the riverbank. She didn't know what Mace had told them, but it couldn't have been good; she'd caught several skeptical glances throughout the journey, and Dyer in particular looked as though he'd swallowed a lemon. As Pen, Mace, and Kelsea moved off to have a private conference on the other side of the knoll, she heard Dyer mutter, "Fucking waste of time."

When Kelsea produced the jewel, it was once again glowing so brightly that the two men needed to cover their eyes.

"Where's it taking you?" Pen asked.

"East."

"Why don't you just take it off?" Mace demanded.

Kelsea, feeling strangely reluctant, reached up and unclasped the necklace. But when she pulled the chain from her neck, she felt diminished. It was a dreadful feeling, like being drained.

"Jesus, she's turning white."

Pen shook his head. "She can't take it off, sir." He took the necklace from Kelsea and clasped it around her neck. Relief flooded her body, the sensation almost narcotic.

What is happening to me?

"Christ's sake, Pen," Mace muttered disgustedly. "What the hell do we do with these magic things?"

"We could follow the Queen, sir. No one needs to know where she's getting her directions from."

"I've got nothing better," Mace muttered, shooting Kelsea an irritated glance. "But it'll cause trouble. The rest are already pissed off about being out here at all."

Kelsea shook her head. "You know, Lazarus, at this moment I don't really care whether you believe me or not. But later on I will remember that you did not."

"Do, Lady. Do that."

They walked back toward the top of the knoll, and Kelsea tucked the sapphire beneath the shirt of her uniform, shielding her eyes from the sun. The blue thread of the Crithe wound its way east; they could barely see the Caddell, miles to the south. The two rivers ran nearly parallel courses, but their beds were dissimilar; the Crithe twisted and turned where the Caddell merely meandered. There was no sign of Thorne along either river, and yet Kelsea wasn't discouraged. The sapphire pulled at her, drawing her toward what she sought.

Mace took the bridle of his stallion from Wellmer, announcing casually, "From now on, the Queen will lead. We follow her."

There was some grumbling from the group, and Dyer pursed his lips and let out a loud, expressive sigh. But it appeared that would be the extent of argument. They mounted up, and Kibb and Coryn resumed the good-natured argument about the quality of their horses that had sustained them for much of the journey. Save for Mace and Dyer, the troop seemed to have resigned themselves to a silly errand, just as if Kelsea had taken it into her head to go pleasure boating on the Crithe.

Fine. So long as it gets me where I'm going.

"We could split, Lady," Mace suggested quietly. "Send you off with four or five men and—"

"No," Kelsea replied, clutching her sapphire. "Don't even try it, Lazarus. Turning aside would drive me mad now."

"Perhaps you're mad already, Majesty. Did that ever occur to you?"

It had occurred to Kelsea, but she wouldn't give him the satisfaction. She gripped the reins and turned her horse east, allowing him to find his own way forward along the river-bank. Immediately the pressure in her chest eased, and she closed her eyes in relief.

The next day, they ran onto the ruts of enormous wheels caked into the mud of the Mort Road. The sight stopped Mace cold, and Kelsea took a spiteful pleasure in his surprise, though she could tell he still wasn't convinced. Sometimes the tracks left the road and crossed the country, but they were always easy to spot, and Kelsea knew where Thorne was going now: cutting a nearly straight line east toward the Argive Pass, the same route always taken by the shipment. There were other places to get a caravan across the border, but the Argive gave direct access to the Pike Hill, a straight slope to Demesne. Speed would be important to Thorne, so it must be important to Kelsea as well. On the first night, when her guard made plans to camp, Kelsea told them firmly that they were welcome to stop, but she would keep riding. The resulting night's travel earned her no friends, but Kelsea didn't care. She was being driven now, driven by a great vein of blue fire in her head that seemed to widen with each passing hour.

On the second night, Mace finally commanded them to stop and rest. Kelsea, realizing that she had pushed herself to exhaustion, made no argument. They camped in an enormous field of wildflowers just beyond the end of the Crithe. Kelsea had never seen such a field; it stretched out like an ocean, dappled with every color of the rainbow. The flowers, unfamiliar to Kelsea, smelled like strawberries, and the grass was so soft that the troop didn't even bother to set up tents; they simply piled onto bedrolls in the field. Kelsea, who had expected to toss and turn for hours with the torment in her head, fell asleep at once. When she woke, she felt restored, and she picked several of the flowers, tucking them into her cloak for luck. Everyone seemed to wake in a good mood, and most of her guards began to treat Kelsea in their old fashion, joking lightly with her as they rode. Even Mhurn, who had been avoiding her since the incident at her audience, dropped back to ride on her left as the morning went on.

"Well met, Mhurn."

"Lady."

"Come to try to talk me out of it as well?"

"No, Lady." Mhurn shook his head. "I know you're telling the truth."

She looked up at him, startled. "You do?"

"Mhurn!" Mace barked from the front of the troop. "Up here now!"

Mhurn shook his reins and his horse darted around several others to reach the front. Kelsea stared after him, and then shook her head. On her other side, Pen was frowning, his hand on his sword, and Kelsea felt a pulse of low, banked anger. She wished she could forgive Pen for that scene in her chamber, but she simply couldn't. He of all people should have believed her; he knew she was no hysteric. Pen seemed to feel her anger, for he turned to give her a defiant look.

"Yes, Lady?"

"If I'd been forced to leave the Keep alone, if Lazarus hadn't allowed any of the Guard to come with me, would you still have come, Pen?"

"I'm sworn, Majesty."

"But sworn to whom? If it came down to a choice between the Captain of Guard and myself, which way would you go?"

"Don't force me to answer that, Lady."

"I won't, Pen, not today. But you either trust me or you don't. And if you don't, I no longer want you as my close guard."

Pen stared at her, his eyes wounded. "Lady, I thought only of your safety."

Kelsea turned away, suddenly furious with him, with all of them . . . except Mhurn. It had been more than a month, and many of them had come to know her, but nothing had really changed. She was still the girl they'd brought like a piece of baggage from Barty and Carlin's cottage, the girl who couldn't ride, who could barely be trusted to put up her own tent. It was Mace they listened to, whose word counted, and in the final judgment even Mace had treated her like a wayward child. When Pen tried to speak to her again, she didn't answer.

The terrible pull of the east only increased as the day progressed, becoming less a physical tug than a mental compulsion. Something was dragging Kelsea's mind along without the slightest concern whether the rest of her followed. Her chest throbbed, the sapphire throbbed, and they seemed to feed each other, the jewel and the anger, each of them growing beyond their own borders until just after noon, when Wellmer called a sudden halt.

The entire company drew rein just over the rise of a small

hill that was covered with wheat and dotted with purple flowers. To the east, Mount Ellyre and Mount Willingham rose to blot out the horizon, the deep blue V between them marking the ravine of the Argive Pass. Wellmer pointed toward the base of the mountains, where the Mort Road disappeared in a series of switchbacks.

"There, Lady."

They all stood in their stirrups, Kelsea craning her neck to get a better view. Some ten miles distant, buried in the foothills, was a long black shadow snaking its way upward.

"A fissure in the rock," Dyer muttered.

"No, sir." Wellmer's face was white, but he firmed his jaw and turned to Kelsea. "Cages, Majesty, all in a line. I can see the bars."

"How many cages?"

"Eight."

"Bullshit!" Elston roared from the back of the troop. "How the hell could Thorne build new cages in secret?"

"It doesn't matter how. It's done." Kelsea felt Mace's eyes on her, but she didn't look at him. On her right, Pen was staring at the foothills, his jaw twitching. "We have to reach them before they get out of the Argive. Once they come down from the mountains, Mort soldiers will be waiting to escort them to Demesne."

"How can you know that, Majesty?" Dyer asked. His tone was remarkably humble; it sounded almost like an honest question.

"I just know."

Now they all turned to Mace, seeking validation. An hour ago, this would have enraged Kelsea all over again, but now she could only stare at the caravan, making its slow way up the foothills. At least one of those cages was filled with children. How many villages like the one she'd seen? How many people?

Mace spoke slowly, refusing to meet Kelsea's gaze. "I apologize, Majesty. Thorne has outsmarted me again, and I promise you, it's the last time."

Kelsea didn't acknowledge his words, only shook her reins, anxious to go on. She stared at the dark line silhouetted against the foothills, shivering, trying not to wonder how she might come out of this on the other side.

East.

The voice was in her mind, but it seemed to be all around her, its words vibrating against her skin. "Let's ride on. We need to catch them by nightfall."

"Do we have a plan, Lady?" Dyer asked.

"Certainly." She had no plan at all. "Come, daylight's wasting."

When Javel wiped his brow, his hand came away soaking wet. The day was brutally, unseasonably hot, and driving the mules forward was exhausting work. Thorne had planned the bulk of their route through the Almont to avoid the most heavily populated towns and villages; sensible enough, but as a consequence they'd sometimes been forced to take rough roads that had seen no repair for a long time. By the time they reached the end of the Crithe, Javel could already feel his sickness over this whole enterprise beginning to overtake him, but he turned forward and thought of Allie.

The people in the cages wouldn't be quiet. They could hardly be expected to, but their pleading was something that Javel had never considered back in New London. Even Thorne might not have considered it, although being

Thorne, he probably didn't care either way. Javel could see him up ahead through the bars of the cage, guiding his horse forward as serenely as a king out for a picnic. Javel pulled the flask from his pocket and took a sip of whiskey, which burned his parched throat. Thorne would give him hell if he saw him drinking, but Javel hardly cared at this point. He'd packed three full flasks into his saddlebags, knowing that he would need them before the journey was over.

Thorne had decided that four men were necessary to guard each cage. There were several nobles in addition to Lord Tare, as well as a fair smattering of the Tearling army. The Baedencourt brothers had also produced two more Caden, Dwyne and Avile; both were well-known fighters, which made the rest of the group feel better. But even for a conspiracy, they were all curiously detached from each other, brought together by a common purpose like a group of wanderers stranded in the Cadarese desert. There was no love, and precious little respect. Brother Matthew and the little pickpocket, Alain, had taken a palpable dislike to each other. Lord Tare kept himself removed, riding ahead as a scout. Javel resented the presence of the Baedencourt brothers, who didn't even appear to have sobered up for the journey, and he'd spent the past few days with one eye on his cage and the other on Keller, who had begun to worry him more and more.

They had raided twelve villages along the shores of the Crithe. There had been almost no young men and so there'd been very little actual fighting. But Javel had noticed that Keller's disappearances into houses and huts took a long time, and that some of the women Keller brought out, particularly the young ones, had seen rough handling, their clothing ripped and stained with blood. Javel had considered raising the subject with Thorne, appealing to him on his level: wouldn't damage to the merchandise mean reduced value? But there had been no opportunity to speak privately with Thorne, and finally Javel had swallowed his disgust, bit by bit, just as he'd been forced to swallow everything else in this business. The progression was terribly easy: one bulwark after another fell inside his mind, like sand castles under the tide, until he worried that one day he might wake up and find himself actually become Arlen Thorne, so debased that everything seemed acceptable.

Allie.

The villages were so isolated that it seemed unlikely anyone would have time to mount a pursuit, but Thorne had insisted on the extra guards all the same, and Javel was forced to admit that Thorne was right. The recent rains had raised the level of the Crithe, and extra men were needed to get the cages across the Beth Ford. It didn't hurt to be overly cautious either, for the cages were vulnerable – made of simple wood, built to undertake only a few journeys, easier to attack.

"Please," a woman whimpered from the cage beside Javel, so close that he jumped. "My sons. Please. Can't they be in here with me?"

Javel shut his eyes and then opened them. The children were the worst part of this business, the worst part of every shipment. But Thorne had explained that the Red Queen valued the children highly, perhaps more than anything else they might bring. Javel himself had seized several: two small girls from Lowell, a toddler and baby boy from Haven, and, in Haymarket, a baby girl right out of her cradle. The children's cages were fourth and fifth in line, right in the center of the shipment, and Javel thanked God that he hadn't been assigned to guard them, though he could hear them well enough. The babies, particularly those too young for weaning, had squalled almost continuously for the first two days of the journey. Now, mercifully, they had fallen silent, and so had nearly all of the prisoners, their throats too dry to beg. Thorne had barely brought enough water for the guards and mules; he said that more than a few liters apiece would slow them down.

Right now I need you, Javel thought, staring at Thorne through the bars of the cage. *But if I ever catch you alone, just once, on a dark night in the Gut ... I won't be fooled again.*

"Please," the woman croaked. "My little one, my baby. He's only five months old."

Javel shut his eyes again, wishing he had put her in a different cage. She had blonde hair, just like Allie's, and when he had yanked her son from her arms, he'd been assaulted by a sudden and terrible certainty: Allie could see him. She could see everything he'd done. The certainty had faded a bit as the caravan moved along and dawn faded into morning, but it had raised a new problem, one that Javel had not considered before: how would he account to Allie for her release? She was a good woman; she would rather die than buy her freedom by the misery of others. What would she say when she found out what he had done?

When Javel was ten, his father had taken him to see the slaughterhouse where he worked, a squat building made of cheap wood. Maybe Father had intended it as a learning experience, or maybe he meant for Javel to follow in his footsteps, but either way, the outing had backfired. The line of steers, dozens of them, had waited dumbly to enter the building through its huge door. But the cows inside the building weren't dumb at all; there was a cacophony of sound, mooing and screeching, and behind that the thudding of heavy blows.

"Where do they come out?" Javel asked. But his father didn't answer, merely looked at him until Javel understood. "You kill them?"

"Where d'you think beef comes from, son? For that matter, where d'you think *money* comes from?"

When they entered the slaughterhouse, the smell had hit Javel instantly, blood and the rich reek of rotten entrails, and he'd lost his breakfast violently all over his father's shoes. He would remember that smell all his life, but it was the door of the slaughterhouse that planted the real hooks in Javel's child's mind: the wide-open door, the yawning darkness beyond. The steers went in, they screamed in the darkness, and they didn't come out again.

Six years ago, when Allie had gone to Mortmesne, Javel had ridden quietly behind the shipment for several days, not knowing what he planned to do. He could see Allie in the fourth cage, her bright blonde hair visible even from a distance, but the bars put infinite miles between them. And even if he found a way to successfully attack the shipment – a feat no one had ever managed – where would they go?

At least the steer didn't know what was coming. Allie's doom had been in her eyes that entire summer; it was one of the few things Javel remembered clearly. Mortmesne would have only one use for such a beautiful woman, just as a slaughterhouse had only one use for steers. They went in, and they didn't come out again. But now he would snatch Allie back. Javel could almost see her now, a dim shape in the darkened doorway, and he no longer heard the woman beside him, begging for her sons. Eventually she stopped.

As the day got hotter, the mules began to act up. They

were Cadarese mules, bred for strain and scorching temperatures, but they seemed to like the cargo no more than Javel did. He'd avoided whipping them throughout the journey, but finally it couldn't be helped, and he and Arne Baedencourt stationed themselves up at the front of the third cage, whips at the ready whenever a mule began to lag. It did no good. The caravan slowed, and then slowed further, until Thorne himself rode toward the cages and yelled at Ian, the mules' handler. "We need to reach Demesne by tomorrow night! What's wrong with your mules?"

"Can't say!" Ian shouted back. "The heat, maybe! They need more water!"

Good luck with that, Javel thought. They'd passed the end of the Crithe yesterday, and now they were more than halfway up the foothills that set the base of the Clayton Mountains. Even after the rains, there was no water this high up. Several hundred feet ahead, they would go through the Argive Pass and then run straight down the Pike Hill to Demesne. If only the damned mules could make it a few more hours, they could rest and it would be an easy trek the rest of the way.

The heat finally reached its pinnacle and held there as the sun began to sink toward the horizon. Several times Javel saw Alain, stationed on the cage ahead of him, sneaking cups of water to the prisoners. Javel thought of reprimanding him; if Thorne caught Alain wasting water that should have gone to the mules, they would all hear about it. But Javel remained silent.

Near sunset, the woman in the cage, who was apparently blessed with a throat of iron, started up again. She was more difficult to ignore this time; soon Javel knew that her sons were named Jeffrey and William, that her husband had been killed in a construction accident two months ago, that she was pregnant once more and sure it was a girl this time. This last fact bothered Javel most of all, though he couldn't say why. Allie had never gotten pregnant; Gate Guards made enough to afford good contraception, and both he and Allie deemed children too much of a risk in uncertain times. The decision had seemed so clear-cut then, but now Javel was merely sorry, and wearier than he could say. He wondered why Thorne hadn't thought of this, that they might take a woman whose pregnancy wasn't visible yet. Very soon she would have little value as a slave; she wouldn't be able to work, and no man wanted a pregnant woman for his toy.

It's Thorne's problem, it's Thorne's problem.

After the last excruciating mile uphill, they finished the rise at dusk and brought the line of cages into the Argive Pass. The sides of the ravine were steep but not sheer, dotted with boulders and outcroppings that jutted sharply from the slope. Broken stonework, the wreck of the Argive Tower, littered the floor of the valley. Greenery had long since deserted the Argive, and the constant trek of shipments had further eroded what arid vegetation was left. In the half-light of dusk, the pass was a deep brown gorge with dim purple sky at the top, stretching nearly a mile from east to west.

The mules were at the end of their strength, but Javel refrained from pointing this out to Thorne. He'd find out soon enough, when the poor beasts simply stopped moving despite all the whips in the world. They would have to stop for the night, although Javel didn't expect to get any sleep, not with those cages only yards away. He thought of Allie again. What would he tell her? Not the truth, certainly; her eyes would take on that brittle, blank look, Allie's form of disappointment.

What if she doesn't care?

But Javel refused to think of how Allie might have changed during the years in Mortmesne. Telling her was out of the question; he would have to come up with a lie.

As the sun set, clouds gathered overhead. Javel heard some grumbling; Dwyne, the leader of the four Caden, muttered loudly to his companions that it was convenient to receive shade just when the sun was gone. The Caden had made this journey many times during the Regency, and it was a comfort to have Dwyne and Avile, if not the dissipated Baedencourts. Yet even Dwyne seemed uneasy. The clouds had gathered fast, and were darkening even faster. If a storm broke overnight, it would slow the caravan's progress down the Pike Hill. But a storm would also give the prisoners some water. Perhaps when they stopped, Javel could even give the pregnant woman some time with her sons. Thorne would never allow it, but Alain had been sneaking around under Thorne's nose all day. Maybe Javel could do the same. He straightened up in his saddle, feeling better at the thought. It was a small thing, but a thing he could do.

The clouds deepened inexorably overhead, and at some point, almost without warning, darkness fell on the pass.

How many?" Mace hissed.

"I count twenty-nine," Wellmer whispered back. "Several more I can't see behind the cages. Wait—"

Kelsea waited, uncomfortably aware of the group of shadows who surrounded her. Mace and Pen were beside her, yes, but anyone could pull a knife in the dark. She was undeniably vulnerable here. She waited, her anxiety increasing, until Wellmer crawled back behind the boulder where half the troop crouched concealed. "Caden down there, sir. Dwyne and another I don't recognize."

"Damn, and they never work in twos. There'll be more of them."

After several seconds of hunting for a pocket, Wellmer tucked his spyglass away in the neck of his army uniform. They had left the horses far behind, at the mouth of the Pass, and everyone seemed to have simultaneously discovered that their uniforms had no pockets. Kelsea pulled at the neck of her own uniform; it was sewn of cheap material that made her skin itch. The army garb seemed to sit strangely on all of the Guard; she'd caught many of them twisting and adjusting themselves all day, even Pen, who seemed to be able to blend like a chameleon into whatever surrounded him.

But the black of the uniforms was good for concealment, since the sky still held the barest hint of a cold amber moon. The other half of Kelsea's guard was about fifteen feet away, tucked behind a second boulder, and Kelsea couldn't even pick them out; they were simply a dark mass against the side of the ravine. She was more worried about concealing her sapphire. The moment they'd entered the Argive Pass, the horrible heat inside her chest had cooled down to a low pulse that was almost pleasant by comparison. The jewel's light had dimmed as well, but Kelsea didn't trust the thin fabric of the uniform to block it entirely.

Metal rasped on leather behind her, the sound of a knife being drawn, and Kelsea drew into herself, trying to compress her body into the tiniest ball possible. Her pulse was thudding now, so loudly that it seemed they would all be able to hear it, and her forehead was chilled with sweat. The wound on her shoulder tightened in remembered agony. Which of the men around her had done it?

"We're outnumbered, Lady," Mace told her. "Not badly,

but we can't simply make a frontal attack. Not with the Caden down there."

"Wellmer, can't you pick them off?"

"I can shoot, Lady, but only two or three before they take cover and douse the light."

Mace tapped Venner on the shoulder, whispered to him, and sent him to the other boulder. "We've got Wellmer and three more decent archers. We'll send two across the pass, so the rest can't take cover behind the cages. If we take the Caden first, that'll even things up a bit."

"They might put out the fires at any point," Pen warned softly. "We should act soon, before we lose the advantage of the light."

Kelsea grabbed Mace's wrist. "The people in the cages are the priority. Make very sure they understand."

Venner crept back, three dark forms behind him. They huddled with Mace, conversing in whispers, and Kelsea wiped her sweating forehead, determined not to give in to the paranoia that had come over her in the dark. "Wellmer, give me your spyglass."

The eight cages had been doubled up in a horseshoe so that their gates faced inward. Kelsea was relieved to see that the cages had no iron. They looked to be hastily assembled affairs of mere wood, and the bars, rather than interlocking links, were thick, vertical wooden planks. Even if the wood was Tearling oak, the bars should be vulnerable to a concerted attack with axes.

Wellmer had spotted outliers stationed around the caravan, but the bulk of Thorne's men were concentrated within the horseshoe. Kelsea squinted through the spyglass, focusing on the men around the campfire. She knew very few of them. There was a well-dressed, heavyset man, clearly a noble, whom she remembered from her first audience, though she couldn't recall his name. Several men whom she thought might be with the Census. A good chunk of her own army, so careless that they hadn't even bothered to wear civilian clothing. And there was the man himself, Arlen Thorne, right in the middle of the circle. Her sapphire gave a small tremor against her chest. Nothing better could be expected from Thorne, but all the same Kelsea felt betrayed, betrayed by the just world she'd understood from her childhood. All of her plans, all of the good she wanted to accomplish . . . could it really be subverted by one man?

"Elston." She passed him the spyglass. "Right at noon around the fire."

"Motherfucker," Elston muttered, peering through the glass. Mace sighed, but he'd given up trying to clean up the guards' speech on this journey. Kelsea had heard many new words in the past few days. From overheard conversations, she knew that Elston hated Arlen Thorne; it was something to do with a woman, but no one would give Kelsea the whole story.

"I want him alive, Elston," she murmured. "Bring him to me, and I'll let you design his dungeon."

Several of her Guard chuckled.

"Five more minutes, Lady, and we can go," Mace whispered. "Give Tom and Kibb time to work their way across."

Kelsea nodded, feeling adrenaline flood her body. The guards drew their swords as quietly as they could, but Kelsea could still hear each rasp of metal against leather, and she fought down a stifling feeling. The sapphire pulsed like a drum against her chest, or maybe inside her chest, she couldn't tell anymore.

"Lady, I ask you for the last time to stay up here with Pen and Venner. If we fail, you can still get away."

"Lazarus." Kelsea smiled gently at his silhouette beside her. "You don't understand."

"I understand more than you think, Lady. You can blame it on your damned jewel if you want, but I understand that the shadow of your mother is making you both angry and reckless. That combination is dangerous to us all."

Kelsea seemed to have no capacity for anger at the moment; all of her energy was directed toward the campsite below. "You have your faults too, Lazarus. You're stubborn, and your life of weapons has closed sections of your mind that would be better left open. And yet I've grown to trust you in spite of all that. Maybe you could trust me as well."

There was no answer in the dark.

"Pen and Venner will stay with me at all times. Yes?"

"Lady," they murmured.

"I'd like you to stay with me as well, Lazarus. All right?"

"Fine. But you're not to engage, Lady. Venner says your footwork is atrocious."

"I won't pick up a weapon, Lazarus. You have my word."

After several minutes, Mace gave a birdlike whistle that faded away easily under the wind. The troop spread out among the boulders, and each began to work his own quiet way down the side of the ravine.

For once, Thorne had taken Javel's advice, and they'd established camp in the narrowest part of the Argive, leaving only two sides of the caravan to defend. Javel had meant to stay awake and see if he could give the pregnant woman some time with her sons, but exhaustion had finally won out. He decided to get at least a few hours' sleep and then deal with the matter. He settled his bedroll and curled up in front of the enormous fire, his legs shuddering in pleasure at the heat. Gate Guards rarely had reason to ride more than a few miles, and the long journey had taxed Javel's weak thigh muscles. He began to drop off toward sleep, dozing in longer and longer intervals, and he'd nearly reached oblivion when the first scream jerked him awake.

Javel sat up. In the dim firelight he could see nothing but the rest of the men, all of them looking around sleepily, as confused as he was.

"Archers!" someone shouted from behind the cages. "They're—" The shout cut off as suddenly as it had begun, reduced to a shallow gurgling.

"Arm yourselves!" Thorne commanded. He was already on his feet, looking as though he hadn't slept at all. Two men sprung up from the fire and tore off into the darkness, but before they got very far one of them went down with an arrow in his back.

Archers, Javel thought, bemused. *On the hillside.* He wondered if he were still asleep. He used to sleepwalk; Allie had told him so. Thoughts of Allie galvanized him, and he jumped up, drawing his sword and staring around wildly, seeing nothing beyond the circle of the firelight. Another arrow hissed through the darkness above his head.

"Put out the fire!" Dwyne shouted. "We're sitting ducks!"

Javel hauled his bedding from the ground and threw it onto the fire pit. The fabric wasn't heavy enough; the bedroll began to smolder, fire blooming through the layers of wool.

"We need more!" Javel waved at the befuddled men around him. "Give me your bedrolls!"

Sleepily, they began to rise and bundle up their blankets. Javel wanted to scream in frustration.

"Move!" Dwyne elbowed past him, carrying a huge pile of bedding, and threw it onto the fire. The light dimmed and then died, the air thick with the smell of scorched wool. Out in the darkness behind the cages, swords clashed and the air was suddenly rent with the high, unbearable scream of a wounded horse.

"Riders west!" someone shouted. "I hear them!"

"We're encircled," Dwyne muttered. "I told that damned bureaucrat it was a poor place to camp."

Javel flushed, hoping Dwyne wouldn't find out that Javel had suggested the pass as a stopping place. Javel had never dealt directly with any of the Caden before; they existed on a high plane, out of reach. Perhaps it was silly, but he still found himself longing for respect from the big man in the red cloak.

Thorne reached them in the darkness and grasped Javel's shoulder, thin breath hissing unpleasantly against Javel's ear. "Dwyne. What do we do? We need light."

"No, we don't. If they're a rescue party, the archers won't risk hitting the prisoners. We have a better chance in the dark."

"But we can't just wait here! When day comes, we'll be easy prey."

The impact of metal on metal rang from all sides now, drowning out Dwyne's reply. A sword glinted in the anemic moonlight, some ten feet away, and Javel raised his own sword in preparation, his heart hammering. Dwyne began to laugh.

"What can possibly be funny?" asked Thorne.

"It's the Tear army, man! Look at the uniforms!"

Javel could see nothing, but he grunted his agreement so Dwyne wouldn't know.

"I can probably deal with all of them by myself, dark or no. Wait here." Dwyne drew his sword and hurried away. When his footsteps had faded, Javel repressed a moment of stifling, amorphous fright. Having Thorne next to him in the dark was no comfort at all.

"He's full of shit," Thorne was muttering again. "We need light. Enough light to—"

He clenched Javel's arm again, hard enough that Javel winced.

"Get a torch."

Kelsea was still crawling forward, Pen and Venner on either side, when the fire went out, robbing them of light.

"The archers took at least four," Mace whispered behind her. "I don't know if they got Dwyne though; be on your guard."

"How are those cages fastened? Could anyone see?"

"No," replied Pen, "but they're definitely not steel. I think they're just plain old wood."

Kelsea was suddenly furious at the unknown builder of the cages. Thorne was no carpenter, but someone had built cages for him, all the same.

"Hooves," Venner whispered. "To the west."

The four went silent, and after a moment Kelsea, too, could hear multiple horsemen, coming down into the valley from the western opening of the pass.

"Three or four," Mace whispered. "If they're more Caden, we're in trouble."

"Should we move, sir?" asked Pen.

Kelsea looked around. In the dim starlight, she could see the outline of a few chunks of stone ahead of them and a large boulder to her left, but nothing else. There was nowhere to go except back up on the hillside.

"No," Mace replied. "Let's move behind that boulder and they should pass right by us. If not, there aren't many of them. We'll be able to cover the Queen's retreat."

The hooves were growing louder. Following Mace's lead, Kelsea crawled along on her belly toward the boulder. The ground was covered with tiny, sharp rocks that bit into her palms, making her hiss. She told herself not to be such a pansy and cursed inside, using Elston's word.

Mace led their crawling train behind the boulder and they leaned back against it, facing the campsite. Kelsea could dimly glimpse the barred silhouette of one of the cages against the deep blue-black sky, nothing else, but she could hear plenty. The sound of steel on steel resonated everywhere, and the night was alive with the groans of the wounded. She remembered her earlier paranoia and felt a flush of hot shame creep across her face. The sapphire, as though sensing her misery, pulsed in response. The hoofbeats drew nearer.

"Where—"

"Quiet." Mace's voice brooked no argument.

Several riders came past the boulder, their silhouettes barely visible against the grey backdrop of the ravine. They halted perhaps twenty feet from Kelsea's hiding place and the air was filled with the sound of overtaxed horses, their breaths whickering in the night.

"What now?" a man asked in a low voice.

"It's a mess," replied another. "We need light."

"We should wait for the fighting to die down a bit."

"No. We'll find Alain first," a new voice commanded, and Kelsea jerked to attention. She scrambled to her feet and moved forward before Mace could stop her. Four black silhouettes turned, drawing swords as she approached, but Kelsea only smiled. Certainty was upon her, a certainty that had nothing to do with the man's voice and everything to do with the sudden bloom of warmth in her chest.

"Well met, Father of Thieves."

"Holy hell." One of the horsemen rode toward her and drew rein some five feet away. Although Kelsea could see nothing but a black shadow against the sky, she could have sworn that he was looking down and seeing her.

Mace reached her then, grabbing her around the waist. "Behind me, Lady."

"No, Lazarus," Kelsea replied, her eyes on the tall shadow in front of her. "Keep your attention elsewhere."

"*What?*"

"Tear Queen," the Fetch remarked quietly. "It seems I did underestimate you, after all."

Kelsea heard Pen and Venner coming up behind her, and she held up a hand. "Both of you, stand down."

The Fetch regarded her in silence. Although Kelsea could see nothing of his face, she sensed that she really had surprised him, maybe for the first time. It comforted her, made her feel less of a child to his adult, and she straightened up, staring back at him defiantly. He dismounted and approached, and Kelsea felt Mace edge up on his toes beside her. She placed a restraining hand on his chest.

"Sir?" Pen asked, his voice high and anxious, younger than Kelsea had ever heard it.

"Christ. Stand down, Pen."

The Fetch reached out with one hand, and Kelsea instinctively drew back. But he only touched the very edges of her hair, cropped close around her head, and spoke softly. "Look what you've done to yourself."

Kelsea wondered how he could see her short hair when she could barely see anything at all. As his words sank in, however, she flushed and snapped, "Why are you here?"

"We've come after Thorne's little tea party. Alain is here somewhere; he's been spying out the lay of the land for weeks."

Alain, the blond man who was so quick with cards. Kelsea hadn't seen him anywhere around the campfire.

"The better question is: why are *you* here, Tear Queen?"

Good question. Even Mace, for all of his grumbling, hadn't asked Kelsea why. She thought for a moment, trying to come up with an honest answer, for she sensed the Fetch would know if she lied. The jewel continued to throb between her breasts, driving her to action, but she willed it to be still. "I'm here to keep my word. I promised this would never happen again."

"You could've kept your word from the Keep, you know. You have an entire army at your disposal these days."

Kelsea flinched at the sarcasm in his voice, but drew herself up to her full height. "A long time ago, before ascending the throne, the king pledged himself to die for his kingdom, if necessary. It was the only way the system worked."

"You're ready to die here?"

"I've been ready to die for this land since the day we met, Father of Thieves."

The Fetch's head tilted to the left. When he spoke, his voice was softer than Kelsea had ever heard it. "I've waited a long time for you, Tear Queen. Longer than you can imagine."

Kelsea blushed and looked away, not understanding what

he meant, only knowing that it wasn't what she wanted him to mean.

"Hold out your hand."

She obeyed and felt him place something cold in her palm. Exploring it with her fingers, she realized it was a necklace, a necklace with a cold pendant that had already begun warming against her skin.

"Whatever comes of this, Tear Queen, you've earned that back."

To Kelsea's left, much closer than the rest of the battle, came the dull, wet slap of a sword hitting flesh, and a man screamed, his voice high and terrified in the dark. Kelsea backed behind Mace, who raised his sword.

"I owe you the Queen's life, rascal," Mace hissed. "I won't hinder you, so long as you pose no threat to her. But clear away now, before you bring them all down on us."

"Agreed," the Fetch replied. "We go." He swung back up on his horse, becoming once more a dark silhouette against the sky. "Luck to you, Tear Queen. May we meet again when this business is done."

Still blushing, Kelsea found the clasp of the second necklace, reached up, and hooked it around her neck. Her heart seemed to jog inside her chest, creating heat that spread throughout her veins. She heard a crackling sound like static electricity, looked down, and found that the second sapphire was glowing like a tiny sun, emitting small flares of light. She tucked the pendant inside her uniform and heard an audible click, like a key turning in a lock. Her sight skewed crazily; she blinked and saw a different world, black buildings against a white skyline, but when she blinked again, it was gone.

The Fetch and his companions turned and rode farther

into the Pass, causing renewed warning cries and several shrieks of terror from the direction of the campfire. Meanwhile, Kelsea and her three guards crept back behind the other side of the boulder, away from the fighting, and sat down, staring outward toward the mouth of the pass.

"Sir?" Pen asked.

"Later, Pen."

Kelsea expected Mace to begin a lecture of some kind, about running away, about the Fetch, about recklessness in general. But he didn't. She could see the gleam of his drawn sword, and another shine of metal that she assumed was his mace. But the gleam was blue, not moonlight. Kelsea looked down and realized that her two jewels were now glowing so brightly that she could see both of them through the fabric of her uniform. She clasped them in her right hand, trying to block the light. Whatever had begun in her chest was steadily progressing now; her heart was hammering away much too fast, and her veins felt as though they'd been pumped full of fire. She was waiting for something terrible to happen, something she couldn't see.

Of course, she realized suddenly. *I only kept the second necklace in my pocket before. I never put it on.*

She closed her eyes and there it was again: a skyline, full of tall buildings, dozens of them, even taller than the Keep. Madness seemed to be there, beckoning, a city of madness that existed only in her head. More screaming came from the center of the battle, bringing Kelsea back to herself. She opened her eyes to merciful darkness, saw Pen peering around the edge of the boulder.

"They've lit the fire again."

"Fools," Mace muttered. "Wellmer will pick them off easily."

Kelsea peeked around Pen. Light glowed against the sky several hundred feet away, right in the center of the campsite. Her jewel was trying to drive her forward, somehow, but she had promised Mace and she willed it to be silent. The screaming from the center of the pass continued, and Kelsea's pulse ratcheted higher, recognizing that this was the terrible thing, the thing she'd been waiting for. She suddenly pinpointed the source of her anxiety. "That's a woman's voice."

Pen moved a few more feet out from the boulder, and even in the dim glow of the distant fire, Kelsea saw his face turn white. "Christ."

"What is it?"

"Women." His voice sounded as though it came through water. "They've lit a cage of women."

Before she had time to think, Kelsea was running.

"Lady! Damn it!" Mace's shouts seemed very far away. Women's screams echoed off the walls of the pass, seeming to fill the night from horizon to horizon. The two sapphires bounced free of her uniform, ablaze now, and Kelsea found that she could see everything, each boulder and blade of grass limned in blue. She'd never been much of a runner, but the jewels were giving her strength and she ran fast, faster than she ever had in her life, sprinting toward the brightening bloom of the fire.

Javel didn't know what had happened. He'd gone to find a torch for Thorne, hardly aware of what he was doing. His mind was still full of Allie, wondering what would happen to her if they failed. He sensed that Thorne's men were losing the battle. They hadn't gotten the fire out quickly enough, and the archers must have done great damage from the hillside because he couldn't move a foot without tripping over a body. More horsemen had arrived while he was searching for the torch; the sound seemed to push Thorne into a panic, so Javel knew they were not part of the plan. They were going to lose the fight, and then what would become of Allie?

Finally Javel found a discarded torch lying on the far side of the fire pit and returned to Thorne, who took the torch without thanks and moved away out of earshot.

Good riddance, Javel thought darkly. But once Thorne disappeared, he didn't know what to do. He was a Gate Guard, not a soldier, and this wasn't the Gut, with its comfort of walls and cramped streets. Javel had always hated nature. The walls of the pass were tall, ghostly boundaries on the world. He didn't want to move, and though he could hear fighting all around him, he recoiled from the idea of engaging an enemy he couldn't see. His experience with combat had been limited to the repulsion of two or three gate crashers, lunatics who showed up intending to fight their way into the Keep. He'd never killed a man before.

Am I a coward?

The prisoners had found their voices again once the attack started, and now they screamed for help, a slaughterhouse sound that made him want to clap his hands to his ears. He thought of trying to get the pregnant woman out, but he could see nothing, and he was afraid. He thought of Keller, of the young girls who filled the caravans. Several had been raped; Javel could no longer deny it now, even to himself. One of them, surely no more than twelve, had done nothing but sob brokenly all the way from Haymarket. Javel thought of those drunken nights in the Gut, nights when he'd idly contemplated finding child traffickers, bringing them to justice, doing heroic things. But morning always came, sunlight and hangovers ruining his best plans. This was different, Javel realized. This was dark work; there was no morning here. And so much could be accomplished in the dark.

He sheathed his sword and pulled the knife from his belt, waiting. Gate Guards always stuck together, and a few minutes later Keller found him, as Javel had known he would.

"Not really our scene, is it, Javel?"

"No," Javel agreed. "Never thought I'd long to be back on the gate in the middle of the night." They stood quietly in the dark for a moment, Javel gathering his courage, feeling adrenaline flood his body. "Does that cage door look loose to you?"

"What door? I can't see anything."

"Over there, to the left."

The moment Keller turned, Javel snaked an arm around his neck. Keller was big, but Javel was quick, and he was able to draw his knife across Keller's throat and dance backward before Keller's hands found him. Keller gurgled, gasping for breath in the dark, then Javel heard a satisfying thump as his huge body collapsed to the ground. Javel's heart blazed with satisfaction, a great dawn breaking inside his mind and flooding his veins with courage. What should he do next?

He knew immediately: he would open the doors. He would open the doors of the cages, just as the Queen had done on the Keep Lawn that day, and let everyone out.

He stumbled toward the caravan, but tripped over another body. Men were still fighting all around him and the ground was littered with corpses. Thorne was right; they needed light.

Just as Javel thought this, he realized that he could see; a thin amber glow illuminated several pairs of fighters and the first few cages on either side of the horseshoe. Someone had lit a fire. Dwyne would be angry, but Javel felt only relief.

That was when the screaming started for real. A woman positively shrieked, her voice ascending in a terrible, eldritch wail that went on and on until Javel had to clap his hands over his ears. He sank to his knees, thinking: *Surely she must run out of breath.* And she might have, but he couldn't tell, because suddenly they were all screaming, an entire world of women crying out.

Javel turned, saw the fire, and realized what Thorne had done.

The fourth cage on the left was aflame at one end, the door already obliterated. Thorne stood perhaps ten feet away, torch in hand, staring at the fire, and Javel saw evil in those bright blue eyes, not malevolence but something much worse: an evil born of lack of self-awareness, an evil that didn't know it was evil and therefore could justify anything.

Evil that did the math.

The women in the cage shrieked as they crushed themselves against the far wall. But the fire was coming for them, inching its way across the floor of the cage. Two women had already caught fire; Javel could see them easily through the crude wooden bars. One was William and Jeffrey's mother. She was beating at the flames that had taken her skirt and screaming at the other women for help, but none of them noticed in their mad push to get away. The second woman was nothing but a blazing torch, a dark, writhing shape with arms that waved madly from inside the fire. While Javel watched, in a span of time that seemed endless, her arms sank to her sides and her body simply collapsed. She had no face anymore, only a blackened thing that burned madly, spreading flame along the cage floor.

The rest of the women continued to scream, a blood-curdling cacophony that Javel knew he would hear in his head for the rest of his life. They screamed endlessly, and all of them seemed to have Allie's voice.

Javel lunged for the Baedencourt brothers' belongings, which lay on the other side of the dead campfire. Hugo Baedencourt always carried an axe; both brothers had been sent out on the first watch, but an axe was no use in combat. Javel tore through the sack of weapons, pushing aside swords and a bow before he came upon the axe, a strong, gleaming thing in his hands. It was too heavy for him, but he found that he could lift it, and once he reached the cage, he found that he could swing it as well. Jeffrey and William's mother was burning now, her hair and face on fire. Her dress had gone up first and Javel knew, in the part of the mind that remained cold and suspended in such situations, that the baby inside her was already dead. But even the flames couldn't stop the woman's iron voice. She screamed and screamed into the night.

Javel swung the first crushing blow against the bars. Wood splintered, but they held.

I'm not strong enough.

He swallowed the thought and swung again, ignoring a rending tear in the muscle of his left shoulder. Allie was upon him, standing there looking at him affectionately, long before they were married, neither of them thinking of the lottery, of anything at all.

Stench had filled the air now, a gut-churning mixture of

burning wool and charred skin. Javel was losing the race against the fire, he knew it, but he couldn't stop swinging the axe. Jeffrey and William's mother died somewhere in the middle of the race; one second she was screaming, the next she was not, and in one cold blink, Javel decided to kill Arlen Thorne. But Thorne was already gone; he'd thrown away his torch and fled into the darkness.

The women were still crushed against the far wall of the cage, but only those in back continued to scream now; smoke had overwhelmed the women closest to the fire and they could only cough wretchedly. Several had flames licking at their skirts. Javel's own eyes were watering, burning with smoke, and the skin on his arms felt as though it was beginning to bake. He ignored everything and swung again, feeling the axe bite cleanly through one of the bars. But only one. It was too late.

Allie I'm so sorry.

His skin was on fire. Javel dropped the axe and sank to his knees. He clapped his hands to his ears but he could still hear them screaming.

Then the world filled with blue light.

Some fifty feet from the burning cage, Kelsea became aware that several riders had moved to flank her as she ran. The Fetch's men, their faces masked in black, and they paced her, launching arrows as they went. She might have been hallucinating but she no longer cared. Nothing mattered now but the cages, the women. Her responsibility. She was the Queen of the Tearling.

Several of Thorne's men tried to approach her as she ran, their swords upraised and murder in their faces. But a series of blue flares enveloped them and took them down. Kelsea felt that the light wasn't coming from the jewels at all, but from inside her own head. She merely thought to kill them and they were gone. Her breath tore at her throat, but she couldn't slow down. The jewels pulled her onward toward the flames.

She skidded around the last boulder and baking heat hit her like a wall, pushing her back. Women had crowded mindlessly at one end of the flaming cage, but the fire had already reached them. A grey-haired man was down in front, attacking the bars with an axe, but he didn't appear to be making a dent.

Tearling oak, Kelsea thought. The women were trapped. Worse yet, flames were already licking at the bars of the next cage; if they couldn't put out the fire, the entire caravan would go up. They needed water, but there was none for miles. Kelsea tightened her fists in despair, so that her nails bit into her palms, drawing blood. If someone had offered her a trade right now, her life for those people in the cage, she would have taken it easily and without fear, just as a mother would unthinkingly trade her life for her child's. But there was no one to trade with. All of Kelsea's good intentions had come to this in the end.

I would give everything if I could, she thought, and knew in that second that it was true.

The two jewels exploded in blue light, and she felt current slam into her body, voltage coursing through every nerve. The force of it shoved her backward. She felt twice her own size, every hair on her body standing on end and her muscles straining against their own walls.

Her despair vanished.

The entire pass was illuminated now, washed in blue, each shadow brighter than the next. Kelsea could see everything, still and quiet and suspended. All around her were struggling figures, frozen in the light.

Wellmer up on the hillside to her left, perched on the edge of a boulder with an arrow nocked into his bow and his jaw clenched in concentration;

Elston, his eyes red with fire and murder, chasing Arlen Thorne along the rocky floor of the ravine;

Alain, back behind one of the cages with a knife in his hand, killing the wounded, his mouth open to shout;

the Fetch, down by the end of the caravan, wearing his horrible mask, fighting a big man in a red cloak;

the man who'd attacked the cages with his axe, on his knees now, weeping, his face consumed with agony, regret that spanned years;

but most of all, the women in the cage, standing right in the path of the flames.

It's better to die clean.

Voltage poured through Kelsea, so much that her body couldn't hold it; it was as though she'd taken a bolt of lightning. If there was a God, he would feel like this, standing astride the world. But Kelsea was terrified, sensing that if she wanted to break the world in half she could do it, of course she could, but there was more here than she knew. Everything came with a price.

Water.

There was no choice here. If there was a price, she would have to pay it. She reached out, her arms stretching far beyond their span. Water was there, she could sense it, almost taste it. She called for it, screamed for it, and felt electricity burst from her, a vast current that had appeared from nowhere and now went the same way.

Thunder shattered above the pass, trembling the ground.

The jewels went cold and dark, and the pass was suddenly covered once more in firelit night. Everything began to move again; women screamed, men shouted, swords clashed. But Kelsea merely stood there in the dark, waiting, with each hair on her body standing on end.

Water cascaded from the sky, a flood so thick that it obscured the moonlight. It fell on Kelsea like a wall, knocking her to the ground and tumbling her along the floor of the ravine, gushing up her nose and into her lungs. But Kelsea drifted pleasantly now, her mind vacant of everything but the need to sleep, an inviting darkness somewhere beyond her vision.

The Crossing, she realized. *The* real *Crossing. I can almost see it.*

Kelsea closed her eyes and crossed.

The Queen of Mortmesne stood on her balcony, staring across her domain. She'd begun to come here when she was wakeful, which was nearly every night now. She wasn't getting enough sleep, and small things had begun to slip. She'd forgotten to sign a set of execution orders one night, and the next morning the crowd had gathered in Cutter's Square and waited . . . and waited. The King of Cadare had invited her for a visit and she'd mistaken the date by a week, confusing her servants and necessitating some unpacking. One night they'd brought her a requested slave and she'd already been fast asleep. These things were small, and Beryll caught most of them, but sooner or later someone besides Beryll would notice and it would become a problem.

It was the girl, always the girl. The Queen wanted a look at the girl, wanted it so badly that she'd even gathered her generals and broached the possibility of a state visit to the

Tearling. They rarely vetoed her suggestions, but they'd done so this time, and the Queen had eventually admitted their point. The overture would be a sign of weakness, and a pointless one; the girl would likely refuse. But even if she accepted, there were hidden dangers. By now the Queen could see that the girl was an unknown quantity, nothing like her mother at all. Worse, the girl's guard was captained by the Mace, who was *not* an unknown quantity. Even Ducarte didn't want to tangle with the Mace yet, not without more information and advantages than they held at present. The Mace was a terror, the girl was a blind spot, and both of these things boded ill.

The Queen liked this balcony; it was two floors above her chambers, at the top of one of the Palais's many turrets. She could see for miles in every direction: across the vastness of her land to Callae in the east, Cadare in the south, and due west to the Tearling. The Tearling, which had given her no trouble for almost twenty years, and now it felt as though she'd stepped into an anthill. It was a disaster. Thorne's shipment would arrive tomorrow, and it would work as a stopgap, but it wouldn't resolve the larger problem. If she allowed the Tearling to evade tribute, it would be only a matter of time before the others followed suit.

The domestic situation was no better. The Queen had ruled her kingdom with an iron grip for over a century, but now the lack of new slaves had created a novel problem: internal unrest. The Queen's spies reported that Mort nobles had been gathering in secret, in larger and larger groups. The commanders of her army weren't so secretive; they voiced their displeasure to anyone who would listen. The northern cities, particularly Cite Marche, had reported increasing levels of popular unrest. Cite Marche was full of young radicals, most of whom had never owned a single slave, but they scented opportunity in the spread of discontent.

I will have to invade the Tearling, the Queen realized, troubled. She moved to the south-west corner of the balcony and looked out beyond the city, to the dark shadow that blanketed the vastness of the Champs Demesne. She had mobilized her army weeks ago but then delayed sending it, something in her gut counseling caution. Invasion was simpler, but also riskier, and the Queen didn't care for unquantified risk. A victory could carry unintended consequences. She didn't want more land to police; she wanted things to go on quietly, as they always had, with each surrounding kingdom paying tribute and doing as it was told. If she were forced to take real military action, it would delay the project, keep things from moving forward.

But she didn't really have a choice anymore. Thorne's assessment was clear: the girl would not be bought. She showed dangerous strains of her grandmother, Arla, and even something more.

Who was the father?

Some mornings, the Queen thought that everything hinged on this question. She was a geneticist, perhaps the most advanced geneticist since the Crossing, and she appreciated the power of bloodlines to create change, even abrupt, aberrant change, from generation to generation. Both Elyssa and her Regent had been so easy to manage, constrained by vanity and lack of imagination. There was no reason the girl should be so different, unless some entirely original strain had been introduced to the mix. The Regent had always refused to tell her the identity of the girl's father; she should have forced the information from him years ago, but it hadn't seemed that critical. Only now, when he had disappeared and her plans had ground to a halt, did she see that the girl's paternity might matter more than anything else.

I've grown complacent, the Queen realized suddenly. Everything had been so easy for so long ... but the complacent ruler stood at the whim of any indignity evolution could produce, even a nineteen-year-old girl who should have been dead years before.

Something was happening on the Tear border.

The Queen narrowed her eyes, trying to understand what she was seeing. It was just past midnight, and the sky was clear all the way to the border, where the two mountains, Willingham and Ellyre, rose high above the forest, their snow-covered peaks visible by a thin sliver of moon. Useful landmarks, those mountains; the Queen had always been grateful to know exactly where the Tear began, to be able to keep an eye on it from a distance.

Now lightning rent the sky above the Argive Pass, illuminating roiling black storm clouds. The Queen was unimpressed; she could summon lightning herself if she cared to, it was a parlor trick. But this lightning wasn't white, it was blue. The bright blue of a sapphire.

Fear trickled inside her, making her belly contract, and she narrowed her eyes at the western horizon, trying desperately to see. But magic, like all strengths, was constrained not only by the user but by the audience, and now she could see nothing. She'd never been able to see the girl, not even once. Only in dreams.

The Queen whirled and left her balcony, startling her guards, who froze for a moment before falling into place behind her. She hurried down the circular staircase toward her quarters, not caring whether they could keep up.

Premonition was suddenly upon her, unbidden, a sense of disaster. Something terrible was happening on the border, some catastrophe that could wreck all of her plans.

Juliette, the Queen's head page, was stationed at the door to her quarters. The Queen would have preferred Beryll for this duty, Beryll whose loyalty was unquestioned. But he was an old man now, and he needed his sleep. Juliette was a tall, muscular blonde of about twenty-five, strong and capable, but so young that the Queen wondered what she could possibly know about anything. The price of a long, long life was suddenly clear, laid out in the younger woman's bright, somehow stupid face.

All of my people have grown old.

"Bring me a child," she snapped at Juliette. "A boy, nine or ten. Drug him hard."

Juliette bowed and went swiftly down the hallway. The Queen passed into her quarters and found that someone had already drawn the curtains. Normally, she loved her room with its curtains closed, so that the walls and ceiling were nothing but an unbroken field of crimson silk. It was like being inside a cocoon, and she'd often taken pride in thinking of herself that way, as a creature who'd broken free of the walls of her prison and emerged stronger than before, stronger than anyone had ever imagined she would be. But now she took no pleasure in her surroundings. The dark thing would be angry at being summoned, and even angrier at a request for help.

There was no other option. Her own gifts had failed.

Her guard had prepared for her return; a large, healthy fire burned in the enormous fireplace. That was good. One less thing to do. The Queen rummaged through her drawers until she found a knife and a clean white towel. Then she cleared away the furniture in front of the fireplace, dragging sofa and chairs away to leave a wide space on the stone hearth. When she finished, she found that she was breathing hard, her pulse thudding in her ears.

I'm afraid, she thought miserably. *It's been a long time.*

Someone knocked. The Queen opened the door and found Juliette standing there, a young Cadarese boy in her arms. He was the right age, but very skinny, his face slack with unconsciousness. When the Queen lifted an eyelid, she found his pupils dilated almost to the rim of the iris.

"Good." The Queen took the child in her arms, not liking the warm feel of his thin body. "No disturbances, not for anything, no matter what you hear."

Juliette bowed again and backed away to the far side of the hall. The night guard stationed against the wall gave Juliette's ass a frankly lascivious glance, and the Queen paused briefly on the threshold, thinking that she should do something about that. Her pages weren't supposed to suffer any sort of harassment; it was one of the perks of a difficult job.

Fuck it, she thought resentfully. Beryll could sort it out tomorrow.

She slammed the door with one shoulder, carried the boy to her bed, and dumped him on top of the coverlet. His breathing was deep and even, and the Queen stared at him for a moment, her thoughts moving in various directions. She didn't particularly like children; they made too much noise and demanded too much energy. She'd never wanted a child herself, not even when she was young. Children were simply a necessary cog in the machine, something to be tolerated. It was only when they were quiet like this that she found them bearable, that she could regret what had to be done.

There were several pedophiles in high positions in her military. The Queen felt a strange, sickly contempt for these men, unable to understand what was wrong with them. Genetics gave her no answers; there was nothing sexual in children. Some people were simply broken, something inside them grown wrong and twisted. These men were diseased, and the Queen made a special point of never touching them, not even to shake hands.

But she needed them, needed them badly. When they weren't being what they were, they were incredibly useful, and Ducarte in particular was invaluable. The trick was not to think of these things, not while she watched the sleeping child in front of her, utterly vulnerable on the bed.

Someday, she thought, *when everything is completed, I'll rid the land of all of them. I'll go from one end of the New World to the other, scraping out the rot, and I'll start in the Fairwitch.*

But for tonight, she needed the child. And she should act quickly, before the drug began to wear off.

Picking up the knife, the Queen reached down and made a shallow slice across the boy's forearm. Blood welled up in a fat line and she blotted it with the towel, soaking the white cotton. The boy didn't even stir; a good sign. Maybe she could get through this more cleanly than last time.

The Queen took off her gown and underclothes, leaving them in a scarlet puddle on the floor behind her. She dropped to her knees on the stone hearth and whispered a few words of a language long gone, then sat back on her heels and waited, gritting her teeth. The stone of the floor was hard and sharp, digging into her knees, but the dark thing liked that, just as it liked to have her naked. It appreciated discomfort, enjoyed it in some way she didn't fully understand. If she kept her panties on, or put down a pillow to soften the floor, it would notice.

A voice spoke from the fire, a low, toneless voice that couldn't be identified as either male or female. At the sound of it, gooseflesh broke out on the Queen's arms.

"What is your need?"

She swallowed, wiping perspiration from her forehead. "I need . . . advice."

"You need help," the dark thing corrected, its voice expectant. "What will you give in return?"

She leaned forward, as far as she dared, and threw the bloody towel into the fire. Despite the heat, her nipples had hardened to tiny points, as though she were cold, or excited. Crackling sounds filled the room as the flames consumed the towel.

"Innocent blood," the dark thing remarked. "It is good to taste."

The air in front of the fireplace began to darken and coalesce. As always, the Queen stared at this phenomenon, trying to understand what she was seeing. The space in front of her was turning a rich black, a dark, fathomless hole opening there. It looked as though oil were condensing right out of the air.

"What troubles you, Mort Queen?"

"The Tearling," the Queen replied, unhappy to find that her voice wasn't entirely steady. The creature in the fire needed her just as much as she needed it, she reminded herself. "The new Queen of the Tearling."

"The Tear heir. You've been unable to yoke her; I have been watching."

"I couldn't see what happened on the border tonight. I can't see the girl at all."

The hole in front of the fire widened now, pulsing blackly in the firelight. "I do not come to listen to you complain. Ask your question."

"What happened on the border tonight?"

"Tonight is nothing. There is no time here."

The Queen pursed her lips and tried again. "Arlen Thorne was bringing a clandestine shipment of Tear across the border. Did something happen?"

"He failed." There was no emotion in its voice, no human tone at all. "There will be no shipment."

"How did he fail? Was the girl there?"

"The Tear heir holds both jewels now."

The Queen's stomach dropped unpleasantly, and she looked down at the hearth, considering various choices. All of them led to the same place. "I must invade the Tearling and kill the girl."

"You will not invade the Tearling."

"I have no choice. I have to kill her before she learns to use them."

The black mass in front of the Queen trembled suddenly, like a door frame struck by a heavy blow. A spear of flame shot from the fire, crossing the hearth to bury itself in the skin of her right hip. She cried out and fell backward, rolling against the carpet until the flames were extinguished. Her hip had burned black, and it squalled in agony when she tried to sit up. She lay on the floor, panting.

When she looked up, the black mass in the air was gone. Instead, a man towered above her, handsome beyond words. His pure black hair swept back from a perfect patrician face, gaunt cheekbones offset by a thick, full-lipped mouth. A beautiful man, but the Queen wasn't fooled by that beauty anymore. Red eyes glittered coldly down at her.

"As high as I set you, I can bring you low," the dark thing informed her steadily. "I have lived longer even than you, Mort Queen. I see the beginning and the end. You will not harm the Tear heir."

"Will I fail?" She couldn't imagine it; the Tearling had no steel and a lounging army with a geriatric commander. Even the girl couldn't change that. "Will an invasion fail?"

"You will not invade the Tearling," the dark thing repeated.

"What am I to do?" she asked in desperation. "My army is restless. The people are restless."

"Your problems are not mine, Mort Queen. Your problems are merely motes of dust in my sight. Now give me my price."

Shaking, the Queen pointed toward the bed. She didn't dare disobey the thing above her, but without new slaves, the situation would continue to worsen. She thought of her recurring dream, which came every night now: the man in grey, the necklace, the girl, the firestorm behind her. The real reason for her insomnia had become painfully obvious; she was afraid to sleep.

Behind her, she heard a slithering noise, the low hiss of the thing's breath. She curled up tightly on the floor, cradling her injured hip, and wrapped an arm around her head, trying not to listen. But it was no good. A gurgling sound came from the direction of the bed, and then the slave boy screamed, his high, unbroken voice echoing around the walls of the chamber. The Queen tightened her arms around her head, tensing the muscles of her ears until there was only a thick roaring inside her eardrums. She stayed that way, eyes and ears shut tightly, until it seemed that hours must have passed, that it must be done.

She rolled over, opened her eyes, and screamed. The dark

thing was right above her, its face inches from her own, its red gaze staring down at her. Its full lips were smeared with blood.

"I sense your disobedience, Mort Queen. Even now, I can taste it in my mouth. But betrayal has a price; I know that better than anyone. Harm the Tear heir, and you will feel *my* wrath, darker than your darkest dream. Do you wish that?"

The Queen shook her head frantically. Her nipples were rock-hard now, almost aching, and she moaned as the thing slithered off her, licking the last of the blood from its lips. The fire went out, plunging the room into darkness.

The Queen rolled to her other side. Grasping the oak foot of her bed, she began the slow process of hauling herself to her feet. Her hip shrieked as she made it into a squat. She explored the deep, angry welt with her fingers . . . a bad burn, one that would scar. A surgeon could fix it, but use of a surgeon would also prove that she could still be injured. No, the Queen realized, she would have to live with the scar.

Crossing the room by touch, she fumbled around at her desk. There was a candle on her bedside table, but she couldn't bear to go over there in the dark. Something brushed her hand and the Queen gave a small squeal of fright. But it was only a spider, scuttling along in its own alien doings. Her other hand closed on the unmistakable shape of a candle and she lit it, gasping with relief. Her chambers were empty. She was alone.

The Queen wiped sweat from her forehead and cheeks; the rest of her naked body was damp as well. But her legs moved as though driven, propelling her to stand beside the bed. Taking a deep breath, she looked down at the boy.

He had been bled. Even by candlelight, she could see the pallor beneath his dark skin. The thing always used the cut she'd made; the first few times, she'd asked her pages to check the bodies for other incisions, but eventually she stopped. It wasn't anything she wanted to know. The boy's spine was arched nearly to breaking, one arm pulled so far from its socket that it hung limp and twisted behind him on the scarlet bedspread. His mouth was wide, frozen in a scream. His eyes were empty sockets, drained even of blood, viscous holes that stared past the Queen at nothing.

What do they see? she wondered. Certainly not the same pretty face the dark thing put on for her. All of them looked like this; there were subtle variations, but it was always the same. If not for the eyes, she might have thought the boy dead from pure fright.

Now her stomach began to churn, bile climbing up the back of her throat. The Queen turned and ran for the bathroom, one hand clamped across her mouth, her eyes wide and hunted.

She nearly made it.

— CHAPTER 13 —

AWAKENING

*In comparing the Glynn Queen to the Red Queen, we find few
similarities. They were very different rulers, and we now know
that they were motivated by very different goals. I should note
that both queens displayed iron will, a shared ability to take the
quickest route to what needed to be done. Yet history also gives
us ample demonstration that the Glynn Queen, unlike the Red
Queen, often tempered her judgments with pity. Indeed, many
historians find this to be the crucial difference between the
two . . .*

—*Professor Jessica Fenn, lecture transcript,*
UNIVERSITY OF THE TEARLING, 458 MARCH

"Lady."

Something cool swiped her forehead, and Kelsea
turned her head, trying to ignore it. Mace had awakened her
out of . . . nothing. No dream she could remember, only a
sleep as cool and dark and endless as she'd ever had in her
life, thousands of miles traveled in unfathomable waters.
Her own Crossing, and she had no urge to return.

"Lady."

Mace's voice was tight with anxiety. She should wake up and let him know she was all right. But the darkness was so warm. It was like being wrapped in velvet.

"She's breathing too slowly. We should get her to a doctor."

"What doctor could help her now?"

"I just thought–"

"They don't train doctors in magic, Pen, only healers, and most of them are frauds anyway. We just have to wait."

Kelsea could hear each of them breathing above her, Mace heavy and Pen shallow. Her senses had sharpened; emerging from the depths one layer at a time, she could hear a man singing softly and the whinny of a horse some distance away.

"Did she bring the flood, sir?"

"God knows, Pen."

"Did the old Queen ever do anything like that?"

"Elyssa?" Mace began to laugh. "Christ, I watched Elyssa wear both jewels for years, and their most extraordinary feat was getting stuck in her dress. We were in the middle of a reception for the Cadarese, and it took us thirty minutes to untangle the damned things with her modesty intact."

"I think the Queen brought the flood. I think it took everything out of her."

"She's breathing, Pen. She's alive. Let's not look beyond that."

"Then why doesn't she wake?"

Pen's voice was filled with something close to grief, and Kelsea realized that it was time now, that she couldn't make them wait any longer. Breaking through the dark warmth in her head, she opened her eyes. Once again she found herself in a blue tent; time might almost have doubled back to that morning when she'd woken and seen the Fetch sitting there.

"Ah, thank Christ," Mace muttered above her. Kelsea's eyes

were drawn first to a bright red patch at his shoulder. His uniform was torn and stained with blood. Pen, kneeling beside him, had no visible wounds, but Kelsea still found Pen the graver case; his eyes were circled dark, the rest of his face ghost-white.

Both of them reached to help her sit up, Pen for her hands and Mace behind her back. Kelsea expected to have a headache, but as she sat up, she found instead that her head felt wonderfully clear, miles wide. She reached up and found both necklaces, still around her neck.

"Don't worry; we didn't dare touch them," Mace told her dryly.

"I hardly dare touch them."

"How do you feel, Lady?"

"Good. Too good. How long did I sleep?"

"A day and a half."

"Are you both all right?"

"We're fine, Lady."

She pointed to Mace's wounded shoulder. "I see someone finally got through your guard."

"There were three of them, Lady, and one was switch-handed. If Venner finds out, I'll never hear the end of it."

"What about the women?"

Mace and Pen looked at each other uncomfortably.

"Speak up!"

"Three lost," Mace replied gruffly.

"But you saved twenty-two, Majesty," Pen added, throwing Mace a dark look that, mercifully, he missed. "Twenty-two women. They're fine, and so are the others. They're on their way home."

"What of the Guard?"

"We lost Tom, Lady." Mace wiped his forehead with one

palm. It was a commonplace gesture, but very expressive in Mace's case; Kelsea thought it was the closest he would let himself come to grief. But she hadn't known Tom well, so she wouldn't shed tears.

"What else?"

"It only stopped raining early this morning, Lady. We were waiting for you to wake up, but I had to make some decisions."

"Your decisions are usually acceptable, Lazarus."

"I sent the caravan back. There were a couple of children left motherless, but a woman from their village said that she would look after them."

Kelsea grabbed his arm, clutching just beneath the elbow. "Is he all right?"

Pen's brow furrowed, but Mace gave her an irritated look; he knew exactly who she meant. She braced herself, anticipating a lecture, but Mace was a good man; he took a deep breath and let it out in a slow sigh. "He's fine, Lady. They all left yesterday, shortly after dawn."

Kelsea's heart sank, but that was nothing Mace needed to know, so she stretched, eliciting several satisfying cracks in her back. As she pushed herself to her feet, she caught the two guards giving each other a hard glance.

"What?"

"There are things to deal with outside, Majesty."

"Fine. Let's go."

Weather could change everything. They'd camped in Thorne's spot, right at the base of the valley that formed the Argive. The entire pass was washed in sunlight, and Kelsea saw that the ravine that had seemed so forbidding at night was actually extraordinarily beautiful, a stark, spare beauty built of bare land and white rock. The walls of the pass gleamed like marble above Kelsea's head.

Her guard was seated around the remains of Thorne's campfire, but upon her approach they stood up, and to her surprise, all of them bowed, even Dyer. Kelsea's black army uniform was streaked and stained with mud, and her hair was undoubtedly a fright, but they didn't seem to care about that. They stood waiting, and after a moment Kelsea realized they weren't waiting for orders from Mace. They were waiting for her.

"Where are the cages? The caravan?"

"I sent it back the way it came, Lady. The prisoners couldn't walk all the way home and most of the mules survived, so we busted off the tops of the cages and turned them into rolling wagons so they could ride comfortably. They should be well into the Almont by now, heading home."

Kelsea nodded, finding this a good solution. Splintered pieces of the roofs and bars still littered the bottom of the pass. At the far side of the ravine, a line of smoke curled into the air. "What's on fire over there?"

"Tom, Lady," Mace replied, his voice tight. "No family, and it's what he would have wanted. No ceremony."

Kelsea looked around at the group, marking a second man missing. "Where's Fell?"

"I sent him back to New London, Lady, with several women who looked like they could use a shopping trip in the big city."

"That's tasteful, Lazarus. They could have died, and you sent them back to spread propaganda."

"It is what it is, Lady. And Fell needed to get indoors anyway; he took some sort of lung illness from the wet."

"Is anyone else injured?"

"Only Elston's pride, Lady," Kibb piped up.

Elston gave his friend a ferocious glare and then looked down at his feet. "Forgive me, Majesty. I failed to take Arlen Thorne. He got away clean."

"You're forgiven, Elston. Thorne's a tough mark."

Bitter laughter erupted from the ground. Looking through several sets of legs, Kelsea saw a man, bound at the wrists, sitting beside the campfire.

"Who's that?"

"Stand, you!" Dyer growled, prodding the prisoner with his foot. The man rose wearily, as though he had a ton of granite between his shoulders. Kelsea's brow quirked, something rippling in her memory. The prisoner wasn't old, perhaps thirty or thirty-five, but his hair was already mostly grey. He looked at her with vacant apathy.

"Javel, Lady. A Gate Guard, and the only survivor who didn't escape. He didn't try to run."

"Well, what am I supposed to do with him?"

"He's a traitor, Lady," Dyer told her. "He's already confessed to opening the Keep Gate for the Graham heir."

"On Thorne's orders?"

"So he says, Lady."

"How did you extract that information?"

"*Extract?* Christ, Lady, we didn't have to do a thing. He would've screamed it in the town square if he could."

Kelsea turned back to the prisoner. In spite of the sun's warmth, a nasty shiver went down her spine. This man looked just as Carroll had looked in the clearing: all hope gone, and something inside him already dead. "How did a Gate Guard get mixed up with Thorne?"

Mace shrugged. "His wife was shipped six years ago. I'm guessing Thorne offered to get her back."

Kelsea's memory was tugging harder now, and she moved

closer, signaling to Coryn and Dyer to back off. The prisoner was clearly no threat to anyone; indeed, he looked like he wanted to do nothing more than fall down dead where he stood.

"He's a traitor, Lady," Dyer repeated. "There's only one fate for a traitor."

Kelsea nodded, knowing this was true. But out of the blur of that night, which now seemed centuries ago, her mind suddenly dug up a vivid picture: this man, an axe in his hand, swinging wildly at the bars of the cage. She waited for a moment, listening, waiting for Carlin to speak up, to tell her what to do. But there was nothing. She hadn't heard Carlin's voice in a long time. She considered the prisoner for a moment longer, then turned to Dyer. "Take him back to the Keep and put him in a cell."

"He's a traitor, Majesty! Make an example of him, and the next bastard Thorne asks will think twice!"

"No," Kelsea replied firmly. Her sapphires gave a light throb, the first thing she'd felt from them since waking. "Take him back, and go easy on him. He won't try to flee."

Dyer's jaw clenched for a moment, but then he nodded. "Lady."

Kelsea had expected Mace to disagree, but he remained oddly silent. "Can we go now?"

"A moment more, Lady." Mace held out an arm, watching while Dyer led Javel away, behind a boulder. "We've business to settle here. Business of the Guard."

Elston and Kibb leaped across the grass and laid hold of Mhurn, who'd already begun to bolt at Mace's words. Elston lifted him bodily off the ground, letting him struggle against the air, while Kibb began to bind his legs.

"What—"

"Our traitor, Lady."

Kelsea's mouth dropped open. "Are you certain?"

"Quite certain, Lady." Mace picked up a saddlebag from the ground and dug through its contents until he produced a leather pouch, carefully rolled and sealed, the way one would pack diamonds or other valuables. Unrolling the pouch, he rifled through it and held one hand out for her inspection. "See here."

Kelsea moved closer, peering at the substance in his palm. It was a fine white powder, almost like flour. "Opium?"

"Not just opium, Lady," Coryn remarked from the campfire. "High-grade morphiate. Someone took a lot of care to cook this stuff. We found needles as well."

Kelsea whirled around, horrified. "*Heroin?*"

"Not quite, Majesty. Not even the Cadarese have been able to synthesize heroin. But they will one day, I have no doubt."

Kelsea closed her eyes, rubbing her temples. When William Tear had sailed from America to create his kingdom on a hill, he'd managed to eradicate narcotics for a brief time. But the drug trade had clawed its way back; humanity would never stop wanting to ride that particular carousel. Heroin . . . it was the worst development Kelsea could imagine.

"How did you find out?"

"Arliss. He and Thorne compete in several markets. Not an ounce of narcotic moves through New London without going through Thorne's backyard, Lady. It's the easiest thing in the world, to suborn an addict by cutting off his supply."

"You had no idea of his addiction?"

"If I had, Lady, he would have been gone."

Kelsea turned and approached Mhurn, who still dangled within Elston's massive arms while Kibb bound his wrists.

"Well, Mhurn, anything to say?"

457

"Nothing, Majesty." He refused to meet her gaze. "Nothing to excuse."

Kelsea stared at him, this man who'd smuggled an assassin into the Queen's Wing, who'd stuck a knife in her back, and found herself remembering that night by the campfire, the tears in his eyes during the ugly scene with Lady Andrews. Carlin had no sympathy for addicts; an addict, she'd told Kelsea, was innately and strategically weak, since his addiction could always be used to break him. Carlin's voice might have fallen silent in Kelsea's mind, but she still knew what Carlin would say: Mhurn was a traitor, and he deserved execution.

Barty had been more lenient about such failings. Once, he'd explained to Kelsea that addiction was like having a crack in your life. "It's a deep crack, and deadly, Kel, but you can build guards around it. You can put up a fence."

Staring at Mhurn now, Kelsea felt no anger, only pity. It would be nearly impossible to conceal such an addiction, since Mace saw everything. Mhurn must have been in constant withdrawal almost every day of his life.

"Do you confess to treachery, Mhurn?"

"Yes."

Kelsea looked around and saw that the rest of the Guard had closed in around them, their gazes cold. She turned back to Mhurn, anxious to forestall them, to prolong his life. "When did you become addicted?"

"What does it matter, at this late date?"

"It matters."

"Two years ago."

"What the hell were you thinking?" Mace roared, unable to contain himself. "A Queen's Guard with a drug habit? Where did you suppose that would end?"

"Here."

"You're a dead man."

"I've been dead since the invasion, sir. It's only the past few years I've begun to rot."

"What a load of shit."

"You've no idea what I've lost."

"We've all lost something, you self-pitying ass." Cold fury laced Mace's voice. "But we're Queen's Guards. We don't sell our honor. We don't abandon our vows."

He turned to Kelsea. "This is best handled out here, Lady, among ourselves. Give us permission to finish him."

"Not yet. Elston, are you getting tired?"

"Are you kidding, Lady? I could hold this faithless bastard all day." Elston flexed his arms, causing Mhurn to groan and struggle. There was an audible snap as one of his ribs broke.

"Enough."

Elston subsided. Kibb had finished tying Mhurn's hands and feet, and now Mhurn merely dangled from Elston's arms like a bound doll, his blond hair hanging limply in his face. Kelsea suddenly recalled something he had said that night out in the Reddick Forest: that the crimes of soldiers came from two sources – situation or leadership. The other prisoner, the Gate Guard, had picked up an axe in the last extremity and tried to right his wrong, but Mhurn had not. His was a difficult situation, to be sure, but was Kelsea's leadership also to blame? From Mace, she knew that Mhurn was a gifted swordsman, not quite of Pen's caliber, but impressive. He was also one of the most levelheaded of the guards, the one Mace trusted when something needed to be done tactfully. It was a terrible loss of a valuable man, and try as she might, Kelsea could feel no anger, only sorrow and the certainty that this tragedy could have been avoided somehow, that she had missed something crucial along the way.

"Coryn, do you know how to inject him with that stuff?"

"I've injected men with antibiotics before, Lady, but I know little of morphia. I might as easily kill him."

"Well, that's neither here nor there now. Give him a decent dose."

"Lady!" Mace barked. "He doesn't deserve that!"

"My decision, Lazarus."

Kelsea watched with covert interest as Coryn went to work, lighting a small flame and heating the white powder in one of his medical tins. As it liquefied, the morphine collapsed into itself like a tiny building. But when Coryn had filled one of his syringes, Kelsea turned away, unable to watch him give Mhurn the injection.

"All done, Lady."

Turning back, she marked the hard angles of Mhurn's face, softened now, and the hazy look in those cold, beautiful eyes. His entire body appeared to have gone limp. How could a drug work so quickly?

"What happened to you in the Mort invasion, Mhurn?"

"You heard me tell it, Majesty."

"I've heard two versions now, Mhurn, and neither was complete. What happened to *you*?"

Mhurn stared dreamily over her shoulder. When he spoke, his voice had a disconnected quality that made Kelsea's stomach clench. "We lived in Concord, Lady, on the shores of the Crithe. Our village was isolated; we didn't even know the Mort were coming until a warning rider came through. But then we could see the shadow on the horizon . . . the smoke from their fires . . . the vultures that followed them in the sky. We fled our village, but we weren't quick enough. My daughter was sick, my wife had never learned to ride, and at any rate we had only one horse. They caught us halfway between the Crithe and the Caddell. My wife was bad, Lady, but Alma, my daughter ... she was taken by Ducarte himself, dragged along in the train of the Mort army for miles. I found her body months later, in the piles of dead left by the Mort after they withdrew from the Keep Lawn. She was covered with bruises ... worse than bruises. I see her always, Lady. Except when I'm on the needle ... that's the only time I'm blind.

"So you're wrong, sir," he continued, turning to Mace, "if you think I care how I die, or when."

"You never told us any of that," Mace snapped back.

"Can you blame me?"

"Carroll would never have taken you into the Guard if he'd known you were so fucked in the head."

Kelsea had heard enough. She reached down and pulled out her knife, the knife that Barty had given her so long ago. Barty had been a Queen's Guard once; would he have wanted this?

Mace's jaw dropped as she straightened. "Lady, any of us would gladly do this for you! You don't have to—"

"Of course I do, Lazarus. This is a traitor to the Crown. I'm the Crown."

Mhurn looked up, his dilated pupils gradually focusing on her knife, and he smiled hazily. "They don't understand, Lady, but I do. You've done me a kindness, and now you mean to do me an honor as well."

Kelsea's eyes filled with tears. She looked up at Elston, seeing his huge form as a blur. "Hold him steady, Elston. I won't be able to do this twice."

"Done, Lady."

Kelsea dashed the tears away, grabbed a handful of Mhurn's blond hair, and yanked his head upright. She spotted his carotid artery, pulsing gently at the corner of his throat. Barty always said to avoid the carotid, if possible; an imprecise cut would end up covering the cutter in blood. She gripped her knife tightly, suddenly sure that this was what Barty would have wanted: for her to do a clean job. She placed the edge of the blade flat against the right side of Mhurn's throat, then drew it across in a quick, sharp movement. Warm crimson spurted over her knife hand but Kelsea ignored it, holding Mhurn's head up long enough to see the widening red smile, the blood beginning to sheet down his throat. His blue eyes stared dreamily into hers for another minute, then she let go of his hair and backed away, watching his head sink slowly toward his chest.

"That's well done, Majesty," Venner remarked. "A good, clean slice."

Kelsea sat down on the ground, crying now, and leaned her head on her crossed arms.

"Leave her alone for a minute," Mace ordered roughly. "Put him on the fire. Coryn, you take charge of the rest of that crap in the pouch; maybe Arliss can make something of it when we get home."

They all moved away then, except for one guard who sat down beside her. Pen.

"Lady," he murmured. "It's time to go."

Kelsea nodded, but it seemed she couldn't stop crying; the tears continued to leak out no matter how she worked to get control. Her breath came in thick, asthmatic gasps. After a moment she felt Pen's hand on hers, gently wiping away the blood.

"Pen!"

Pen's hand vanished.

"Get her up! We've stayed too long already!"

Pen's reached beneath Kelsea's arm, his touch impersonal now, and lifted her from the ground. He held her up as she stumbled along, heading for the pile of boulders where the horses waited inside their makeshift paddock. When she reached Dyer, who was holding her horse, she climbed up automatically, wiping her face on her sleeve.

"Can we go, Lady?"

Kelsea turned to stare behind them, toward the eastern end of the pass. She could see nothing beyond; the rise was too steep. There was no time, but she had the sudden urge to tiptoe up to the edge of the slope, to peek over and behold Mortmesne, this land she'd seen only in dreams. But they were all waiting for her. She wiped the last tears from her cheeks. Mhurn's face was in her mind, but she clenched the reins in her fist and wiped that image clean as well. "All right. Let's go home."

O nce they got out of the Argive, they made good time. The pass itself was sticky with mud, but as soon as they started downhill, the land quickly became dry as a bone. It had only rained over the pass. From time to time, Kelsea reached up and clutched the sapphires beneath her shirt. She could feel nothing from them today, but she wasn't deceived; they wouldn't stay quiet for long. She thought of the nausea she'd felt on the outward journey, the way her mind had been forced forward. The dying sensation when she tried to take one of them off.

What will they do to me?

From their vantage in the foothills, they could see the dark train of the caravan, perhaps half a day's ride ahead, snaking its way across the grasslands. Mace had questioned the villagers well into the night while Kelsea slept, eliciting several interesting facts. Thorne had raided a total of twelve villages along the shores of the Crithe, villages where the men went off together each spring to trade goods in New London. Thorne's men had come the very night after the men had departed, setting fires to create confusion before they broke into houses and grabbed women and children.

Kelsea felt a chill steal down her spine, remembering that bitterly cold morning in the village, the screams of the woman as she lost her sons. She had no urge to intercept the caravan, but she worried about all of those women and children, alone without guard. It seemed important to keep them within sight.

And what could you do if they were attacked, you and your fifteen guards? her mind jeered.

I could do a lot, Kelsea replied darkly, remembering the vast blue light, the voltage that had flared inside her. *I could do plenty*.

But deep down, she was sure there was no danger out here anymore. Coryn had had the good sense to loose Thorne's horses; the few men who'd escaped would be stuck on foot, and it was a very long walk to anywhere. They'd found several of the horses already, grazing in the foothills, and Mace had been able to slip a rope around their necks. He'd given one of the extra horses to the Gate Guard, Javel, though Dyer had tied the man's legs to his saddle and now remained close behind him, watching him with a hawk's eye. Kelsea didn't think it was necessary. In her mind, she saw Javel hacking at the burning cage, his face bathed in soot.

There's something more to him, she thought, *and Mace sees it too.*

When they drew even with the caravan, still a thin shadow several miles to the north, Mace allowed the troop to slow down and keep pace. The sun had crossed a good part of the sky, and they'd covered more than half the distance back to the Crithe when Mace called a halt.

"What is it?"

"A rider," he replied, staring toward the caravan. "Wellmer, get up here!"

It was indeed a single rider, galloping for all he was worth across the countryside from the north. He rode so fast that he left a cloud of dust behind him, despite the fact that the country was mostly grass.

Elston, Pen, and Mace drew together in a triangle around Kelsea, who felt her stomach tightening. What could have gone wrong now?

"He's Caden," Pen murmured. "I see the cloak."

"But only a messenger," Mace remarked thoughtfully. "I'm going to guess we're in a lot of trouble for the death of Dwyne."

"He's dead?" Kelsea asked.

Mace's eyes never left the rider. "Your friend killed him. But the Caden have no way of knowing that. They'll think it was us."

"Well, they've tried to kill me before. I can't be in more trouble than I was already."

"It's not like the Caden to send one man for anything, Lady. Let's err on the side of caution and just wait here."

Kelsea scanned the country around them: wide stretches of grassland and wheat, with some patches of rock, all the way to the blue line of the Crithe. It seemed almost a different country now, but the change wasn't in the land; it was in Kelsea.

"Sir?" Wellmer rode up from the rear with his bow already in hand. "He's got a Caden cloak, all right, but he has a child with him."

"What?"

"A small boy, maybe five or six years old."

Mace frowned for a moment, thinking. Then his brow smoothed out and he smiled, that genuinely pleased smile that Kelsea saw so rarely. "Fortune, you happy bitch."

"What is it?"

"Many of the Caden have bastards around the kingdom, Lady, but Caden aren't particularly suited for fatherhood. The more decent ones usually just give the woman a sum of money and leave."

"Good for them."

"You don't see affection very often," Mace continued, as though Kelsea hadn't spoken, "but I've heard tell of a few Caden who try to live a secret life on the side, a normal life with a woman and family concealed. They're very careful about it, for it would be a fantastic piece of leverage. I think Thorne may have been stupid enough to snatch a Caden's child. Who is it, Wellmer?"

"I don't know all of them by sight yet, sir."

"Describe him."

"Sandy hair. A bruiser. He has a sword and short knife. And an ugly scar across his forehead."

Elston, Pen, and Mace turned to stare at each other, and an entire conversation passed between them in the space of a few seconds.

"What?" Kelsea asked.

"Let's see what he does," Mace told Elston, then turned to Pen. "You watch only the Queen's safety, understand? Nothing else."

The Caden pulled his horse to a halt perhaps fifty yards away. Kelsea saw that he did indeed have a small child tucked in one arm; he lowered the boy carefully toward the ground before climbing down himself. "Who is he?"

"Merritt, Lady," Mace replied. "The Caden don't have a single leader; they're too factional. But Merritt wields considerable power among them, even more than Dwyne."

"If the child was a secret, there's probably a woman in one of those villages as well," Elston cautioned. "We need to handle this carefully."

"Agreed."

Now Merritt took his horse's bridle in one hand, his son's hand in the other, and began to walk toward Kelsea, his movements slow and cautious. He was indeed blond and heavily built, towering over the child beside him. But there was clear affection between them; it was obvious in the way the man shrank his strides to match the boy's, the way the boy looked up at him every few moments, as though to be sure he was still there.

"Extraordinary," Mace remarked quietly, then raised his voice. "Come no closer!"

Merritt stopped short. His son stared at him in confusion, and Merritt picked him up and set him in the crook of his arm. Kelsea could see the scar on Merritt's forehead now, a truly nasty gash that had apparently seen no stitches. It wasn't the distended wound that a childhood injury would leave; rather, it looked fairly recent, an ugly red line against his pale forehead.

"Is the Queen with you?"

"I am!"

"Pen," Mace growled, "stay sharp."

Merritt murmured to his son for a moment and then set

him down. He raised his hands in the air in a gesture of surrender and ventured a few steps closer. Kelsea expected Mace to object, but he merely drew his sword and moved to stand in front of her as Merritt approached.

"I'm Merritt of the Caden, Majesty."

"Well met. Did you come to kill me?"

"We no longer seek your death, Majesty. There's no profit in it."

The small boy had crept up behind his father to wrap an arm around his leg, and now Merritt reached down without thinking and picked him up again. "According to Sean, it's you I have to thank for his life."

"Many lives were saved last night. I'm glad your boy is one of them."

"Will the Mace allow me to come a bit closer?"

Mace nodded. "You may come within five feet, if you keep your arms around your son at all times."

"That's a lot of care for someone traveling openly across flat country in daylight."

Mace bristled, but said nothing. As Merritt came closer, Kelsea saw that the boy was falling asleep, his dark head tucked into the curve of his father's neck. Merritt halted perhaps seven feet away, and Kelsea's gaze was drawn automatically to the scar on his forehead, but when he looked her in the eye, she found that she couldn't look away. Despite his bruiser's build, his eyes were a bright and perceptive grey.

"I'll be gone from New London for a time, Majesty, perhaps a month, to hide my family. But I'm an honorable man, and you've given me my son's life. So you have my word: I will never raise a hand against you, and if it's within my power to do you a similar favor, I will."

He gestured toward the caravan on the northern horizon. "I apologize also for those of my brothers you found in this business. They were working on their own. I doubt we'd have approved this action if it had come to a vote."

Kelsea raised her eyebrows, surprised. She wouldn't have thought of the Caden as a democratic body.

"Should you need my assistance, find a baker's boy named Nick down in the Wells," Merritt continued, speaking to Mace now. "He'll know how to get a message to me, and he'll do it quietly."

He bowed to Kelsea and turned to walk back to his horse, his gait slow so as not to wake the child. He remounted with the boy still in the crook of one arm (how strong he must be! Kelsea thought; she could barely haul herself and her own armor into a saddle) and began to trot west.

"Well, that was something," Kelsea remarked.

"More than something, Lady," Mace replied. "The Caden bow to no one. I think he meant every word."

They watched Merritt until he was no more than a speck against the tan of the grasslands, and only then did Mace seem to relax. He snapped his fingers, particularly at Kibb, who showed signs of climbing down from his horse. "Back at it!"

They rode west. The shining cerulean line of the Crithe grew closer as they traveled, until it resolved itself into a bright ribbon of water running alongside them. The caravan would need to ford the Crithe, and that would take some effort, yet Kelsea found that she wasn't worried about anything at the moment. She'd checked her sapphires often, but they simply hung there, heavy and cold. For today, at least, they were only jewels.

They kept within sight of the caravan until it reached the close-set group of villages along the Crithe. Mace had directed the villagers to cut weight as they went, leaving empty cages behind, and Wellmer assured Kelsea that the caravan was gradually being dismantled from village to village. No one would use Thorne's handiwork again, not for anything but firewood.

But he can always build more, Kelsea's mind warned. The thought made her jaw clench; if only they'd managed to take Thorne! She couldn't be angry at Elston, but she didn't underestimate the danger of having Thorne out there, on the loose. It might take him some time to regroup, but he wouldn't be idle for long.

When the caravan reached the final village, Kelsea and her Guard finally turned away and headed for New London, rejoining the Mort Road. Their travel was uneventful. The guards talked quietly among themselves during the journey. Coryn, who'd had the presence of mind to gather all the water he could carry in the Argive, periodically passed around bottles. A couple of times they were treated to the truly horrible sound of Kibb singing riding songs, until Kelsea finally threatened to throw him out of her Guard if he didn't shut up.

She spent much of the journey talking to Wellmer, with whom she'd had little conversation before. He told her that he'd been fifteen, living on the streets of New London and earning his bread by hustling games of darts, when Mace had found him. "He taught me to shoot, Lady. He said there wasn't that much difference between archery and darts, and there isn't. It's in the eye."

Kelsea looked up ahead, to where Mace led the company. "What if you failed to make the switch? Would he have thrown you back to the streets?"

"Probably. Dyer always says there's no room for dead-weight in the Queen's Guard."

That sounded like Dyer, fair but hard, probably true. Looking around her, Kelsea saw no signs of grief over Mhurn; indeed, her guards didn't discuss him at all, and Kelsea wondered if he meant nothing to them now, if Queen's Guards were able to cut their deadweight as easily as the caravan. She couldn't forget about Mhurn so easily; the image of his empty, drug-hazed eyes recurred to her constantly as they traversed the Mort Road. She looked at the land around her, the deep amber of the wheat cut by the yellow line of the road, and wished that she could make it a softer world.

On the final night of the journey, they camped within sight of New London, atop a shallow rise on the banks of the Caddell. Her guards fell gratefully to their bedrolls, but Kelsea, who had slept soundly each night since they'd left the Argive, found herself wakeful. She tossed and fidgeted for perhaps an hour, then finally got up, wrapped herself in her cloak, and crept away from Pen, proud when he failed to wake.

She found Mace sitting some twenty feet down the side of the hill, looking out across the Caddell and the Almont Plain beyond, a pale blue shadow in the darkness. He didn't even turn around as she approached.

"Can't sleep, Lady?"

Feeling around on the ground, Kelsea found a broad, flat rock that would hold her comfortably and sat down beside him. "I never know what I'll see when I sleep these days, Lazarus."

"Where's Pen?"

"Sleeping."

"Ah." He looped his arms around his legs. "We'll undoubtedly discuss that at some point, but for now, I'm glad you found me alone, Lady. It's time for me to offer my resignation."

"Why?"

Mace chuckled bitterly. "You know, Lady, all those years I watched Carroll do this job, I envied him. I was better than him at so many things, you see . . . I could read people better, I was a better fighter, I had better discipline. Each time the Regent tried to disband us, to cut off our salaries, I was the one who made sure it didn't happen. I always assumed that when my turn came, I would be a better captain than Carroll. But pride has done me in."

Kelsea bit her lip. Despite the events of the past week, she had never even considered asking Mace to resign. Who else could possibly do his job? She opened her mouth to tell him so, and then closed it. Maudlin sentiment would cut no ice here. "You've had several spectacular failures in security lately, Lazarus."

"Indeed, Lady."

"Disappointing, and yet I forgive you those failures."

"You shouldn't have to."

Kelsea thought for a moment, then continued, "That day in my chamber, when you and Pen grabbed hold of me, I could have killed you. Did you know that?"

"Not at the time, Majesty. But now I don't doubt that it's so."

"I could kill you now, Lazarus, for all your vaunted prowess with sword and mace. And before I asked you to resign, I *would* kill you. I'm safest with you here beside me, not out there beside someone else."

"I'm sworn to you, Lady. That doesn't end when I resign."

"So you say now. But even you can't predict what circumstance may do. I won't take the chance, and I don't accept your resignation."

She grabbed his arm, not hard, but not too gently either. "But make no mistake: if you ever refuse to obey a direct order of mine again, I will kill you. Anger almost made me do it once, and could easily make me do it again. I'm not a child any longer, Lazarus, nor am I a fool. I'm either the Queen or I'm not . . . there can be no grey."

Mace swallowed; she heard it clearly in the dark. "You're the Queen, Lady."

"I'm sorry to threaten you, Lazarus. It's not what I want."

"I don't fear death, Lady."

She nodded. Mace didn't fear anything; she already knew that.

"But I don't want to die at your hands."

Kelsea's lips parted, and she stared at the twinkling line of the Caddell, unable to respond.

"What now, Lady?"

"Now we continue, Lazarus. We prepare for the war that we both know is coming. We figure out how to feed and educate and doctor all of these people. But even more than that . . ." She turned back to him. "I've been thinking for a long time about the shipment, about all those Tear in Mortmesne."

You have? her mind asked, bewildered. *When?* And it came to Kelsea: while she'd slept. Something from that dark period strained to break the surface, but then it faded without a ripple, and the pool in her head lay still. She *had* dreamed; she'd dreamed of so many things that her mind had wiped itself clean.

"Many of the allotted are dead now, Lady. Worked to death or killed for their organs."

"I know that. But organs can't be the primary use for Mort slaves; Arliss says the transplant surgery hasn't been perfected. There's no money in it yet. No, it'll be the two old standbys: labor and sex. I'm sure many of them are dead, but humanity always finds a way to survive this ordeal. I think more must still be alive."

"So?"

"I don't know yet. But something, Lazarus. Something."

Mace shook his head. "I have several spies in Demesne, Lady, but none where you're talking about, which is the Auctioneer's Office. The Mort are a population under the boot; it's difficult to turn them."

"Carlin always used to tell me that people under tyranny needed only a swift kick to awaken them."

Mace remained silent for a long moment.

"What?"

"Lady, your foster parents are dead."

The words hit Kelsea like a punch to the stomach. She turned to him, opening her mouth, but nothing came out.

"Dyer found them there, Lady, when he went for the books. Both of them, some weeks dead."

"How?"

"They were sitting in their parlor, mugs of tea in front of them, a bottle of cyanide on the table. Dyer's no detective, but it was an easy scene to read. They waited until you left, poured their tea, and laced it. They would've been dead by the time the Caden reached the cottage."

Kelsea stared at the river, feeling the warmth of tears on her cheeks. She should have known. She remembered Barty and Carlin in the weeks before her departure, the haphazard way they'd packed, the lack of urgency. The awful whiteness of their faces that morning in front of the cottage. All of their talk of Petaluma had been a show for Kelsea's benefit. They had never planned to leave.

"Did you know this when you came to the cottage?"

"No."

"Why wouldn't they tell me?"

"For the same reason I haven't told you, Lady: to save you anguish. Believe me, theirs was an honorable act. No matter where they went or how well they hid themselves, Barty and the Lady Glynn would always have been a danger to you."

"Why?"

"They raised you, Lady. They had the sort of information no one else could discover: your likes and dislikes, what moves you, your weaknesses, who you really are."

"What could anyone do with that?"

"Ah, Lady, that's the sort of information that enemies value most. I use such intelligence myself, to suborn spies and create havoc. Pressure points are incredibly valuable. Moreover, Lady, what if someone had captured your foster parents, offered them to you for ransom, threatened them with harm? What would you have been willing to give?"

Kelsea had no answer. She couldn't seem to get beyond the fact that she would never see Barty again. She thought of her chair, of Kelsea's Patch, which sat right in the sunlight through the cottage window. More tears came now, burning like acid behind her eyelids.

"The Lady Glynn was a historian of the pre-Crossing, Lady, and Barty was a Queen's Guard. They knew what they were getting into eighteen years ago, when I delivered you to their door."

"You said you didn't know!"

"I didn't, Lady, but they did. Listen closely, for I will only tell this tale once." Mace considered for a moment, then continued. "Eighteen years ago, I rode up to that cottage in the Reddick with you strapped to my chest. It was raining hard; we'd been on the road for three straight days, and it had rained the entire time. We rigged up a waterproof sling for me to carry you in, but even so, by the end of the journey, you were nearly wet through."

Despite her grief, Kelsea was fascinated. "Did I cry?"

"Not a bit, Lady. You absolutely loved that sling. The burn on your arm was still healing, but so long as we were riding along, you never cried once. The only time I had to quiet you was when you began to laugh.

"When we got to the cottage, it was the Lady Glynn who answered the door. You did cry a bit when I unstrapped you from the sling; I've always thought that, even then, you knew somehow that the ride was over. But when I handed you to the Lady Glynn, you quieted instantly and went to sleep in her arms."

"Carlin held me?" This seemed so unlikely that Kelsea wondered whether Mace was making up the entire story.

"She did, Lady. Barty offered me dinner, much to his lady's displeasure, so we sat down to eat. By the end of the meal, I could see that Barty had already fallen in love with you; it was plain in his face."

Kelsea closed her eyes, feeling more tears trickle from beneath the lids.

"When we were done eating, Barty offered to let me spend the night, but I wanted to be gone before the rain would no longer hide my tracks. When I'd repacked my saddle, I went in to bid them goodbye and found the three of you in the front room. I think they'd forgotten I was there. They saw nothing but you."

Kelsea's stomach gave a slow, sick lurch.

"Barty said, 'Let me hold her.' So the Lady Glynn handed you to him, and then – I'll never forget, Lady – she said, 'From now on, it will be you . . . the love must come from you.'

"Barty looked as baffled as I was, until she explained. 'This is our great work, Barty. Children need love, but they also need stiffening, and you'll be no help with that. Give her whatever she wants, and she'll turn into her mother. She has to hate one of us, at least a little, so that she can walk out the door and not look back.'"

Kelsea closed her eyes.

"They knew, Lady. They always knew. They made a sacrifice, and you should weep, but you should also honor them for it."

Kelsea wept, glad that Mace neither sought to comfort her nor tried to leave. He merely sat beside her, his arms wrapped around his knees, staring at the Caddell, until Kelsea's tears reduced themselves to hitching gasps, then to slow breaths that whistled in and out of her throat.

"You should return to your bed, Lady. We get an early start tomorrow."

"I can't sleep."

"Try, and I'll go easy on Pen for letting you sneak away."

Kelsea opened her mouth to tell him that she didn't care about Pen, and then closed it. Somewhere on the return journey, all of her anger at Pen had faded away. It had been a child's anger, she realized, implacable and unproductive . . . the sort that had always disappointed Carlin the most.

Putting a hand on Mace's shoulder, Kelsea boosted herself

up, wiping her face. But five steps away, she turned around. "What have you lost, Lazarus?"

"Lady?"

"You told Mhurn that you'd all lost something. What have *you* lost?"

"Everything."

Kelsea shrank from the bitterness in his voice. "Have you gained something now?"

"I have, Lady, and I value it. Go to sleep."

CHAPTER 14
THE QUEEN OF THE TEARLING

Here is Tearling, here is Mortmesne,
One of black and the other red,
One of light and one of darkness,
One of living, the other dead.

Here is Glynn Queen, here is Red Queen,
One to perish beyond recall,
The Lady moves, the Witch despairs,
Glynn Queen triumph and Red Queen fall.
—CHILD'S GAMING VERSE, PROMINENT DURING
THE MIDDLE TEAR EMPIRE

Two days later, a strange thing happened.

Kelsea was sitting at her desk in the library, copying one of Father Tyler's volumes of history. Father Tyler sat at the desk beside her, also assiduously copying away. Mace had procured four clerks, but Kelsea and Father Tyler both wrote faster, and on the priest's visiting days they often sat there together, talking occasionally while they worked. Kelsea had never expected to feel comfortable with a priest, but it *was* comfortable, the way Kelsea imagined school would have felt if she'd been allowed to go.

Father Tyler knew a great deal about the Crossing. This was useful, for the Crossing had been on Kelsea's mind since they'd returned from the Argive. What had it been like for Tear's utopians, braving the worst ocean imaginable, not knowing if they would ever reach land, if there was any land to reach? Father Tyler told Kelsea that after the waves had capsized the White Ship, there had been survivors in the water, doctors and nurses waiting for rescue. But the other ships had insufficient control, the ocean too wild and the weather too disastrous for them to turn around. They'd been forced to leave the survivors behind, all of those people, first struggling in the water and then bobbing gently until they slipped beneath the waves. Kelsea couldn't get the image out of her head; she even dreamed about it, dreams of treading water, freezing, her struggles growing fainter and fainter, watching as the rest of the ships disappeared over the horizon toward a new world. Toward the Tearling.

Kelsea had read the same two paragraphs several times now, and she finally put down her pen. She wondered if there was any word yet about Thorne. He had disappeared into the vastness of the Tearling without a trace, but Mace would find him. Mace and Elston, who seemed to have taken it as a mortal affront that Thorne had escaped. They would find him and bring him here. Kelsea trembled at the thought, rage mixing with excitement inside her head.

Peeking over at Father Tyler, she saw that he was

distracted as well. Two deep furrows had appeared in his forehead, and he had stopped copying, now merely stared at the bookshelves in the corner.

"You're idling, Father," she prompted him.

The priest looked up and smiled a timid, pleasant smile. They'd begun to joke with each other from time to time, a development that pleased Kelsea. "I was woolgathering, Lady. I apologize."

"What's wrong?"

Father Tyler's lips pressed together for a moment, then he shrugged and said, "I suppose you will find out eventually, Majesty. The Holy Father has fallen ill with pneumonia again, and they say that this is the final illness."

"I'm sorry."

"You are not sorry, Majesty. I wish you wouldn't say so."

Kelsea looked sharply at him, as did Pen, sitting in the corner. She thought about reproving the priest but, finding his frankness valuable, decided not to. "So what happens now?"

"All of the cardinals are returning for conclave, to select a new Holy Father."

"Who are the candidates?"

Father Tyler's mouth tightened again. "On paper, Lady, there are several candidates, but the deal is done. They say that Cardinal Anders will be the new Holy Father within a month."

Kelsea didn't know much about Cardinal Anders, only that Mace considered him a nasty piece of work. "And that bothers you?"

"He's a competent administrator, Lady. Perhaps not truly devout." Father Tyler straightened and clamped his mouth shut, his default reaction when he thought he'd said too much. Kelsea dipped pen in ink and prepared to resume her work.

"Be careful, Lady."

"What?"

"I know . . . I have not told them . . . that Your Majesty has no more religion than a housecat. Cardinal Anders is . . . I fear for Your Majesty. I fear for all of us."

Kelsea drew back, amazed at this outburst from the normally taciturn priest. "What did he do to you?"

"Not me, Majesty." He stared at her with wide eyes. "But I believe the cardinal capable of terrible things. I believe—"

Mace and Wellmer entered the library, and Father Tyler fell silent. Kelsea shot Mace an annoyed glance, checking her watch; she was supposed to have at least another twenty minutes with the priest before meeting with Arliss.

"Lady, there's something you should see."

"Now?"

"Yes, Lady. Out on the balcony."

Kelsea sighed, looking at the priest with real regret. She had no idea what he'd been about to say, but it had sounded worth hearing. "I believe that's our time together, Father. Have a safe trip back to Arvath, and my best wishes for the Holy Father's health."

"Thank you, Majesty." Father Tyler folded up his bound copybook, his eyes darting to Mace. He still looked worried, so much so that Kelsea leaned closer and whispered, "Have no fear, Father; I underestimate no one, certainly not your cardinal."

He gave her the briefest of nods, his white face still troubled. According to Mace, who had several spies in the

Arvath, the Holy Father was displeased with Father Tyler, who wasn't giving him the information he wanted. Kelsea wondered how bad things were really getting for Father Tyler in the Arvath, but they hadn't yet reached a place where she could ask him outright.

When the priest had gone, Mace and Wellmer led Kelsea down the hallway to the balcony room. Jordan, her herald, emerged sleepily from one of the rooms at the end of the hall. "You wanted me, sir?"

Mace crooked a finger at him, and Jordan followed them into the room, scratching the back of his head. Mace now kept two guards on the balcony doors, and today it was Coryn and Dyer, both of whom bowed as Kelsea entered the room.

"Out here, Lady." Mace threw the doors open, admitting cold sunlight. Winter was just beginning to melt into spring, but the sky looked like summer, pure blue all the way to the horizon. Kelsea stepped out into the sunlight and shuddered with pleasure; the heat on her skin was an extraordinary feeling after the darkness of the Queen's Wing. Mace beckoned her forward and pointed over the parapet. "Down there."

Kelsea peeked over the edge and immediately regretted it; the height was dizzying. They must be very near the top of the Keep, but she found that she wanted to look up even less than she wanted to look down.

Far below lay the Keep Lawn, covered with people, crowds that stretched from the moat all the way to the crest of the hill, a breathing, murmuring organism some three hundred yards wide. Kelsea remembered the day of the shipment, a month and a lifetime ago, but today there were no lines, no cages. After a moment, however, she noticed an odd treelike figure that poked high above the crowd. "My eyes are terrible. What is that?"

"That, Lady, is a head on a pike," replied Wellmer.

"Whose head?"

"Your uncle's, Lady. I went down there just to make sure. The pike is hung with a placard that says 'A gift for the Tear Queen, compliments of the Fetch.' "

Despite the gruesome nature of the offering, Kelsea smiled. She looked to Mace and found the corners of his mouth tucked downward, holding in a smile as well, and she suddenly understood. It was like that day with the books, the library. Mace intended this moment as a gift for Kelsea, but he couldn't admit it, any more than he could drop the mantle of suspicion that shrouded his entire life. This was as far as he could come. She wished she could hug him, as she would have hugged Barty, but she knew he wouldn't want that. She wrapped her arms around herself instead, as though she were cold, but continued to watch Mace out of the corner of her eye.

What made him this way? What happened to him?

Wellmer continued. "The pike's buried deep, so the crowd can't get at it unless they brought shovels. The head is in immaculate condition, Lady; someone's treated it with a fixative so it won't rot."

"Useful lawn ornament," Mace remarked.

Kelsea looked over the edge again, certain that the Fetch was down there now. He would have delivered the gift himself, hiding in plain sight. She wished she could see him, tell him that their bargain had borne even better fruit than he could have imagined. "What do all these people want?"

"You, Lady," Mace told her. "Your mother never dared to

go out into the city proper; she would use this balcony for announcements. The crowd began gathering yesterday when they found out you were back in the Keep. My man on the gate says most of them spent the night out there."

"I don't have anything to announce."

"Come up with something, Lady. I don't think they're going away."

Kelsea peeked over the balcony again. The people did appear to have settled in; she could see tents of various colors and smell roasting meat. Snatches of song drifted up from far below. There were so many people.

"Speak up, Jordan. Let's tell them she's here."

Jordan cleared his throat, emitting a phlegmy rumble that seemed to fit a much older man. "Sorry, Lady," he muttered, blushing. "I've had a cold."

Taking a deep breath, he leaned over the parapet and shouted, "The Queen of the Tearling!"

The entire lawn looked upward, erupting in a roar so powerful that Kelsea felt it shake the stone beneath her. She was looking down at a sea of faces now, all of them upturned, all staring at her. Placing both hands on the balcony, she leaned far over the edge, so far that Pen took a preemptive hold on the back of her dress. Kelsea held up her hands for silence, waiting until the echoes died down. That day on the Keep Lawn seemed like another lifetime, but now, just as then, she found that words had filled her throat.

"I am Kelsea Raleigh, child of Elyssa Raleigh!"

The crowd remained silent, waiting.

"But I am also the adopted child of Bartholemew and Carlin Glynn!"

A thick carpet of susurrations and whispering rose from

the lawn below. Kelsea closed her eyes and saw Barty and Carlin, as clearly as she had ever seen them in life, standing in the kitchen of the cottage, Barty holding his plant kit and Carlin holding a book. Kelsea had known they were dead; somewhere deep inside, she had known. She hadn't heard either Carlin's or Barty's voice in her head for weeks. They had been gradually fading, replaced with another voice, that grim, determined voice that spoke up when things were dire, when she didn't know what to do.

My own voice, Kelsea realized in wonder. *Not Carlin's, not Barty's, but mine.*

"My foster parents made me what I am and gave their lives in my service!" she shouted hoarsely. "Therefore I change my name! From this day forward, I am Kelsea Raleigh Glynn! My throne will be Glynn, my children will be Glynn, and I will not be a Raleigh queen, but a Glynn queen!"

This time, the roar nearly knocked her backward, trembling the parapet and making the door frame rattle behind her. Kelsea didn't have anything more to say, could only wave at them, but that seemed to be all right. They continued to cheer for long minutes, as though that was all they wanted, just to see her, to know she was there.

I'm not alone, she realized, her eyes filling with tears. *Barty was right after all.*

She wiped the moisture away and muttered to Mace, "They're easily pleased."

"No, Lady. They're not."

The crowd had erupted in some song now, but from this height Kelsea couldn't catch most of the words, only her name. She stared out across her country, a truly spectacular view. The horizon cut the land perhaps halfway across the

Almont Plain, but still Kelsea felt that the entire Tearling was laid out before her. Despite her poor vision, she could see every inch of her land, every detail, north to the Fairwitch and east to the Mort border, even to the rocky crags of the Border Hills where Hall and his battalion were preparing for invasion, constructing defenses on the hillsides. She blinked and saw Mortmesne, just as she'd seen it before, miles of forest broken by well-kept roads. The roads were crammed with long, black lines of soldiers, with wagons and siege towers, with cannons that gleamed in the sun, all of them marching inexorably toward the Tearling.

But now Kelsea's vision blurred and she was no longer looking even at Mortmesne. She could see much farther, across mountains and borders, to seas that existed on no map of the New World, to the skyline of a city that was crumbling into dust. Geography had altered and the land was in upheaval. Kelsea glimpsed wonders, so briefly that she didn't have the time to understand them, or even to mourn their passing. She could see everything, the future and the past, her vision stretching into a place where time and land merged into one.

Then it was all abruptly gone. Kelsea blinked again, her eyes filled with tears, and saw only her own kingdom, farming plains running out before her to meet the sky. Her heart ached, the same vague sensation of loss she felt upon waking from a dream she couldn't remember. She was Kelsea Glynn, a girl who'd grown up in the forest, who loved to study history and read fiction. But she was something else, something more than Kelsea, and so she remained there for a moment longer, watching over her country, straining to see the danger beyond the horizon.

My responsibility, she thought, and the idea brought no fear now, only an extraordinary sense of gratitude.

My kingdom.

Acknowledgments

My first and greatest thanks must go to Dorian Karchmar: not only superagent, but friend and gifted editor, who put in extraordinary effort to get this book ready for the world. Thanks also to Cathryn Summerhayes, Simone Blaser, Laura Bonner, Ashley Fox, Michelle Feehan, and the rest of the incredibly helpful people at William Morris Endeavor. All have been great.

Thank you to Maya Ziv, Jonathan Burnham, and everyone at Harper, for placing a great deal of faith in a first-time author. Seabiscuit particularly thanks Maya for shepherding this book down the stretch. Similar thanks to the crew at Transworld Publishers, especially Simon Taylor; if there's a better man to lunch and talk books with, I haven't found him yet.

Thank you, Dad and Deb, for being supportive and understanding of the long and circuitous life trajectory that brought me to this point. And big thanks to Christian and Katie, who constantly remind me that love really does move the wide world.

Thanks and love to Shane Bradshaw, who keeps my crazy under control, accommodates my knitting addiction, and reminds me that things will be all right.

I'm sure many writers can produce good work without having a mentor, but I'm not one of them. Thank you to all teachers out there, but particularly to Edward Carey, Chris Offutt, and others who share their gifts at the Iowa Writers' Workshop, as well as the incomparable Professor Betsy Bolton of Swarthmore College. Thank you also to Jonas Honick, the world's greatest history teacher; I'm not sure what my sense of social justice (or Kelsea's, for that matter) would look like without you.

Last but not least, thank you, readers. I hope you had a good time here.

The thrilling story of Kelsea Glynn and the
Tearling kingdom continues in

THE
INVASION
OF THE
TEARLING

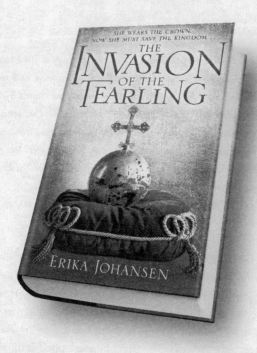

Here's a taster . . .

Chapter 1

Hall

The Second Mort Invasion had all the makings of a slaughter. On one side was the vastly superior Mort army, armed with the best weapons available in the New World and commanded by a man who would balk at nothing. On the other was the Tear army, one-fourth the size and bearing weapons of cheaply forged iron that would break under the impact of good steel. The odds were not so much lopsided as catastrophic. There seemed no way for the Tearling to escape disaster.

—*The Tearling as a Military Nation*, CALLOW THE MARTYR

Dawn came quickly on the Mort border. One minute there was nothing but a hazy line of blue against the horizon, and the next, bright streaks stretched upward from eastern Mortmesne, drenching the sky. The luminous reflection spread across Lake Karczmar until the surface was nothing but a glowing sheet of fire, an effect only broken when a light breeze lapped at the shores and the smooth surface divided into waves.

The Mort border was a tricky business in this region. No one knew precisely where the dividing line was drawn. The Mort asserted that the lake was in Mort territory, but the Tear staked its own claim to the water, since a noted Tear explorer named Martin Karczmar had discovered the lake in the first place. Karczmar had been laid in his grave nearly three centuries since, but the Tearling had never quite relinquished its shaky claim to the lake. The water itself was of little value, filled with predatory fish that were no good to eat, but the lake was an important spot, the only concrete geographical landmark on the border for miles to the north or south. Both kingdoms had always been anxious to establish a definitive claim. At one point, long ago, there had been some talk of negotiating a specific treaty, but nothing had ever come of it. The eastern and southern edges of the lake were salt flats, the territory alternating between silt and marshland. These flats stretched eastward for miles before they ran into a forest of Mort pine. But on the western edge of Lake Karczmar, the salt flats continued for only a few hundred feet before they climbed abruptly into the Border Hills, steep slopes covered with a thick layer of pine trees. The trees wrapped up and over the Hills, descending on the other side into the Tearling proper and flattening out into the northern Almont Plain.

Although the steep eastern slopes of the Border Hills were uninhabited forest, the hilltops and western slopes were dotted with small Tear villages. These villages did some foraging in the Almont, but they mostly bred livestock—sheep and goats—and dealt in wool and milk and mutton, trading primarily with each other. Occasionally they would pool their resources and send a heavily guarded shipment to New London, where goods—particularly wool—fetched a greater price, and the payment was not in barter but in coin. The villages stretched across the hillside: Woodend, Idyllwild, Devin's Slope, Griffen . . . easy pickings, their inhabitants armed with wooden weapons and burdened with animals they were unwilling to leave behind.

Colonel Hall wondered how it was possible to love a stretch

of land so much and yet thank great God for the fate that had taken you away. Hall had grown up the son of a sheep farmer in the village of Idyllwild, and the smell of those villages—wet wool caked with a generous helping of manure—was such a fixed part of his memory that he could smell it even now, though the nearest village was on the western side of the Border Hills, several miles away and well out of sight.

Fortune had taken Hall away from Idyllwild, not good fortune, but the backhanded sort that gave with one hand while it stabbed with the other. Their village was too far north to have suffered badly in the first Mort invasion; a party of raiders had come one night and taken some of the sheep from an unguarded paddock, but that was all. When the Mort Treaty was signed, Idyllwild and its neighbor villages had thrown a festival. Hall and his twin brother, Simon, had gotten roaring drunk and woken up in a pig-pen in Devin's Slope. Father said their village had gotten off easy, and Hall thought so too, until eight months later, when Simon's name was pulled in the second public lottery.

Hall and Simon were fifteen, already men by border lights, but their parents forgot that fact over the next three weeks. Mum made Simon's favorite foods, Pa relieved both boys from work. Near the end of the month they made the journey to New London, just as so many families had made since, with Pa weeping in the front of the wagon, Mum grim and silent, and Hall and Simon working hard to produce a forced gaiety on the way.

His parents hadn't wanted Hall to see the shipment. They'd left him in a pub on the Great Boulevard, with three pounds and instructions to stay there until they returned. But Hall wasn't a child, and he left the pub and followed them to the Keep Lawn. Pa had collapsed shortly before the shipment departed, leaving Mum to try to revive him, so in the end it was only Hall who saw the shipment leave, only Hall who saw Simon disappear into the city and out of their lives forever.

Their family stayed in New London that night, in one of the filthiest inns the Gut had to offer. The horrendous smell finally drove Hall outside, and he wandered the Gut, looking for a horse to steal, determined to follow the cages down the Mort Road, break Simon out or die trying. He found a horse tied outside one of the pubs and was working on the complicated knot when a hand fell on his shoulder.

"What do you think you're doing, country rat?"

The man was big, taller than Hall's father, and covered in armor and weapons. Hall thought he would likely die within moments, and part of him was glad. "I need a horse."

The man looked at him shrewdly. "Someone in the shipment?"

"None of your business."

"It certainly is my business. It's my horse."

Hall drew his knife. It was a sheep-shearing knife, but he hoped the stranger wouldn't know. "I don't have time to argue with you. I need your horse."

"Put that away, boy, and stop being a fool. The shipment is guarded by eight Caden. I'm sure you've heard of the Caden, even out in whatever shithole town you come from. They could break your puny little knife with their teeth."

The stranger made to grab the horse's bridle, but Hall held the knife up higher, blocking his path. "I am sorry to be a thief, but that's the way it is. I have to go."

The stranger gazed at him for a long moment, assessing. "You've got stones, boy, I'll give you that. What are you, farmer?"

"Shepherd."

The stranger considered him for another moment and then said, "All right, boy. Here's how it plays out. I will *lend* you my horse. His name, appropriately enough, is Favor. You ride him down the Mort Road and take a look at that shipment. If you're smart, you'll realize that it's a no-win proposition, and then you have two choices. You can die senselessly, achieving nothing. Or

495

you can turn around and ride to the army barracks in the Wells, so we can talk about your future."

"What future?"

"As a soldier, boy. Unless you want to spend the rest of your life stinking of sheep shit."

Hall eyed him uncertainly, wondering if his words were a trick. "What if I just ride off with your horse?"

"You won't. You've a sense of obligation in you, or you'd never be off on this fool's errand in the first place. Besides, I have an entire army's worth of horses if I need to come after you."

The stranger turned and headed back into the pub, leaving Hall standing there at the hitching post.

"Who are you?" Hall called after him.

"Major Bermond, of the Right Front. Ride fast, boy. And if any harm comes to my horse, I'll take it out of your miserable sheep-loving hide."

After a hard night's ride, Hall caught up to the shipment and found that Bermond was right: it was a fortress. Soldiers surrounded each cage, their formations dotted by the red cloaks of the Caden. Hall didn't have a sword, but he wasn't fool enough to believe that a sword would make any difference. He couldn't even get close enough to distinguish Simon; when he tried to approach the cages, one of the Caden launched an arrow that missed him by no more than a foot. It was just as the Major had said.

Still, he considered charging the shipment and ending everything, the terrible future he had already sensed on the trip to New London, a future in which his parents looked at him and only saw Simon missing. Hall's face would not be a comfort to them, only a terrible reminder. He tightened his grip on the reins, preparing to charge, and then something happened that he would never be able to explain: through the mass of tightly packed prisoners in the sixth cage, he suddenly glimpsed Simon. The cages were too far away for Hall to have seen anything, but seen it he had, all the same: his brother's face. His own face. If he rode to his death, there would be nothing left of Simon, nothing to even mark his passage. And then Hall saw that this was not about Simon at all, but about his own guilt, his own sorrow. Selfishness and self-destruction, riding hand in hand, as they so often did.

Hall turned the horse, rode back to New London, and joined the Tear army. Major Bermond was his sponsor, and although Bermond would never admit it, Hall thought that the Major must have spoken a word in someone's ear, because even during Hall's years in the unranked infantry, he had never been pulled for shipment duty. He sent a portion of his earnings home each month, and on his rare journeys to Idyllwild, his parents surprised him by being gruff but proud of their soldier son. He rose quickly through the ranks, becoming the General's Executive Officer by the young age of thirty-one. It wasn't rewarding work; a soldier's life under the Regency consisted of breaking up brawls and hunting down petty criminals. There was no glory in it. But this . . .

"Sir."

Hall looked up and saw Lieutenant-Colonel Blaser, his second-in-command. Blaser's face was darkened with soot.

"What is it?"

"Major Caffrey's signal, sir. Ready on your command."

"A few more minutes."

The two of them sat in a bird's nest deep on the eastern slope of the Border Hills. Hall's battalion had been out here for several weeks now, working steadily, as they watched the dark mass move across the Mort Flats. The sheer size of the Mort army hindered its progress, but it had come, all the same, and now the encampment sprawled along the southern edge of Lake Karczmar, a black city that stretched halfway to the horizon.

Through his spyglass, Hall could see only four sentries, posted at wide lengths on the western edge of the Mort camp. They were dressed to blend in with the dark, silty surface of the salt flats, but Hall knew the banks of this lake well, and outliers were easy to spot in the growing light. Two of them weren't even patrolling; they'd dozed off at their posts. The Mort were resting easy, just as they should. The Mace's reports said that the Mort army numbered over twenty thousand, and their swords and armor were good iron, tipped with steel. And by any measure, the Tear army was weak. Bermond was partly to blame. Hall loved the old man like a father, but Bermond had become too accustomed to peacetime. He toured the Tearling like a farmer inspecting his acres, not a soldier preparing for battle. The Tear army wasn't ready for war, but now it was upon them, all the same.

Hall's attention returned, as it had so often in the past week, to the cannons, which sat in a heavily fortified area right in the center of the Mort camp. Until Hall had seen them with his own eyes, he hadn't believed the Queen, though he didn't doubt that she'd had some sort of vision. But now, as the light brightened in the east, it gleamed off the iron monsters, accentuating their smooth, cylindrical shapes, and Hall felt the familiar twist of anger in his gut. He was as comfortable with a sword as any man alive, but a sword was a limited weapon. The Mort were trying to bend the rules of warfare as Hall had known it all of his life.

"Fine," he murmured, tucking away his spyglass, unaware that he spoke aloud. "So will we."

He descended the ladder from the bird's nest, Blaser right behind him, each dropping the last ten feet to the ground before they began to climb the hill. In the past twelve hours Hall had quietly deployed more than seven hundred men, archers and infantry, over the eastern slopes. But after weeks of hard physical work, his men found it difficult to remain still and simply lie in wait, particularly in the dark. One sign of increased activity on the hillside would have the Mort wide awake and on their guard, and so Hall had spent most of the night going from post to post, making sure his soldiers didn't simply jump out of their skins.

The slope grew steeper, until Hall and Blaser were forced to scrabble for handholds among the rocks, their feet slipping in pine needles. Both of them wore thick leather gloves and climbed carefully, for it was dangerous terrain here. The rocks were riddled with tunnels and small caves, and rattlesnakes liked to use the caves for their dens. Border rattlers were tough brutes, the result of millennia spent grappling for survival in an unforgiving place. Thick, leathery skins rendered them nearly impervious to fire and their fangs delivered a carefully controlled dose of venom. One wrong handhold on this slope and it was your life. When Hall and Simon were ten years old, Simon had once captured a rattler with a cage trap and tried to make it into a pet, but the game had lasted less than a week. No matter how well Simon fed the snake, it could not be tamed, and would attack any movement. Finally Hall and Simon had let the snake go, opening the cage and then running for their lives back up the eastern slope. No one knew how long border rattlers lived; Simon's snake might even be here somewhere, slithering among its brethren just behind the rocks.

Simon.

Hall shut his eyes, opened them again. The smart man trained his imagination not to venture too far down the Mort Road, but in these past few weeks, with all of western Mortmesne spread out before him, Hall had found himself thinking of his twin brother more often than usual: where Simon might be, who owned him now, how he had been used. Probably labor; Simon was considered one of the best shearers on the western slope. It would be wasteful to use such a man for anything besides heavy labor; Hall told himself this again and again, but probability held no sway. His mind dwelled constantly on the small percentage, the chance that Simon might have been sold for something else.

"Bastard."

Blaser's quiet curse brought Hall back to himself, and he snuck a look back over his shoulder to make sure his lieutenant hadn't been bitten. But Blaser had only slipped slightly before regaining his hold. Hall continued to climb, shaking his head to clear it of unwanted thoughts. The shipment was a wound, one that did not heal with the passage of time.

Hall gained the top of the rise and broke into the clearing to find his men waiting, their gazes expectant. Over the last month they had worked quickly, with none of the complaining that usually marked a military construction project, and had finished so early that Hall was able to test the entire operation multiple times before the Mort army had even reached the flats. The hawk handler, Jasper, was also waiting, his twelve hooded charges tethered to a long perch at the crest of the hill. The hawks had cost a pretty penny, but the Queen had listened carefully and then approved the cost without blinking.

Hall walked over to one of the catapults and placed a hand on its arm, feeling a fierce stab of pride as he touched the smooth wood. Hall was a lover of mechanisms, of gadgets. He constantly sought ways to do things faster and better. In his early career, he had invented a stronger yet more flexible longbow that was now favored by the Tear archers. On loan to a civilian construction project, he had tested and proved a pump-based irrigation system that now carried water from the Caddell to a vast, parched portion of the southern Almont. But these were his crowning achievement: five catapults, each sixty feet long, with thick arms made of Tear oak and lighter cups of pine. Each catapult could fling at least two hundred pounds, with a range of nearly four hundred yards into the wind. The arms were secured to the bases with rope, and on either side of each arm stood a soldier with an axe.

Peeking into the cup of the first catapult, Hall saw fifteen large, bulky canvas bundles, each wrapped in a thin layer of sky-blue fabric. Hall had originally planned to fling boulders, like the siege catapults of old, and flatten a significant portion of the Mort encampment. But these bundles, which had been Blaser's idea, were much better, well worth several weeks of unpleasant work. The topmost bundle shifted slightly in the wind, its canvas sides rippling, and Hall backed away, raising a clenched hand into the stillness of the morning. His axemen grabbed their weapons and heaved them high over their shoulders.

Blaser had begun humming. He always hummed to himself in tight situations: an annoying tic. Hall, listening with half an ear, identified the tune: "The Queen of the Tearling," the notes badly off-key but recognizable all the same. The song had taken hold with his men; Hall had heard it more than once in the past few weeks as they sanded lumber or sharpened blades.

My gift to you, Queen Kelsea, he thought, and dropped his hand toward the ground.

Axes hissed through the air, and then the stillness of the morning wrenched wide open, the hillside echoing with an enormous creaking and cracking as the arms of the catapults realized they were free. One by one they levered upward, gaining speed as they lunged into the sky, and Hall felt his heart lift in a pure joy that never evaporated, a joy he'd felt even as a small child testing his first rabbit trap.

My design! It works!

The arms of the catapults reached their limits and halted, with a boom that echoed across the hillside. That would wake the Mort, but it was already too late.

Hall socketed his spyglass and followed the progress of the light-blue bundles as they hurtled toward the Mort camp. They reached their zenith and began to drop, seventy-five of them in all, the sky-blue parachutes unraveling as they caught the wind, their canvas burdens swinging innocuously in the breeze.

The Mort were moving about now. Hall spied knots of activity: soldiers emerging from tents with weapons, sentries withdrawing into the camp in preparation for an attack.

"Jasper!" he called. "Two minutes!"

Jasper nodded and began to pull the hoods from his hawks, feeding each bird a small piece of meat. Major Caffrey, with his uncanny gift for recognizing a dependable mercenary, had found Jasper in a Mort border village three weeks ago. Hall didn't like Mort hawks any more now than he had as a child, when the birds used to swoop across the hillside looking for easy prey, but he still had to admire Jasper's skill with his charges. The hawks watched their handler attentively, heads cocked, like dogs waiting for their master to throw a stick.

A warning shout went up from the Mort camp. They had spotted the parachutes, which dropped faster now as wind resistance decreased. Hall watched through his spyglass, counting under his breath, as the first bundle disappeared behind one of the tents. Twelve seconds had elapsed when the first scream echoed across the flats.

More of the parachutes descended on the camp. One landed on an ordnance wagon, and Hall watched, fascinated despite himself, as the ropes relaxed. The bundle shivered for a moment, then sprang open as five furious rattlesnakes realized they were free. Their mottled skins curled and streaked over the pikes and arrows, dropping from the wagon and disappearing from sight.

Screams echoed against the hillside, and in less than a minute, the camp devolved into utter chaos. Soldiers ran into each other; half-dressed men stabbed wildly at their own feet with swords. Some tried to climb to higher ground, the tops of wagons and tents, even each other's backs. But most of them fled for the boundaries of the camp, desperate to get clear. Officers shouted orders, to no avail; panic had taken hold, and now the Mort army began to pour from the camp on all sides, fleeing west toward the Border Hills or away to the east and south, across the flats. Some even sprinted mindlessly north and splashed into the shallows of Lake Karczmar. They had no armor or weapons; many were stark naked. Several had cheeks still covered with shaving cream.

"Jasper!" Hall called. "Time!"

One by one, Jasper coaxed his hawks onto the thick leather glove that covered his arm from thumb to shoulder and sent them into the air. Hall's men watched the birds uneasily as they gained altitude, but the hawks were well trained; they ignored the Tear soldiers entirely, soaring down the hillside toward the Mort camp. They dove directly into the exodus of men who streamed from the southern and eastern ends of the campsite, talons opening as they dropped, and Hall watched the first of them seize the neck of a fleeing man who wore only a half-buttoned pair of trousers. The hawk ripped out his jugular, spraying the morning sunlight with a fine mist of blood.

On the west side of the camp, wave after wave of Mort soldiers sprinted mindlessly toward the trees at the foot of the hillside. But fifty Tear archers were scattered among the treetops, and now the Mort went down in droves, their bodies riddled with arrows, sinking into the mud of the flats. New screams came from the lake; the men who'd sought shelter there had discovered their error and now they thrashed back toward the shore, bellowing in pain. Hall smiled with a touch of nostalgia. Going into the lake was a rite of passage among the children of Idyllwild, and Hall still had the scars on his legs to prove it.

By now the bulk of the Mort army had deserted the camp. Hall cast a regretful eye toward the ten cannons, which sat entirely unattended. But there was no way to get to them now; everywhere he looked, rattlesnakes slithered among the tents, seeking a good place to nest. He wondered where General Genot was, whether he had fled along with his men, whether he could be one of the hundreds of corpses lying piled at the bottom of the slope. Hall had developed a healthy respect for Genot, but he knew the man's limitations, many of the same limitations that Bermond suffered himself. Genot wanted his warfare quiet and rational. He didn't make allowances for extraordinary bravado or crushing incompetence. Yet Hall knew that any army was riddled with such anomalies.

"Jasper!" he called. "Your birds have done good work. Bring them back."

Jasper gave a loud, piercing whistle and waited, tightening the straps that bound the leather glove to his forearm. Within seconds, the hawks began to soar back in, circling over the hilltop. Jasper whistled intermittently, a different note each time, and one by one each bird dropped to settle on his forearm, where it was rewarded with several pieces of rabbit before being hooded and placed back on the perch.

"Pull the archers," Hall told Blaser. "And find Emmett. Have him send messengers to the General and the Queen."

"What message, sir?"

"Tell them I've bought us time. At least two weeks until the Mort can regroup."

Blaser departed, and Hall turned back to stare across the surface of Lake Karczmar, a blinding sheet of red fire in the rising sun. This sight, which used to fill him with longing as a child, now seemed like a terrible warning. The Mort were scattered, true, but not for long, and if Hall's men lost the hillside, there was nothing to prevent the Mort from shredding Bermond's carefully assembled defensive lines. Just over the hill sprawled the Almont Plain: thousands of square miles of flat land with little room for maneuver, its farms and villages isolated and defenseless. The Mort had four times the numbers, twice the quality of arms, and if they made it down into the Almont, there was only one endgame: slaughter.

Ewen had been the Keep's Jailor for several years, ever since his Da retired out of the job, and in all that time, he had never had a prisoner that he considered truly dangerous. Most of them had been men who disagreed with the Regent, and these men generally entered the dungeons too starved and beaten to do more than totter into their cells and collapse. Several of them had died in Ewen's care, although Da had told him that he was not to blame. Ewen had disliked coming in and finding their bodies cold on their cots, but the Regent hadn't seemed to care either way. One night the Regent had even marched down the dungeon steps dragging one of his own women, a red-haired lady so beautiful that she seemed like something out of one of Da's fairy stories. But she had a rope tied around her neck. The Regent led her into a cage himself, calling her bad names the entire way, and snarled at Ewen, "No food or water! She doesn't come out until I say!"

Ewen didn't like having a woman prisoner. She did not talk or even weep, only gazed stonily at the wall of her cell. Ignoring the Regent's orders, Ewen had given her food and water, keeping a careful eye on the clock. He could tell that the rope around her neck was hurting her, and finally, unable to bear it any longer, he went in and loosened the noose. He wished he was a healer, able to fix the circle of raw red flesh on her throat, but Da had taught him only the most basic first aid, for cuts and such. Da had always been patient with Ewen's slowness, even when it caused trouble. But it didn't take a smart brain to keep a woman alive for the night, and Da would have been disappointed in Ewen had he failed. When the Regent came to collect the woman the next day, Ewen had felt great relief. The Regent had said he was sorry, but the woman had swept out of the dungeon without giving him so much as a glance.

Ever since the new Queen took the throne, there hadn't been much for Ewen to do. The Queen had freed all of the Regent's prisoners, which confused Ewen, but Da had explained that the Regent liked to put men in the dungeon for saying things he didn't like, and the Queen only put men in the dungeon for doing bad things. Da said this was sensible, and after thinking it over for a while, Ewen decided that Da was right.

Twenty-seven days ago (Ewen had noted it in the book), three Queen's Guards had burst into the dungeon leading a bound prisoner, a grey-haired man who looked exhausted but—Ewen noted gratefully—uninjured. The three guards didn't ask Ewen's permission before hauling the prisoner through the open door of Cell Three, but Ewen didn't mind. He'd never been so close to Queen's Guards before, but he'd heard all about them from Da: they protected the Queen from danger. To Ewen, this sounded like the most wonderful and important job in the world. He was grateful to be Head Jailor, but if he'd just been born smarter, he would have wanted most of all to be one of these tall, hard men in their grey cloaks.

"Treat him well," ordered the leader, a man with a head of bright red hair. "Queen's orders."

Though the guard's hair fascinated him, Ewen tried not to stare, for he didn't like it when people stared at him. He locked the cell, noting that the prisoner had already lain down on the cot and closed his eyes.

"What's his name and crime, sir? I have to write it in the book."

"Javel. His crime is treason." The red-haired leader stared through the cage bars for a moment, then shook his head. Ewen watched as the men tromped off toward the stairwell, their voices drifting down the hallway behind them.

"I'd have cut his throat."

"Is he safe with the dummy, you think?"

"That's between the Queen and the Mace."

"He must know his job. No one's ever escaped."

"Still, she can't have an idiot as a jailor forever."

Ewen flinched at the word. Bullies used to call him that, before he got so big, and he had learned to allow the word to roll right off him, but it hurt more from a Queen's Guard. And now he had something new and terrible to think about: the possibility of being replaced. When Da had retired, Da had gone to speak directly to the Regent, to make sure that Ewen could stay on. But Ewen didn't think Da had ever spoken to the Queen.

The new prisoner, Javel, was one of the easiest charges Ewen had ever had. He barely spoke, only a few words to tell Ewen when he had finished his meals or run out of water or needed the bucket emptied. For long hours Ewen even forgot that Javel was there, but then Ewen could think of little but being dismissed from his post. What would he do if that happened? He couldn't even bring himself to tell Da what the Queen's Guard had called him. He didn't want Da to know.

Five days after Javel came to the dungeon, three more Queen's Guards stomped down the stairs. One of them was Lazarus of the Mace, a recognizable figure even to Ewen, who rarely left his cells. Ewen had heard plenty of stories about the Mace from Da, who claimed that the Mace was fairy-born, that no cell would hold him. ("A jailor's nightmare, Ew!" Da would cackle over his tea.) If the other Queen's Guards had been impressive, the Mace was ten times so, and Ewen studied him as closely as he dared. The Captain of Guard in his dungeon! He couldn't wait to tell Da.

The other two guards carried a prisoner between them like a sack of grain, and after Ewen unlocked Cell One, they threw the man on the cot. The Mace stood looking at the prisoner for what seemed to Ewen a very long time. Finally he straightened, cleared something deep in his throat, and spat, a great glob of yellow slime that landed square on the prisoner's cheek.

Ewen thought this unkind; whatever the man's crime, surely he had suffered enough. He was a miserable, shriveled creature, starved and dehydrated. Mud had caked into the thick welts over his legs and torso. More welts, deep red rivets, crossed his wrists. Great hanks of hair had been pulled from his head, leaving patches of scabbed flesh. Ewen couldn't imagine what had happened to him.

The Mace turned to Ewen and snapped his fingers. "Jailor!"

Ewen stepped forward, trying to stand as tall as he could. Da had chosen Ewen as his apprentice, even over Ewen's smarter brothers, for exactly this reason: Ewen was big and strong. But he still only came up to the Mace's nose. He wondered if the Mace knew he was slow.

"You watch this one closely, Jailor. No visitors. No little field trips outside the cell for exercise. Nothing."

"Yes, sir," Ewen replied, wide-eyed, and watched the group of guards exit the dungeon. No one called him any names this time, but it was only after they'd departed that Ewen realized he had forgotten to ask for the man's name and crime for the book. Stupid! The Mace would surely notice such things.

The next day, Da had come to visit. Ewen was tending the new prisoner as best he could, though the man's wounds were well beyond the power of anything but time or magic. But Da had taken one look at the man on his cot and spat, just like the Mace.

"Don't bother trying to cure this bastard, Ew."

"Who is he?"

"A carpenter." Da's bald head gleamed, even in the dim torchlight, and Ewen saw with some uneasiness that the skin of Da's forehead was getting thin, like linen. Even Da would die eventually, Ewen knew that, deep in a dark place in his mind. "A builder."

"What did he build, Da?"

"Cages," Da replied shortly. "Be very careful, Ew."

Ewen looked around, confused. The dungeon was full of cages. But Da didn't seem to want to talk about it, and so Ewen stored the facts in his mind alongside the rest of the mysteries he didn't understand. Once in a while, usually when Ewen wasn't even trying, he would solve a mystery, and that was a great and extraordinary feeling, the way he imagined birds would feel as they swooped across the sky. But no matter how he stared at the man in the cell, no answers were forthcoming.

After that, Ewen thought he was prepared for anyone to enter his dungeon, but he was wrong. Two days before, two men in the black uniform of the Tear army had burst in, dragging a woman between them. But this was no fancy woman like the Regent's redhead; she spat and kicked, shouting curses at the two men who dragged on her arms. Ewen had never seen anything like her. She seemed all white, from head to toe, as if her flesh had lost all of its color. Her hair was similarly faded, like hay that had sat too long in the sunlight. Even her dress was white, though Ewen thought it might once have been light blue. She looked like a ghost. The soldiers tried to force her through the open door of Cell Two, but she grabbed at the bars and hung on.

"Don't make this any harder than it needs to be," the taller soldier panted.

"Fuck you, you limp prawn!"

The soldier kept patient pressure on her hands, trying to peel back her locked fingers, while the other soldier worked on hauling her into the cage. Ewen hung back, not sure whether to get involved. The woman's eyes fell on him, and he went cold inside. Her irises were circled pink, but deep in the center was a blue so light that it glittered like ice. Ewen saw something terrible there, animal and sick. The woman opened her mouth, and Ewen knew what was coming, even before she spoke.

"I know all about you, boy. You're the halfwit."

"Give us some help, for Christ's sake!" one of the soldiers snarled.

Ewen jumped forward. He didn't want to touch any part of the ghost-woman, so he took hold of her dress and began to tug her backward. With both soldiers free to work on her fingers, they finally succeeded in prying her loose from the bars and then flung her into the cage, where she ran into the cot and fell to the ground. Ewen was barely able to get the door closed before the woman hurled herself against the bars, spewing more curses at the three of them.

"Christ, what a job!" one of the soldiers muttered. He wiped his brow, where a mole grew like a small mushroom. "Locked in, though, she shouldn't give you too much trouble. She's blind as a mouse."

"Only watch out when the owl comes hunting," the other remarked, and they chuckled together.

"What's her name and crime?"

"Brenna. Her crime . . ." The soldier with the mole looked at his friend. "Hard to say. Treason, probably."

Ewen wrote the crime in the book, and the soldiers left the dungeon, cheerful now, their work done. The soldiers had said that the ghost-woman was blind, but Ewen quickly discovered that wasn't so. When he moved, she turned her head and her blue-pink eyes followed him across the dungeon. When he looked up, he found her gaze pinned on him, a horrible smile stretching her mouth. Ewen usually brought his prisoners their food in their cells, for he was too big to be physically overpowered by an unarmed man. But now he was glad of the little door on the front of the cell that allowed him to slide the woman's food trays through. He wanted the comfort of bars between them. Cell Two was the best cell for dangerous prisoners, since it faced directly into Ewen's small living quarters; he was a light sleeper. But now, when it came time for bed, he found that he could not sleep with that awful gaze upon him, and he finally moved his cot into the corner so that the doorway blocked the view. Still, he could sense the woman, sleepless and malevolent, even in the dark, and for the past few days his sleep had been uneasy, frequently broken.

Tonight, after Ewen had finished his dinner and inspected the empty cells for rats or rot (there was neither; he cleaned his cell-block thoroughly every other day), he settled down with his pictures. He tried constantly to paint the things he saw, but he always failed. It seemed like an easy business, with the right paper and some good paints and brushes—Da had given him these for his last birthday—but the images always escaped somewhere between his thoughts and the paper. Ewen couldn't see why it had to be that way, but it was. He was trying to paint Javel, the prisoner in Cell Three, when the door at the top of the steps crashed open.

For a few moments, Ewen had a bad fright, worried about jailbreak. Da had warned him about jailbreak, the worst shame that could befall a jailor. Two soldiers were stationed outside the door at the top of the steps, but Ewen was all alone down in the dungeon. He didn't know what he would do if someone had forced his way in. He grabbed the knife that lay on his desk.

But the crash of the door was followed by many voices and footsteps, such unexpected sounds that Ewen could only sit at his desk and wait to see what would come down the hallway. After a few moments a woman entered the dungeon, a tall woman with short-cropped brown hair and a silver crown on her head. Two great blue jewels hung on fine, glittering silver chains around her neck, and she was surrounded by five Queen's Guards. Ewen considered these things for a few seconds, then bolted to his feet: the Queen!

She went first to stare through the bars of Cell Three. "How have you been, Javel?"

The man on the cot looked up at her with empty eyes. "Fine, Majesty."

"Nothing else to say?"

"No."

The Queen put her hands on her hips and huffed, a sound of disappointment that Ewen recognized from Da, then moved over to Cell One to gaze at the wounded man who lay there.

"What a miserable-looking creature."

The Mace laughed. "He's endured rough handling, Lady. Rougher, maybe, than even I could have devised. The villagers took him in Devin's Slope when he tried to barter carpentry for food. They bound him to a wagon for the trip to New London, and when he finally collapsed, they dragged him the rest of the way."

"You paid these villagers?"

"All two hundred, Majesty. It's a lucky break; we need the loyalty of those border villages, and the money will probably keep Devin's Slope for a year. They don't see a lot of coin out there."

The Queen nodded. She didn't look like the queens in Da's stories, who were always delicate, pretty women like the Regent's redhead. This woman looked . . . tough. Maybe it was her short hair, short like a man's, or maybe just the way she stood, with her feet spread and one hand tapping impatiently on her hip. A favorite phrase of Da's popped into Ewen's head: she looked like no one to fiddle with.

"You! Bannaker!" The Queen snapped her fingers at the man on the cot.

The prisoner groaned, putting his hands to his head. The welts on his arms had begun to scab over and heal, but he still seemed very weak, and despite Da's words, Ewen felt a moment's pity.

"Give it up, Lady," the Mace remarked. "You won't get anything out of him for a while. Men's minds can break from a journey like that. It's usually the point."

The Queen cast around the dungeon and her deep green eyes found Ewen, who snapped to attention. "Are you my Jailor?"

"Yes, Majesty. Ewen."

"Open this cell."

TO BE CONTINUED